The Giant's Robe by F. Anstey

F. Anstey was the pseudonym of Thomas Anstey Guthrie who was born in Kensington, London on August 8th, 1856, to Augusta Amherst Austen, an organist and composer, and Thomas Anstey Guthrie., a prosperous military tailor

Anstey was educated at King's College School and then at Trinity Hall, Cambridge. Although his education was first rate Anstey could only manage a third-class degree; A Gentlemen's degree as it was euphemistically known.

In 1880 he was called to the bar. However this career path rapidly fell away in his desire to become an author. The successful publication of Vice Versa, in 1882, with the premise of a substitution of a father for his schoolboy son, made his name and reputation as a refreshing and original humorist.

The following year he published a rather more serious work, The Giant's Robe. Interestingly the story is about a plagiarist and Anstey was, ironically, accused of plagiarism in writing the work. Despite good reviews both he and his public knew that his writing career was to be that of a humorist.

In the following years he published prolifically beginning with; The Black Poodle (1884), The Tinted Venus (1885), A Fallen Idol (1886), and Baboo Jabberjee B.A. (1897).

Anstey worked not only as a novelist and short story writer but was also a valued member of the staff at the humorous Punch magazine, in which his voces populi and his parodies of a reciter's stock-piece (Burglar Bill) represent perhaps his best work.

In 1901, his successful farce, The Man from Blankleys, based on a story that originally appeared in Punch, was first produced on stage at the Prince of Wales Theatre, in London.

Anstey had become a writer, and a successful one at that, of many talents.

Many more of his stories were made into plays and films over the years. Others were simply taken for the premise alone, usually with no credit to the original author.

By the end of the First World War Anstey's original publications had slowed to a crawl and he seemed rather more interested in translating and publishing some works of Moliere.

Thomas Anstey Guthrie died of pneumonia on March 10th, 1934 in London.

His self-deprecating autobiography, A Long Retrospect, was published in 1936.

Index of Contents
PREFACE
CHAPTER I - AN INTERCESSOR
CHAPTER II - A LAST WALK

CHAPTER III - GOOD-BYE
CHAPTER IV - MALAKOFF TERRACE
CHAPTER V - NEIGHBOURS
CHAPTER VI - SO NEAR AND YET SO FAR
CHAPTER VII - IN THE FOG
CHAPTER VIII - BAD NEWS
CHAPTER IX - A TURNING-POINT
CHAPTER X - REPENTE TURPISSIMUS
CHAPTER XI - REVOLT
CHAPTER XII - LAUNCHED
CHAPTER XIII - A 'THORN AND FLOWER PIECE'
CHAPTER XIV - IN THE SPRING
CHAPTER XV - HAROLD CAFFYN MAKES A DISCOVERY
CHAPTER XVI - A CHANGE OF FRONT
CHAPTER XVII - IN WHICH MARK MAKES AN ENEMY AND RECOVERS A FRIEND
CHAPTER XVIII - A DINNER PARTY
CHAPTER XIX - DOLLY'S DELIVERANCE
CHAPTER XX - A DECLARATION—OF WAR
CHAPTER XXI - A PARLEY WITH THE ENEMY
CHAPTER XXII - STRIKING THE TRAIL
CHAPTER XXIII - PIANO PRACTICE
CHAPTER XXIV - A MEETING IN GERMANY
CHAPTER XXV - MABEL'S ANSWER
CHAPTER XXVI - VISITS OF CEREMONY
CHAPTER XXVII - CLEAR SKY—AND A THUNDERBOLT
CHAPTER XXVIII - MARK KNOWS THE WORST
CHAPTER XXIX - ON BOARD THE 'COROMANDEL'
CHAPTER XXX - THE WAY OF TRANSGRESSORS
CHAPTER XXXI - AGAG
CHAPTER XXXII - AT WASTWATER
CHAPTER XXXIII - IN SUSPENSE
CHAPTER XXXIV - ON THE LAUFENPLATZ
CHAPTER XXXV - MISSED FIRE
CHAPTER XXXVI - LITTLE RIFTS
CHAPTER XXXVII - MARK ACCEPTS A DISAGREEABLE DUTY
CHAPTER XXXVIII - HAROLD CAFFYN MAKES A PALPABLE HIT
CHAPTER XXXIX - CAFFYN SPRINGS HIS MINE
CHAPTER XL - THE EFFECTS OF AN EXPLOSION
CHAPTER XLI - A FINAL VICTORY
CHAPTER XLII - FROM THE GRAVE
CONCLUSION
F. ANSTEY — A CONCISE BIBLIOGRAPHY

PREFACE

It has been my intention from the first to take this opportunity of stating that, if I am indebted to any previous work for the central idea of a stolen manuscript, such obligation should be ascribed to a short tale, published some time ago in one of the Christmas numbers—the only story upon the subject which I have read at present.

It was the story of a German student who, having found in the library of his university an old scientific manuscript, by a writer long since dead and forgotten, produced it as his own; and it is so probable that the recollection of this incident became quite unconsciously the germ of the present book that, although the matter is not of general importance, I feel it only fair to mention it here.

I trust, nevertheless, that it is not necessary to insist upon any claim to the average degree of originality; for if the book does not bear the traces of honest and independent work, that is a defect which is scarcely likely to be removed by the most eloquent and argumentative of prefaces.

CHAPTER I

AN INTERCESSOR

In the heart of the City, but fended off from the roar and rattle of traffic by a ring of shops, and under the shadow of a smoke-begrimed classical church, stands—or rather stood, for they have removed it recently—the large public school of St. Peter's.

Entering the heavy old gate, against which the shops on both sides huddled close, you passed into the atmosphere of scholastic calm which, during working hours, pervades most places of education, and saw a long plain block of buildings, within which it was hard to believe, so deep was the silence, that some hundreds of boys were collected.

Even if you went down the broad stair to the school entrance and along the basement, where the bulk of the class-rooms was situated, there was only a faint hum to be heard from behind the numerous doors—until the red-waistcoated porter came out of his lodge and rang the big bell which told that the day's work was over.

Then nervous people who found themselves by any chance in the long dark corridors experienced an unpleasant sensation, as of a demon host in high spirits being suddenly let loose to do their will. The outburst was generally preceded by a dull murmur and rustle, which lasted for a few minutes after the clang of the bell had died away—then door after door opened and hordes of boys plunged out with wild shrieks of liberty, to scamper madly down the echoing flagstones.

For half an hour after that the place was a Babel of unearthly yells, whistles, and scraps of popular songs, with occasional charges and scuffles and a constant tramp of feet.

The higher forms on both the classical and modern sides took no part of course in these exuberances, and went soberly home in twos or threes, as became 'fellows in the Sixth.' But they were in the minority, and the Lower School boys and the 'Remove'—that bodyguard of strong limbs and thick heads which it seemed hopeless to remove any higher—were quite capable of supplying unaided all the noise that might be considered necessary; and, as there was no ill-humour and little roughness in their japes, they were very wisely allowed to let their steam off without interference. It did not last very long, though it died out gradually enough: first the songs and whistles became more isolated and distinct, and the hallooing and tramping less continued, until the charivari toned down almost entirely, the frightened silence came stealing back again, and the only sounds at last were the hurried run of the delinquents who had been 'run in' to the detention room, the slow footsteps of some of the masters, and the brooms of the old ladies who were cleaning up.

Such was the case at St. Peter's when this story begins. The stream of boys with shiny black bags had poured out through the gate and swelled the great human river; some of them were perhaps already at home and enlivening their families with the day's experiences, and those who had further to go were probably beguiling the tedium of travel by piling one another up in struggling heaps on the floors of various railway carriages, for the entertainment of those privileged to be their fellow-passengers.

Halfway down the main corridor I have mentioned was the 'Middle-Third' class-room, a big square room with dingy cream-coloured walls, high windows darkened with soot, and a small stained writing-table at one end, surrounded on three sides by ranks of rugged seasoned forms and sloping desks; round the walls were varnished lockers with a number painted on the lid of each, and a big square stove stood in one corner.

The only person in the room just then was the form-master, Mark Ashburn; and he was proposing to leave it almost immediately, for the close air and the strain of keeping order all day had given him a headache, and he was thinking that before walking homeward he would amuse himself with a magazine, or a gossip in the masters' room.

Mark Ashburn was a young man, almost the youngest on the school staff, and very decidedly the best-looking. He was tall and well made, with black hair and eloquent dark eyes, which had the gift of expressing rather more than a rigid examination would have found inside him—just now, for example, a sentimental observer would have read in their glance round the bare deserted room the passionate protest of a soul conscious of genius against the hard fate which had placed him there, whereas he was in reality merely wondering whose hat that was on the row of pegs opposite.

But if Mark was not a genius, there was a brilliancy in his manner that had something very captivating about it; an easy confidence in himself, that had the more merit because it had hitherto met with extremely small encouragement.

He dressed carefully, which was not without effect upon his class, for boys, without being overscrupulous in the matter of their own costume, are apt to be critical of the garments of those in authority over them. To them he was 'an awful swell'; though he was not actually overdressed—it was only that he liked to walk home along Piccadilly with the air of a man who had just left his club and had nothing particular to do.

He was not unpopular with his boys: he did not care twopence about any of them, but he felt it pleasant to be popular, and his careless good-nature secured that result without much effort on his part. They had a great respect for his acquirements too, speaking of him among themselves as 'jolly clever when he liked to show it'; for Mark was not above giving occasional indications of deep learning which were highly impressive. He went out of his way to do it, and was probably aware that the learning thus suggested would not stand any very severe test; but then there was no one there to apply it.

Any curiosity as to the last hat and coat on the wall was satisfied while he still sat at his desk, for the door, with its upper panels of corrugated glass protected by stout wire network—no needless precaution there—opened just then, and a small boy appeared, looking rather pale and uncomfortable, and holding a long sheet of blue foolscap in one hand.

'Hullo, Langton,' said Mark, as he saw him; 'so it's you; why, haven't you gone yet, eh? How's that?'

'Please sir,' began the boy, dolorously, 'I've got into an awful row—I'm run in, sir.'

'Ah!' said Mark; 'sorry for you—what is it?'

'Well, I didn't do anything,' said he. 'It was like this. I was going along the passage, and just passing Old Jemmy's—I mean Mr. Shelford's—door, and it was open. And there was a fellow standing outside, a bigger fellow than me, and he caught hold of me by the collar and ran me right in and shut the door and bolted. And Mr. Shelford came at me and boxed my ears, and said it wasn't the first time, and I should have a detention card for it. And so he gave me this, and I'm to go up to the Doctor with it and get it signed when it's done!'

And the boy held out the paper, at the top of which Mark read in old Shelford's tremulous hand—'Langton. 100 lines for outrageous impertinence. J. Shelford.'

'If I go up, you know, sir,' said the boy, with a trembling lip, 'I'm safe for a swishing.'

'Well, I'm afraid you are,' agreed Mark, 'but you'd better make haste, hadn't you? or they'll close the Detention Room, and you'll only be worse off for waiting, you see.'

Mark was really rather sorry for him, though he had, as has been said, no great liking for boys; but this particular one, a round-faced, freckled boy, with honest eyes and a certain refinement in his voice and bearing that somehow suggested that he had a mother or sister who was a gentlewoman, was less objectionable to Mark than his fellows. Still he could not enter into his feelings sufficiently to guess why he was being appealed to in this way.

Young Langton half turned to go, dejectedly enough; then he came back and said, 'Please, sir, can't you help me? I shouldn't mind the—the swishing so much if I'd done anything. But I haven't.'

'What can I do?' asked Mark.

'If you wouldn't mind speaking to Mr. Shelford for me—he'd listen to you, and he won't to me.'

'He will have gone by this time,' objected Mark.

'Not if you make haste,' said the boy, eagerly.

Mark was rather flattered by this confidence in his persuasive powers: he liked the idea, too, of posing as the protector of his class, and the good-natured element in him made him the readier to yield.

'Well, we'll have a shot at it, Langton,' he said. 'I doubt if it's much good, you know, but here goes—when you get in, hold your tongue and keep in the background—leave it to me.'

So they went out into the long passage with its whitewashed walls and rows of doors on each side, and black barrel-vaulting above; at the end the glimmer of light came through the iron bars of the doorway, which had a prison-like suggestion about them, and the reflectors of the unlighted gas lamps that projected here and there along the corridor gave back the glimmer as a tiny spark in the centre of each metal disc.

Mark stopped at the door of the Upper Fourth Classroom, which was Mr. Shelford's, and went in. It was a plain room, not unlike his own, but rather smaller; it had a daïs with a somewhat larger desk for the master, and a different arrangement of the benches and lockers, but it was quite as gloomy, with an outlook into a grim area giving a glimpse of the pavement and railings above.

Mr. Shelford was evidently just going, for as they came in he had put a very large hat on the back of his head, and was winding a long grey comforter round his throat; but he took off the hat courteously as he saw Mark. He was a little old man, with a high brick-red colour on his smooth, scarcely wrinkled cheeks, a big aquiline nose, a wide thin-lipped mouth, and sharp little grey eyes, which he cocked sideways at one like an angry parrot.

Langton retired to a form out of hearing, and sat down on one end of it, nursing his detention paper anxiously.

'Well, Ashburn,' began the Reverend James Shelford, 'is there anything I can do for you?'

'Why,' said Mark, 'the fact is, I—'

'Eh, what?' said the elder. 'Wait a minute—there's that impident fellow back again! I thought I'd seen the last of him. Here, you sir, didn't I send you up for a flogging?'

'I—I believe you did, sir,' said Langton with extreme deference.

'Well, why ain't you getting that flogging—eh, sir? No impidence, now—just tell me, why ain't you being flogged? You ought to be in the middle of it now!'

'Well, you see,' said Mark, 'he's one of my boys—'

'I don't care whose boy he is,' said the other, testily; 'he's an impident fellow, sir.'

'I don't think he is, really,' said Mark.

'D'ye know what he did, then? Came whooping and shouting and hullabalooing into my room, for all the world as if it was his own nursery, sir. He's always doing it!'

'I never did it before,' protested Langton, 'and it wasn't my fault this time.'

'Wasn't your fault! You haven't got St. Vitus' dance, have you? I never heard there were any Tarantula spiders here. You don't go dancing into the Doctor's room, do you? He'll give you a dancing lesson!' said the old gentleman, sitting down again to chuckle, and looking very like Mr. Punch.

'No, but allow me,' put in Mark; 'I assure you this boy is—'

'I know what you're going to tell me—he's a model boy, of course. It's singular what shoals of model boys do come dancing in here under some irresistible impulse after school. I'll put a stop to it now I've caught one. You don't know 'em as well as I do, sir, you don't know 'em—they're all impident and all liars—some are cleverer at it than others, and that's all.'

'I'm afraid that's true enough,' said Mark, who did not like being considered inexperienced.

'Yes, it's cruel work having to do with boys, sir—cruel and thankless. If ever I try to help a boy in my class I think is trying to get on and please me, what does he do? Turn round and play me some scurvy trick, just to prove to the others he's not currying favour. And then they insult me—why, that very boy has been and shouted "Shellfish" through my keyhole many a time, I'll warrant!'

'I think you're mistaken,' said Mark, soothingly.

'You do? I'll ask him. Here, d'ye mean to tell me you never called out "Shellfish" or—or other opprobrious epithets into my door, sir?' And he inclined his ear for the answer with his eyes fixed on the boy's face.

'Not "Shellfish,"' said the boy; 'I did "Prawn" once. But that was long ago.'

Mark gave him up then, with a little contempt for such injudicious candour.

'Oh!' said Mr. Shelford, catching him, but not ungently, by the ear. '"Prawn," eh? "Prawn"; hear that, Ashburn? Perhaps you wouldn't mind telling me why "Prawn"?'

A natural tendency of the youthful mind to comparative physiology had discovered a fancied resemblance which justified any graceful personalities of this kind; but Langton probably felt that candour had its limits, and that this was a question that required judgment in dealing with it.

'Because—because I've heard other fellows call you that,' he replied.

'Ah, and why do they call me Prawn, eh?'

'I never heard them give any reason,' said the boy, diplomatically.

Mr. Shelford let the boy go with another chuckle, and Langton retired to his form again out of earshot.

'Yes, Ashburn,' said old Jemmy, 'that's the name they have for me—one of 'em. "Prawn" and "Shellfish"—they yell it out after me as I'm going home, and then run away. And I've had to bear it thirty years.'

'Young ruffians!' said Mark, as if the sobriquets were wholly unknown to the masters' room.

'Ah, they do though; and the other day, when my monitor opened the desk in the morning, there was a great impident kitten staring me in the face. He'd put it in there himself, I dare say, to annoy me.'

He did not add that he had sent out for some milk for the intruder, and had nursed it on his old knees during morning school, after which he showed it out with every consideration for its feelings; but it was the case nevertheless, for his years amongst boys had still left a soft place in his heart, though he got little credit for it.

'Yes, it's a wearing life, sir, a wearing life,' he went on with less heat, 'hearing generations of stoopid boys all blundering at the same stiff places, and worrying over the same old passages. I'm getting very tired of it; I'm an old man now. "Occidit miseros crambe"—eh, you know how it goes on?'

'Yes, yes,' said Mark, 'quite so,'—though he had but a dim recollection of the line in question.

'Talking of verses,' said the other, 'I hear we're to have the pleasure of seeing one of your productions on Speech-night this year. Is that so?'

'I was not aware anything was settled,' said Mark, flushing with pleasure. 'I did lay a little thing of my own, a sort of allegorical Christmas piece—a masque, don't you know—before the Doctor and the Speeches Committee, but I haven't heard anything definite yet.'

'Oh, perhaps I'm premature,' said Mr. Shelford; 'perhaps I'm premature.'

'Do you mind telling me if you've heard anything said about it?' asked Mark, thoroughly interested.

'I did hear some talk about it in the luncheon hour. You weren't in the room, I believe, but I think they were to come to a decision this afternoon.'

'Then it will be all over by now,' said Mark; 'there may be a note on my desk about it. I—I think I'll go and see, if you'll excuse me.'

And he left the room hastily, quite forgetting his original purpose in entering: something much more important to him than whether a boy should be flogged or not, when he had no doubt richly deserved it, was pending just then, and he could not rest until he knew the result.

For Mark had always longed for renown of some sort, and for the last few years literary distinction had seemed the most open to him. He had sought it by more ambitious attempts, but even the laurels which the performance of a piece of his by boy-actors on a Speech-day might bring him had become desirable; and though he had written and submitted his work confidently and carelessly enough, he found himself not a little anxious and excited as the time for a decision drew near.

It was a small thing; but if it did nothing else it would procure him a modified fame in the school and the masters' room, and Mark Ashburn had never felt resigned to be a nonentity anywhere.

Little wonder, then, that Langton's extremity faded out of his mind as he hurried back to his class-room, leaving that unlucky small boy still in his captor's clutches.

The old clergyman put on the big hat again when Mark had gone, and stood up peering over the desk at his prisoner.

'Well, if you don't want to be locked up here all night, you'd better be off,' he remarked.

'To the Detention Room, sir?' faltered the boy.

'You know the way, I believe? If not, I can show you,' said the old gentleman politely.

'But really and truly,' pleaded Langton, 'I didn't do anything this time. I was shoved in.'

'Who shoved you in? Come, you know well enough; you're going to lie, I can see. Who was he?'

It is not improbable that Langton was going to lie that time—his code allowed it—but he felt checked somehow. 'Well, I only know the fellow by name,' he said at last.

'Well, and what's his name? Out with it; I'll give him a detention card instead.'

'I can't tell you that,' said the boy in a lower voice.

'And why not, ye impident fellow? You've just said you knew it. Why not?'

'Because it would be sneakish,' said Langton boldly.

'Oh, "sneakish," would it?' said old Jemmy. '"Sneakish," eh? Well, well, I'm getting old, I forget these things. Perhaps it would. I don't know what it is to insult an old man—that's fair enough, I dare say. And so you want me to let you off being whipped, eh?'

'Yes, when I've done nothing.'

'And if I let you off you'll come gallopading in here as lively as ever to-morrow, calling out "Shellfish"—no, I forgot—"Prawn's" your favourite epithet, ain't it?—calling out "Prawn" under my very nose.'

'No, I shan't,' said the boy.

'Well, I'll take your word for it, whatever that's worth,' and he tore up the compromising paper. 'Run off home to your tea, and don't bother me any more.'

Langton escaped, full of an awed joy at his wonderful escape, and old Mr. Shelford locked his desk, got out the big hook-nosed umbrella, which had contracted a strong resemblance to himself, and went too.

'That's a nice boy,' he muttered—'wouldn't tell tales, wouldn't he? But I dare say he was taking me in all the time. He'll be able to tell the other young scamps how neatly he got over "old Jemmy." I don't think he will, though. I can still tell when a boy's lying—I've had plenty of opportunities.'

Meanwhile Mark had gone back to his class-room. One of the porters ran after him with a note, and he opened it eagerly, only to be disappointed, for it was not from the committee. It was dated from Lincoln's Inn, and came from his friend Holroyd.

'Dear Ashburn,' the note ran, 'don't forget your promise to look in here on your way home. You know it's the last time we shall walk back together, and there's a favour I want to ask of you before saying good-bye. I shall be at chambers till five, as I am putting my things together.'

'I will go round presently,' he thought. 'I must say good-bye some time to-day, and it will be a bore to turn out after dinner.'

As he stood reading the note, young Langton passed him, bag in hand, with a bright and grateful face.

'Please, sir,' he said, saluting him, 'thanks awfully for getting Mr. Shelford to let me off; he wouldn't have done it but for you.'

'Oh, ah,' said Mark, suddenly remembering his errand of mercy, 'to be sure, yes. So, he has let you off, has he? Well, I'm very glad I was of use to you, Langton. It was a hard fight, wasn't it? That's enough, get along home, and let me find you better up in your Nepos than you were yesterday.'

Beyond giving the boy his company in facing his judge for the second time, Mark, as will have been observed, had not been a very energetic advocate; but as Langton was evidently unaware of the fact, Mark himself was the last person to allude to it. Gratitude, whether earned or not, was gratitude, and always worth accepting.

'By Jove,' he thought to himself with half-ashamed amusement, 'I forgot all about the little beggar; left him to the tender mercies of old Prawn. All's well that ends well, anyhow!'

As he stood by the grille at the porter's lodge, the old Prawn himself passed slowly out, with his shoulders bent, and his old eyes staring straight before him with an absent, lack-lustre expression in them. Perhaps he was thinking that life might have been more cheerful for him if his wife Mary had lived, and he had had her and boys like that young Langton to meet him when his wearisome day was over, instead of being childless and a widower, and returning to the lonely, dingy house which he occupied as the incumbent of a musty church hard by.

Whatever he thought of, he was too engaged to notice Mark, who followed him with his eyes as he slowly worked his way up the flight of stone steps which led to the street level. 'Shall I ever come to that?' he thought. 'If I stay here all my life, I may. Ah, there's Gilbertson—he can tell me about this Speech-day business.'

Gilbertson was a fellow-master, and one of the committee for arranging the Speech-day entertainment. For the rest he was a nervously fussy little man, and met Mark with evident embarrassment.

'Well, Gilbertson,' said Mark, as unconcernedly as he could, 'settled your programme yet?'

'Er—oh yes, quite settled—quite, that is, not definitely as yet.'

'And—my little production?'

'Oh, ah, to be sure, yes, your little production. We all liked it very much—oh, exceedingly so—the Doctor especially—charmed with it, my dear Ashburn, charmed!'

'Very glad to hear it,' said Mark, with a sudden thrill; 'and—and have you decided to take it, then?'

'Well,' said Mr. Gilbertson, looking at the pavement all round him, 'you see, the fact is, the Doctor thought, and some of us thought so too, that a piece to be acted by boys should have a leetle more— eh? and not quite so much—so much of what yours has, and a few of those little natural touches, you know—but you see what I mean, don't you?'

'It would be a capital piece with half that in it,' said Mark, trying to preserve his temper, 'but I could easily alter it, you know, Gilbertson.'

'No, no,' said Gilbertson, eagerly, 'you mustn't think of it; you'd spoil it; we couldn't hear of it, and—and it won't be necessary to trouble you. Because, you see, the Doctor thought it was a little long, and not quite light enough; and not exactly the sort of thing we want, but we all admired it.'

'But it won't do? Is that what you mean?'

'Why—er—nothing definite at present. We are going to write you a letter about it. Good-bye, good-bye! Got a train to catch at Ludgate Hill.'

And he bustled away, glad to escape, for he had not counted upon having to announce a rejection in person.

Mark stood looking after him, with a slightly dazed feeling. That was over, then. He had written works which he felt persuaded had only to become known to bring him fame; but for all that it seemed that he was not considered worthy to entertain a Speech-night audience at a London public school.

Hitherto Mark's life had contained more of failure than success. From St. Peter's he had gone to a crammer's to be prepared for the Indian Civil Service, and an easy pass had been anticipated for him even at the first trial. Unfortunately, however, his name came out low down on the list—a disaster which he felt must be wiped out at all hazards, and, happening to hear of an open scholarship that was to be competed for at a Cambridge college, he tried for it, and this time was successful. A well-to-do uncle, who had undertaken the expenses hitherto, was now induced to consent to the abandonment of the Civil Service in favour of a University career, and Mark entered upon it accordingly with fair prospects of distinction, if he read with even ordinary steadiness.

This he had done during his first year, though he managed to get a fair share of enjoyment out of his life, but then something happened to change the whole current of his ambitions—he composed a college skit which brought him considerable local renown, and from that moment was sought as a contributor to sundry of those ephemeral undergraduate periodicals which, in their short life, are so universally reviled and so eagerly read.

Mark's productions, imitative and crude as they necessarily were, had admirers who strengthened his own conviction that literature was his destiny; the tripos faded into the background, replaced by the more splendid vision of seeing an accepted article from his pen in a real London magazine; he gave frantic chase to the will o' the wisp of literary fame, which so many pursue all their lives in vain, fortunate if it comes at last to flicker for awhile over their graves.

With Mark the results were what might have been expected: his papers in his second year examinations were so bad that he received a solemn warning that his scholarship was in some danger, though he was not actually deprived of it, and finally, instead of the good class his tutor had once expected, he took a low third, and left Cambridge in almost as bad a plight as Arthur Pendennis.

Now he had found himself forced to accept a third-form mastership in his old school, where it seemed that, if he was no longer a disciple, he was scarcely a prophet.

But all this had only fanned his ambition. He would show the world there was something in him still; and he began to send up articles to various London magazines, and to keep them going like a juggler's oranges, until his productions obtained a fair circulation, in manuscript.

Now and then a paper of his did gain the honours of publication, so that his disease did not die out, as happens with some. He went on, writing whatever came into his head, and putting his ideas out in every variety of literary mould—from a blank-verse tragedy to a sonnet, and a three-volume novel to a society paragraph—with equal ardour and facility, and very little success.

For he believed in himself implicitly. At present he was still before the outwork of prejudice which must be stormed by every conscript in the army of literature: that he would carry it eventually he did not doubt. But this disappointment about, the committee hit him hard for a moment; it seemed like a forecast of a greater disaster. Mark, however, was of a sanguine temperament, and it did not take him long to remount his own pedestal. 'After all,' he thought, 'what does it matter? If my "Sweet Bells Jangled" is only taken, I shan't care about anything else. And there is some of my best work in that, too. I'll go round to Holroyd, and forget this business.'

CHAPTER II

A LAST WALK

Mark turned in from Chancery Lane under the old gateway, and went to one of the staircase doorways with the old curly eighteenth-century numerals cut on the centre stone of the arch and painted black. The days of these picturesque old dark-red buildings, with their small-paned dusty windows, their turrets and angles, and other little architectural surprises and inconveniences, are already numbered. Soon the sharp outline of their old gables and chimneys will cut the sky no longer; but some unpractical persons will be found who, although (or it may be because) they did not occupy them, will see them fall with a pang, and remember them with a kindly regret.

A gas jet was glimmering here and there behind the slits of dusty glass in the turret staircase as Mark came in, although it was scarcely dusk in the outer world; for Old Square is generally a little in advance in this respect. He passed the door laden with names and shining black plates announcing removals, till he came to an entrance on the second floor, where one of the names on a dingy ledge above the door was 'Mr. Vincent Holroyd.'

If Mark had been hitherto a failure, Vincent Holroyd could not be pronounced a success. He had been, certainly, more distinguished at college; but after taking his degree, reading for the Bar, and being called, three years had passed in forced inactivity—not, perhaps, an altogether unprecedented circumstance in a young barrister's career, but with the unpleasant probability, in his case, of a continued brieflessness. A dry and reserved manner, due to a secret shyness, had kept away many whose friendship might have been useful to him; and, though he was aware of this, he could not overcome the feeling; he was a lonely man, and had become enamoured of his loneliness. Of the interest popularly believed to be indispensable to a barrister he could command none, and, with more than the average amount of ability, the opportunity for displaying it was denied him; so that when he was suddenly called upon to leave England for an indefinite time, he was able to abandon prospects that were not brilliant without any particular reluctance.

Mark found him tying up his few books and effects in the one chamber which he had sub-rented, a little panelled room looking out on Chancery Lane, and painted the pea-green colour which, with a sickly buff, seem set apart for professional decoration.

His face, which was dark and somewhat plain, with large, strong features, had a pleasant look on it as he turned to meet Mark. 'I'm glad you could come,' he said. 'I thought we'd walk back together for the last time. I shall be ready in one minute. I'm only getting my law books together.'

'You're not going to take them out to Ceylon with you, then?'

'Not now. Brandon—my landlord, you know—will let me keep them here till I send for them. I've just seen him. Shall we go now?'

They passed out through the dingy, gas-lit clerk's room, and Holroyd stopped for a minute to speak to the clerk, a mild, pale man, who was neatly copying out an opinion at the foot of a case. 'Good-bye, Tucker,' he said, 'I don't suppose I shall see you again for some time.'

'Good-bye, Mr. 'Olroyd, sir. Very sorry to lose you. I hope you'll have a pleasant voy'ge, and get on over there, sir, better than you've done 'ere, sir.'

The clerk spoke with a queer mixture of patronage and deference: the deference was his ordinary manner with his employer in chief, a successful Chancery junior, and the patronage was caused by a pitying contempt he felt for a young man who had not got on.

'That 'Olroyd'll never do anything at the Bar,' he used to say when comparing notes with his friend the clerk to the opposite set of chambers. 'He's got no push, and he's got no manner, and there ain't nobody at his back. What he ever come to the Bar for at all, I don't know!'

There were some directions to be given as to letters and papers, which the mild clerk received with as much gravity as though he were not inwardly thinking, 'I'd eat all the papers as ever come in for you, and want dinner after 'em.' And then Holroyd left his chambers for the last time, and he and Mark went down the rickety winding stair, and out under the colonnade of the Vice-Chancellors' courts, at the closed doors of which a few clerks and reporters were copying down the cause list for the next day.

They struck across Lincoln's Inn Fields and Long Acre, towards Piccadilly and Hyde Park. It was by no means a typical November afternoon: the sky was a delicate blue and the air mild, with just enough of autumn keenness in it to remind one, not unpleasantly, of the real time of year.

'Well,' said Holroyd, rather sadly, 'you and I won't walk together like this again for a long time.'

'I suppose not,' said Mark, with a regret that sounded a little formal, for their approaching separation did not, as a matter of fact, make him particularly unhappy.

Holroyd had always cared for him much more than he had cared for Holroyd, for whom Mark's friendship had been a matter of circumstance rather than deliberate preference. They had been quartered in the same lodgings at Cambridge, and had afterwards 'kept' on the same staircase in college, which had led to a more or less daily companionship, a sort of intimacy that is not always strong enough to bear transplantation to town.

Holroyd had taken care that it should survive their college days; for he had an odd liking for Mark, in spite of a tolerably clear insight into his character. Mark had a way of inspiring friendships without much effort on his part, and this undemonstrative, self-contained man felt an affection for him which was stronger than he ever allowed himself to show.

Mark, for his part, had begun to feel an increasing constraint in the company of a friend who had an unpleasantly keen eye for his weak points, and with whom he was always conscious of a certain inferiority which, as he could discover no reason for it, galled his vanity the more.

His careless tone wounded Holroyd, who had hoped for some warmer response; and they walked on in silence until they turned into Hyde Park and crossed to Rotten Row, when Mark said, 'By the way, Vincent, wasn't there something you wanted to speak to me about?'

'I wanted to ask a favour of you; it won't give you much trouble,' said Holroyd.

'Oh, in that case, if it's anything I can do, you know—but what is it?'

'Well,' said Holroyd, 'the fact is—I never told a soul till now—but I've written a book.'

'Never mind, old boy,' said Mark, with a light laugh; for the confession, or perhaps a certain embarrassment with which it was made, seemed to put Holroyd more on a level with himself. 'So have lots of fellows, and no one thinks any the worse of them—unless they print it. Is it a law book?'

'Not exactly,' said Holroyd; 'it's a romance.'

'A romance!' cried Mark. 'You!'

'Yes,' said Holroyd, 'I. I've always been something of a dreamer, and I amused myself by putting one of my dreams down on paper. I wasn't disturbed.'

'You've been called though, haven't you?'

'I never got up,' said Holroyd, with a rather melancholy grimace. 'I began well enough. I used to come up to chambers by ten and leave at half-past six, after noting up reports and text-books all day; but no solicitor seemed struck by my industry. Then I sat in court and took down judgments most elaborately, but no leader ever asked me to take notes for him, and I never got a chance of suggesting anything to the court as amicus curiæ, for both the Vice-Chancellors seemed able to get along pretty well without me. Then I got tired of that, and somehow this book got into my head, and I couldn't rest till I'd got it out again. It's finished now, and I'm lonely again.'

'And you want me to run my eye over it and lick it into shape a little?' asked Mark.

'Not quite that,' said Holroyd; 'it must stand as it is. What I'm going to ask you is this: I don't know any fellow I would care to ask but yourself. I want it published. I shall be out of England, probably with plenty of other matters to occupy me for some time. I want you to look after the manuscript for me while I'm away. Do you mind taking the trouble?'

'Not a bit, old fellow,' said Mark, 'no trouble in the world; only tying up the parcel each time, sending it off again. Well, I didn't mean that; but it's no trouble, really.'

'I dare say you won't be called upon to see it through the press,' said Holroyd; 'but if such a thing as an acceptance should happen, I should like you to make all the arrangements. You've had some experience in these things, and I haven't, and I shall be away too.'

'I'll do the best I can,' said Mark. 'What sort of a book is it?'

'It's a romance, as I said,' said Holroyd. 'I don't know that I can describe it more exactly: it—'

'Oh, it doesn't matter,' interrupted Mark. 'I can read it some time. What have you called it?'

'"Glamour,"' said Holroyd, still with a sensitive shrinking at having to reveal what had long been a cherished secret.

'It isn't a society novel, I suppose?'

'No,' said Holroyd. 'I'm not much of a society man; I go out very little.'

'But you ought to, you know: you'll find people very glad to see you if you only cultivate them.'

There was something, however, in Mark's manner of saying this that suggested a consciousness that this might be a purely personal experience.

'Shall I?' said Holroyd. 'I don't know. People are kind enough, but they can only be really glad to see any one who is able to amuse them or interest them, and that's natural enough. I can't flatter myself that I'm particularly interesting or amusing; any way, it's too late to think about that now.'

'You won't be able to do the hermit much over in Ceylon, will you?'

'I don't know. My father's plantation is in rather a remote part of the island. I don't think he has ever been very intimate with the other planters near him, and as I left the place when I was a child I have fewer friends there than here even. But there will be plenty to do if I am to learn the business, as he seems to wish.'

'Did he never think of having you over before?'

'He wanted me to come over and practise at the Colombo Bar, but that was soon after I was called, and I preferred to try my fortune in England first. I was the second son, you see, and while my brother John was alive I was left pretty well to my own devices. I went, as you know, to Colombo in my second Long, but only for a few weeks of course, and my father and I didn't get on together somehow. But he's ill now, and poor John died of dysentery, and he's alone, so even if I had had any practice to leave I could hardly refuse to go out to him. As it is, as far as that is concerned, I have nothing to keep me.'

They were walking down Rotten Row as Holroyd said this, with the dull leaden surface of the Serpentine on their right, and away to the left, across the tan and the grey sward, the Cavalry Barracks, with their long narrow rows of gleaming windows. Up the long convex surface of the Row a faint white mist was crawling, and a solitary, spectral-looking horseman was cantering noiselessly out of it towards them. The evening had almost begun; the sky had changed to a delicate green tint, merged towards the west in a dusky crocus, against which the Memorial spire stood out sharp and black; from South Kensington came the sound of a church bell calling for some evening service.

'Doesn't that bell remind you somehow of Cambridge days?' said Mark. 'I could almost fancy we were walking up again from the boats, and that was the chapel bell ringing.'

'I wish we were,' said Holroyd with a sigh: 'they were good old times, and they will never come back.'

'You're very low, old fellow,' said Mark, 'for a man going back to his native country.'

'Ah, but I don't feel as if it was my native country, you see. I've lived here so long. And no one knows me out there except my poor old father, and we're almost strangers. I'm leaving the few people I care for behind me.'

'Oh, it will be all right,' said Mark, with the comfortable view one takes of another's future; 'you'll get on well enough. We shall have you a rich coffee planter, or a Deputy Judge Advocate, in no time. Any fellow has a chance out there. And you'll soon make friends in a place like that.'

'I like my friends ready-made, I think,' said Holroyd; 'but one must make the best of it, I suppose.'

They had come to the end of the Row; the gates of Kensington Gardens were locked, and behind the bars a policeman was watching them suspiciously, as if he suspected they might attempt a forcible entry.

'Well,' said Mark, stopping, 'I suppose you turn off here?' Holroyd would have been willing to go on with him as far as Kensington had Mark proposed it, but he gave no sign of desiring this, so his friend's pride kept him silent too.

'One word more about the—the book,' he said. 'I may put your name and address on the title-page, then? It goes off to Chilton and Fladgate to-night.'

'Oh yes, of course,' said Mark, 'put whatever you like.'

'I've not given them my real name, and, if anything comes of it, I should like that kept a secret.'

'Just as you please; but why?'

'If I keep on at the Bar, a novel, whether it's a success or not, is not the best bait for briefs,' said Holroyd; 'and besides, if I am to get a slating, I'd rather have it under an alias, don't you see? So the only name on the title-page is "Vincent Beauchamp."'

'Very well,' said Mark, 'none shall know till you choose to tell them, and, if anything has to be done about the book, I'll see to it with pleasure, and write to you when it's settled. So you can make your mind easy about that.'

'Thanks,' said Holroyd; 'and now, good-bye, Mark.'

There was real feeling in his voice, and Mark himself caught something of it as he took the hand Vincent held out.

'Good-bye, old boy,' he said. 'Take care of yourself—pleasant voyage and good luck. You're no letter-writer, I know, but you'll drop me a line now and then, I hope. What's the name of the ship you go out in?'

'The "Mangalore." She leaves the Docks to-morrow. Good-bye for the present, Mark. We shall see one another again, I hope. Don't forget all about me before that.'

'No, no,' said Mark; 'we've been friends too long for that.'

One more good-bye, a momentary English awkwardness in getting away from one another, and they parted, Holroyd walking towards Bayswater across the bridge, and Mark making for Queen's Gate and Kensington.

Mark looked after his friend's tall strong figure for a moment before it disappeared in the dark. 'Well, I've seen the last of him,' he thought. 'Poor old Holroyd! to think of his having written a book—he's one of those unlucky beggars who never make a hit at anything. I expect I shall have some trouble about it by-and-by.'

Holroyd walked on with a heavier heart. 'He won't miss me,' he told himself. 'Will Mabel say good-bye like that?'

CHAPTER III

GOOD-BYE

On the same afternoon in which we have seen Mark and Vincent walk home together for the last time, Mrs. Langton and her eldest daughter Mabel were sitting in the pretty drawing-room of their house in Kensington Park Gardens.

Mrs. Langton was the wife of a successful Q.C. at the Chancery Bar, and one of those elegantly languid women with a manner charming enough to conceal a slight shallowness of mind and character; she was pretty still, and an invalid at all times when indisposition was not positively inconvenient.

It was one of her 'at home' days, but fewer people than usual had made their appearance, and these had filtered away early, leaving traces of their presence behind them in the confidential grouping of seats and the teacups left high and dry in various parts of the room.

Mrs. Langton was leaning luxuriously back in a low soft chair, lazily watching the firebeams glisten through the stained-glass screen, and Mabel was on a couch near the window trying to read a magazine by the fading light.

'Hadn't you better ring for the lamps, Mabel?' suggested her mother. 'You can't possibly see to read by this light, and it's so trying for the eyes. I suppose no one else will call now, but it's very strange that Vincent should not have come to say good-bye.'

'Vincent doesn't care about "at homes,"' said Mabel.

'Still, not to say good-bye—after knowing us so long, too! and I'm sure we've tried to show him every kindness. Your father was always having solicitors to meet him at dinner, and it was never any use; and he sails to-morrow. I think he might have found time to come!'

'So do I,' agreed Mabel. 'It's not like Vincent, though he was always shy and odd in some things. He hasn't been to see us nearly so much lately, but I can't believe he will really go away without a word.'

Mrs. Langton yawned delicately. 'It would not surprise me, I must say,' she said. 'When a young man sets himself—' but whatever she was going to say was broken off by the entrance of her youngest daughter Dolly, with the German governess, followed by the man bearing rose-shaded lamps.

Dolly was a vivacious child of about nine, with golden locks which had a pretty ripple in them, and deep long-lashed eyes that promised to be dangerous one day. 'We took Frisk out without the leash, mummy,' she cried, 'and when we got into Westbourne Grove he ran away. Wasn't it too bad of him?'

'Never mind, darling, he'll come back quite safe—he always does.'

'Ah, but it's his running away that I mind,' said Dolly; 'and you know what a dreadful state he always will come back in. He must be cured of doing it somehow.'

'Talk to him very seriously about it, Dolly,' said Mabel.

'I've tried that—and he only cringes and goes and does it again directly he's washed. I know what I'll do, Mabel. When he comes back this time, he shall have a jolly good whacking!'

'My dear child,' cried Mrs. Langton, 'what a dreadful expression!'

'Colin says it,' said Dolly, though she was quite aware that Colin was hardly a purist in his expressions.

'Colin says a good many things that are not pretty in a little girl's mouth.'

'So he does,' said Dolly cheerfully. 'I wonder if he knows? I'll go and tell him of it—he's come home.' And she ran off just as the door-bell rang.

'Mabel, I really think that must be some one else coming to call after all. Do you know, I feel so tired and it's so late that I think I will leave you and Fräulein to talk to them. Papa and I are going out to dinner to-night, and I must rest a little before I begin to dress. I'll run away while I can.'

Mrs. Langton fluttered gracefully out of the room as the butler crossed the hall to open the door, evidently to a visitor, and presently Mabel heard 'Mr. Holroyd' announced.

'So you really have come after all,' said Mabel, holding out her hand with a pretty smile of welcome. 'Mamma and I thought you meant to go away without a word.'

'You might have known me better than that,' said Holroyd.

'But when your last afternoon in England was nearly over and no sign of you, there was some excuse for thinking so; but you have come at last, so we won't scold you. Will you have some tea? It isn't very warm, I'm afraid, but you are so very late, you know. Ring, and you shall have some fit to drink.'

Vincent accepted tea, chiefly because he wanted to be waited upon once more by her with the playful, gracious manner, just tinged with affectionate mockery, which he knew so well; and then he talked to her and Fräulein Mozer, with a heavy sense of the unsatisfactory nature of this triangular conversation for a parting interview.

The governess felt this too. She had had a shrewd suspicion for some time of the state of Holroyd's feelings towards Mabel, and felt a sentimental pity for him, condemned as he was to disguise them under ordinary afternoon conversation.

'He is going away,' she thought; 'but he shall have his chance, the poor young man. You will not think it very rude, Mr. Holroyd,' she said, rising: 'it will not disturb you if I practise? There is a piece which I am to play at a school concert to-morrow, and do not yet know it.'

'Vincent won't mind, Ottilia dear,' said Mabel. 'Will you, Vincent?' So the governess went to the further room where the piano stood, and was soon performing a conveniently noisy German march. Vincent sat still for some moments watching Mabel. He wished to keep in his memory the impression of her face as he saw it then, lighted up by the soft glow of the heavily shaded lamp at her elbow; a spirited and yet tender face, with dark-grey eyes, a sensitive, beautiful mouth, and brown hair with threads of gold in it which gleamed in the lamplight as she turned her graceful head.

He knew it would fade only too soon, as often happens with the face we best love and have reason chiefly to remember. Others will rise unbidden with the vividness of a photograph, but the one face eludes us more and more, till no effort of the mind will call it up with any distinctness.

Mabel was the first to speak. 'Are you very fond of music, Vincent?' she said a little maliciously. 'Would you rather be allowed to listen in peace, or talk? You may talk, you know.'

'I came late on purpose to see as much of you as possible,' said poor Vincent. 'This is the last time I shall be able to talk to you for so long.'

'I know,' said Mabel, simply; 'I'm very sorry, Vincent.' But there was only a frank friendliness in her eyes as she spoke, nothing more, and Vincent knew it.

'So am I,' he said. 'Do you know, Mabel, I have no photograph of you. Will you give me one to take away with me?'

'Of course, if I have one,' she said, as she went to a table for an album. 'Oh, Vincent, I'm so sorry. I'm afraid there's not one left. But I can give you one of mother and father and Dolly, and I think Colin too.'

'I should like all those very much,' said Vincent, who could not accept this offer as a perfect substitute, 'but can't you find one of yourself, not even an old one?'

'I think I can give you one after all,' said Mabel; 'wait a minute.' And as she came back after a minute's absence she said, 'Here's one I had promised to Gilda Featherstone, but Gilda can wait and you can't. I'll give you an envelope to put them all in, and then we will talk. Tell me first how long you are going to be away?'

'No longer than I can help,' said Vincent, 'but it depends on so many things.'

'But you will write to us, won't you?'

'Will you answer if I do?'

'Of course,' said Mabel. 'Don't you remember when I was a little girl, and used to write to you at school, and at Trinity too? I was always a better correspondent than you were, Vincent.'

Just then Dolly came, holding a cage of lovebirds. 'Champion said you were here,' she began. 'Vincent, wait till I put Jachin and Boaz down. Now you can kiss me. I knew you wouldn't go away without saying good-bye to me. You haven't seen my birds, have you? Papa gave them to me. They're such chilly birds, I've brought them in here to get warm.'

'They're very much alike,' said Vincent, looking into the cage, upon which each bird instantly tried to hide its head in the sand underneath the other.

'They're exactly the same,' said Dolly, 'so I never know which is Jachin and which is Boaz; but they don't know their own names, and if they did they wouldn't answer to them, so it doesn't matter so very much after all, does it?'

As it never occurred to Dolly that anybody could have the bad taste to prefer any one else's conversation to her own, she took entire possession of Vincent, throwing herself into the couch nearest to him, and pouring out her views on lovebirds generally to his absent ear.

'They don't know me yet,' she concluded, 'but then I've only had them six months. Do you know, Harold Caffyn says they're little humbugs, and kiss one another only when people look at them. I have caught them fighting dreadfully myself. I don't think lovebirds ought to fight. Do you? Oh, and Harold says that when one dies I ought to time the other and see how long it takes him to pine away; but Harold is always saying horrid things like that.'

'Dolly dear,' cried the governess from the inner room, 'will you run and ask Colin if he has taken away the metronome to the schoolroom?'

Dolly danced out to hunt for that prosaic instrument in a desultory way, and then forget it in some dispute with Colin, who generally welcomed any distraction whilst preparing his school-work—a result which Fräulein Mozer probably took into account, particularly as she had the metronome by her side at the time. 'Poor Mr. Vincent!' she thought; 'he has not come to talk with Dolly of lovebirds.'

'You will be sure to write and tell us all about yourself,' said Mabel. 'What do you mean to do out there, Vincent?'

'Turn coffee-planter, perhaps,' he said gloomily.

'Oh, Vincent!' she said reproachfully, 'you used to be so ambitious. Don't you remember how we settled once that you were going to be famous? You can't be very famous by coffee-planting, can you?'

'If I do that, it is only because I see nothing else to do. But I am ambitious still, Mabel. I shall not be content with that, if a certain venture of mine is successful enough to give me hopes of anything better. But it's a very big "if" at present.'

'What is the venture?' said Mabel. 'Tell me, Vincent; you used to tell me everything once.'

Vincent had very few traces of his tropical extraction in his nature, and his caution and reserve would have made him disposed to wait at least until his book were safe in the haven of printer's ink before confessing that he was an author.

But Mabel's appeal scattered all his prudence. He had written with Mabel as his public; with the chief hope in his mind that some day she would see his work and say that it was well done. He felt a strong impulse to confide in her now, and have the comfort of her sympathy and encouragement to carry away with him.

If he had been able to tell her then of his book, and his plans respecting it, Mabel might have looked upon him with a new interest, and much that followed in her life might have been prevented. But he hesitated for a moment, and while he hesitated a second interruption took place. The opportunity was gone, and, like most opportunities in conversation, once missed was gone for ever. The irrepressible Dolly was the innocent instrument: she came in with a big portfolio of black and white papers, which she put down on a chair. 'I can't find the metronome anywhere, Fräulein,' she said. 'I've been talking to Colin: he wants you to come and say good-bye before you go, Vincent. Colin says he nearly got "swished" to-day, only his master begged him off because he'd done nothing at all really. Wasn't it nice of him? Ask him to tell you about it. Oh, and, Vincent, I want your head for my album. May I cut it out?'

'I want it, myself, Dolly, please,' said Vincent; 'I don't think I can do without it just yet.'

'I don't mean your real head,' said Dolly, 'I believe you know that—it's only the outline I want!'

'It isn't a very dreadful operation, Vincent,' said Mabel. 'Dolly has been victimising all her friends lately, but she doesn't hurt them.'

'Very well, Dolly, I consent,' said Vincent; 'only be gentle with me.'

'Sit down here on this chair against the wall,' said Dolly, imperiously. 'Mabel, please take the shade off the lamp and put it over here.' She armed herself with a pencil and a large sheet of white paper as she spoke. 'Now, Vincent, put yourself so that your shadow comes just here, and keep perfectly still. Don't move, or talk, or anything, or your profile will be spoilt!'

'I feel very nervous, Dolly,' said Vincent, sitting down obediently.

'What a coward you must be! Why, one of the boys at Colin's school said he rather liked it. Will you hold his head steady, Mabel, please?—no, you hold the paper up while I trace.'

Vincent sat still while Mabel leaned over the back of his chair, with one hand lightly touching his shoulder, while her soft hair swept across his cheek now and then. Long after—as long as he lived, in fact—he remembered those moments with a thrill.

'Now I have done, Vincent,' cried Dolly, triumphantly, after some laborious tracing on the paper. 'You haven't got much of a profile, but it will be exactly like you when I've cut it out. There!' she said, as she held up a life-size head cut out in curling black paper; 'don't you think it's like you, yourself?'

'I don't know,' said Vincent, inspecting it rather dubiously, 'but I must say I hope it isn't.'

'I'll give you a copy to take away with you,' said Dolly, generously, as she cut out another black head with her deft little hands. 'There, that's for you, Vincent—you won't give it away, will you?'

'Shall I promise to wear it always next to my heart, Dolly?'

Dolly considered this question. 'I think you'd better not,' she said at last: 'it would keep you warm certainly, but I'm afraid the black comes off—you must have it mounted on cardboard and framed, you know.'

At this point Mrs. Langton came rustling down, and Vincent rose to meet her, with a desperate hope that he would be asked to spend the whole of his last evening with them—a hope that was doomed to disappointment.

'My dear Vincent,' she said, holding out both her hands, 'so you've come after all. Really, I was quite afraid you'd forgotten us. Why didn't somebody tell me Vincent was here, Mabel? I would have hurried over my dressing to come down. It's so very provoking, Vincent, but I have to say good-bye in a hurry. My husband and I are going out to dinner, and he wouldn't come home to change, so he will dress at his chambers, and I have to go up and fetch him. And it's so late, and they dine so ridiculously early where we're going, and he's sure to keep me waiting such a time, I mustn't lose another minute. Will you see me to the carriage, Vincent? Thanks. Has Marshall put the footwarmer in, and is the drugget down? Then we'll go, please; and I wish you every success in—over there, you know, and you must be careful of yourself and bring home a nice wife.—Lincoln's Inn, tell him, please.—Good-bye, Vincent, good-bye!'

And she smiled affectionately and waved her long-gloved hand behind the window as the carriage rolled off, and all the time he knew that it would not distress her if she never saw him again.

He went slowly back to the warm drawing-room, with its delicate perfume of violets. He had no excuse for lingering there any longer—he must say his last words to Mabel and go. But before he could make up his mind to this another visitor was announced, who must have come up almost as Mrs. Langton had driven off.

'Mr. Caffyn,' said Champion, imposingly, who had a graceful way of handing dishes and a dignified deference in his bow which in his own opinion excused certain attacks of solemn speechlessness and eccentricity of gait that occasionally overcame him.

A tall, graceful young man came in, with an air of calm and ease that was in the slightest degree exaggerated. He had short light hair, well-shaped eyes, which were keen and rather cold, and a firm, thin-lipped mouth; his voice, which he had under perfect control, was clear and pleasant.

'Do you mean this for an afternoon call, Harold?' asked Mabel, who did not seem altogether pleased at his arrival.

'Yes, we're not at home now, are we Mabel?' put in audacious Dolly.

'I was kept rather late at rehearsal, and I had to dine afterwards,' explained Caffyn; 'but I shouldn't have come in if I had not had a commission to perform. When I have done it you can send me away.'

Harold Caffyn was a relation of Mrs. Langton's. His father was high up in the consular service abroad, and he himself had lately gone on the stage, finding it more attractive than the Foreign Office, for which he had been originally intended. He had had no reason as yet to regret his apostasy, for he had obtained almost at once an engagement in a leading West-end theatre, while his social prospects had not been materially affected by the change; partly because the world has become more liberal of late in these matters, and partly because he had contrived to gain a tolerably secure position in it already, by the help of a pleasant manner and the musical and dramatic accomplishments which had led him to adopt the stage as his profession.

Like Holroyd, he had known Mabel from a child, and as she grew up had felt her attraction too much for his peace of mind. His one misgiving in going on the stage had been lest it should lessen his chance of finding favour with her.

This fear proved groundless: Mabel had not altered to him in the least. But his successes as an amateur had not followed him to the public stage; he had not as yet been entrusted with any but very minor rôles, and was already disenchanted enough with his profession to be willing to give it up on very moderate provocation.

'Why, Holroyd, I didn't see you over there. How are you?' he said cordially, though his secret feelings were anything but cordial, for he had long seen reason to consider Vincent as a possible rival.

'Vincent has come to say good-bye,' explained Dolly. 'He's going to India to-morrow.'

'Good-bye!' said Caffyn, his face clearing: 'that's rather sudden, isn't it, Holroyd? Well, I'm very glad I am able to say good-bye too' (as there is no doubt Caffyn was). 'You never told me you were off so soon.'

Holroyd had known Caffyn for several years: they had frequently met in that house, and, though there was little in common between them, their relations had always been friendly.

'It was rather sudden,' Holroyd said, 'and we haven't met lately.'

'And you're off to-morrow, eh? I'm sorry. We might have managed a parting dinner before you went—it must be kept till you come back.'

'What was the commission, Harold?' asked Mabel.

'Oh, ah! I met my uncle to-day, and he told me to find out if you would be able to run down to Chigbourne one Saturday till Monday soon. I suppose you won't. He's a dear old boy, but he's rather a dull old pump to stay two whole days with.'

'You forget he's Dolly's godfather,' said Mabel.

'And he's my uncle,' said Caffyn; 'but he's not a bit the livelier for that, you know. You're asked, too Juggins.' (Juggins was a name he had for Dolly, whom he found pleasure in teasing, and who was not deeply attached to him.)

'Would you like to go, Dolly, if mother says yes?' asked Mabel.

'Is Harold going?' said Dolly.

'Harold does not happen to be asked, my Juggins,' said that gentleman blandly.

'Then we'll go, Mabel, and I shall take Frisk, because Uncle Anthony hasn't seen him for a long time.'

Holroyd saw no use in staying longer. He went into the schoolroom to see Colin, who was as sorry to say good-bye as the pile of school-books in front of him allowed, and then he returned to take leave of the others. The governess read in his face that her well-meant services had been of no avail, and sighed compassionately as she shook hands. Dolly nestled against him and cried a little, and the cool Harold felt so strongly that he could afford to be generous now, that he was genial and almost affectionate in his good wishes.

His face clouded, however, when Mabel said 'Don't ring, Ottilia. I will go to the door with Vincent—it's the last time.' 'I wonder if she cares about the fellow!' he thought uneasily.

'You won't forget to write to us as soon as you can, Vincent?' said Mabel, as they stood in the hall together. 'We shall be thinking of you so often, and wondering what you are doing, and how you are.'

The hall of a London house is perhaps hardly the place for love-passages—there is something fatally ludicrous about a declaration amongst the hats and umbrellas. In spite of a consciousness of this, however, Vincent felt a passionate impulse even then, at that eleventh hour, to tell Mabel something of what was in his heart.

But he kept silence: a surer instinct warned him that he had delayed too long to have any chance of success then. It was the fact that Mabel had no suspicion of the real nature of his feelings, and he was right in concluding as he did that to avow it then would come upon her as a shock for which she was unprepared.

Fräulein Mozer's inclination to a sentimental view of life, and Caffyn's tendency to see a rival in every one, had quickened their insight respectively; but Mabel herself, though girls are seldom the last to discover such symptoms, had never thought of Vincent as a possible lover, for which his own undemonstrative manner and procrastination were chiefly to blame.

He had shrunk from betraying his feelings before. 'She can never care for me,' he had thought; 'I have done nothing to deserve her—I am nobody,' and this had urged him on to do something which might qualify him in his own eyes, until which he had steadily kept his own counsel and seen her as seldom as possible.

Then he had written his book; and though he was not such a fool as to imagine that any woman's heart could be approached through print alone, he could not help feeling on revising his work that he had done that which, if successful, would remove something of his own unworthiness, and might give him a new recommendation to a girl of Mabel's literary sympathy.

But then his father's summons to Ceylon had come—he was compelled to obey, and now he had to tear himself away with his secret still untold, and trust to time and absence (who are remarkably overrated as advocates by the way) to plead for him.

He felt the full bitterness of this as he held both her hands and looked down on her fair face with the sweet eyes that shone with a sister's—but only a sister's—affection. 'She would have loved me in time,' he thought; 'but the time may never come now.'

He did not trust himself to say much: he might have asked and obtained a kiss, as an almost brother who was going far away, but to him that would have been the hollowest mockery.

Suppressed emotion made him abrupt and almost cold, he let her hands drop suddenly, and with nothing more than a broken 'God bless you, Mabel, good-bye, dear, good-bye!' he left the house hurriedly, and the moment after he was alone on the hill with his heartache.

'So he's gone!' remarked Caffyn, as she re-entered the drawing-room after lingering a few moments in the empty hall. 'What a dear, dull old plodder it is, isn't it? He'll do much better at planting coffee than he ever did at law—at least, it's to be hoped so!'

'You are very fond of calling other people dull, Harold,' said Mabel, with a displeased contraction of her eyebrows. 'Vincent is not in the least dull: you only speak of him like that because you don't understand him.'

'I didn't say it disparagingly,' said Caffyn. 'I rather admire dulness; it's so restful. But as you say, Mabel, I dare say I don't understand him: he really doesn't give a fellow a fair chance. As far as I know him, I do like him uncommonly; but, at the same time, I must confess he has always given me the impression of being, don't you know, just a trifle heavy. But very likely I'm wrong.'

'Very likely indeed,' said Mabel, closing the subject. But Caffyn had not spoken undesignedly, and had risked offending her for the moment for the sake of producing the effect he wanted; and he was not altogether unsuccessful. 'Was Harold right?' she thought later. 'Vincent is very quiet, but I always thought there was power of some sort behind; and yet—would it not have shown itself before now? But if poor Vincent is only dull, it will make no difference to me; I shall like him just as much.'

But, for all that, the suggestion very effectually prevented all danger of Vincent's becoming idealised by distance into something more interesting than a brother—which was, indeed, the reason why Caffyn made it.

Vincent himself, meanwhile, unaware—as all of us would pray to be kept unaware—of the portrait of himself, by a friend, which was being exhibited to the girl he loved, was walking down Ladbroke Hill to spend the remainder of his last evening in England in loneliness at his rooms; for he had no heart for anything else.

It was dark by that time. Above him was a clear, steel-blue sky; in front, across the hollow, rose Campden Hill, a dim, dark mass, twinkling with lights. By the square at his side a German band was playing the garden music from 'Faust,' with no more regard for expression and tunefulness than a German band is ever capable of; but distance softened the harshness and imperfection of their rendering, and Siebel's air seemed to Vincent the expression of his own passionate, unrequited devotion.

'I would do anything for her,' he said, half aloud, 'and yet I dared not tell her then.... But if I ever come back to her again—before it is too late—she shall know all she is and always will be to me. I will wait and hope for that.'

CHAPTER IV

MALAKOFF TERRACE

After parting from Vincent at the end of Rotten Row, Mark Ashburn continued his walk alone through Kensington High Street and onwards, until he came to one of those quiet streets which serve as a sort of backwater to the main stream of traffic, and, turning down this, it was not long before he reached a row of small three-story houses, with their lower parts cased in stucco, but the rest allowed to remain in the original yellow-brown brick, which time had mellowed to a pleasant warm tone. 'Malakoff Terrace,' as the place had been christened (and the title was a tolerable index of its date), was rather less depressing in appearance than many of its more modern neighbours, with their dismal monotony and pretentiousness. It faced a well-kept enclosure, with trim lawns and beds, and across the compact laurel hedges in the little front gardens a curious passer-by might catch glimpses of various interiors which in nearly every case left him with an impression of cosy comfort. The outline of the terrace was broken here and there by little verandahs protecting the shallow balconies and painted a deep Indian-red or sap-green, which in summer time were gay with flowers and creepers, and one seldom passed there then on warm and drowsy afternoons without undergoing a well-sustained fire from quite a masked battery of pianos, served from behind the fluttering white curtains at most of the long open windows on the first floor.

Even in winter and at night the terrace was cheerful, with its variety of striped and coloured blinds and curtains at the illuminated windows; and where blinds and curtains were undrawn and the little front rooms left unlighted, the firelight flickering within on shining bookcases and picture frames was no less pleasantly suggestive. Still, in every neighbourhood there will always be some houses whose exteriors are severely unattractive; without being poverty-stricken, they seem to belong to people indifferent to all but the absolutely essential, and incapable of surrounding themselves with any of the characteristic contrivances that most homes which are more than mere lodgings amass almost unconsciously. It was before a house of this latter kind that Mark stopped—a house with nothing in the shape of a verandah to relieve its formality. Behind its front railings there were no trim laurel bushes—only an uncomfortable bed of equal parts of mould and broken red tiles, in which a withered juniper was dying hard; at the windows were no bright curtain-folds or hanging baskets of trailing fern to give a touch of colour, but dusty wire blinds and hangings of a faded drab.

It was not a boarding-house, but the home in which Mark Ashburn lived with his family, who, if they were not precisely gay, were as respectable as any in the terrace, which is better in some respects than mere gaiety.

He found them all sitting down to dinner in the back parlour, a square little room with a grey paper of a large and hideous design. His mother, a stout lady with a frosty complexion, a cold grey eye, and an injured expression about the mouth and brow, was serving out soup with a touch of the relieving officer in her manner; opposite to her was her husband, a mild little man in habitually low spirits; and the rest of the family, Mark's two sisters, Martha and Trixie, and his younger brother, Cuthbert, were in their respective places.

Mrs. Ashburn looked up severely as he came in. 'You are late again, Mark,' she said; 'while you are under this roof' (Mrs. Ashburn was fond of referring to the roof) 'your father and I expect you to conform to the rules of the house.'

'Well, you see, mother,' explained Mark, sitting down and unfolding his napkin, 'it was a fine afternoon, so I thought I would walk home with a friend.'

'There is a time for walking home with a friend, and a time for dinner,' observed his mother, with the air of quoting something Scriptural.

'And I've mixed them, mother? So I have; I'm sorry, and I won't do it again. There, will that do?'

'Make haste and eat your soup, Mark, and don't keep us all waiting for you.'

Mrs. Ashburn had never quite realised that her family had grown up. She still talked to Mark as she had done when he was a careless schoolboy at St. Peter's; she still tried to enforce little moral lessons and even petty restrictions upon her family generally; and though she had been long reduced to blank cartridges, it worried them.

The ideal family circle, on re-assembling at the close of the day, celebrate their reunion with an increasing flow of lively conversation; those who have been out into the great world describe their personal experiences, and the scenes, tragic or humorous, which they have severally witnessed during the day; and when these are exhausted, the female members take up the tale and relate the humbler incidents of domestic life, and so the hours pass till bedtime.

Such circles are in all sincerity to be congratulated; but it is to be feared that in the majority of cases the conversation of a family whose members meet every day is apt, among themselves, to become frightfully monosyllabic. It was certainly so with the Ashburns. Mark and Trixie sometimes felt the silences too oppressive to be borne, and made desperate attempts at establishing a general discussion on something or anything; but it was difficult to select a topic that could not be brought down by an axiom from Mrs. Ashburn, which disposed of the whole subject in very early infancy. Cuthbert generally came back from the office tired and somewhat sulky; Martha's temper was not to be depended upon of an evening; and Mr. Ashburn himself rarely contributed more than a heavy sigh to the common stock of conversation.

Under these circumstances it will be readily believed that Mark's 'Evenings at Home' were by no means brilliant. He sometimes wondered himself why he had borne them so long; and if he had been able to procure comfortable lodgings at as cheap a rate as it cost him to live at home, he would probably have taken an early opportunity of bursting the bonds of the family dulness. But his salary was not large, his habits were expensive, and he stayed on.

The beginning of this particular evening did not promise any marked increase in the general liveliness. Mrs. Ashburn announced lugubriously to all whom it might concern that she had eaten no lunch; Martha mentioned that a Miss Hornblower had called that afternoon—which produced no sensation, though Cuthbert seemed for a moment inclined to ask who Miss Hornblower might happen to be, till he remembered in time that he really did not care, and saved himself the trouble. Then Trixie made a well-meant, but rather too obvious, effort to allure him to talk by an inquiry (which had become something of a formula) whether he had 'seen any one' that day, to which Cuthbert replied that he had noticed one or two people hanging about the City; and Martha observed that she was glad to see he still kept up his jokes, moving him to confess sardonically that he knew he was a funny dog, but when he saw them all—and particularly Martha—rollicking round him, he could not help bubbling over with merriment himself.

Mrs. Ashburn caught the reply, and said severely: 'I do not think, Cuthbert, that either I or your father have ever set you the example of "rollicking," as you call it, at this table. Decent mirth and a cheerful tone of conversation we have always encouraged. I don't know why you should receive a mother's remarks with laughter. It is not respectful of you, Cuthbert, I must say!'

Mrs. Ashburn would probably have proceeded to further defend herself and family from the charge of rollicking, and to draw uncomplimentary parallels from the Proverbs between the laughter of certain persons and the crackling of thorns under a pot, when a timely diversion was effected by a sounding knock at the little front door. The maid put down the dish she was handing and vanished; after which there were sounds of a large body entering the passage, and a loud voice exclaiming, 'All in, hey? and at dinner, are they? Very well, my dear; tell 'em I'm here. I know my way in.'

'It's Uncle Solomon!' went round the table. They refrained from any outward expression of joy, because they were naturally a quiet family.

'Well,' said Mrs. Ashburn, who seemed to put her own construction on this reserve, 'and I'm sure if there is any table at which my only brother Solomon should be a welcome guest, it's this table.'

'Quite so, my dear; quite so,' said Mr. Ashburn, hastily. 'He was here last week; but we're all glad to see him at any time, I'm sure.'

'I hope so, indeed! Go in, Trixie, and help your uncle off with his coat,' for there were snorting and puffing signs from the next room, as if their relative were in difficulties; but before Trixie could rise the voice was heard again, 'That's it, Ann, thanky—you're called Ann, aren't you? I thought so. Ah, how's the baker, Ann—wasn't it the baker I caught down the airy now? wasn't it, hey?'

And then a large red-faced person came in, with a puffy important mouth, a fringe of whiskers meeting under his chin, and what Trixie, in speaking privately of her relative's personal appearance, described as 'little piggy eyes,' which had, however, a twinkle of a rather primitive kind of humour in them.

Solomon Lightowler was a brother of Mrs. Ashburn's, a retired business man, who had amassed a considerable fortune in the hardware trade.

He was a widower and without children, and it was he who, fired with the ambition of placing a nephew in the Indian Civil Service as a rising monument to his uncle's perception, had sent Mark to the crammer's—for Mr. Ashburn's position in the Inland Revenue Office would scarcely have warranted such an outlay.

Mark's performances at his first examination, as has been said, had not been calculated to encourage his uncle's hopes, but the latter had been slightly mollified by his nephew's spirit in carrying off the Cambridge scholarship soon afterwards, and with the idea of having one more attempt to 'see his money back,' Mr. Lightowler had consented to keep him for the necessary time at the University. When that experiment also had ended in disaster, Uncle Solomon seemed at one time to have given him up in disgust, only reserving himself, as the sole value for his money, the liberty of reproach, and Mark was of opinion that he had already gone far towards recouping himself in this respect alone.

'Hah! phew—you're very hot in here!' he remarked, as an agreeable opening—he felt himself rich enough to be able to remark on other people's atmospheres; but Cuthbert expressed a sotto voce wish that his uncle were exposed to an even higher temperature.

'We can't all live in country houses, Solomon,' said his sister, 'and a small room soon gets warm to any one coming in from the cold air.'

'Warm!' said Mr. Lightowler, with a snort; 'I should think you must all of you be fired like a set of pots! I don't care where I sit, so long as I'm well away from the fire. I'll come by you, Trixie, eh—you'll take care of your uncle, won't you?'

Trixie was a handsome girl of about eighteen, with abundant auburn hair, which was never quite in good order, and pretty hands of which most girls would have been more careful; she had developed a limp taste for art of late, finding drawing outlines at an art school less irksome than assisting in the housekeeping at home. Uncle Solomon always alarmed her because she never knew what he would say next; but as it was a family rule to be civil to him, she made room for him with great apparent alacrity.

'And how are you all, boys and girls, eh?' asked Uncle Solomon, when he was comfortably seated; 'Mark, you've got fuller in the waist of late; you don't take 'alf enough exercise. Cuthbert, lad, you're looking very sallow under the eyes—smoking and late hours, that's the way with all the young men nowadays! Why don't you talk to him, eh, Matthew? I should if he was a boy o' mine. Well, Martha, has any nice young man asked you to name a day yet?—he's a long time coming forward, Martha, that nice young man; why, let me see, Jane, she must be getting on now for—she was born in the year fifty-four, was it?—four it was; it was in the war time, I remember, and you wanted her christened Alma, but I said an uncommon name is all very well if she grows up good-looking, but if she's plain it only sounds ridiklous; so, very fortunately as things turn out, you had her christened Martha. There's nothing to bite your lips over, my dear; no one blames you for it, we can't be all born 'andsome. It's Trixie here who gets all the love-letters, isn't it, Trixie?—ah, I thought I should see a blush if I looked! Who is it now, Trixie, and where do we meet him, and when is the wedding? Come, tell your old uncle.'

'Don't put such nonsense into the child's head, Solomon,' said his sister, in a slightly scandalised tone.

'That would be coals to Newcastle with a vengeance,' he chuckled; 'but you mustn't mind my going on— that's my way; if people don't like it I can't help it, but I always speak right out.'

'Which is the reason we love him,' came in a stage aside from Cuthbert, who took advantage of a slight deafness in one of his uncle's ears.

'Well, Mr. Schoolmaster,' said the latter, working round to Mark again, 'and how are you gettin' on? If you'd worked harder at College and done me credit, you'd 'a' been a feller of your college, or a judge in an Indian court, by this time, instead of birching naughty little boys.'

'It's a detail,' said Mark; 'but I don't interfere in that department.'

'Well, you are young to be trusted with a birch. I'm glad they look at things that way. If you're satisfied with yourself, I suppose I ought to be, though I did look forward once to seeing a nephew of mine famous. You've 'ad all your fame at Cambridge, with your papers, and your poems, and your College skits—a nice snug little fame all to yourself.'

Martha tittered acidly at this light badinage, but it brought a pained look into Trixie's large brown eyes, who thought it was a shame that poor Mark should never be allowed to hear the last of his Cambridge fiasco.

Even Mrs. Ashburn seemed anxious to shield Mark. 'Ah, Solomon,' she said, 'Mark sees his folly now; he knows how wrong he was to spend his time in idle scribbling to amuse thoughtless young men, when he ought to have studied hard and shown his gratitude to you for all you have done for him.'

'Well, I've been a good friend to him, Jane, and I could have been a better if he'd proved deserving. I'm not one to grudge any expense. And if I thought, even now, that he'd really given up his scribbling—'

Mark thought it prudent to equivocate: 'Even if I wished to write, uncle,' he said, 'what with my school-work, and what with reading for the Bar, I should not have much time for it; but mother is right, I do see my folly now.'

This pleased Uncle Solomon, who still clung to the fragments of his belief in Mark's ability, and had been gratified upon his joining one of the Inns of Court by the prospect of having a nephew who at least would have the title of barrister; he relaxed at once: 'Well, well, let bygones be bygones, you may be a credit to me yet. And now I think of it, come down and stay Sunday at "The Woodbines" soon, will you? it'll be a rest for you, and I want you to see some of that 'Umpage's goings on at the church.' (Uncle Solomon not unfrequently dropped an 'h,' but with a deliberation that seemed to say that he was quite aware it was there, but did not consider it advisable to recognise it just then.) 'He's quite got round the Vicar; made him have flowers and a great brass cross and candles on the Communion table, and 'Umpage all the time a feller with no more religion inside him than'—here he looked round the table for a comparison—'ah, than that jug has! He's talked the Vicar into getting them little bags for collections now, all because he was jealous at the clerk's putting the plate inside my pew reg'lar for me to hold. It isn't that I care about 'olding a plate, but to see 'Umpage smirking round with one of them red velvet bags makes me downright sick—they'll drive me to go over and be a Baptist one of these fine days.'

'You don't like Mr. Humpage, do you, uncle?' said Trixie.

''Umpage and me are not friendly—though contiguous,' said he; 'but as for liking, I neither like nor dislike the man; we 'old no intercourse, beyond looking the other way in church and 'aving words across the fence when his fowls break through into my garden—he won't have the hole seen to, so I shall get it done myself and send the bill in to him—that's what I shall do.—A letter for you, Matthew? read away, don't mind me,' for the maid had come in meanwhile with a letter, which Matthew Ashburn opened and began to read at this permission.

Presently he rubbed his forehead perplexedly: 'I can't make head or tail of it,' he said feebly; 'I don't know who they are, or what they write all this to me for!'

''And it over to me, Matthew; let's see if I can make it any plainer for you,' said his brother-in-law, persuaded that to his powerful mind few things could long remain a mystery.

He took the letter, solemnly settled his double eyeglasses well down on his broad nose, coughed importantly, and began to read: 'Dear Sir,' he began in a tone of expounding wisdom—'well, that's straightforward enough—Dear Sir, we have given our best consideration to the—hey!' (here his face began to grow less confident) 'the sweet—what?—ah, sweet bells, sweet bells jangled. What have you been jangling your bells about, eh, Matthew?'

'I think they're mad,' said poor Mr. Ashburn; 'the bells in this house are all right, I think, my dear?'

'I'm not aware that any of them are out of order; they rehung the bell in the area the other day—it's some mistake,' said Mrs. Ashburn.

'Which,' continued Uncle Solomon, 'you 'ave been good enough to submit to us (pretty good that for a bell-'anger, hey?) We regret, however, to say that we do not find ourselves in a position to make any overtures to you in the matter. Well,' he said, though not very confidently, 'you've been writing to your landlord about the fixtures, and these are his lawyers writing back—isn't that it now?'

'What should I write to him for?' said Mr. Ashburn; 'that's not it, Solomon—go on, it gets worse by-and-by!'

'Your one fair daughter also (hullo, Trixie!) we find ourselves compelled to decline, although with more reluctance; but, in spite of some considerable merits, there is a slight roughness (why, her complexion's clear enough!), together with a certain immaturity and total lack of form and motive (you are giddy, you know, Trixie, I always told you so), which are in our opinion sufficient to prevent us from making any proposals to you in the matter.'

Uncle Solomon laid down the letter at this point, and looked around open-mouthed: 'I thought I could make out most things,' he said; 'but this is rather beyond me, I must say.'

''Ere are these people—what's their names? Leadbitter and Gandy (who I take it are in the gas-fitting and decorating line)—writing to say in the same breath that they can't come and see to your bells, and they don't want to marry your daughter. Who asked them?—you ain't come down so low in the world to go and offer Trixie to a gas-fitter, I should 'ope, Matthew!—and yet what else does it mean—tell me that, and I'll thank you.'

'Don't ask me,' said the unhappy father; 'they're perfect strangers.'

'Trixie, you know nothing about it, I hope?' said Mrs. Ashburn, rather suspiciously.

'No, ma dear,' said Trixie; 'but I don't want to marry either Mr. Leadbitter or Mr. Gandy.'

The situation had become too much for Mark; at first he had hoped that by holding his tongue he might escape being detected, while the rejection of both the novels from which he had hoped so much was a heavy blow which he felt he could scarcely bear in public; but they seemed so determined to sift the matter to the end that he decided to enlighten them at once, since it must be only a question of time.

But his voice was choked and his face crimson as he said, 'I think perhaps I can explain it.'

'You!' they all cried, while Uncle Solomon added something about 'young men having grown cleverer since his young days.'

'Yes, that letter is addressed to me—M. Ashburn, you see, stands for Mark, not Matthew. It's from—from a firm of publishers,' said the unlucky Mark, speaking very hoarsely; 'I sent them two novels of mine—one was called "One Fair Daughter," and the other "Sweet Bells Jangled"—and they, they won't take them—that's all.'

There was a 'sensation,' as reporters say, at this announcement: Martha gave a sour little laugh of disgust; Cuthbert looked as if he thought a good deal which brotherly feeling forbade him to put in words; but Trixie tried to take Mark's hand under the table—he shrank from all sympathy, however, at such a moment, and shook her off impatiently, and all she could do was to keep her eyes in pity from his face.

Mrs. Ashburn gave a tragic groan and shook her head: to her a young man who was capable of writing novels was lost; she had a wholesome horror of all fiction, having come from a race of Dissenters of the strict old-fashioned class, whose prejudices her hard dull nature had retained in all their strength. Her husband, without any very clear views of his own, thought as she did as soon as he knew her opinions, and they all left it to Mr. Lightowler to interpret the 'evident sense of the house.'

He expanded himself imposingly, calling up his bitterest powers of satire to do justice to the occasion: 'So that's all, is it?' he said; 'ah, and quite enough, too, I should think; so it was the bells on your cap that were jingling all the time?'

'Since you put it in that pleasant way,' said Mark, 'I suppose it was.'

'And that's how you've been studying for the Bar of evenings, this is the way you've overcome your fondness for scribbling nonsense? I've spent all the money I've laid out on you' (it was a way of his to talk as if Mark had been a building estate), 'I've given you a good education, all to 'ave you writing novels and get 'em "returned with thanks!"—you might have done that much without going to College!'

'Every writer of any note has had novels declined at some time,' said Mark.

'Well,' said Uncle Solomon, ponderously, 'if that's all, you've made a capital start. You can set up as a big littery pot at once, you can, with a brace of 'em. I 'ope you're satisfied with all this, Jane, I'm sure?'

'It's no use saying anything,' she said; 'but it's a bad return after all your kindness to him.'

'A return with thanks,' put in Cuthbert, who was not without some enjoyment of Mark's discomfiture; he had long had a certain contempt for his elder brother as a much overrated man, and he felt, with perfect justice, that had Fortune made him his uncle's favourite, he had brains which would have enabled him to succeed where Mark had failed; but he had been obliged to leave school early for a City office, which had gone some way towards souring him.

'There's an old Latin proverb,' said Mr. Ashburn, with a feeling that it was his turn—'an old Latin proverb, "Nec suetonius ultra crepitam."'

'No, excuse me, you 'aven't quite got it, Matthew,' said his brother-in-law, patronisingly; 'you're very near it, though. It runs, if I don't make a mistake, "Ne plus ultra sutorius (not suetonius—he was a Roman emperor)—crepitam," a favourite remark of the poet Cicero—"Cobbler stick to your last," as we have it more neatly. But your father's right on the main point, Mark. I don't say you need stick to the schoolmastering, unless you choose. I'll see you started at the Bar; I came this very evening to 'ave a talk with you on that. But what do you want to go and lower yourself by literature for? There's a littery man down at our place, a poor feller that writes for the "Chigbourne and Lamford Gazette," and gets my gardener to let him take the measure of my gooseberries; he's got a hat on him my scarecrow wouldn't be seen in. That's what you'll come to!'

'There's some difference,' said Mark, getting roused, 'between the reporter of a country paper and a novelist.'

'There's a difference between you and him,' retorted his uncle; 'he gets what he writes put in and paid so much a line for—you don't. That's all the difference I can see.'

'But when the books are accepted, they will be paid for,' said Mark, 'and well paid for too.'

'I always thought that dog and the shadow must ha' been a puppy, and now I know it,' said his uncle, irritably. 'Now look here, Mark, let's have no more nonsense about it. I said I came here to have a little talk with you, and though things are not what I expected, 'ave it I will. When I saw you last, I thought you were trying to raise yourself by your own efforts and studying law, and I said to myself, "I'll give him another chance." It seems now that was all talk; but I'll give you the chance for all that. If you like to take it, well and good; if not, I've done with you this time once for all. You go on and work 'ard at this Law till you've served your time out, or kept your terms, or whatever they call it, and when you get called you can give 'em notice to quit at your school. I'll pay your fees and see you started in chambers till you're able to run alone. Only, and mind this, no more of your scribbling—drop that littery rubbish once for all, and I stand by you; go on at it, and I leave you to go to the dogs your own way. That's my offer, and I mean it.'

There are few things so unpleasantly corrective to one's self-esteem as a letter of rejection such as had come to Mark—the refusal of the school committee was insignificant in comparison; only those who have yielded to the subtle temptation to submit manuscript to an editor or a publisher's reader, and have seen it return in dishonour, can quite realise the dull anguish of it, the wild, impotent rebellion that follows, and the stunned sense that all one's ideas will have somehow to be readjusted; perhaps an artist whose pictures are not hung feels something of it, but there one's wounded vanity can more easily find salves.

Mark felt the blow very keenly; for weeks he had been building hopes on these unfortunate manuscripts of his; he had sent both to a firm under whose auspices he was particularly anxious to come before the world, in the hope that one at least would find favour with them, and now the two had been unequivocally declined; for a moment his confidence in himself was shaken, and he almost accepted the verdict.

And yet he hesitated still: the publisher might be wrong; he had heard of books riding out several such storms and sailing in triumphantly at last. There was Carlyle, there was Charlotte Brontë, and other instances occurred to him. And he longed for speedy fame, and the law was a long avenue to it.

'You hear what your uncle says?' said his mother. 'Surely you won't refuse a chance like this.'

'Yes, he will,' said Martha. 'Mark would rather write novels than work, wouldn't you, Mark? It must be so amusing to write things which will never be read, I'm sure.'

'Leave Mark alone, Martha,' said Trixie. 'It's a shame—it is.'

'I don't know why you should all be down on me like this,' said Mark; 'there's nothing positively immoral in writing books—at least when it never goes any further. But I daresay you're right, and I believe you mean to be kind at any rate, uncle. I'll take your offer. I'll read steadily, and get called, and see if I'm good for anything at the Bar, since it seems I'm good for nothing else.'

'And you'll give up the writing, hey?' said his uncle.

'Oh, yes,' said Mark, irritably, 'anything you please. I'm a reformed character; I'll take the pledge to abstain from ink in all forms if you like.' It was not a very gracious way of accepting what was by no means an unhandsome offer; but he was jarred and worried, and scarcely knew what he said.

Mr. Lightowler was not sensitive, and was too satisfied at having gained his object to cavil at Mark's manner of yielding. 'Very well; that's settled,' he said. 'I'm glad you've come to your senses, I'm sure. We'll have you on the Woolsack yet, and we'll say no more about the other business.'

'And now,' said Mark, with a forced smile, 'I think I'll say good night. I'll go and attack the law-books while I'm in the humour for them.'

Upstairs in his room he got out his few elementary text-books, and began to read with a sort of sullen determination; but he had not gone very far in the 'descent of an estate-tail,' before he shut the book up in a passion: 'I can't read to-night,' he said savagely; 'it isn't easy to hug my chains all at once; it will be a long time before I come out strong on estates-tail. If Holroyd (who says he likes the jargon) can't get a living by it, there's not much hope for me. I loathe it! I'm sure I had a chance with those books of mine, too; but that's all over. I must burn them, I suppose— Who's there?' for there was a tap at the door.

'It's me, Mark—Trixie—let me in.' Mark rose and opened the door to Trixie, in a loose morning wrapper. 'Mark, I'm so sorry, dear,' she said softly.

'Sorry! you ought to rejoice, Trixie,' said Mark, with a bitter laugh. 'I'm a brand from the burning—a repentant novelist, I've seen my errors and am going to turn Lord Chancellor.'

'You mustn't be angry with them,' said Trixie. 'Dear ma is very strict; but then she is so anxious to see you making a living, Mark, and you know they don't give you very much at St. Peter's. And Martha and Cuthbert can't help saying disagreeable things. Don't you think, perhaps,' she added timidly, 'that it's better for you to give up thinking about writing any more?'

'Well, I've done it, Trixie, at any rate. I'm not so bad as that fellow Delobelle, in "Fromont Jeune," with his "Je n'ai pas le droit de renoncer au théâtre!" am I? I've renounced my stage. I'm a good little boy, and won't make a mess with nasty ink and pens any more. When I get those confounded books back they shall go into the fire—by Jove they shall!'

'No, Mark, don't, it would be such a pity,' cried Trixie. 'I'm sure they were beautifully written; quite as well as some that get printed. I wish you could write novels and be Lord Chancellor too, Mark.'

'Bring out Acts in three volumes, and edit Judicature Rules in fancy covers for railway reading? It would be very nice, Trixie, wouldn't it? But I'm afraid it wouldn't do, even if I wrote them in secret, under the Woolsack. If I write anything now, it must be a smart spicy quarto on Bankruptcy, or a rattling digest on the Law of Settlement and Highways. My fictions will be all legal ones.'

'I know you will do your best,' said Trixie, simply.

Mark dreamed that night—much as other disappointed literary aspirants have dreamed before him—that a second letter had come from the publishers, stating that they had reconsidered their decision, and offering repentantly to publish both novels on fabulous terms. He was just rushing to call Trixie, and tell her the good news, when the dream faded, and he awoke to the consciousness of his very different circumstances.

Literature had jilted him. The Law was to be his mistress henceforth: a bony and parchment-faced innamorata, with a horsehair wig; and he thought of the task of wooing her with a shudder.

CHAPTER V

NEIGHBOURS

More than a week had passed since the scene in Malakoff Terrace described in my last chapter—a week spent by Mark in the drudgery of school work, which had grown more distasteful than ever now he could indulge in no golden dreams of a glorious deliverance; for he could not accept his new prospects as an adequate substitute, and was beginning to regret his abandonment of his true ambitions with a longing that was almost fierce.

He had gone down to 'The Woodbines,' his uncle's villa at Chigbourne, in pursuance of the invitation given him; and Mr. Lightowler's undisguised recovery of the feeling of proprietorship in him, and his repeated incitements to pursue his studies with unwearying ardour, only increased Mark's disgust with himself and his future, as he walked along the lanes with his relative towards the little church beyond the village on the last Sunday in November.

It was a bright clear frosty day, with a scarlet sun glowing through dun-coloured clouds, and a pale blue sky beyond the haze above their heads; the country landscape had suggestions of Christmas cheeriness, impossible enough to Londoners who cannot hope to share in country-house revels à la Mr. Caldecott, but vaguely exhilarating notwithstanding.

Mark knew that his Christmas would be passed in town with his family, who would keep it, as they observed Sunday, and refrain from any attempt at seasonable jollity; yet he began to feel elated by its approach, or the weather, or some instinct of youth and health which set his blood tingling and drove away his dissatisfaction with every step he took.

Uncle Solomon had come out in broadcloth, and a large hat with such an ecclesiastical brim that it influenced his conversation, causing it to be more appropriate than Sunday talk will sometimes be, even amongst the best people. He discoursed of Ritualism, and deplored the hold it had acquired on the vicar, and the secret manoeuvres of the detested Humpage in the vestry.

'I was brought up a Baptist,' he said, 'and I'd go back to 'em now, if I didn't know how they'd all crow about it; and they're a poor lot at Little Bethel, too, not a penny-piece among 'em.'

'When we get into the church,' he continued, 'you give a look left of the chancel, close by the door where the shelf is with the poor-loaves. You'll see a painted winder there which that 'Umpage got put up to his aunt—that's his ostentation, that is. I don't believe he ever had an aunt; but I don't wish to judge him. Only you look at that window, and tell me how it strikes you afterwards. He's got the artist to do him as the Good Samaritan there! I call it scandalous!—there's no mistake about it; the 'air's not the same colour, and the Eastern robes hide it a bit; but he's there for all that. I don't relish seeing 'Umpage figurin' away in painted glass and a great gaudy turban every time I look up, he's quite aggravating enough in his pew. If I chose to go to the expense, I could put up a winder too, and 'ave myself done.'

'As a saint?' suggested Mark.

'Never you mind. If I liked to be a saint on glass I could, I suppose—I'm a churchwarden, and there's no reason why 'Umpage should 'ave all the painted winders to himself; but I shouldn't care to make myself so conspicuous. 'Umpage, now, he likes that sort of thing.'

This brought them to the church, a perpendicular building with a decidedly 'Early English' smell in it, and Uncle Solomon led the way to his pew, stopping to nudge Mark as they passed the memorial to his enemy's meretricious aunt; he nudged him again presently, after he had retired behind the ecclesiastical hat and emerged again to deal out some very large prayer and hymn books as if they were cards.

'That's him—that's 'Umpage,' he said in a loud whisper.

Mark looked up in time to see an old gentleman advance to the door of the pew in front of them—a formidable-looking old gentleman, with a sallow face, long iron-grey locks, full grey eyes, a hook-nose, and prominent teeth under a yellowish-grey moustache and beard.

He felt a sudden shame, for behind Mr. Humpage came a pretty child with long floating light hair, with a staid fresh-faced woman in grey, and last a girl of about nineteen or twenty, who seemed to have caught the very audible whisper, for she glanced in its direction as she passed in with the slightest possible gleam of amused surprise in her eyes and a lifting of her delicate eyebrows.

A loud intoned 'Amen' came from the vestry just then, the organ played a voluntary, and the vicar and curate marched in at the end of a procession of little surpliced country boys, whose boots made a very undevotional clatter over the brasses and flagstones.

As a Low Churchman Mr. Lightowler protested against this processional pomp by a loud snort, which expression of opinion he repeated at any tendency to genuflexion on the part of the clergyman during the service, until the little girl turned round and gazed at him with large concerned eyes, as if she thought he must be either very devout or extremely unwell.

Mark heard little of the service; he was dimly aware of his uncle singing all the psalms and responses with a lusty tunelessness, and coming to fearful grief in gallant attempts to follow the shrill little choristers over a difficult country of turns and flourishes. He explained afterwards that he liked to set an example of 'joining in.'

But Mark saw little else but the soft shining knot of hair against the dark sables of the hat and tippet of his beautiful neighbour, and a glimpse of her delicate profile now and then, as she turned to find the places for her little sister, who invariably disdained assistance as long as possible. He began to speculate idly on her probable character. Was she proud?—there was a shade of disdain about her smile when he first saw her. Self-willed?—the turn of her graceful head was slightly imperious. She could be tender with it all—he inferred that from the confidence with which the child nestled against her as the sermon began, and the gentle protecting hand that drew her closer still.

Mark had been in and out of love several times in his life; his last affair had been with a pretty, shallow flirt with a clever manner picked up at secondhand, and though she had come to the end of her répertoire and ceased to amuse or interest him long before they parted by mutual consent, he chose to believe his heart for ever blighted and proof against all other women, so that he was naturally in the most favourable condition for falling an easy victim.

He thought he had never seen any one quite like this girl, so perfectly natural and unaffected, and yet with such an indefinable air of distinction in her least movement. What poems, what books might not be written, with such an influence to inspire them, and then Mark recollected with a pang that he had done with all that for ever now. That most delicate form of homage would be beyond his power, even if he ever had the opportunity of paying it, and the thought did not tend to reconcile him to his lot.

Would chance ever bring him within the sphere of his new-found divinity? Most probably not. Life has so many of these tantalising half-glimpses, which are never anything more. 'If she is Humpage's daughter,' he thought, 'I'm afraid it's hopeless; but she shall not pass out of my life if I can help it!' and so he dreamed through the sermon, with the vicar's high cracked voice forming a gentle clacking accompaniment, which he quite missed when the benediction came upon him unexpectedly.

They came out of church into bright November sunshine; the sun had disengaged itself now from the dun clouds, melted the haze, and tempered the air almost to the warmth of early spring. Mark looked round for Mr. Humpage and his party, but without success; they had lingered behind, perhaps, as he could not help fearing, designedly. He determined, however, to find out what he could about them, and approached the subject diplomatically.

'I saw the window,' he began; 'that was the Good Samaritan in front, of course. I recognised him by the likeness at once.'

'He took care it should be like,' said Uncle Solomon, with a contemptuous sniff.

'That was his family with him, I suppose?' Mark asked carelessly.

''Umpage is a bachelor, or gives himself out for such,' said his uncle, charitably.

'Then those young ladies—are they residents here?'

'Which young ladies?'

'In his pew,' said Mark, a little impatiently, 'the little girl with the long hair, and—and the other one?'

'You don't go to church to stare about you, do you? I didn't take any notice of them; they're strangers here—friends of 'Umpage, I daresay. That was his sister in grey; she keeps house for him, and they say he leads her a pretty life with his tempers. Did you see that old woman behind in a black coalscuttle? That was old widow Barnjum; keeps a sweetstuff shop down in the village. I've seen her that far in liquor sometimes she can't find her way about and 'as to be taken 'ome in a barrow. You wouldn't think it to look at her, would you? I shall give the vicar the 'int to tell old John Barker he ought to stay away till he's got over that cough of his; it's enough to make anybody ill to listen to him. I've a good mind to tell him of it myself; and I will, too, if I come across him. The Colonel wasn't in church again. They tell me he's turned Atheist, and loafs about all Sunday with a gun. I've seen him myself driving a dog-cart Sunday afternoons in a pot 'at, and I knew then what would come of that. Here we are again!' he said, as they reached the palings of 'The Woodbines.' 'We'll just stroll round to get an appetite for dinner before we go in.'

Uncle Solomon led the way into the stables, where he lingered to slap his mare on the back and brag about her, and then Mark had to be introduced to the pig. 'What I call a 'andsome pig, yer know,' he remarked; 'a perfect picture, he is' (a picture that needed cleaning, Mark thought)—'you come down to me in another three weeks or so, and we'll try a bit off of that chap'—an observation which seemed to strike the pig as in very indifferent taste, for he shook his ears, grunted, and retired to his sty in a pointed manner.

After that there was plenty to do and see before Mark was allowed to dine: Lassie, the colley, had to be unfastened for a run about the 'grounds,' of which a mechanical mouse might have made the tour in five minutes; there was a stone obelisk to be inspected that Uncle Solomon had bought a bargain at a sale and set up at a corner of the lawn inscribed with the names of his favourites living and dead—a remarkably scratch team, by the way; then he read out sonorous versions of the Latin names of most of his shrubs, which occupied a considerable time until, at last, by way of the kitchen-garden and strawberry beds, they came to a little pond and rustic summer-house, near which the boundary fence was unconcealed by any trees or shrubs.

'See that gap?' said Mr. Lightowler, pointing to a paling of which the lower half was torn away; 'that's where 'Umpage's blathering old gander gets through. I 'ate the sight of the beast, and I'd sooner 'ave a traction-engine running about my beds than him! I've spoke about it to 'Umpage till I'm tired, and I shall 'ave to take the law into my own hands soon, I know I shall. There was Wilcox, my gardener, said something about some way he had to serve him out—but it's come to nothing. And now we'll go in for a wash before dinner.'

Uncle Solomon was a widower; a niece of his late wife generally lived with him and superintended his domestic affairs—an elderly person, colourless and cold, who, however, had a proper sense of her position as a decayed relative on the wife's side, and made him negatively comfortable; she was away just then, which was partly the reason why Mark had been invited to bear his uncle company.

They dined in a warm little room, furnished plainly but well; and after dinner Uncle Solomon gave Mark a cigar, and took down a volume of American Commentaries on the Epistles, which he used to give a Sunday tone to his nap; but before it could take effect, there were sounds faintly audible through the closed windows, as of people talking at the end of the grounds.

Mr. Lightowler opened his drooping eyelids: 'There's some one in my garden,' he said. 'I must go out and put a stop to that—some of those urchins out of the village—they're always at it!'

He put on an old garden-hat and sallied out, followed by Mark: 'The voices seem to come down from 'Umpage's way, but there's no one to be seen,' he said, as they went along. 'Yes, there is, though; there's 'Umpage himself and his friends looking across the fence at something! What does he want to go staring on to my land for—like his confounded impudence!'

When they drew a little nearer, he stopped short and, turning to Mark with a face purple with anger, said, 'Well, of all the impudence—if he isn't egging on that infernal gander now—put him through the 'ole himself, I daresay!'

On arriving at the scene, Mark saw the formidable old gentleman of that morning glaring angrily over the fence; by his side was the fair and slender girl he had seen in church, while at intervals her little sister's wondering face appeared above the top of the palings, a small dog uttering short sharp barks and yelps behind her.

They were all looking at a large grey gander, which was unquestionably trespassing at that moment; but it was unjust to say, as Mr. Lightowler had said, that they were giving it any encouragement; the prevailing anxiety seemed to be to recover it, but as the fence was not low, and Mr. Humpage not young enough to care to scale it, they were obliged to wait the good pleasure of the bird.

And Mark soon observed that the misguided bird was not in a condition to be easily prevailed upon, being in a very advanced stage of solemn intoxication; it was tacking about the path with an erratic stateliness, its neck stretched defiantly, and its choked sleepy cackle said, 'You lemme 'lone now, I'm all ri', walk shtraight enough 'fiwan'to!' as plainly as bird-language could render it.

As Uncle Solomon bore down on it, it put on an air of elaborate indifference, meant to conceal a retreat to the gap by which it had entered, and began to waddle with excessive dignity in that direction, but from the way in which it repeatedly aimed itself at the intact portions of the paling, it seemed reasonable to infer that it was under a not infrequent optical illusion.

Mr. Lightowler gave a short and rather savage laugh. 'Wilcox has done it, then!' he said. Mark threw away his cigar, and slightly lifted his hat as he came up: he felt somewhat ashamed and strongly tempted to laugh at the same time; he dared not look at the face of Mr. Humpage's companion, and kept in the background as a dispassionate spectator.

Mr. Lightowler evidently had made up his mind to be as offensive as possible. 'Afternoon, Mr. 'Umpage,' he began; 'I think I've 'ad the pleasure of seeing this bird of yours before; he's good enough to come in odd times and assist my gardener; you'll excuse me for making the remark, however, but when he's like this I think he ought to be kep' indoors.'

'This is disgraceful, sir,' the other gentleman retorted, galled by this irony; 'disgraceful!'

'It's not pretty in a gander, I must say,' agreed Uncle Solomon, wilfully misunderstanding. 'Does it often forget itself in this way, now?'

'Poor dear goose,' chanted the little girl, reappearing at this juncture, 'it's so giddy; is it ill, godpa?'

'Run away, Dolly,' said Mr. Humpage; 'it's no sight for you; run away.'

'Then Frisk mustn't look either; come away, Frisk,' and Dolly vanished again.

When she had gone, the old gentleman said, with a dangerous smile that showed all his teeth, 'Now, Mr. Lightowler, I think I'm indebted to you for the abominable treatment of this bird?'

'Somebody's been treating it, it's very plain,' said the other, looking at the bird, which was making a feeble attempt to spread out its wings and screech contemptuously at the universe.

'You're equivocating, sir; do you think I can't see that poison has been laid in your grounds for this unhappy bird?'

'It's 'appy enough; don't you be uneasy, Mr. 'Umpage, there's been no worse poison given to it than some of my old Glenlivat,' said Mr. Lightowler; 'and, let me tell you, it's not every man, let alone every gander, as gets the luck to taste that. My gardener must have laid some of it down for—for agricultural purposes, and your bird, comin' in through the 'ole (as you may p'raps remember I've spoke to you about before), has bin makin' a little too free with it, that's all. It's welcome as the flowers in May to it, only don't blame me if your bird is laid up with a bad 'eadache by-and-by, not that there's an 'eadache in the whole cask.'

At this point Mark could not resist a glance at the fair face across the fence. In spite of her feminine compassion for the bird and respect for its proprietor, Mabel had not been able to overcome a sense of the absurdity of the scene, with the two angry old gentlemen wrangling across the fence over an intoxicated gander; the face Mark saw was rippling with subdued amusement, and her dark grey eyes met his for an instant with an electric flash of understanding; then she turned away with a slight increase of colour in her cheeks. 'I'm going in, Uncle Anthony,' she said; 'do come, too, as soon as you can; don't quarrel about it any more—ask them to give you back the poor goose, and I'll take it into the yard again; it ought to go at once.'

'Let me manage it my own way,' said Mr. Humpage, testily. 'May I trouble you, Mr. Lightowler, to kindly hand me over that bird—when you have quite finished with it?' he added.

'That bird has been taking such a fancy to my manure heap that I'll ask to be excused,' said Mr. Lightowler. 'If you was to whistle to it now I might 'ead it through the 'ole; but it always finds it a good deal easier to come through than it does to come back, even when it's sober. I'm afraid you'll have to wait till it comes round a bit.'

At this the gander lurched against a half-buried flower pot, and rolled helplessly over with its eyes closed. 'Oh, the poor thing,' cried Mabel, 'it's dying!'

'Do you see that?' demanded its owner, furiously; 'it's dying, and you've had it poisoned, sir; that soaked bread was put there by you or your orders—and, by the Lord, you shall pay for it!'

'I never ordered or put it there either,' said his enemy doggedly.

'We shall see about that—we shall see,' said Mr. Humpage; 'you can say that by-and-by.'

'It's no good losing your temper, now—keep cool, can't you?' roared Uncle Solomon.

'It's likely to make a man cool, isn't it? to come for a quiet stroll on Sunday afternoon, and find that his gander has been decoyed into a neighbour's garden and induced to poison itself with whisky?'

'Decoyed? I like that! pretty innercent, that bird of yours! too timid to come in without a reg'lar invitation, wasn't he?' jeered Mr. Lightowler; 'quite 'ad to press him to step in and do the garden up a bit. You and your gander!'

Mabel had already escaped; Mark remained trying to persuade his uncle to come away before the matter ceased to be farcical.

'I shall take this matter up, sir! I shall take it up!' said Mr. Humpage, in a white rage; 'and I don't think it will do you credit as a churchwarden, let me tell you!'

'Don't you go bringing that in here, now!' retorted Uncle Solomon. 'I'll not be spoken to as a churchwarden by you, Mr. 'Umpage, sir, of all parties!'

'You'll not be spoken to by anybody very soon—at any rate, as a churchwarden. I mean to bring this affair before the magistrates. I shall take out a summons against you for unlawfully ill-treating and abusing my gander, sir!'

'I tell you I never ill-treated him; as for abuse, I don't say. But that's neither here nor there. He ain't so thin-skinned as all that, your gander ain't. And if I choose to put whisky, or brandy, or champagne-cup about my grounds, I'm not obliged to consult your ridik'lous gander, I do hope. I didn't ask him to sample 'em. I don't care a brass button for your summonses. You can summon me till you're black in the face!'

But in spite of these brave words Mr. Lightowler was really not a little alarmed by the threat.

'We shall see about that,' said the other again, viciously. 'And now, once more, will you give me back my poor bird?'

Mark thought it had gone far enough. He took up the heavy bird, which made some maudlin objections, and carried it gingerly to the fence. 'Here's the victim, Mr. Humpage,' he said lightly. 'I think it will be itself again in a couple of hours or so. And now, perhaps, we can let the matter drop for the present.'

The old gentleman glared at Mark as he received his bird: 'I don't know who you may be, young sir, or what share you've had in this disgraceful business. If I trace it to you, you shall repent of it, I promise you! I don't wish to have any further communication with you or your friend, who's old enough to know his duty better as a neighbour and a Christian. You will let him know, with my compliments, that he'll hear more of this.'

He retired with the outraged bird under his arm, leaving Uncle Solomon, who had of course heard his parting words, looking rather ruefully at his nephew.

'It's all very well for you to laugh,' he said to Mark, as they turned to go into the house again; 'but let me tell you if that hot-tempered old idiot goes and brings all this up at Petty Sessions, it may be an awkward affair for me. He's been a lawyer, has 'Umpage, and he'll do his worst. A pretty thing to 'ave my name in all the papers about 'ere as torturing a goose! I dessay they'll try and make out that I poured the whisky down the brute's throat. It's Wilcox's doings, and none of mine; but they'll put it all on me. I'll drive over to Green & Ferret's to-morrow, and see how I stand. You've studied the law. What do you think about it, come? Can he touch me, eh? But he hasn't got a leg to stand on, like his gander—it's all nonsense, ain't it?'

If there had ever been a chance, Mark thought bitterly, after comforting his uncle as well as his very moderate acquaintance with the law permitted, of anything like intimacy between himself and the girl whose face had fascinated him so strangely, it was gone now: that bird of evil omen had baulked his hopes as effectually as its ancestors frustrated the aspiring Gaul.

The dusk was drawing on as they walked across the lawn, from which the russet glow of the sunset had almost faded; the commonplace villa before them was tinted with violet, and in the west the hedges and trees formed an intricate silhouette against a background of ruddy gold and pale lemon; one or two flamingo-coloured clouds still floated languidly higher up in a greenish blue sky; over everything the peace and calm had settled that mark the close of a perfect autumn day, with the additional stillness which always makes itself perceptible on a Sunday.

Mark felt the influence of it all, and was vaguely comforted—he remembered the passing interchange of glances across the fence, and it consoled him.

At supper that evening his uncle, too, recovered his spirits: 'If he brings a summons, they'll dismiss it,' he said confidently; 'but he knows better than that as a lawyer—if he does, he'll find the laugh turned against him, hey? I'm not answerable for what Wilcox chooses to do without my orders. I never told him he wasn't to—but that ain't like telling him to go and do it, is it now? And where's the cruelty, either?—a blend like that, too. Just try a glass, now, and say what you think—he'll be dropping in for more of it if he's the bird I take him for!'

But as they were going upstairs to bed, he stopped at the head of the staircase and said to Mark, 'Before I forget it, you remind me to get Wilcox to find out, quietly, the first thing to-morrow, how that gander is.'

CHAPTER VI

SO NEAR AND YET SO FAR

When Mark awoke next morning the weather had undergone one of those sudden and complete changes which form one of the chief attractions of our climate; there had been a frost, and with it a thin white mist, which threw its clinging veil over the landscape; the few trees which were near enough to be seen were covered with a kind of thick grey vegetation, that gave them a spectral resemblance to their summer selves. Breakfast was early, as Mark had to be down at St. Peter's as soon after morning chapel as possible, and he came down shivering to find his uncle already seated. 'The dog-cart will be round in five minutes,' said the latter gentleman, with his mouth full; 'so make the most of your time. You'll have a cold drive. I'll take you over to the station myself, and go on and see Ferret after.'

The too-zealous Wilcox brought the trap round. ''Ave you been round to see about that bird next door?' Mr. Lightowler asked rather anxiously, as the man stood by the mare's head. 'Yessir,' said Wilcox, with a grin; 'I went and saw Mr. 'Umpage's man, and he say the old gander was werry bad when they got 'im 'ome, but he ain't any the worse for what he 'ad this mornin', sir; though the man, he dew say as the gander seem a bit sorry for 'isself tew. They tough old birds 'a' got strong 'eads, sir; I knowed it 'ud do him no 'arm, bless ye!'

'Well, don't you go trying it again, Wilcox, that's all. Mind what I say,' said Uncle Solomon, with visible relief, 'else you and me'll 'ave words and part. Let her go,' and they drove off.

He gave Mark much good advice on the way, such as wealthy uncles seem to secrete and exude almost unconsciously, as toads yield moisture; but Mark paid only a moderate degree of attention to it as they spun past the low dim edges; he hardly noticed what could be seen along the road even, which was not much—a gable-end or a haystack starting out for an instant from the fog, or a shadowy labourer letting himself through a gate—he was thinking of the girl whose eyes had met his the afternoon before.

He had dreamed of her all that night—a confused ridiculous dream, but with a charm about it which was lingering still; he thought they had met and understood one another at once, and he had taken her to the village church where he had first seen her, and they had a private box, and Uncle Solomon took the chair, while old Mr. Shelford, Trixie, and young Langton were all in the choir, which was more like an orchestra. It was not particularly connected or reverent, but she had not been included in the general travesty—his sleeping brain had respected her image even in its waywardness, and presented it as vivid and charming as in life, so that the dream with all its absurdity seemed to have brought her nearer to him, and he could not resist the fancy that she might have some recollection of it too.

A low hum in the still air, and distant reports and choked railway whistles told them they were near the station, but the fog had grown so much denser that there was no other indication of it, until Mr. Lightowler brought up sharply opposite the end of an inclined covered staircase, which seemed to spring out of nothing and lead nowhere, where they left the dog-cart in charge of a flyman and went up to the platform.

There a few old gentlemen with rosy faces were stamping up and down and slapping their chests, exchanging their 'Raw morning this, sir's,' 'Ah, it is indeed's,' with an air of good men bearing up under an undeserved persecution.

'Sharp morning this to stand about in,' said Uncle Solomon; 'let's go into the waiting-room, there's a fire there.' The waiting-room was the usual drab little room, with a bottle of water and tumblers on a bare stained table, and local advertisements on the dingy walls; the gas was lighted, and flickered in a sickly white fishtail flame, but the fire was blazing cheerfully, giving a sheen to the silver-grey fur of a child in a crimson plush hat who stood before it embracing a small round basket out of which a Skye terrier's head was peering inquisitively.

The firelight shone, too, on the graceful form of a girl, who was bending towards it holding out her slender hands to the blaze. Mark scarcely needed to glance at the face she turned towards the newcomers to recognise that fortune had allowed him one more chance: Mr. Humpage's visitors were evidently returning to town by the same train as himself, and the old gentleman in person was standing with his back to them examining a time-table on the wall.

Uncle Solomon, in his relief at Wilcox's information that morning, did not perceive any awkwardness in the encounter, but moved about and coughed noisily, as if anxious to attract his enemy's attention. Mark felt considerably embarrassed, dreading a scene; but he glanced as often as he dared at the lady of his thoughts, who was drawing on her gloves again with a dainty deliberation.

'Godpapa,' said the little girl, suddenly, 'you never told me if Frisk had been good. Has he?'

'So good that he kept me awake thinking of him all night,' said the old gentleman drily, without turning.

'Did he howl, godpapa? He does sometimes when he's left out in the garden, you know.'

'He did,' said Mr. Humpage. 'Oh, yes—he howled; he's a clever dog at that.'

'And you really like him to?' said Dolly. 'Some people don't.'

'Narrow-minded of 'em, very,' growled the old gentleman.

'Isn't it?' said Dolly, innocently. 'Well, I'm glad you like it, godpapa, because now I shall bring him to see you again. When there's a moon he can howl much louder. I'll bring him when the next moon comes, shall I?'

'We'll see, Chuckie, we'll see. I shouldn't like to keep him sitting up all night to howl on my account; it wouldn't be good for his health. But the very next blue moon we have down in these parts, I'll send up for him—I promise you that.'

Dolly was evidently about to inquire searchingly into the nature of this local phenomenon, but before she could begin the old gentleman turned and saw that they were not alone.

'Mornin', Mr. 'Umpage,' said Uncle Solomon, clearing his throat; and Mark felt a pang of regret for the lost aspirate.

'Good morning to you, sir,' said the other, distantly.

The elder girl returned the bow which Mark risked, though without giving any sign of remembrance; but Dolly remarked audibly, 'Why, that's the old man next door that gave your goose something to make it giddy, isn't it, godpapa?'

'I hope,' said Uncle Solomon, 'that now you've had time to think over what 'appened yesterday afternoon, you'll see that you went too far in using the terms that fell from you, more particularly as the bird's as well as ever, from what I hear this morning?'

'I don't wish to reopen that affair at present,' said the other, stiffly.

'Well, I've heard about enough of it, too; so if you'll own you used language that was unwarrantable, I'm willing to say no more about it for my part.'

'I've no doubt you are, Mr. Lightowler, but you must excuse me from entering into any conversation on the subject. I can't dismiss it as lightly as you seem to do—and, in short, I don't mean to discuss it here, sir.'

'Very well, just as you please. I only meant to be neighbourly—but it don't signify. I can keep myself to myself as well as other parties, I daresay.'

'Then have the goodness to do it, Mr. Lightowler. Mabel, the train is due now. Get your wraps and things and come along.'

He walked fiercely past the indignant Uncle Solomon, followed by Mabel and Dolly, the former of whom seemed a little ashamed of Mr. Humpage's behaviour, for she kept her eyes lowered as she passed Mark, while Dolly looked up at him with childish curiosity.

'Confound these old fools!' thought Mark, angrily; 'what do they want to squabble for in this ridiculous way? Why, if they had only been on decent terms, I might have been introduced to her—to Mabel—by this time; we might even have travelled up to town together.'

'Regular old Tartar, that!' said his uncle, under his breath. 'I believe he'll try and have the law of me now. Let him—I don't care! Here's your train at last. You won't be in by the time-table this morning with all this fog about.'

Mark got into a compartment next to that in which Mr. Humpage had put Mabel and her sister; it was as near as he dared to venture. He could hear Mabel's clear soft voice saying the usual last words at the carriage window, while Uncle Solomon was repeating his exhortations to study and abstinence from any 'littery nonsense.'

Then the train, after one or two false starts on the greasy rails, moved out, and Mark had a parting glimpse of the neighbours turning sharply round on the platform with an elaborate affectation of being utter strangers.

He had no paper to amuse him, for the station was not important enough for a bookstall, and there was nothing to be seen out of the windows, which were silvered with frozen moisture. He had the compartment to himself, and lay back looking up rather sentimentally at the bull's-eye, through which he heard occasional snatches of Dolly's imperious treble.

'I know her name now,' he thought, with a quite unreasonable joy—'Mabel. I shall remember that. I wonder if they are going all the way to town, and if I could offer to be of any use to them at King's Cross? At all events, I shall see her once more then.'

It was not a very long journey from Chigbourne to the terminus, but, as will be seen hereafter, it was destined to be a land mark in the lives of both Mark and Mabel, though the meeting he looked forward to at the end of it never took place.

CHAPTER VII

IN THE FOG

Mark was roused from his reverie in the railway carriage by the fact that the train, after slackening speed rather suddenly, had come to a dead standstill. 'Surely we can't be in already,' he said to himself, wondering at the way in which his thoughts had outstripped the time. But on looking out he found that he was mistaken—they were certainly not near the metropolis as yet, nor did they appear to have stopped at any station, though from the blank white fog which reigned all around, and drifted in curling wreaths through the window he had let down, it was difficult to make very sure of this.

Along the whole length of the train conversation, no longer drowned by the motion, rose and fell in a kind of drone, out of which occasional scraps of talk from the nearer carriages were more distinctly audible, until there came a general lull as each party gave way to the temptation of listening to the other—for the dullest talk has an extraordinary piquancy under these circumstances, either because the speakers, being unseen, appeal to our imagination, or because they do not suppose that they are being so generally overheard.

But by-and-by it seemed to be universally felt that the stoppage was an unusual one, and windows went down with a clatter along the carriages while heads were put out inquiringly. Every kind of voice demanded to be told where they were, and why they were stopping, and what the deuce the Company meant by it—inquiries met by a guard, who walked slowly along the line, with the diplomatic evasiveness which marks the official dislike to admit any possible hitch in the arrangements.

'Yes,' he said, stolidly; 'there might be a bit of a stoppage like; they'd be going on presently; he couldn't say how long that would be; something had gone wrong with the engine; it was nothing serious; he didn't exactly know what.'

But he was met just under Mark's window by the guard from the break at the end of the train, when a hurried conference took place, in which there was no stolidity on either side. 'Run back as quick as you can and set the detonators—there ain't a minute to lose, she may be down on us any time, and she'll never see the other signals this weather. I'd get 'em all out of the train if I was you, mate—they ain't safe where they are as it is, that they ain't!'

The one guard ran back to his break, and then on to set the fog-signals, while the other went to warn the passengers. 'All get out 'ere, please; all get out!' he shouted.

There was the usual obstructive person in the train who required to be logically convinced first of the necessity for disturbing himself; he put his head angrily out of a window near Mark's: 'Here, guard!' he shouted importantly; 'what's all this? Why am I to get out?' 'Because you'd better,' said the guard, shortly. 'But why—where's the platform? I insist on being taken to a platform—I'm not going to break my leg getting out here.' Several people, who had half opened their doors, paused on the steps at this, as if recalled to a sense of their personal dignity. 'Do as you please, sir,' said the official; 'the engine's broke down, and we may be run into any minute in this fog; but if you'd be more comfortable up there—' There was no want of alacrity after that, the obstructive man being the first down; all the rosy-faced gentlemen hopped out, some of the younger ones still grasping half-played hands of 'Nap' or 'Loo,' and made the best of their way down the embankment, and several old ladies were got out in various stages of flutter, narrowly escaping sprained ankles in the descent.

Mark, who had seen his opportunity from the first, had rushed to the door of the next compartment, caught Dolly in his arms as she jumped down, and, hardly believing in his own good fortune, held Mabel's hand in his for one happy moment as she stepped from the high and awkward footboard.

'Down the slope, quick,' he cried to them; 'get as far from the line as you can in case of a smash.'

Mabel turned a little pale, for she had not understood till then that there was any real danger. 'Keep close to me, Dolly,' she said, as they went down the slope; 'we're safe here.'

The fog had gathered thick down in the meadows, and nothing could be seen of the abandoned train when they had gone a few paces from the foot of the embankment; the passengers were moving about in excited groups, not knowing what horrors they might not be obliged to witness in the next few minutes. The excitement increased as one of them declared he could hear the noise of an approaching train. 'Only just in time—God help them if they don't pull up!' cried some, and a woman hoped that 'the poor driver and stoker were not on the engine.'

Dolly heard this and broke from Mabel with a loud cry—'Mabel, we've left Frisk!' she sobbed; 'he'll be killed—oh, my dog will be killed—he mustn't be left behind!'

And, to Mark's horror, she turned back, evidently with the idea of making for the point of danger; he ran after her and caught the little silvery-grey form fast in his arms. 'Let me go!' cried Dolly, struggling; 'I must get him back—oh, I must!'

'He'll have jumped out by this time—he's quite safe,' said Mark in her ear.

'He was sound asleep in his basket, he'll never wake if I don't call to him—why do you hold me? I tell you I will go!' persisted Dolly.

'No, Dolly, no,' said Mabel, bending over her; 'it's too late—it's hard to leave him, but we must hope for the best.' She was crying, too, for the poor doomed dog as she spoke.

Mark was hardly a man from whom anything heroic could be very confidently expected; he was no more unselfish than the generality of young men; as a rule he disliked personally inconveniencing himself for other people, and in cooler moments, or without the stimulus of Mabel's presence, he would certainly have seen no necessity to run the risk of a painful death for the sake of a dog.

But Mabel was there, and the desire of distinguishing himself in her eyes made a temporary hero out of materials which at first sight were not promising. He was physically fearless enough, and given to acting on impulses without counting the consequences; the impulse seized him now to attempt to rescue this dog, and he obeyed it blindly.

'Wait here,' he said to Mabel; 'I'll go back for him.'

'Oh, no—no,' she cried; 'it may cost you your life!'

'Don't stop him, Mabel,' entreated Dolly; 'he is going to save my dog.'

Mark had gone already, and was half-way up the slope, slippery as it was, with the grass clumped and matted together by the frost, and scored in long brown tracks by the feet that had just descended it.

Mabel was left to console and encourage the weeping Dolly as best she might, with a terrible suspense weighing on her own heart the while, not altogether on Frisk's account. At the point where the train had broken down, the line took a bold curve, and now they could hear, apparently close upon them, the roar of a fast train sweeping round through the fog; there were some faint explosions, hoarse shouting, a long screeching whistle,—and after that the dull shock of a collision; but nothing could be seen from where they stood, and for some moments Mabel remained motionless, almost paralysed by the fear of what might be hidden behind the fog curtain.

Mark clambered painfully up the glistening embankment, hoping to reach the motionless carriages and escape with his object effected before the train he could hear in the distance ground into them with a hideous crash.

He knew his danger, but, to do him justice, he scarcely gave it a thought—any possible suffering seemed as remote and inconsiderable just then as the chance of a broken leg or collar-bone had been to him when running for a touchdown in his football days; the one idea that filled his brain was to return to Mabel triumphant with the rescued dog in his arms, and he had room for no others.

He went as directly as he could to the part of the train in which was the carriage he had occupied, and found it without much difficulty when he was near enough to make out forms through the fog; the door of Mabel's compartment was open, and, as he sprang up the footboard, he heard the train behind rattling down on him with its whistle screeching infernally, and for the first time felt an uneasy recollection of the horribly fantastic injuries described in accounts of so many railway collisions.

But there was no time to think of this; at the other end of the carriage was the little round wicker-basket he had seen in Dolly's hands at the Chigbourne waiting-room, and in it was the terrier, sleeping soundly as she had anticipated. He caught up the little drowsy beast, which growled ungratefully, and turned to leap down with it to the ballast, when there was a sharp concussion, which sent a jangling forward shock, increasing in violence as it went, along the standing train, and threw him violently against the partition of the compartment.

Meanwhile the passengers of the first train, now that the worst was apparently over, and the faint shouts and screams from the embankment had calmed down, began to make their way in the direction of the sounds, and Mabel, holding Dolly fast by the hand, forced herself to follow them, though she was sick and faint with the dread of what she might see.

The first thing they saw was a crowd of eager, excited faces, all questioning and accusing the badgered officials of both trains at the same time. 'Why was an empty train left on the rails unprotected in this way? they might have been all killed.—It was culpable negligence all round, and there should be an inquiry—they would insist on an inquiry—they would report this to the traffic manager,' and so on.

The faces looked pale and ghastly enough in the fog, but all the speakers were evidently sound in wind and limb, and, as far as could be seen, neither train had left the rails—but where was the young man who had volunteered to recover the dog? 'Oh, Mabel,' cried Dolly, again and again. 'Frisk is killed, I'm sure of it, or he'd come to me—something has happened—ask, do ask.'

But Mabel dared not, for fear of hearing that a life had been nobly and uselessly sacrificed; she could only press through the crowd with the object of making her way to the carriage where the suspense would be ended.

'There's someone in one of the carriages!' she heard a voice saying as she got nearer, and her heart beat faster; and then the crowd parted somehow, and she saw Mark Ashburn come out of it towards her, with a dazed, scared smile on his pale face, and the little trembling dog safe under one arm.

Fortunately for Mark, the fog-signals had been set in time to do their work, and the second train was fitted with powerful brakes which, but for the state of the rails, would have brought it to without any collision at all; as it was, the shock had not been severe enough to damage the rolling-stock to any greater extent than twisting or straining a buffer or coupling-chain here and there, though it had thrown him against the corner of the net-rail with sufficient violence to slightly graze his forehead, and leave him stunned and a little faint for a few moments.

After sitting down for a short time to recover himself, he picked up the terrier from the cushions on which it was crouching and shivering, having dropped from his hand at the concussion, and feeling himself still rather giddy and sick, got down amongst the astonished crowd, and came towards Mabel and Dolly as we have seen.

It was the best moment, as he thought afterwards, in his life. Every one, probably, with any imagination at all likes to conceive himself at times as the performer of some heroic action extorting the admiration he longs for from some particular pair of eyes, but opportunities for thus distinguishing oneself are sadly rare nowadays, and often when they come are missed, or, if grasped with success, the fair eyes are looking another way and never see it.

But Mark had a satisfied sense of appearing to the utmost advantage as he met the little girl and placed the dog in her arms. 'There's your dog; he's quite safe, only a little frightened,' he said, with a pleasant sympathy in his voice.

Dolly was too overcome for words; she caught Frisk up with her eyes swimming, and ran away with him to pour her self-reproach and relief into his pricked ears, without making any attempt to express her thanks to his rescuer. Her sister, however, made him ample amends.

'How can we thank you?' she said, with a quiver in her voice and an involuntary admiration in her eyes; 'it was so very, very brave of you—you might have been killed!'

'I thought at first it was going to be rather a bad smash,' said Mark—he could not resist the impulse now to make all the capital he could out of what he had done—'I was knocked down—and—and unconscious for a little while after it; but I'm not much hurt, as you see. I don't think I'm any the worse for it, and at all events your little sister's dog isn't—and that's the main point, isn't it?' he added, with a feeling that his words were equal to the occasion.

'Indeed it isn't,' said Mabel warmly; 'if you had been seriously hurt I should never have forgiven myself for letting you go—but are you sure you feel no pain anywhere?'

'Well,' he admitted, 'I fancy I was cut a little about the head' (he was afraid she might not have noticed this), 'but that's a trifle.'

'There is a cut on your forehead,' said Mabel; 'it has been bleeding, but I think it has stopped now. Let me bind it up for you in case it should break out again.'

It was in truth a very small cut, and had hardly bled at all, but Mark made light of it elaborately, as the surest means of keeping her interest alive. 'I am afraid it must be giving you pain,' she said, with a pretty, anxious concern in her eyes as she spoke; and Mark protested that the pain was nothing—which was the exact truth, although he had no intention of being taken literally.

They had gone down the embankment again and were slowly crossing the dim field in which they had first taken refuge. No one was in sight, the other passengers being still engaged in comparing notes or browbeating the unhappy guards above; and as Mark glanced at his companion he saw that her thoughts had ceased to busy themselves about him, while her eyes were trying to pierce the gloom which surrounded her.

'I was looking for my little sister,' she exclaimed, answering the question in his eyes. 'She ran off with the dog you brought back to her, and it is so easy to lose oneself here. I must find out where she is—oh, you are ill!' she broke off suddenly, as Mark staggered and half fell.

'Only a slight giddiness,' he said; 'if—if I could sit down somewhere for a moment—is that a stile over there?'

'It looks like one. Can you get so far without help?' she said compassionately. 'Will you lean on me?'

He seemed to her like some young knight who had been wounded, as it were, in her cause, and deserved all the care she could give him.

'If you will be so very good,' said Mark. He felt himself a humbug, for he could have leaped the stile with ease at that very moment. He had very little excuse for practising in this way on her womanly sympathy, except that he dreaded to lose her just yet, and found such a subtle intoxication in being tended like this by a girl from whom an hour ago he had scarcely hoped to win another careless glance; if he exaggerated his symptoms, as it is to be feared he did, there may be some who will forgive him under the circumstances.

So he allowed Mabel to guide him to the stile, and sat down on one of its rotten cross-planks while she poured eau-de-Cologne or some essence of the kind on a handkerchief, and ordered him to bathe his forehead with it. They seemed isolated there together on the patch of hoary grass by a narrow black ditch half hidden in rank weeds, which alone could be distinguished in the prevailing yellowish whiteness, and Mark desired nothing better at that moment.

'I wonder,' said Mabel, 'if there's a doctor amongst the passengers. There must be, I should think. I am sure you ought to see one. Let me see if I can find one and bring him to you.'

But Mark declared he was quite himself again, and would have begged her not to leave him if he had dared; and as there really did not seem to be anything serious the matter, Mabel's uneasiness about Dolly returned. 'I can't rest till I find her,' she said, 'and if you really are strong again, will you help me? She cannot have gone very far.'

Mark, only too glad of any pretence to remain with her, volunteered willingly.

'Then will you go round the field that way,' she said, 'and I will go this, and we will meet here again?'

'Don't you think,' said Mark, who had not been prepared for this, 'that if—she might not know me, you see—I mean if I was not with you?'

'Yes, she will,' said Mabel impatiently; 'Dolly won't forget you after what you have done, and we are losing time. Go round by there, and call her now and then; if she is here she will come, and if not then we will try the next field.'

She went off herself as she spoke, and Mark had nothing for it but to obey, as she so evidently expected to be obeyed. He went round the field, calling out the child's name now and then, feeling rather forlorn and ridiculous as his voice went out unanswered on the raw air. Presently a burly figure, grotesquely magnified by the mist, came towards him, and resolved itself into an ordinary guard.

'You one of the gentlemen in my train, sir?' he said, 'the train as broke down, that is?'

'Yes,' said Mark; 'why?'

"Cause we've got the engine put to rights, sir; nothing much the matter with her, there wasn't, and we're goin' on directly, sir; I'm gettin' all my passengers together.'

Mark was in no hurry to leave that field, but his time was not his own; he ought to have been at St. Peter's long ago, and was bound to take the first opportunity of getting back. It would not be pleasant, as it was, to have to go and fetch down his class from the sixth form room, where the headmaster had probably given them a temporary asylum.

He had never forgotten a morning on which he had overslept himself, and the mortification he had felt at the Doctor's blandly polite but cutting reception of his apologies. He had a better excuse this time, but even that would not bear overtaxing.

He hesitated a moment, however. 'I'll go in a minute,' he said, 'but there's a lady and a little girl with a dog somewhere about. They mustn't be left behind. Wait while I go and tell them, will you?'

'Never you fear, sir,' said the guard, 'we won't go without them, but I'll call 'em; they'll mind me more than they will you, beggin' your pardon, sir, and you'd better run on, as time's short, and keep places for 'em. You leave it all to me; I'll take care on 'em.'

Mark heard faint barks across the hedge in the direction Mabel had taken. The child was evidently found. The best thing, he thought, to do now was to secure an empty compartment, and with that idea, and perhaps a little from that instinctive obedience to anything in a uniform which is a characteristic of the average respectable Englishman, he let himself be persuaded by the guard, and went back to the train.

To his great joy he found that the compartment Mabel had occupied had no one in it; he stood waiting by the door for Mabel and her sister to come up, with eager anticipations of a delightful conclusion to his journey. 'Perhaps she will tell me who she is,' he thought; 'at all events she will ask me who I am. How little I hoped for this yesterday!'

He was interrupted by a guard—another guard, a sour-looking man with a grizzled beard, who was in charge of the front van. 'Get in, sir, if you mean to travel by this 'ere train,' he said.

'I'm waiting for a young lady,' said Mark, rather ingenuously, but it slipped out almost without his knowledge. 'The other guard promised me—'

'I don't know nothing about no young ladies,' said the guard obdurately; 'but if you mean my mate, he's just give me the signal from his end, and if you don't want to be left be'ind you'd better take your seat while you can, sir, and pretty sharp, too.'

There was nothing else to do; he could not search for Mabel along the train; he must wait till they got to King's Cross; but he took his seat reluctantly and with a heavy disappointment, thinking what a fool he had been to let himself be persuaded by the burly guard. 'But for that, she might have been sitting opposite to me now!' he thought bitterly. 'What a fool I was to leave her. How pretty she looked when she wanted me to see a doctor; how charming she is altogether! Am I in love with her already? Of course I am; who wouldn't be? I shall see her again. She will speak to me once more, and, after all, things might be worse. I couldn't have counted on that when we started.'

And he tried to console himself with this, feeling an impatient anger at the slow pace of the train as it crept cautiously on towards the goal of his hopes. But the breakdown had not happened very far from town, and, tedious as the time seemed to Mark, it was not actually long before the colour of the atmosphere (there was no other indication) proved that they were nearing the terminus.

It changed by slow gradations from its original yellow-whiteness to mustard colour, from that to a smoky lurid red, and from red to stinging, choking iron-grey, and the iron-grey pall was in full possession of King's Cross, where the sickly moonlight of the electric lamps could only clear small halos immediately around their globes.

Mark sprang out before the train had stopped; he strained his eyes in watching for the form he hoped to see there, but in vain; there were no signs in all that bustle of Mabel or Dolly, or the little dog to whom he owed so much.

He sought out the guard who had deluded him and found him superintending the clearing of the luggage van. He hardly knew whether it was merely a fancy that the official, after making a half-step forward to meet him, and fumbling in all his pockets, turned away again as if anxious to avoid meeting his eye.

Mark forced him to meet him, however, willing or not. 'Where is the lady?' he said sharply. 'You left her behind after all, it seems?'

'It wasn't my fault, sir,' said the guard wheezily, 'nor it wasn't the lady's fault, leastways on'y the little lady's, sir. Both on us tried all we could, but the little missy, her with the tarrier dawg, was nervous-like with it all, and wouldn't hear of getting in the train again; so the young lady, she said, seeing as they was so near London, they could get a fly or a cab or summat, and go on in that.'

'And—did she give you no message for me?' said Mark.

There was such evident expectation in his face that the guard seemed afraid to disappoint it. 'I was to give you her respecks and compliments,' he said slowly—'or was it her love, now?' he substituted quickly, after a glance at Mark's face, 'and you was not to be in a way about her, and she'd be seein' of you again before very long, and—'

'That's all a lie, you know,' said Mark, calmly.

'Well, then, she didn't say nothing, if that warn't it,' said the guard, doggedly.

'Did she—did she leave any directions about luggage or anything?' said Mark.

'Brown portmanty to go in the left-luggage room till called for,' said the guard. 'Anything else I can do for you, sir; no? Good mornin', then, and thanky, sir!'

'Never did such a thing as that in my life afore,' he muttered, as he went back to his van; 'to go and lose a bit o' paper with writing on it, d'reckly I got it, too; I'm afraid my head's a-leavin' me; they ain't keepin' company, that's plain. I made a mess o' that, or he wouldn't have wanted her direction. I saw what he was up to—well, they'd make a good-looking pair. I'm sorry I lost that there paper; but it warn't no use a-tellin' of him.'

As for Mark, this lame and impotent conclusion brought back all his depression again. 'She never even asked my name!' he thought, bitterly. 'I risked my life for her—it was for her, and she knew it: but she has forgotten that already. I've lost her for ever this time; she may not even live in London, and if she did

I've no clue to tell me where, and if I had I don't exactly see what use it would be; I won't think about her—yes, I will, she can't prevent me from doing that, at any rate!'

By this time he had left the City station of the Metropolitan Railway, and was going back to his underground labours at St. Peter's, where he was soon engaged in trying to establish something like discipline in his class, which the dark brown fog seemed to have inspired with unaccountable liveliness. His short holiday had not served to rest and invigorate him as much as might have been expected; it had left him consumed with a hopeless longing for something unattainable. His thirst for distinction had returned in an aggravated form, and he had cut himself off now from the only means of slaking it. As that day wore on, and with each day that succeeded it, he felt a wearier disgust with himself and his surroundings.

CHAPTER VIII

BAD NEWS

It was Christmas week, and Mrs. Langton and her daughters were sitting, late one afternoon, in the drawing-room where we saw them first. Dolly was on a low stool at her mother's feet, submitting, not too willingly, to have the bow in her hair smoothed and arranged for her. 'It must be all right now, mother!' she said, breaking away rebelliously at last.

'It's worse than ever, Dolly,' said Mrs. Langton plaintively; 'it's slipped over to the left now!'

'But it doesn't matter, it never will keep straight long.'

'Well, if you like to run about like a little wild child,' was the resigned answer.

'Little wild children don't wear bows in their hair; they wear—well, they don't wear anything they've got to be careful and tidy about. I think that must be rather nice,' said Dolly, turning round from where she knelt on the hearthrug. 'Wake up, Frisk, and be good-tempered directly. Mother, on Christmas Day I'm going to tie a Christmas card round Frisk's neck, and send him into papa's dressing-room to wish him a Merry Christmas, the first thing in the morning—you won't tell him before the time, will you?'

'Not if you don't wish it, darling,' said Mrs. Langton, placidly.

'I mightn't have had him to tie a card to,' said Dolly, taking the dog up and hugging him fondly, 'if that gentleman had not fetched him out of the train for me; and I never said "thank you" to him either. I forgot somehow, and when I remembered he was gone. Should you think he will come to see me, Mabel; you told him that mother would be glad to thank him some time, didn't you, on the paper you gave the guard for him?'

'Yes, Dolly,' said Mabel, turning her head a little away; 'but you see he hasn't come yet.'

'My dear,' said her mother, 'really I think he shows better taste in keeping away; there was no necessity to send him a message at all, and I hope he won't take any advantage of it. Thanking people is so tiresome and, after all, they never think you have said enough about it. It was very kind of the young man, of course, very—though I can't say I ever quite understood what it was he did—it was something in a fog, I know,' she concluded vaguely.

'We told you all about it, mother,' explained Dolly; 'I'll tell you all over again. There was a fog and our train stopped, and we all got out, and I left Frisk behind, and there he was in the carriage all alone, and then the gentleman ran back and got him out and brought him to me. And another train came up behind and stopped too.'

'Dolly tells it rather tamely,' said Mabel, her cheeks flushing again. 'At the time he ran back for the dog, we could all hear the other train rushing up in the fog, mamma, and nobody knew whether there might not be a frightful collision in another minute.'

'Then I think it was an extremely rash thing for him to do, my dear; and if I were his mother I should be very angry with him.'

'He was very good-looking, wasn't he, Mabel?' said Dolly, irrelevantly.

'Was he, Dolly? Well, yes, I suppose he was, rather,' said Mabel, with much outward indifference, and an inward and very vivid picture of Mark's face as he leaned by the stile, his fine eyes imploring her not to leave him.

'Well, perhaps, he doesn't care about being thanked, or doesn't want to see us again,' said Dolly; 'if he did, he'd call, you know; you wrote the address on the paper.'

Mabel had already arrived at the same conclusion, and was secretly a little piqued and hurt by it; she had gone slightly out of her way to give him an opportunity of seeing her again if he wished, and he had not chosen to take advantage of it; it had not seriously disturbed her peace of mind, but her pride was wounded notwithstanding. At times she was ready to believe that there had been some mistake or miscarriage with her message, otherwise it was strange that the admiration which it had not been difficult to read in his eyes should have evaporated in this way.

'Why, here's papa—home already!' cried Dolly, as the door opened and a tall man entered. 'How do you do, papa? you've rumpled my bow—you didn't think I meant it, did you? you can do it again if you like— I don't mind a bit; mother does.'

He had duly returned the affectionate hug with which Dolly had greeted him, but now he put her aside with a rather preoccupied air, and went to his wife's chair, kissing the smooth forehead she presented, still absently.

'You are early, Gerald,' she said; 'did the courts rise sooner to-day?'

'No,' he said conscientiously, 'it's the Vacation now—I left chambers as soon as I could get away,' and he was folding and unfolding the evening paper he had brought in with him, as he stood silent before the fire.

Mr. Langton was not much over fifty, and a handsome man still, with full clear eyes, a well-cut chin and mouth, iron-grey whiskers, and a florid complexion which years spent in stifling law-courts and dust and black laden chambers had not done much to tone down. Young barristers and solicitors' clerks were apt to consider him rather a formidable personage in Lincoln's Inn; and he was certainly imposing as he rustled along New Square or Chancery Lane, his brows knitted, a look of solemn importance about his tightly-closed lips, and his silk gown curving out behind him like a great black sail. He had little imperious ways in court, too, of beckoning a client to come to him from the well, or of waving back a timid junior who had plucked his gown to draw his attention to some suggestion with a brusque 'Not now—I can't hear that now!' which suggested immeasurable gulfs between himself and them. But at home he unbent, a little consciously, perhaps, but he did unbend—being proud and fond of his children, who at least stood in no fear of him. Long years of successful practice had had a certain narrowing effect upon him; the things of his profession were almost foremost in his mind now, and when he travelled away from them he was duller than he once promised to be—his humour had slowly dwindled down until he had just sufficient for ordinary professional purposes, and none at all for private consumption.

In his favour it may be added that he was genial to all whom he did not consider his inferiors, a good though not a demonstrative husband; that as a lawyer he was learned without the least pedantry; and that he was a Bencher of his Inn, where he frequently dined, and a Member of Parliament, where he never spoke, even on legal matters.

Mabel's quick eyes were the first to notice a shade on his face and a constraint in his manner; she went to his side and said in an undertone, 'You are not feeling ill, papa, are you, or has anything worried you to-day?'

'I am quite well. I have news to tell you presently,' he said in the same tone.

'Come and see my Christmas cards before I do them up,' said Dolly from a side-table; 'I'm going to send one to each of my friends, except Clara Haycraft, or if I do send her one,' she added thoughtfully, 'it will be only a penny one, and I shall write her name on the back so that she can't use it again. Clara has not behaved at all well to me lately. If I sent one to Vincent now, papa, would he get it in time?'

'No—no,' said her father, a little sharply, 'and look here, Pussy, run away now and see how Colin is getting on.'

'And come back and tell you?' inquired Dolly; 'very well, papa.'

'Don't come back till I send for you,' he said. 'Mind that now, Dolly, stay in the schoolroom.'

He shut the door carefully after her, and then, turning to his wife and daughter, he said, 'You haven't either of you seen the papers to-day, I suppose?'

'No,' said Mrs. Langton; 'you know I never read daily papers. Gerald,' she cried suddenly, with a light coming into her eyes, 'is another judge dead?' Visions of her husband on the Bench, a town-house in a more central part of London, an increase of social consideration for herself and daughters, began to float into her brain.

'It's not that—if there was, I'm not likely to be offered a judgeship just yet; it's not good news, Belle, I'm afraid it's very bad,' he said warningly, 'very bad indeed.'

'Oh, papa,' cried Mabel, 'please don't break it to us—tell it at once, whatever it is!'

'You must let me choose my own course, my dear; I am coming to the point at once. The "Globe" has a telegram from Lloyd's agent reporting the total loss of the "Mangalore."'

'Vincent's ship!' said Mabel. 'Is—is he saved?'

'We cannot be certain of anything just yet—and—and these disasters are generally exaggerated in the first accounts, but I'm afraid there is very grave reason to fear that the poor boy went down with her—not many passengers were on board at the time, and only four or five of them were saved, and they are women. We can hope for the best still, but I cannot after reading the particulars feel any confidence myself. I made inquiries at the owners' offices this afternoon, but they could tell me very little just yet, though they will have fuller information by to-morrow—but from what they did say I cannot feel very hopeful.'

Mabel hid her face, trying to realise that the man who had sat opposite to her there scarcely a month ago, with the strange, almost prophetic, sadness in his eyes, was lying somewhere still and white, fathoms deep under the sea—she was too stunned for tears just yet.

'Gerald,' said Mrs. Langton, 'Vincent is drowned—I'm sure of it. I feel this will be a terrible shock to me by-and-by; I don't know when I shall get over it—poor, poor dear fellow! To think that the last time I saw him was that evening we dined at the Gordons'—you remember, Gerald, a dull dinner—and he saw me into the carriage, and stood there on the pavement saying good-bye!' Mrs. Langton seemed to consider that these circumstances had a deep pathos of their own; she pressed her eyes daintily with her handkerchief before she could go on. 'Why didn't he sail by one of the safe lines?' she murmured; 'the P. and O. never lost a single life; he might have gone in one of them and been alive now!'

'My dear Belle,' said her husband, 'we can't foresee these things, it—it was to be, I suppose.'

'Is nothing more known?' said Mabel, with a strong effort to control her voice.

'Here is the account—stay, I can give you the effect of it. It was in the Indian Ocean, not long after leaving Bombay, somewhere off the Malabar coast; and the ship seems to have grazed a sunken reef, which ripped a fearful hole in her side, without stopping her course. They were not near enough to the land to hope to reverse the engines and back her on shore at full speed. She began to settle down fast by the head, and their only chance was in the boats, which unfortunately had nearly all become jammed in the davits. Every one appears to have behaved admirably. They managed at last to launch one of the boats, and to put the women into it; and they were trying to get out the others, when the vessel went down suddenly, not a quarter of an hour after striking the reef.'

'Vincent could swim, papa,' said Mabel, with gleaming eyes.

'He was not a first-rate swimmer,' said Mr. Langton, 'I remember that, and even a first-rate swimmer would have found it hard work to reach the shore, if he had not been drawn down with the ship, as seems to have been the fate of most of the poor fellows. Still of course there is always hope.'

'And he is dead! Vincent dead! It seems so hard, so very, very sad,' said Mabel, and began to cry softly.

'Cry, darling,' said Mrs. Langton, 'it will do you good. I'm sure I wish I could cry like that, it would be such a relief. But you know papa says we may hope yet; we won't give up all hope till we're obliged to; we must be brave. You really don't care about coming in to dinner? You won't have a little something sent up to your room? Well, I feel as if food would choke me myself, but I must go in to keep papa company. Will you tell this sad news to Dolly and Colin, and ask Fräulein to keep them with her till bedtime? I can't bear to see them just yet.'

Mr. Langton's decorous concern did not interfere with his appetite, and Mrs. Langton seemed rather relieved at being able to postpone her grief for the present, and so Mabel was left to break the disaster, and the fate there was too much reason to fear for Vincent, to her younger brother and sister—a painful task, for Holroyd had been very dear to all three of them. Fräulein Mozer, too, wept with a more than sentimental sorrow for the young man she had tried to help, who would need her assistance never again.

The tidings had reached Mark early that same afternoon. He was walking home through the City from some 'holiday-classes' he had been superintending at St. Peter's, when the heading 'Loss of a passenger steamer with — lives' on the contents-sheets of the evening papers caught his eye, and led him, when established with a 'Globe' in one of the Underground Railway carriages, to turn with a languid interest to the details. He started when he saw the name of the vessel, and all his indifference left him as he hurriedly read the various accounts of the disaster, and looked in vain for Vincent's name amongst the survivors.

The next day he, too, went up to the owners' offices to make inquiries, and by that time full information had come in, which left it impossible that any but those who had come ashore in the long-boat could have escaped from the ship. They had remained near the scene of the wreck for some time, but without picking up more than one or two of the crew; the rest must all have been sucked down with the ship, which sank with terrible suddenness at the last.

Vincent was certainly not amongst those in the boat, while, as appeared from the agent's list, he was evidently on board when the ship left Bombay. It was possible to hope no longer after that, and Mark left the offices with the knowledge that Holroyd and he had indeed taken their last walk together; that he would see his face and take his hand no more.

It came to him with a shock, the unavoidable shock which a man feels when he has suddenly to associate the idea of death with one with whom he has had any intimacy. He told himself he was sorry, and for a moment Vincent's fate seemed somehow to throw a sort of halo round his memory, but very soon the sorrow faded, until at last it became little more than an uneasy consciousness that he ought to be miserable and was not.

Genuine grief will no more come at command than genuine joy, and so Mark found, not without some self-reproach; he even began to read 'In Memoriam' again with the idea of making that the keynote for his emotions, but the passionate yearning of that lament was pitched too high for him, and he never finished it. He recognised that he could not think of his lost friend in the way their long intimacy seemed to demand, and solved the difficulty by not thinking of him at all, compounding for his debt of inward mourning by wearing a black tie, which, as he was fond of a touch of colour in his costume, and as the emblem in question was not strictly required of him, he looked upon as, so to speak, a fairly respectable dividend.

Caffyn heard the news with a certain satisfaction. A formidable rival had been swept out of his path, and he could speak of him now without any temptation to depreciate his merits, so much so that when he took an opportunity one day of referring to his loss, he did it so delicately that Mabel was touched, and liked him better for this indication of feeling than she had ever been able to do before.

Her own sorrow was genuine enough, requiring no artificial stimulus and no outward tokens to keep it alive, and if Vincent could have been assured of this it would have reconciled him to all else. No callousness nor forgetfulness on the part of others could have had power to wound him so long as he should live on in the memory of the girl he had loved.

But it is better far for those who are gone that they should be impervious alike to our indifference and our grief, for the truest grief will be insensibly deadened by time, and could not long console the least exacting for the ever-widening oblivion.

CHAPTER IX

A TURNING-POINT

Mark came down to the little back parlour at Malakoff Terrace one dull January morning to find the family already assembled there, with the exception of Mrs. Ashburn, who was breakfasting in bed—an unusual indulgence for her.

'Mark,' said Trixie, as she leaned back in her chair, and put up her face for his morning greeting, 'there's a letter for you on your plate.'

It was not difficult to observe a suppressed excitement amongst all the younger members of his family concerning this letter; they had finished their breakfast and fallen into some curious speculations as to Mark's correspondent before he came in. Now three pairs of eyes were watching him as he strolled up to his seat; Mr. Ashburn alone seemed unconscious or indifferent.

Of late Mark had not had very many letters, and this particular one bore the name of 'Chilton & Fladgate' on the flap of the envelope. The Ashburns were not a literary family, but they knew this as the name of a well-known firm of publishers, and it had roused their curiosity.

Mark read the name too. For a moment it gave him a throb of excitement, the idea coming to him that, somehow, the letter concerned his own unfortunate manuscripts. It was true that he had never had any communication with this particular firm, but these wild vague impressions are often independent of actual fact; he took it up and half began to open it.

Then he remembered what it probably was, and, partly with the object of preserving Vincent's secret still as far as possible, but chiefly, it must be owned, from a malicious pleasure he took in disappointing the expectation he saw around him, put the letter still unopened in his pocket.

'Why don't you open it?' asked Trixie impatiently, who was cherishing the hope that some magnificent literary success had come at last to her favourite brother.

'Manners,' explained Mark, laconically.

'Nonsense,' said Trixie, 'you don't treat us with such ceremony as all that.'

'Not lately,' said Mark; 'that's how it is—it's bad for a family to get lax in these little matters of mutual courtesy. I'm going to see if I can't raise your tone—this is the beginning.'

'I'm sure we're very much obliged to you,' from Martha; 'I'm quite satisfied with my own tone, it's quite high enough for me, thank you.'

'Yes, I forgot,' said Mark, 'I've heard it very high indeed sometimes. I wronged you, Martha. Still, you know, we might (all except you, Martha) be more polite to one another without causing ourselves any internal injury, mightn't we?'

'Well, Mark,' said Trixie, 'all you have to do is to ask our leave to open the letter, if you're really so particular.'

'Is that in the Etiquette Book?' inquired Mark.

'Don't be ridiculous—why don't you ask our leave?'

'I suppose because I want to eat my breakfast—nothing is so prejudicial, my love, to the furtherance of the digestive process as the habit of reading at meals, any medical man will tell you that.'

'Perhaps,' suggested Martha, 'Mark has excellent reasons for preferring to read his letter alone.'

'Do you know, Martha,' said Mark, 'I really think there's something in that?'

'So do I,' said Martha, 'more than you would care for us to know, evidently; but don't be afraid, Mark, whether it's a bill, or a love-letter, or another publisher's rejection; we don't want to know your secrets—do we, Cuthbert?'

'Very amiable of you to say so,' said Mark. 'Then I shan't annoy you if I keep my letter to myself, shall I? Because I rather thought of doing it.'

'Eh? doing what? What is Mark saying about a letter?' broke in Mr. Ashburn. He had a way of striking suddenly like this into conversations.

'Somebody has written me a letter, father,' said Mark; 'I was telling Martha I thought I should read it—presently.'

But even when he was alone he felt in no hurry to possess himself of the contents. 'I expect it's the usual thing,' he thought. 'Poor Vincent is out of all that now. Let's see how they let him down!' and he read:—

'DEAR SIR,—We have read the romance entitled "Glamour" which you have done us the honour to forward some time since. It is a work which appears to us to possess decided originality and merit, and which may be received with marked favour by the public, while it can hardly fail in any case to obtain a reception which will probably encourage its author to further efforts. Of course, there is a certain risk attending its reception which renders it impossible for us to offer such terms for a first book as may be legitimately demanded hereafter for a second production by the same pen. We will give you ...' (and here followed the terms, which struck Mark as fairly liberal for a first book by an unknown author). 'Should you accept our offer, will you do us the favour to call upon us here at your earliest convenience, when all preliminary matters can be discussed.

'We are, &c.,

'CHILTON & FLADGATE.'

Mark ran hurriedly through this letter with a feeling, first of incredulous wonder, then of angry protest against the bull-headed manner in which Fortune had dealt out this favour.

Vincent had been saved the dreary delays, the disappointments and discouragements, which are the lot of most first books; he had won a hearing at once—and where was the use of it? no praise or fame among men could reach him now.

If he had been alive, Mark thought bitterly; if a letter like this would have rescued him from all he detested, and thrown open to him the one career for which he had any ambition, he might have waited for it long and vainly enough. But he began by being indifferent, and, if Fortune had required any other inducement to shower her gifts on him, his death had supplied it.

He chafed over this as he went up to the City, for there was another holiday-class that day at St. Peter's; he thought of it at intervals during the morning, and always resentfully. What increased his irritation above everything was the fact that the publishers evidently regarded him as the author of the book, and he would have the distasteful task put upon him of enlightening them.

When the day's duties were over he found himself putting on his hat and coat in company with the Rev. Mr. Shelford, who was also in charge of one of the classes formed for the relief of parents and the performance of holiday work, and the two walked out together; Mark intending to call at once and explain his position to Messrs. Chilton & Fladgate.

'What are you going to do with yourself, Ashburn, now?' said Mr. Shelford in his abrupt way as they went along. 'Going to be a schoolmaster and live on the crambe repetita all your life, hey?'

'I don't know,' said Mark sullenly; 'very likely.'

'Take my advice (I'm old enough to offer it unasked); give yourself a chance while you can of a future which won't cramp and sour and wear you as this will. If you feel any interest in the boys—'

'Which I don't,' put in Mark.

'Exactly, which you don't—but if you did—I remember I did once, in some of 'em, and helped 'em on, and spoke to the headmaster about 'em, and so on. Well, they'll pass out of your class and look another way when they meet you afterwards. As for the dullards, they'll be always with you, like the poor, down at the bottom like a sediment, sir, and much too heavy to stir up! I can't manage 'em now, and my temper gets the better of me, God forgive me for it, and I say things I'm sorry for and that don't do me or them any good, and they laugh at me. But I've got my parish to look after; it's not a large one, but it acts as an antidote. You're not even in orders, so there's no help for you that way; and the day will come when the strain gets too much for you, and you'll throw the whole thing up in disgust, and find yourself forced to go through the same thing somewhere else, or begin the world in some other capacity. Choose some line in which hard work and endurance for years will bring you in a more substantial reward than that.'

'Well,' said Mark, for whom this gloomy view of his prospects reflected his own forebodings, 'I am reading for the Bar. I went up for my call-examination the other day.'

'Ah, is that so? I'm glad to hear of it; a fine profession, sir; constant variety and excitement—for the pleader, that is to say' (Mr. Shelford shared the lay impression that pleading was a form of passionate appeal to judge and jurymen), 'and of course you would plead in court. The law has some handsome prizes in its disposal, too. But you should have an attorney or two to push you on, they say. Perhaps you can count on that?'

'I wish I could,' said Mark, 'but the fact is my ambition doesn't lie in a legal direction at all. I don't care very much about the Bar.'

'Do you care very much about anything? Does your ambition lie anywhere?'

'Not now; it did once—literature, you know; but that's all over.'

'I remember, to be sure. They rejected that Christmas piece of yours, didn't they? Well, if you've no genuine talent for it, the sooner you find it out the better for you. If you feel you've something inside of you that must out in chapters and volumes, it generally comes, and all the discouragement in the world won't keep it down. It's like those stories of demoniacal possession in the "Anatomy"—you know your Burton, I daresay? Some of the possessed brought "globes of hair" and "such-like baggage" out of themselves, but others "stones with inscriptions." If the demon gets too strong for you, try and produce a stone with a good readable inscription on it—not three globes of hair for the circulating libraries.'

'We shall see,' said Mark laughing. 'I must leave you here. I have an appointment with Chilton & Fladgate just by.'

'Ay, ay,' said the old gentleman, wagging his head; 'publishers, aren't they? Don't tell me your ambition's dead if it's taken you as far as that. But I won't ask any more questions. I shall hope to be able to congratulate you shortly. I won't keep you away from your publishers any longer.'

'They are not my publishers yet,' said Mark; 'they have made me some proposals, but I have not accepted them at present.'

He knew what a false impression this would leave with his companion, bare statement of fact as it was, but he made it deliberately, feeling almost as much flattered by the unconscious increase of consideration in the other's voice and manner as if there had been the slightest foundation for it.

They said good-bye, and the old clergyman went on and was swallowed up in the crowd, thinking as he went, 'Publishing, eh? a good firm, too. I don't think he could afford to do it at his own expense. Perhaps there's more ballast in him after all than I gave him credit for. I can't help liking the young fellow somehow, too. I should like to see him make a good start.'

Mark, having sent up his name by one of the clerks behind the imposing mahogany counters, was shown through various swinging glass doors into a waiting-room, where the magazines and books symmetrically arranged on the table gave a certain flavour of dentistry to the place.

Mark turned them over with a quite unreasonable nervousness, but the fact was he shrank from what he considered the humiliation of explaining that he was a mere agent; it occurred to him for the first time, too, that Holroyd's death might possibly complicate matters, and he felt a vague anger against his dead friend for leaving him in such a position.

The clerk returned with a message that Mr. Fladgate would be happy to see Mark at once, and so he followed upstairs and along passages with glimpses through open doors of rooms full of clerks and desks, until they came to a certain room into which Mark was shown—a small room with a considerable litter of large wicker trays filled with proofs, packets and rolls of manuscripts of all sizes, and piles of books and periodicals, in the midst of which Mr. Fladgate was sitting with his back to the light, which was admitted through windows of ground-glass.

He rose and came forward to meet Mark, and Mark saw a little reddish-haired and whiskered man, with quick eyes, and a curious perpendicular fold in the forehead above a short, blunt nose, a mobile mouth, and a pleasantly impulsive manner.

'How do you do, Mr. Beauchamp?' he said heartily, using the nom de plume with an air of implied compliment; 'and so you've made up your mind to entrust yourself to us, have you? That's right. I don't think you'll find any reason to regret it, I don't indeed.'

Mark said he was sure of that.

'Well, now, as to the book,' continued Mr. Fladgate; 'I've had the pleasure of looking through it myself, as well as Mr. Blackshaw, our reader, and I must tell you that I agree with him in considering that you have written a very remarkable book. As we told you, you know, it may or may not prove a pecuniary success, but, however that may be, my opinion of it will remain the same; it ought, in my judgment, to ensure you a certain standing at once—at once.'

Mark heard this with a pang of jealousy. Long before, he had dreamed of just such an interview, in which he should be addressed in some such manner—his dream was being fulfilled now with relentless mockery!

'But there is a risk,' said Mr. Fladgate, 'a decided risk, which brings me to the subject of terms. Are you satisfied with the offer we made to you? You see that a first book—'

'Excuse me for one moment,' said Mark desperately, 'I'm afraid you imagine that—that I wrote the book?'

'That certainly was my impression,' said Mr. Fladgate, with a humorous light in his eye; 'the only address on the manuscript was yours, and I came to the not unnatural conclusion that Mr. Ashburn and Mr. Beauchamp were one and the same. Am I to understand that is not the case?'

'The book,' said Mark—what it cost him to say this,—'the book was written by a friend of mine, who went abroad some time ago.'

'Indeed? Well, we should prefer to treat with him in person, of course, if possible.'

'It isn't possible,' said Mark, 'my friend was lost at sea, but he asked me to represent him in this matter, and I believe I know his wishes.'

'I've no doubt of it; but you see, Mr.—Mr. Ashburn, this must be considered a little. I suppose you have some authority from him in writing, to satisfy us (merely as a matter of business) that we are dealing with the right person?'

'I have not indeed,' said Mark, 'my friend was very anxious to retain his incognito.'

'He must have been—very much so,' said Mr. Fladgate, coughing; 'well, perhaps you can bring me some writing of his to that effect? You may have it among your papers, eh?'

'No,' said Mark, 'my friend did not think it necessary to give me one—he was anxious to—'

'Oh, quite so—then you can procure me a line or two perhaps?'

'I told you that my friend was dead,' said Mark a little impatiently.

'Ah, so you did, to be sure, I forgot. I thought—but no matter. Well, Mr. Ashburn, if you can't say anything more than this—anything, you understand, which puts you in a position to treat with us, I'm afraid—I'm afraid I must ask time to think over this. If your friend is really dead, I suppose your authority is determined. Perhaps, however, his—ahem—anxiety to preserve his incognito has led him to allow this rumour of his death to be circulated?'

'I don't think that is likely,' said Mark, wondering at an undercurrent of meaning in the publisher's tone, a meaning which had nothing sinister in it, and yet seemed urging him to contradict himself for some reason.

'That is your last word, then?' said Mr. Fladgate, and there was a sharp inflection as of disappointment and irritation in his voice, and the fold in his forehead deepened.

'It must be,' said Mark, rising, 'I have kept you too long already.'

'If you really must go,' said Mr. Fladgate, not using the words in their conventional sense of polite dismissal. 'But, Mr. Ashburn, are you quite sure that this interview might not be saved from coming to nothing, as it seems about to do? Might not a word or two from you set things right again? I don't wish to force you to tell me anything you would rather keep concealed—but really, this story you tell about a Mr. Vincent Beauchamp who is dead only ties our hands, you understand—ties our hands!'

'If so,' said Mark, uncomfortably, 'I can only say I am very sorry for it—I don't see how I can help it.'

He was beginning to feel that this business of Holroyd's had given him quite trouble enough.

'Now, Mr. Ashburn, as I said before, I should be the last man to press you—but really, you know, really—this is a trifle absurd! I think you might be a little more frank with me, I do indeed. There is no reason why you should not trust me!'

Was this man tempting him, thought Mark. Could he be so anxious to bring out this book that he was actually trying to induce him to fabricate some story which would get over the difficulties that had arisen?

As a mere matter of fact, it may be almost unnecessary to mention that no such idea had occurred to worthy Mr. Fladgate, who, though he certainly was anxious to secure the book if he could, by any legitimate means, was anything but a publishing Mephistopheles. He had an object, however, in making this last appeal for confidence, as will appear immediately; but, innocent as it was, Mark's imagination conjured up a bland demon tempting him to some act of unspeakable perfidy; he trembled—but not with horror. 'What do you mean?' he stammered.

Mr. Fladgate gave a glance of keen amusement at the pale troubled face of the young man before him. 'What do I mean?' he repeated. 'Come, I've known sensitive women try to conceal their identity, and even their sex, from their own publishers; I've known men even persuade themselves they didn't care for notoriety—but such a determined instance of what I must take leave to call the literary ostrich I don't think I ever did meet before! I never met a writer so desperately anxious to remain unknown that he would rather take his manuscript back than risk his secret with his own publisher. But don't you see that you have raised (I don't use the term in the least offensively) the mask, so to speak—you should have sent somebody else here to-day if you wished to keep me in the dark. I've not been in business all these years, Mr. Ashburn, without gaining a little experience. I think, I do think, I am able to know an author when I see him—we are all liable to error, but I am very much mistaken if this Mr. Vincent Beauchamp (who was so unfortunately lost at sea) is not to be recovered alive by a little judicious dredging. Do think if you can't produce him; come, he's not in very deep water—bring him up, Mr. Ashburn, bring him up!'

'You make this very difficult for me,' said Mark, in a low voice; he knew now how greatly he had misjudged the man, who had spoken with such an innocent, amiable pride in his own surprising discernment; he also felt how easy and how safe it would be to take advantage of this misunderstanding, and what a new future it might open to him—but he was struggling still against the temptation so unconsciously held out to him.

'I might retort that, I think. Now, be reasonable, Mr. Ashburn. I assure you the writer, whoever he may be, has no cause to be ashamed of the book—the time will come when he will probably be willing enough to own it. Still, if he wishes to keep his real name secret, I tell him, through you, that he may surely be content to trust that to us. We have kept such secrets before—not very long, to be sure, as a general rule; but then that was because the authors usually relieved us from the trouble—the veil was never lifted by us.'

'I think you said,' began Mark, as if thinking aloud, 'that other works by—by the same author would be sure of acceptance?'

'I should be very glad to have an opportunity, in time, of producing another book by Mr. Vincent Beauchamp—but Mr. Beauchamp, as you explained, is unhappily no more. Perhaps these are earlier manuscripts of his?'

Mark had been seized with the desire of making one more attempt, in spite of his promise to his uncle, to launch those unhappy paper ships of his—'Sweet Bells Jangled' and 'One Fair Daughter.' For an instant it occurred to him that he might answer this last question in the affirmative; he had little doubt that if he did his books would meet with a very different reception from that of Messrs. Leadbitter and Gandy; still, that would only benefit Holroyd—not himself, and then he recollected, only just in time, that the difference in handwriting (which was very considerable) would betray him. He looked confused and said nothing.

Mr. Fladgate's patience began to tire. 'We don't seem to be making any way, do we?' he said, with rather affected pleasantry. 'I'm afraid I must ask you to come to a decision on this without any more delay. Here is the manuscript you sent us. If the real author is dead we are compelled to return it with much regret. If you can tell me anything which does away with the difficulty, this is the time to tell it. Of course you will do exactly as you please, but after what you have chosen to tell us we can hardly see our way, as I said, to treat with you without some further explanation. Come, Mr. Ashburn, am I to have it or not?'

'Give me a little time,' said Mark faintly, and the publisher, as he had expected, read the signs of wavering in his face, though it was not of the nature he believed it to be.

Mark sat down again and rested his chin on his hand, with his face turned away from the other's eyes. A conflict was going on within him such as he had never been called upon to fight before, and he had only a very few minutes allowed him to fight it.

Perhaps in these crises a man does not always arrange pros and cons to contend for him in the severely logical manner with which we find him doing it in print. The forces on the enemy's side can generally be induced to desert. All the advantages which would follow if he once allowed himself to humour the publisher's mistake were very prominently before Mark's mind—the dangers and difficulties kept in the background. He was incapable of considering the matter coolly; he felt an overmastering impulse upon him, and he had never trained himself to resist his impulses for very long. There was very little of logical balancing going on in his brain; it began to seem terribly, fatally easy to carry out this imposition. The fraud itself grew less ugly and more harmless every instant.

He saw his own books, so long kept out in the cold by ignorant prejudice, accepted on the strength of Holroyd's 'Glamour,' and, once fairly before the public, taking the foremost rank in triumph and rapidly eclipsing their forerunner. He would be appreciated at last, delivered from the life he hated, able to lead the existence he longed for. All he wanted was a hearing; there seemed no other way to obtain it; he had no time to lose. How could it injure Holroyd? He had not cared for fame in life; would he miss it after his death? The publishers might be mistaken; the book might be unnoticed altogether; he might prove to be the injured person.

But, as Mr. Fladgate seemed convinced of its merit, as he would evidently take anything alleged to come from the same source without a very severe scrutiny, there was nothing for it but to risk this contingency.

Mark was convinced that publishers were influenced entirely by unreasoning prejudices; he thoroughly believed that his works would carry all before them if any firm could once overcome their repugnance to his powerful originality, and here was one firm at least prepared to lay that aside at a word from him. Why should he let it go unsaid?

The money transactions caused him the most hesitation. If he took money for another man's work, there was a name, and a very ugly name, for that. But he would not keep it. As soon as he learnt the names of Holroyd's legal representatives, whoever they might be, he would pay the money over to them without mentioning the exact manner in which it had become due. In time, when he had achieved a reputation for himself, he could give back the name he had borrowed for a time—at least he told himself he could do so.

He stood in no danger of detection, or, if he did, it was very slight. Vincent was not the man to confide in more than one person; he had owned as much. He had been reticent enough to conceal his real surname from his publishers, and now he could never reveal the truth.

All this rushed through his mind in a hurried, confused form; all his little vanities and harmless affectations and encouragements of false impressions had made him the less capable of resisting now.

'Well?' said Mr. Fladgate at last.

Mark's heart beat fast. He turned round and faced the publisher. 'I suppose I had better trust you,' he said awkwardly, and with a sort of shamefaced constraint that was admirably in keeping with his confession, though not artificial.

'I think so. Then you are the man—this book "Glamour"'s your own work?'

'If you must have it—yes,' said Mark desperately.

The words were spoken now, and for good or ill he must abide by them henceforth to the end.

CHAPTER X

REPENTE TURPISSIMUS

No sooner had Mark declared himself the author of his dead friend's book than he would have given anything to recall his words, not so much from conscience (though he did feel he had suddenly developed into a surprisingly finished scoundrel), as from a fear that his lie might after all be detected. He sat staring stupidly at Mr. Fladgate, who patted him on the shoulder with well-meant encouragement; he had never seen quite so coy an author before. 'I'm very glad to make Mr. Vincent Beauchamp's acquaintance—at last,' he said, beaming with honest pride at the success of his tactics, 'and now we can come to terms again.'

He did not find Mark more difficult to deal with than most budding authors, and in this case Mark was morbidly anxious to get the money part of the transaction over as soon as possible; he could not decide whether his conscience would be better or worse satisfied if he insisted on the best pecuniary terms he could obtain, so in his indecision he took the easier course of agreeing to everything.

'About the title now?' said Mr. Fladgate, when the terms had been reduced to a formal memorandum. 'I don't think I quite like your present one; too moonshiny, eh?'

Mark owned that it did sound a little moonshiny.

'I think, too, I rather think, there's something very like it out already, and that may lead to unpleasantness, you know. Now, can you suggest something else which will give a general idea of the nature of the book?'

As Mark had absolutely no idea what the book was about, he could not.

'Well, Mr. Blackshaw suggested something like "Enchantment," or "Witchery."'

'I don't care about either of those,' said Mark, who found this sort of dissembling unexpectedly easy.

'No,' said Mr. Fladgate, 'No. I think you're right. Now, I had a notion—I don't know what you will think of it—but I thought you might call it "A Modern Merlin," eh?'

'"A Modern Merlin,"' repeated Mark thoughtfully.

'Yes, it's not quite the right thing, perhaps, but it's taking, I think, taking.'

Mark said it was taking.

'Of course your hero is not exactly a magician, but it brings in the "Vivien" part of the story, don't you see?' Of course Mark did not see, but he thought it best to agree. 'Well,' continued Mr. Fladgate, who was secretly rather proud of his title, 'how does it strike you now? it seems to me as good a title as we are likely to hit upon.'

After all, Mark thought, what did it matter? it wasn't his book, except in name. 'I think it's excellent,' he said, 'excellent; and, by the way, Mr. Fladgate,' he added, 'I should like to change the nom de plume: it's a whim of mine, perhaps, but there's another I've been thinking lately I should like better.'

'By all means,' said the other, taking up a pencil to make the necessary alteration on the manuscript, 'but why not use your real name? I prophesy you'll be proud of that book some day; think over it.'

'No,' said Mark, 'I don't wish my real name to appear just yet' (he hardly knew why; perhaps a lingering sense of shame held him back from this more open dishonesty). 'Will you strike out "Vincent Beauchamp," and put in "Cyril Ernstone," please?' For 'Cyril Ernstone' had been the pseudonym which he had chosen long ago for himself, and he wished to be able to use it now, since he must not use his own.

'Very well, then, we may consider that settled. We think of bringing out the book as soon as possible, without waiting for the spring season; it will go to press at once and we will send you the proofs as soon as we get them in.'

'There's one thing, perhaps, I'd better mention,' said Mark suddenly; after he had turned to go a new danger had occurred to him, 'the handwriting of the manuscript is not mine. I—I thought it as well to tell you that beforehand; it might lead to mistakes. I had it copied out for me by—by a friend.'

Mr. Fladgate burst out laughing. 'Pardon me,' he said, when he had finished, 'but really I couldn't help it, you do seem to have been so bent on hoodwinking us.'

'And yet you have found me out, you see,' said Mark, with a very unmirthful smile.

Mr. Fladgate smiled, too, making a little gesture of his hand, thinking very possibly that few precautions could be proof against his sagacity, and they parted.

Mark went down the stairs and through the clerks' room into the street, with a dazed and rather awestruck feeling upon him. He hardly realised the treachery he had been guilty of, the temptation had burst upon him so suddenly, his fall had been made so easy for him, that he scarcely felt his dishonour, nor was he likely to feel it very keenly so long as only good results should flow from it. But he was vaguely conscious that he was not the same Mark Ashburn who had parted from old Shelford not an hour ago in the street there; he was a man with a new hope in his breast, and it might be a new fear, but the hope was near and bright, the fear shadowy and remote as yet: he had only to keep his own counsel and be patient for a while, and the course of events would assuredly bring him the stake he had played so high for.

At home that evening he took down his manuscript novels (which of course he had not burnt) and read them again carefully. Yes; there was power in them, he felt it, a copious flow of words, sparkling wit, and melting pathos. The white heat at which the lines were written surprised even himself. It was humiliating to think that without the subterfuge that had been forced upon him he might have found it impossible to find publishers who would appreciate these merits, for after Messrs. Leadbitter & Gandy's refusal he had recognised this to the full; but now, at least, they were insured against any such fate. A careful reading was absolutely necessary to a proper estimation of them, and a careful reading they had never had as yet, and would receive at last, or, if they did not, it would only be because the reputation he had appropriated would procure them a ready acceptance without any such preliminary ordeal. The great point gained was that they would be published, and after that he feared nothing.

If anything whispered to him that he might have accomplished even this by honourable means; that in time and with economy he could have produced them at his own expense; that perhaps a little more perseverance might even have discovered a firm with sufficient faith to take the risk upon themselves; if these doubts suggested themselves to him he had little difficulty in arguing them down. They might have had some weight once, but they came too late; the thing was done now and could never be recalled; his whole interest lay in persuading himself that what he had done was the only thing that could be done, unless he was content to resign his ambition for ever, and Mark succeeded in persuading himself of this.

Very soon his chief feeling was one of impatience for Holroyd's book to come out and make way for his own: then any self-reproach he might still feel would be drowned in a sense of triumph which would justify the means he had taken; so he waited eagerly for the arrival of the first proofs.

They arrived at last. As he came back one evening to Malakoff Terrace, Trixie ran to meet him, holding up two tightly rolled parcels, with a great curiosity in her eyes. 'They came this afternoon,' she whispered, 'and oh, Mark, I couldn't help it; I tore one end a little and peeped; are they really part of a book—is it yours?'

Mark thought he had better accustom himself to this kind of thing as early as possible. 'Yes, Trixie,' he said, 'they're the first proofs of my book.'

'O-oh!' cried Trixie, with a gasp of delight, 'not "Sweet Bells Jangled," Mark?'

'No, not "Sweet Bells Jangled," it—it's a book you don't know about—a little thing I don't expect very much from, but my publishers seem to like it, and I can follow it up with the "Bells" afterwards.'

He was turning over the rough greyish pages as he spoke, and Trixie was peeping greedily at them, too, with her pretty chin dug into his shoulder.

'And did you really write all that?' she said; 'how interesting it looks, you clever boy! You might have told me you were doing it, though. What's it about?'

'How can I tell you before I know myself,' said Mark, quite forgetting himself in his impatience. 'I—I mean, Trixie, that I can't correct these proofs as they ought to be corrected while you stay here chattering.'

'I'll go in a minute, Mark; but you won't have time to correct them before dinner, you know. When did you write it?'

'What does it matter when I wrote it!' said Mark irritably; 'if it hadn't been written the proofs wouldn't be here, would they? Is there anything else you would like to know—how I wrote it, where I wrote it, why I wrote it? You seem to think it a most extraordinary thing that anything I write should be printed at all, Trixie.'

'I don't know why you should speak like that, Mark,' said Trixie, rather hurt; 'you know a little while ago you never expected such a thing yourself. I can't help wanting to know all I can about it. What will you say to Uncle Solomon?' she added, with a little quiver of laughter in her voice. 'You promised him to give up literature, you know.'

'Don't you remember the Arab gentleman in the poem?' said Mark lightly. 'He agreed to sell his steed, but when the time came it didn't come off—he didn't come off, either—he "flung them back their gold," and rode away. I shall fling Uncle Solomon back his gold, metaphorically, and gallop off on my Pegasus.'

'Ma won't like that,' prophesied Trixie, shaking her head wisely.

'No; mother objects to that kind of horse-exercise, and, ahem, Trixie, it might be as well to say nothing about it to any of them just at present. There will only be a fuss about it, and I can't stand that.'

Trixie promised silence. 'I'm so glad about it, though, you can't think, Mark,' she said; 'and this isn't one of your great books, either, you said, didn't you?'

'No,' said Mark; 'it's not one of them. I haven't put my best work into it.'

'You put your best work into the two that came back, didn't you?' asked Trixie naively. 'But they won't come back any more, will they? They'll be glad of them if this is a success.'

'Fladgate will be glad of them, I fancy, in any case. I've got a chance at last, Trixie. A chance at last!'

Later that night he locked himself in the room which he used as a sitting-room and bedroom combined, and set himself, not without repugnance, to go steadily through the proofs, and make the acquaintance of the work he had made his own.

Much has been said of the delight with which an author reads his first proofs, and possibly the sensation is a wholly pleasurable one to some; to others it is not without its drawbacks. Ideas that seemed vivid and bright enough when they were penned have a bald tame look in the new form in which they come back. The writer finds himself judging the work as a stranger's, and forming the worst opinions of it. He sees hideous gaps and crudities beyond all power of correction, and for the first time, perhaps, since he learned that his manuscript was accepted, his self-doubts return to him.

But Mark's feelings were much more complicated than this; all the gratified pride of an author was naturally denied to him, and it was thoroughly distasteful to him to carry out his scheme of deception by such sordid details as the necessary corrections of printers' errors.

But he was anxiously eager to find out what kind of a literary bantling was this which he had fathered so fraudulently; he had claimed it in blind reliance on the publisher's evident enthusiasm—had he made a mistake after all? What if it proved something which could do him no credit whatever—a trap into which his ambition had led him! The thought that this might be so made him very uneasy. Poor Holroyd, he thought, was a very good fellow—an excellent fellow, but not exactly the man to write a book of extraordinary merit—clever, perhaps, but clever in an unobtrusive way—and Mark's tendency was to judge, as he expected to be judged himself, by outsides.

With these misgivings crowded upon him, he sat down to read the opening chapters; he was not likely to be much overcome by admiration in any case, for his habitual attitude in studying even the greatest works was critical, as he felt the presence of eccentricities or shortcomings which he himself would have avoided.

But at least, as he read on, his greatest anxiety was set at rest—if he could judge by the instalment before him, and the book was not in any danger of coming absolutely to grief—it would do his reputation no harm. It was not, to be sure, the sort of book he would have written himself, as he affected the cynical mode of treatment and the indiscriminate satire which a rather young writer feels instinctively that the world expects from him. Still, it was not so bad. It was slightly dreamy and mystical in parts, the work of a man who had lived more amongst books than in the world, but some of the passages glowed with the rich imagery of a true poet, and here and there were indications of a quiet and cultivated humour which would recommend itself to all who do not consider the humorous element in literature as uncanny, if not personally offensive. The situations were strong, too, and as nearly new as situations can be and retain any probability in this over-plagiarised world; and at least one of the characters was obviously studied from life with a true and tender observation.

All of this Mark did not see, nor was he capable of seeing, but he thought that, with a little 'weeding' and 'writing-up,' the book would do, and set himself to supply what was wanting with a laudable self-devotion. His general plan of accomplishing this may be described here once for all.

He freshened up chapters with touches of satire, and gave them a more scholarly air by liberal allusions to the classics; he rewrote some of the more descriptive and romantic passages, putting his finest and most florid epithets into them with what he felt was very like disinterestedness, and a reckless waste of good material. And he cut down the dialogue in places, or gave it a more colloquial turn, so as to suit the tastes of the average reader, and he worked up some of the crises which struck him as inadequately treated.

After that he felt much easier; either considering that these improvements constituted a sort of atonement, or that they removed any chance of failure. As this book was to go forth and herald his own, it was vitally important that it should make as imposing an appearance as possible.

CHAPTER XI

REVOLT

One afternoon, early in the year, Mark had betaken himself to the 'Cock,' where he was to lunch with his uncle by appointment before going with him to the steward's office of his Inn to pay his fees for the privilege of being called to the Bar. For Mark had duly presented himself for the not very searching ordeal by which the public is guaranteed against the incompetence of practitioners, and, rather to his own surprise, had not been required to try again. 'Call night' was announced in the windows of the law wig-makers, and Uncle Solomon, in high delight, resolved that his nephew should join the next batch of barristers, had appointed this day for choosing the wig and gown and settling all other preliminaries—he had been so much pleased, in fact, as to inclose a handsome cheque in the letter which conveyed his desires.

So Mark waited by the hoardings of the New Law Courts, until his relative should join him. Mark was not at ease—he was nerving himself to make a statement which he felt would come upon his uncle as a far from gratifying surprise—he had put it off from time to time, out of weakness, or, as he had told himself, from diplomacy. Now he could do so no longer. Uncle Solomon had hinted terrible things in his letter of a certain brief with which his own solicitor was to entrust the brand-new barrister the morning after his call! But for this, Mark might have let things drift, as he would strongly have preferred to do, but this threat of immediate employment drove him to declare himself. He firmly believed that his true vocation was the one he had secured at such cost to his self-respect; he was willing enough to bear the title of barrister, but he had no intention of devoting himself seriously to the profession; he saw little more attraction in the Bar than in teaching, and the most self-confident man might have recoiled at having work thrust into his hands before he had undergone the slightest practical training for conducting it. And Mark's imagination saw his first brief bringing others in its train, until he should sink in a sea of blue foolscap, helpless and entangled in clinging tentacles of red-tape. Perhaps this was a groundless alarm, but he had planned out a particular career for himself, a career of going about and observing (and it is well known that what a man of genius calls 'observing' is uncommonly like ordinary people's enjoyment), being famous and flattered, and sitting down in moments of inspiration to compose with a clear head and a mind unhampered by all other considerations. Now the responsibility of legal work would hamper him—he felt his muse to be of that jealous disposition which will suffer no rival—if he meant to be free at all, he must strike the blow at once. And so, as has been said, he was not at his ease.

Mr. Lightowler appeared as St. Clement Danes struck half-past one; he was in high good-humour, jubilant, and ruddy. 'Well, Master Barrister,' he said, chuckling; 'to think o' my living to see you figurin' about in a wig and gown—you must cut off that moustache of yours, though, Mark: none of the young barrister fellows I see goin' up in the train of a mornin' wear 'em. I'm told the judges don't consider too much 'air respectful, hey? Well, s'pose we go in and have a bit of something, eh? The "Cock" is it? Ah, I haven't been in here—I haven't been in here not since I was a young man "on the road," as we used to call it. I don't mean I was ever in the Dick Turpin line, but a commercial gentleman, you know. Well, I've made my way since. You'll have to make yours, with more help than I ever had, though.'

Mark led the way up a steep little passage and into the well-known room, with its boxes darkened by age, its saw-dusted floor and quaint carved Jacobean mantelpiece. He chose a compartment well down at the bottom of the room.

'What's your partickler preference, eh?' said Uncle Solomon, rather as if he was treating a schoolboy. 'What's their speciality 'ere, now? Well, you can give me,' he added to the waiter, with the manner of a man conferring a particular favour, 'you can give me a chump chop, underdone, and a sausage. And bring this young gentleman the same. I don't care about anything 'eavier at this time o' day,' he explained.

Mark talked on all kinds of topics with desperate brilliancy for some time; he wanted time before approaching the subject.

Uncle Solomon broached it for him. 'You'll want a regler set o' chambers by-and-by,' he said; 'I've seen a room down Middle Temple Lane that'll do for you for the present. When the briefs begin to come in, we'll see about something better. I was talkin' about you to Ferret the other day,' he went on. 'It'll be all right; he's goin' to instruct their London agent to send you in a little something that you can try your 'prentice hand at directly. Isn't that be'aving like an uncle to you, eh? I hope you will go and do me credit over it; that's the only way you can pay me back a little—I ask but that of you, Mark.'

For all his bumptiousness and despotism, there was a real kindness, possibly not of the purest and most unselfish order, but still kindness in his manner, and Mark felt a pang at having to reward it as he must.

The meal was over now, and Uncle Solomon was finishing the glass of whisky and water before him. 'Well,' he said, as he set it down, 'we'd better be off to the place where I'm to pay the fees for you. Ah, what you young fellows cost to start nowadays!'

'That's it,' said Mark; 'I—I would rather not cost you anything, uncle.'

'It's rather late in the day to be partickler about that, I should say.'

'It is. I feel that; but I mean, I don't want to cost you any more.'

'What d'ye mean by that?'

'I mean that I don't care about being called to the Bar at present.'

'Don't you? Well, I do, so let that be enough for you. If I'm willing to pay, I don't see what you 'ave to say against it. All you've got to do is to work.'

'Uncle,' said Mark in a low voice, 'I must tell you what I feel about this. I—I don't want to cause you to spend your money on false pretences.'

'You'd better not: that's all I can tell you!'

'Precisely,' said Mark; 'so I'll be quite frank with you beforehand. If you set your mind on it, I will take my call to the Bar.'

'Will yer, though? That's very affable of you, now!'

'Yes, I will; but I shall never practise; if Ferret's agent sends me this brief, I shall decline it.'

'I would; that's the way to get on at the Bar; you're a sharp feller, you are!'

'I don't want to get on at the Bar. I don't mean to take it up; there, if you choose to be angry, I can't help it. I've told you.'

'Then may I take the liberty of inquirin' 'ow you purpose to live?' demanded Uncle Solomon.

'I mean to live by literature,' said Mark; 'I know I promised I wouldn't write any more: well, as far as that goes, I've kept my word; but—but a former book of mine has been accepted on very liberal terms, I see my way now to making a living by my pen, and though I'm sorry, of course, if it disappoints you, I mean to choose my life for myself, while I can.'

It must be highly annoying when one has, after infinite labour, succeeded in converting a clown, to see him come to chapel with a red-hot poker and his pockets full of stolen sausages; but even that shock is nothing to Uncle Solomon's.

He turned deadly pale and sank back in the box, glaring at Mark and opening his mouth once or twice with a fish-like action, but without speaking. When he could articulate, he called the waiter, giving Mark reason for a moment to fear that he was going to pour out his rage and disappointment into the ears of one of the smug and active attendants.

'Take for me and this young man, will yer?' was all he said, however. When the waiter had reckoned up the sum in the time-honoured manner and departed, Uncle Solomon turned and began to struggle into his great-coat. 'Let me help you,' said Mark, but Mr. Lightowler indignantly jerked himself away. 'I don't want to be helped into my coat by you,' he said; 'you've helped me into my grave by what you've done this day, you have; let that be sufficient for you!'

When he had rendered himself rather conspicuous by his ineffectual attempts to put on the coat, and was reduced to accept the assistance of two waiters who shook him into it obsequiously, he came back to the box where Mark was sitting in a relieved but still vaguely uncomfortable frame of mind.

'I don't want to 'ave many words with you about this,' he began with a sternness that was not unimpressive. 'If I was to let myself out in 'ere, I should go too far. I'll only just tell you this much; this is the second time you've played me this trick, and it's the last! I warned you before that I should have done with you if you did it again: you'll 'ave no more chances like the last, so mind that. Take care of that cheque, you needn't fear I shall stop it, but you won't get many more out o' me. And now I'll bid you good-day, young gentleman; I'm goin' to Kensington, and then I shall do a little littery composing on my own account, since it's so pop'lar, and get Ferret to help me with it. I'm not one of your littery men, but I dessey I can compose something yet that'll be read some day with a good deal of interest; it won't be pleasant reading for you, though, I can tell yer!'

He went noisily out, the waiters staring after him and the people looking up from their boxes as he passed, and Mark was left to his own reflections, which were of a mixed order.

He had accomplished his main object—his slavery was over, and he felt an indescribable relief at the thought; still, he could not avoid the suspicion that his freedom might have been dearly purchased. His uncle's words had pointed to a state of things in which he would have benefited to a considerable extent under his will, and that was over now. Would it not have been worth while to endure a little longer—but Mark felt strongly that it would not. With such prospects as he now saw opening before him, the idea of submitting himself to an old man's ambitious whims for the sake of a reward which might, after all, be withheld at last was utterly revolting. He felt a certain excitement, too, at the idea of conquering the world single-handed.

When he left the 'Cock' he walked slowly and irresolutely down the Strand. 'If I go home now I shall find him blustering there. I don't feel equal to any more of him just now,' he thought.

He had no club to go to at that time, so he went and read the papers, and drank coffee at a cigar divan until it was late enough to dine, and after dinner tried to drown his care by going to see one of those anomalous productions—a 'three-act burlesque'—at a neighbouring theatre, which he sat through with a growing gloom, in spite of the pretty faces and graceful dances which have now, with some rare exceptions, made plot and humour so unnecessary. Each leading member of the clever company danced his or her special pas seul as if for a competitive examination, but left him unthrilled amidst all the enthusiasm that thundered from most parts of the house. It is true that there were faces there—and young men's faces—quite as solemn as his own, but then theirs was the solemnity of an enjoyment too deep for expression, while Mark's face was blank from a depression he could not shake off.

He went away at the end of the second act with a confused recollection of glowing groups of silk-clad figures, forming up into a tableau for no obvious dramatic reason, and, thinking it better to face his family before the morning, went straight home to Malakoff Terrace. He could not help a slight nervousness as he opened the gate and went up the narrow path of flagstones. The lower window was dark, but there were no lights in the upper rooms, so that he guessed that the family had not retired. Mrs. Ashburn was entirely opposed to the latch-key as a domestic implement, and had sternly refused to allow such a thing to pass her threshold, so that Mark refrained from making use of the key—which of course he had—in all cases where it was not absolutely necessary, and he knocked and rang now.

Trixie came to the door and let him in. 'They've sent Ann to bed,' she whispered, 'but ma and pa are sitting up for you.'

'Are they though?' said Mark grimly, as he hung up his hat.

'Yes,' said Trixie; 'come in here for a minute, Mark, while I tell you all about it. Uncle Solomon has been here this afternoon and stayed to dinner and he's been saying, oh, such dreadful things about you. Why weren't you here?'

'I thought I should enjoy my dinner more if I dined out,' said Mark. 'Well, and what's the end of it all, Trixie?'

'I'm sure I don't know what it will be. Uncle Solomon actually wanted me to come and live with him at Chigbourne, and said he would make it worth my while in the end, if I would promise not to have anything more to do with you.'

'Ah, and when are you going?' said Mark, with a cynicism that was only on the surface.

'When!' said Trixie indignantly, 'why, never. Horrid old man! As if I cared about his money! I told him what I thought about things, and I think I made him angrier. I hope so, I'm sure.'

'Did he make the same offer to Martha or Cuthbert?' asked Mark; 'and were they indignant too?'

'They weren't asked. I don't think Uncle Solomon cares about them much; you're his favourite, Mark.'

'Yes, I'm his favourite,' said Mark; 'but I'm not proud, Trixie. Besides, I rather think all that is over now.'

Here the door of the next room opened, and Mrs. Ashburn's voice was heard saying, 'Trixie, tell your brother Mark that, if he is in a condition to be spoken to, his father and I have something to say to him at once.'

'Encouraging that,' said Mark. 'Well, Trixie, here goes. You'd better go to bed. I'm afraid we are going to have a scene in there.'

He went in with a rather overdone cheerfulness. 'Well, mother,' he began, attempting to kiss her, 'I didn't dine at home to-night because—'

'I know why you didn't dine at home,' she said. 'I wish for no kisses from you, Mark. We have seen your uncle.'

'So have I,' said Mark; 'I lunched with him.'

'It is useless to trifle now,' she said; 'we know all.'

'I assure you I did lunch with him; we had chops,' said Mark, who sometimes found the bland and childlike manner very useful in these emergencies. It did not serve him then, however.

'How could you deceive your uncle in such a manner?' she resumed.

'I didn't. I undeceived him.'

'You have disappointed all his plans for you; thrown up the Bar, your position at St. Peter's, all your prospects in life—and for what?'

'For fun, of course, mother. I don't know what I'm fit for or what I want; it's pure idiotic recklessness, isn't it?'

'It is; but don't talk to me in that ribald tone, Mark; I have enough to bear as it is. Once for all I ask you, Is it true what my brother tells me, that you have returned to the mire like the sow in the Scriptures; that you are going to let your name be connected with—with a novel, after all you have promised?'

'Quite true,' said Mark; 'I hope to be connected with many novels.'

'Mark,' said his mother, 'you know what I think about that. I implore you to pause while there's time still, before doing what you can never recall. It's not only from worldly motives that I ask it. Surely you can sacrifice a contemptible vanity to your duty towards your mother. I may be wrong in my prejudices, but still I have a right to expect you to regard them. I ask you once more to withdraw from this. Are you going to refuse me?'

Mrs. Ashburn's harsh tones carried a very genuine feeling and concern. She truly believed that the paths of fiction would lead to her son's spiritual as well as his material ruin, and Mark had sense enough to recognise the reality of this belief of hers, and drop the levity he had assumed for defensive purposes.

His father had, as usual, taken no part in the interview; he sat looking dolefully at the fire, as if anxious to remain neutral as long as possible; he had long been a mere suzerain, and, like some other suzerains, felt a very modified resentment at a rebellion against an authority that was only nominally his own.

So Mark addressed himself to his mother only. 'I'm sorry if it grieves you, mother,' he said, gently enough; 'but you really must let me go my own way in this—it is no use at all asking me to withdraw now.... I have gone too far.... Some day you will see that I was not so very foolish after all. I promise you that. Wouldn't you rather think of me as living the life I could be happy in—being famous, perhaps, even, some day—than dragging out my days in a school or slaving at a profession I can never care for? Of course you would! And a novel isn't such an awful thing, if you could only bring yourself to think so. You never will read one, you know, so you can't be a very impartial judge.'

Mrs. Ashburn read very little of any literature; what she did read being chiefly the sermons and biographies of Dissenting divines, and she had never felt any desire to stimulate her imagination by anything much more exciting, especially by accounts of things that never happened, and were consequently untruthful. Her extreme horror of fiction was a form of bigotry now almost extinct, but she had grown up in it and retained it in all the old Puritan vigour.

She showed no signs of being at all impressed by Mark's remonstrance; her eyes were severely cold, and her voice measured and loud as she replied, without looking at him.

'You won't make me change my opinion in the least, Mark, if you were to talk till daylight. If you set yourself against my wishes in this, we have quite made up our minds how to act, have we not, Matthew?'

'Yes, quite,' said Mr. Ashburn, uneasily, 'quite; but I hope, Mark, my boy, I hope you won't cross your mother in this, when you see how strongly she feels about it. I want to keep my children about me while I can; I don't wish anyone to go if it can be arranged—if it can be arranged.'

'Do you mean, mother, that if I don't do as Uncle Solomon and you wish, I am to go?' asked Mark.

'I do,' said his mother. 'I won't encourage any son of mine against my conscience and my principles. If you choose to live a life of frivolity and idleness, you shall not lead it under my roof; so you know what to expect if you persist in disobeying me—us, I mean.'

'I think I had better go,' said Mark; 'I don't quite see what enormity I have been guilty of, but if you look at things in that light, there is no more to be said. I have chosen my life, and I don't mean to go back from it. I will see about finding lodgings as soon as I can, and you shall not be troubled with me any longer than I can help.'

'Mark, don't be headstrong—don't let your passion get the better of you!' cried his mother, moved out of all her stoniness—for she had not quite expected this, believing that the amount of Mark's salary and his expenses made him practically dependent on her. She had forgotten his uncle's cheque, and did not believe in any serious profits to be gained from literature.

'I'm not in the least angry,' he said; 'I don't wish to go, if you wish me to stay, but if you meant what you said just now, I have no choice.'

His mother was much too proud to weaken her authority by retracting. She still hoped that he would yield if she remained firm, but yielding was out of the question with Mark then, and, besides, independence had its charms, though he would not have been the first to loosen the tie.

'Blame your wicked pride and selfishness, Mark, not your mother, who is only anxious for your good. Go, if you will, but don't dare to expect a blessing on your disobedience.'

'Do you say go, too, father?' said Mark.

'You hear what your mother says. What else can I say?' he answered feebly; 'it's very painful to me—all this—but you must take your own course.'

'I see I must,' said Mark, and left the room.

'You've been very hard with the boy, Jane,' said her husband, when they were alone, and she had sat for some time with a book open but unread before her; 'I really do think you've been very hard.'

'Do you want to encourage him against his mother?' she asked.

'No, no, you know I don't, Jane. Anything you think right—but I think you were hard.'

'If I was, it was for his good,' she said; 'I have done what I thought right, and we have sat up long enough. We can do no good by talking over it any more, Matthew. Perhaps Mark will think differently to-morrow.'

Trixie had been waiting for Mark in the adjoining room into which she beckoned him as he passed the door. 'How did it end?' she whispered. 'You were very quiet in there; is it settled?'

'Yes, it's settled,' he said, 'I'm to go, Trixie; I shall have to shift for myself. They won't have me here any longer!'

'Oh, Mark!' cried Trixie. 'Take me with you, do, it will be so horrid at home with only Martha and Cuthbert. You and I always got on together; let me come too!'

'I can't,' said Mark, 'not yet—by-and-by, perhaps, Trixie, when I'm a rich man, you know, we can manage it—just now I shall hardly be able to keep myself.'

'I'll work hard at my drawing and get into the Academy. I've begun features already, and I shall soon get into the antique—then we can be famous together, you know.'

'We shall see,' said Mark; 'and in the meantime, Trixie, I think we had better both go to bed.'

When he was alone again and had time to think over the day which had proved so eventful, he could not find it in him to regret what had happened. He had got rid of Uncle Solomon, he had cast off the wig and gown which were to him as the garb of slavery, and the petty restraints of his home life were gone as well; he had no sentimental feelings about his banishment, the bosom of his family had not been a very appreciative or sympathetic one, and he had always intended to go forth from it as soon as he could afford it.

If he had really committed the offence for which he was to be driven from home, he could have considered himself a most interesting martyr; he did his best to do so as it was, but not with complete success. Betraying a dead man's trust is scarcely heroic, and even Mark felt that dimly, and could not dwell on his ill-treatment as he would dearly like to have done.

But there was something exciting for him, notwithstanding, in the future; he was to go out into the world and shift for himself, and conquer; he would have a part, and it might be a difficult one, to play for a season; but after that he could resume his own character and take the place he meant to fill in the world, feeling at last that the applause he won was his by right.

Vincent Holroyd had been unselfish in life; Mark had always recognised that trait in his character, though the liking he had for the man had not been much the stronger on that account—if now Vincent could see any brief and fleeting fame which his book might gain used as the stepping-stone to his friend's advancement, surely, Mark told himself, he would scarcely grudge it.

But he hardly cared to justify to himself what he had done by any casuistry of this kind; he preferred to shut his eyes resolutely to the morality of the thing; he might have acted like the basest scoundrel, very likely he had. Still, no one did, no one need, suspect him. All he had to do was to make the best use of the advantage he had snatched; when he could feel that he had done that, then he would feel justified; meanwhile he must put up with a few natural twinges of conscience now and then, when he was not feeling well.

The next morning breakfast passed without any reference to the scene of the night before; Martha and Cuthbert both knew of what had happened, but kept silence, and if Mrs. Ashburn had any hopes that Mark would recant, she was disappointed.

That evening he informed them that he had taken rooms, and should not remain at Malakoff Terrace for more than a few days longer; his announcement being met by a grim 'Very well, Mark, just as you please,' from his mother; and though her heart sank at his words, and her last hope of prevailing died away, she never returned to the charge in any way, recognising that it was useless.

When the day for his departure came, there were no scenes; even Trixie, who felt it most, was calm, for, after all, Mark would not be so very far away, he had said she might come and see him sometimes; the other two were civil, and cold, there being that curious latent antipathy between them and him which sometimes exists between members of a family.

Mr. Ashburn had mumbled his good-byes with a touch of emotion and even shame in his manner as he shuffled away to his office. 'I don't want you to feel we've cast you off,' he had said nervously. 'Your mother says rather more than she exactly feels at times; but it's better for you to go, my boy, better for all parties concerned. Only, if you find yourself in—in any difficulties, come back to us, or—that is,' he amended, 'write, or come to me at the office, that will be better, perhaps.'

But Mrs. Ashburn's last words were, 'Good-bye, Mark. I never thought to part with a son of mine in anger; we may never meet again, but you may live to be sorry for the grief you have caused your mother, when you stand one day over her grave.'

This would have been more impressive if Mrs. Ashburn had not been so much addicted to indulging in such doleful predictions on less adequate occasions that she had discounted much of the effect that properly belonged to them; even as it was, however, they cut Mark for the moment; he half offered to embrace his mother, but she made no response, and after waiting for a while, and finding that she made no sign, he went out with a slight shrug of expostulation.

When he had left the room, she half rose as if to follow, but stopped half way irresolute, while the cab which he had engaged to take himself and his luggage to his new quarters drove off, and then she went upstairs and shut herself in her bedroom for half-an-hour, and the maid, who was 'doing the rooms' hard by, reported afterwards to the cook that she had 'heard missus takin' on awful in there, a-sobbin', and groanin', and prayin' she was, all together like, it quite upset her to 'ear it.'

There were no traces of emotion on her face, however, when she came down again, and only an additional shade of grimness in her voice and manner to tell of the half-hour's agony in which her mother's heart had warred against her pride and her principles.

CHAPTER XII

LAUNCHED

Mark had now cut himself adrift and established himself in rooms in one of the small streets about Connaught Square, where he waited for his schemes to accomplish themselves. He still retained his mastership at St. Peter's, although he hoped to be able to throw that up as soon as he could do so with any prudence, and the time that was not occupied by his school duties he devoted to the perfecting of his friend's work. It was hardly a labour of love, and he came to it with an ever-increasing weariness; all the tedious toiling through piles of proofs and revised proofs, the weeding out of ingenious perversions which seemed to possess a hydra-like power of multiplication after the first eradication, began to inspire him with an infinite loathing of this book which was his and not his own.

It had never interested him; he had never been able to feel the slightest admiration for any part of it, and at times he ceased to believe in it altogether, and think that, after all, he had transgressed to no purpose, and that his own book would have been a stronger staff to lean upon than this reed he had borrowed. But he had to go on with it now, and trust to his good-luck for the consequences; but still there were moments when he trembled at what he had done, and could not bear to be so constantly reminded of it.

There was a little story in the book which one of the subordinate characters told to a child, the distressing history of a small sugar prince on a Twelfth-cake, who believed himself to be a fairy and was taken tenderly away from a children's party by a little girl who, as the prince supposed, would restore him somehow to his proper position in Fairyland; instead of which, however, she took him home to an ordinary nursery and ate him.

Mark was doubtful of the wisdom of retaining this story in the book at all—it seemed to him out of place there—but as he had some scruples about cutting it out, he allowed it to remain, a decision which was not without after-effect upon his fortunes.

The title of the book underwent one more change, for Mr. Fladgate's mind misgave him at the last moment as to his own first suggestion, and it was finally settled that the book should be called 'Illusion,' which suited Mark quite as well as anything else.

And so in due time Mark read, with a certain curious thrill, the announcement that 'Illusion,' a romance by Cyril Ernstone, was 'now ready at all libraries;' he sent no presentation copies, not even to Trixie—he had thought of doing so, but when it came to the point he could not.

It was early one Saturday afternoon in March, Mark had walked back by a long round from the school to his lodgings through the parks, and the flower-beds were gay with the lilac, yellow and white of crocus and snowdrop, the smoke-blackened twigs were studded with tiny spikes of tender green, and the air was warm and subtly aromatic with the promise of spring—even in the muddy tainted streets the Lent-lilies and narcissus flowers in the street-sellers' baskets gave touches of passing sweetness to the breeze.

Mark felt a longing to get further away from the town and enjoy what remained of the afternoon on higher ground and in purer air; he would go up to Hampstead, he thought, and see the lights sweeping over the rusty bracken on the heath, or walk down over Highgate Hill, and past the quaint old brick houses with their high-trim laurel hedges and their last century wrought-iron gateways and lamps in which the light of other days no longer burns.

But he did not go to either place that afternoon, for when he ran up to his rooms to change his hat and coat, he saw that on his table which made him forget his purpose altogether. It was a packet inclosed in a wrapper which bore the name of his publishers on the outside, and he knew at once before opening it that it contained reviews. He tore off the wrapper eagerly, for now at last he would learn whether he had made a bold and successful stroke, or only a frightful mistake.

Beginners have taken up reviews before now, cowering in anticipation before the curse of Balaam, to receive an unexpected benediction; but perhaps no one could be quite so unprepared for this pleasant form of surprise as Mark, for others have written the works that are criticised, and though they may have worked themselves up into a surface ferment of doubt and humility, deep down in their hearts there is a wonderfully calm acceptance, after the first shock, of the most extravagant eulogy.

The opening paragraphs of the first critique were enough to relieve Mark's main anxiety; Holroyd's book was not a failure—there could be no doubt of that—it was treated with respectful consideration as the work of a man who was entitled to be taken seriously; if reviews had any influence (and it can scarcely be questioned that a favourable review has much) this one alone could not fail to bring 'Illusion' its fair share of attention.

Mark laid down the first paper with a sense of triumph. If a very ordinary book like poor Holroyd's was received in this way, what might he not expect when he produced his own!

Then he took up the next. Here the critic was more measured in his praise. The book he pronounced to be on the whole a good and very nearly a great one, a fine conception fairly worked out, but there was too strong a tendency in parts to a certain dreamy mysticism (here Mark began to regret that he had not been more careful over the proofs), while the general tone was a little too metaphysical, and the whole marred by even more serious blemishes.

'The author,' continued the reviewer, 'whose style is for the most part easy and dignified, with a praiseworthy absence of all inflation or bombast, seems at times to have been smitten by a fatal desire to "split the ears of the groundlings" and produce an impression by showy parades of a not overwhelmingly profound scholarship; and the effect of these contrasts would be grotesque in the extreme, were it not absolutely painful in a work of such high average merit. What, for instance, will be thought of the taste of a writer who could close a really pathetic scene of estrangement between the lovers by such a sentence as the following?...'

The sentence which followed was one of those which Mark had felt it due to himself to interpolate. This was but one example, said the inexorable critic, there were other instances more flagrant still—and in all of these the astonished Mark recognised his own improvements!

To say that this was for the moment an exceedingly unpleasant shock to his self-satisfaction is to state a sufficiently obvious fact; but Mark's character must have been very imperfectly indicated if it surprises anyone to hear that it did not take him long to recover from the blow.

Perhaps he had been wrong in grafting his own strong individuality on an entirely foreign trunk—he had not been careful enough to harmonise the two styles—it was merely an odd coincidence that the reviewer, struck naturally enough by the disparity, should have pitched upon him as the offender. By-and-by he grew to believe it a positive compliment that the reviewer (no doubt a dull person) had simply singled out for disapproval all the passages which were out of his depth—if there had been nothing remarkable about them, they would not have been noticed at all.

And so, as it is a remarkable peculiarity in the mind of man, that it can frequently be set at ease by some self-constructed theory which would not bear its own examination for a minute—as if a quack were to treat himself with his own bread-pills and feel better—Mark, having convinced himself that the reviewer was a crass fool whose praise and blame were to be read conversely, found the wound to his self-love begin to heal from that moment.

That same Saturday afternoon Mabel was sitting in the little room at the back of the house, in which she received her own particular friends, wrote her letters, and read; just then she was engaged in the latter occupation, for the books had come in from the library that day, and she had sat down after luncheon to skim them through before selecting any which seemed worth more careful reading.

Mabel had grown to be fastidious in the matter of fiction, the natural result of a sense of humour combined with an instinctive appreciation of style. There had been a time of course, when, released from the strict censorship of a boarding-school under which all novels on the very lengthy index expurgatorius had to be read in delicious stealth, she had devoured eagerly any literature which was in bright covers and three volumes—but that time was past now.

She could not cry over cheap pathos, or laugh at secondhand humour, or shudder at sham cynicism any longer—desperate escapes and rescues moved her not, and she had wearied of beautiful wicked fiends and effeminate golden-haired guardsmen, who hold a Titanic strength in reserve as their one practical joke, but the liberty she had enjoyed had done her no particular harm, even if many mothers might have thought it their duty to restrict it, which Mrs. Langton was too languid or had too much confidence in her daughter to think of attempting.

Mabel had only returned to the works of the great masters of this century with an appreciation heightened by contrast, and though her new delight in them did not blind her—as why should it?—to the lesser lights in whom something may be found to learn or enjoy, she now had standards by which she could form her opinions of them.

Amongst the books sent in that week was 'Illusion,' a romance by Cyril Ernstone, and Mabel had looked at its neat grey-green covers and red lettering with a little curiosity, for somebody had spoken of it to her the day before, and she took it up with the intention of reading a chapter or two before going out with her racket into the square, where the tennis season had already set in on the level corner of the lawn.

But the afternoon wore on, and she remained by the window in a low wicker chair, indifferent to the spring sunshine outside, to the attractions of lawn tennis, or the occasional sounds of callers, reading on with parted lips and an occasional little musical laugh or involuntary sigh, as Holroyd had once dreamed of seeing his book read by her.

His strong and self-contained nature had unfolded all its deepest tenderness and most cherished fancies in that his first book, and the pages had the interest of a confession. Mabel felt that personal affection for the unknown writer which to have aroused must be the crown of crowns to those who love their art.

The faults of style and errors of taste here and there which jarred upon her were still too rare or too foreign to the general tone of the book to prejudice her seriously, and she put down the book half finished, not from weariness but with an unusual desire to economise the pleasure it gave her.

'I wonder what "Cyril Ernstone" is like,' she thought, half unconsciously.

Perhaps, by the way, a popular but plain author who finds it necessary to cultivate society, would discover, if he would go about veiled or engage a better-looking man to personate him, a speedy increase in the circulation of his next work, and, if at all sensitive as to his own shortcomings, he would certainly be spared a considerable amount of pain, for it is trying for a man who rather enjoys being idolised to be compelled to act as his own iconoclast.

While Mabel was speculating on the personal appearance of the author of 'Illusion,' Dolly darted in suddenly. 'Oh, there you are, Mabel,' she said, 'how lazy of you! Mother thought you were playing tennis, and some people have called, and she and I had to do all the talking to them!'

'Come and rest then, Dolly,' said Mabel, putting an arm up and drawing her down to a low stool by her chair.

'I've got my new sash on,' said Dolly warningly.

'I'll be careful,' said Mabel, 'and I've found a little story in this book I am going to read to you, Dolly, if you care about it.'

'Not a long story, is it, Mab?' inquired Dolly rather dubiously. But she finally settled herself comfortably down to listen, with her bright little face laid against Mabel's side, while she read the melancholy fate of the sugar fairy prince.

Dolly heard it all out in silence, and with a growing trouble in her eyes. When it was all over, and the heartless mortal princess had swallowed the sugar prince, she turned half away and said softly, 'Mabel, that was me.'

Mabel laughed. 'What do you mean, Dolly?' she said.

'I thought he was plain sugar,' Dolly protested piteously; 'how was I to know? I never heard of sugar fairies before. And he did look pretty at first, but I spilt some tea over him, and the colour got all mixed up, just as the story says it did, and so I ate him.'

'It's only a story, Dolly, you know; you needn't make yourself unhappy about it—it isn't true really.'

'But it must be true, it's all put down exactly as it happened.... And it was me.... I've eaten up a real fairy prince.... Mabel, I'm a greedy pig. If I hadn't done it, perhaps we could have got him out of the sugar somehow, and then Colin and I would have had a live fairy to play with. That's what he expected me to do, and I ate him instead. I know he was a fairy, Mabel, he tasted so nice.... Poor, poor little prince!'

Dolly was so evidently distressed that Mabel tried hard to convince her that the story was about another little girl, the prince was only a sugar one, and so on; but she did not succeed, until the idea struck her that a writer whose book seemed to indicate a sympathetic nature would not object to the trouble of removing the childish fears he had aroused, and she said: 'Listen, Dolly; suppose you write a letter to Mr. Ernstone—at his publishers', you know—I'll show you how to address it, but you must write the rest yourself, and ask him to tell you if the sugar prince was really a fairy, and then you will know all about it; but my own belief is, Dolly, that there aren't any fairies—now, at any rate.'

'If there weren't,' argued Dolly, 'people wouldn't write books about them. I've seen pictures of them lots of times.'

'And they dance in rows at the pantomime, don't they, Dolly?' said Mabel.

'Oh, I know those aren't fairies—only thin little girls,' said Dolly contemptuously. 'I'm not a baby, Mabel, but I would write to Mr.—what you said just now—only I hate letter-writing so—ink is such blotty, messy stuff—and I daresay he wouldn't answer after all.'

'Try him, dear,' said Mabel.

Dolly looked obstinate and said nothing just then, and Mabel did not think it well to refer to the matter again. But the next week, from certain little affectations of tremendous mystery on Dolly's part, and the absence of the library copy of 'Illusion' from the morning-room during one whole afternoon, after which it reappeared in a state of preternatural inkiness, Mabel had a suspicion that her suggestion was not so disregarded as it had seemed.

And a few days afterwards Mark found on his breakfast table an envelope from his publisher, which proved to contain a letter directed to 'Mr. Ciril Ernstone,' at the office. The letter was written in a round childish hand, with scrapings here and there to record the fall of a vanquished blot.

'Dear Mr. Ciril Ernstone,' it ran, 'I want you to tell me how you knew that I ate that sugar prince in your story, and if you meant me really. Perhaps you made that part of it up, or else it was some other girl, but please write and tell me who it was and all about it, because I do so hate to think I've eaten up a real fairy without knowing it.—DOROTHY MARGARET LANGTON.'

This poor little letter made Mark very angry; if he had written the story he would, of course, have been amused if not pleased by the naïve testimony to his power; but, as it was, it annoyed him to a quite unreasonable extent.

He threw Dolly's note pettishly across the table; 'I wish I had cut that sugar prince story out; I can't tell the child anything about it. Langton, too—wonder if it's any relation to my Langton—sister of his, perhaps—he lives at Notting Hill somewhere. Well, I won't write; if I do I shall put my foot in it somehow.... It's quite likely that Vincent knew this child. She can't be seriously unhappy about such a piece of nonsense, and if she is, it's not my fault.'

Mark had never quite lost the memory of that morning in the fog, his brief meeting with Mabel, and the untimely parting by the hedge. Subsequent events had naturally done something to efface the impression which her charm and grace had made upon him then; but even yet he saw her face at times as clearly as ever, and suffered once more the dull pain he had felt when he first knew that she had gone from him without leaving him the faintest hope of being ever privileged to know her more intimately or even see her again.

Sometimes, when he dreamed most wildly of the brilliant future that was to come to him, he saw himself, as the author of several famous and successful works (amongst which 'Illusion' was entirely obscured), meeting her once more, and marking his sense of her past ingratitude by a studied coldness. But this was a possibility that never, even in his most sanguine moments, was other than remote.

If he had but known it, there had long been close at hand—in the shape of young Langton—a means which, judiciously managed, might have brought that part of his dream to pass immediately, and now he had that which would realise it even more surely and effectually.

But he did not know, and let the appeal lie unanswered that was due to Mabel's suggestion—'the moral of which,' as Alice's Duchess might say, is that one should never neglect a child's letter.

CHAPTER XIII

A 'THORN AND FLOWER PIECE'

'Illusion' had not been very long published before Mark began to have uncomfortable anticipations that it might be on the way to achieve an unexpected success, and he was nearer the truth in this than he himself believed as yet. It might not become popular in the wider and coarser sense of the word, being somewhat over the heads of the large class who read fiction for the 'story;' it might never find its way to railway bookstalls (though even this, as will appear, befell it in time,) or be considered a profitable subject for Transatlantic piracy; but it was already gaining recognition as a book that people of any culture should, for their own sakes, at least assume to have read and appreciated.

Mark was hailed by many judges of such things as a new and powerful thinker, who had chosen to veil his theories under the garb of romance, and if the theory was dissented from in some quarters, the power and charm of the book were universally admitted. At dinner parties, and in all circles where literature is discussed at all, 'Illusion' was becoming a standard topic; friendships were cemented and intimacies dissolved over it; it became a kind of 'shibboleth.'

At first Mark had little opportunity of realising this to the full extent, for he went out seldom if at all. There had been a time in his life—before he had left Cambridge, that is—when he had mixed more in society; his undergraduate friends had been proud to present to their family circle a man with his reputation for general brilliancy, and so his engagements in the vacations had been frequent. But this did not last; from a feeling that his own domestic surroundings would scarcely bear out a vaguely magnificent way he had of alluding to his 'place' and his 'people'—a way which was not so much deliberate imposition as a habit caught from associates richer and higher up in the social scale—from this feeling, he never offered to return any of these hospitalities, and though this was not rigorously expected of him, it did serve to prevent any one of his numerous acquaintanceships from ripening into something more. When the crash came, and it was generally discovered that the reputed brilliant man of his year was a very ordinary failure, Mark found himself speedily forgotten, and in the first soreness of disappointment was not sorry to remain in obscurity for a season.

But now a reaction in his favour was setting in; his publishers were already talking of a second edition of 'Illusion,' and he received, under his name of 'Cyril Ernstone,' countless letters of congratulation and kindly criticism, all so pleasantly and cordially worded, that each successive note made him angrier, the only one that consoled him at all being a communication in a female hand which abused the book and its writer in the most unmeasured terms. For his correspondent's estimate of the work was the one which he had a secret wish to see more prevalent (so long, of course, as it did not interfere with the success of his scheme), and he could almost have written to thank her—had she not, by some unfortunate oversight, forgotten to append her name and address.

The next stage in the career of the book was a discovery on someone's part that the name of its author was an assumed one, and although there are many who would as little think of looking for the name of the man who wrote the play they see or the book they read as they would for that of the locomotive behind which they travel, there are still circles for whom the first two matters at least possess an interest.

And so several set out to run the actual author to earth, well assured that, as is fabled of the fox, he himself would enjoy the sport as much as his pursuers; and it is the fact that Mark might have given them a much longer run had he been anxious to do so, but, though he regretted it afterwards, the fruits of popularity were too desirable to be foregone.

There were some false cries at first. A 'London correspondent' knew for a fact that the book was written by an old lady at a lunatic asylum in her lucid intervals; while a ladies' journal had heard that the author was a common carpenter and entirely self-educated; and there were other similar discoveries. But before they had time to circulate widely, it became somehow common knowledge that the author was a young schoolmaster, and that his real name was Mark Ashburn.

And Mark at once began to reap the benefit. His old friends sought him out once more; men who had passed him in the streets with a careless nod that was almost as bad as a cut direct, or without even the smallest acknowledgment that a time had been when they were inseparables, now found time to stop him and ask if the rumours of his début in literature were really true.

By-and-by cards began to line his mantelpiece as in the old days; he went out once more, and met everywhere the kindness and courtesy that the world of London, whatever may be said against it, is never chary of showing towards the most insignificant person who has once had the good fortune to arouse its interest.

Mark liked it all at first, but as he saw the book growing more and more in favour, and the honours paid to himself increasing, he began to be uneasy at his own success.

He would not have objected to the book's securing a moderate degree of attention, so as to prepare the public mind for the blaze of intellect he had in reserve for it—that he had expected, or at least hoped for—but the mischief of this ridiculous enthusiasm which everyone he met seemed to be affecting over this book of Holroyd's was that it made an anticlimax only too possible when his own should see the light.

Mark heard compliments and thanks with much the annoyance a practised raconteur must feel with the feeble listener who laughs heartily, while the point of the story he is being told is still in perspective.

And soon he wished heartily that the halo he felt was burning round his undeserving head could be moderated or put out, like a lamp—it was such an inconvenience. He could never escape from Holroyd's book; people would talk to him about it.

Sooner or later, while talking to the most charming persons, just when he was feeling himself conversationally at his very best, he would see the symptoms he dreaded warning him that the one fatal topic was about to be introduced, which seemed to have the effect of paralysing his brain. He would struggle hard against it, making frantic efforts to turn the subject, and doubling with infinite dexterity;

but generally his interlocutor was not to be put off, 'running cunning,' as it were, like a greyhound dead to sporting instincts, and fixing him at once with a 'Now, Mr. Ashburn, you really must allow me to express to you some of the pleasure and instruction I have received from your book,' and so on; and then Mark found himself forced to listen with ghastly smiles of sham gratification to the praises of his rival, as he now felt Holroyd was after all becoming, and had to discuss with the air of a creator this book which he had never cared to understand, and soon came cordially to detest.

If he had been the real author, all this would of course have been delightful to him; it was all so kind and so evidently sincere for the most part, that only a very priggish or cynical person could have affected to undervalue it, and any other, even if he felt it overstrained now and then, would have enjoyed it frankly while it lasted, remembering that, in the nature of things, it could not last very long.

But unfortunately, Mark had not written 'Illusion,' which made all the difference. No author could have shrunk more sensitively in his inmost soul than he did from the praise of his fellow-men, and his modesty would have been more generally remarked had he not been wise enough to perceive that modesty, in a man, is a virtue with a dangerous streak of the ridiculous about it.

And so he braced himself to go through with it and play out his part. It would not be for long; soon he would have his own book to be complimented upon and to explain. Meanwhile he worked hard at 'Illusion,' until he came to have a considerable surface acquaintance with it; he knew the names of all the more important characters in it now, and hardly ever mixed them up; he worked out most of the allusions, and made a careful analysis of the plot and pedigrees of some of the families. It was much harder work than reading law, and quite as distasteful; but then it had to be done if he meant to preserve appearances at all.

His fame had penetrated to St. Peter's, where his fellow-masters treated him with an unaccustomed deference, only partially veiled by mild badinage on the part of the younger men; while even the boys were vaguely aware that he had distinguished himself in the outer world, and Mark found his authority much easier to maintain.

'How's that young rascal—what's his name? Langton?—the little scamp who said he called me "Prawn," but not "Shellfish," the impident fellow! How's he getting on, hey?' said Mr. Shelford to Mark one day about this time.

Mark replied that the boy had left his form now, but that he heard he was doing well, and had begun to acquire the graceful art of verse-making. 'Verse-making? ay, ay; is he indeed? You know, Ashburn, I often think it's a good thing there are none of the old Romans alive now. They weren't a yumorous nation, taken as a whole; but I fancy some of our prize Latin verses would set the stiffest of 'em sniggering. And we laugh at "Baboo English," as they call it! But you tell Langton from me, when you see him, that if he likes to try his hand at a set of elegiacs on a poor old cat of mine that died the other day, I'll look 'em over if he brings them to me after school some day, and if they're what I consider worthy of the deceased's many virtues, I'll find some way of rewarding him. She was a black Persian and her name was "Jinks," but he'll find it Latinise well as "Jinxia," tell him. And now I think of it,' he added, 'I never congratulated you on the effort of your muse. It's not often I read these things now, but I took your book up, and—maybe I'm too candid in telling you so—but it fairly surprised me. I'd no idea you had it in you.'

Mark found it difficult to hit the right expression of countenance at such a compliment, but he did it. 'There are some very fine things in that book, sir,' continued Mr. Shelford, 'some very noble words; remarkable for so young a man as you must be. You have lived, Ashburn, it's easy to see that!'

'Oh, well,' said Mark, 'I—I've knocked about, you know.'

'Ah, and you've knocked something into you, too, which is more to the purpose. I'd like to know now when you found time to construct your theories of life and conduct.'

Mark began to find this embarrassing; he said he had hit upon them at odd times ('very odd times,' he could not help remembering), and shifted his ground a little uneasily, but he was held fast by the buttonhole. 'They're remarkably sound and striking, I must say that, and your story is interesting, too. I found myself looking at the end, sir, ha, ha! to see what became of your characters. Ah, I knew there was something I wanted to ask you. There's a heading you've got for one of your chapters, a quotation from some Latin author, which I can't place to my satisfaction; I mean that one beginning "Non terret principes."'

'Oh, that one?' repeated Mark blankly.

'Yes, it reads to me like later Latin; where did you take it from? One of the Fathers?'

'One of them, I forget which,' said Mark quickly, wishing he had cut the quotations out.

'That ægritudo, now, "ægritudo superveniens," you know—how do you understand that?'

Mark had never troubled himself to understand it at all, so he stared at his interrogator in rather a lost way.

'I mean, do you take it as of the mind or body (that's what made me fancy it must be later Latin). And then there's the correxit?'

Mark admitted that there was the 'correxit.' 'It's mind,' he said quickly. 'Oh, decidedly the mind, not body, and—er—I think that's my 'bus passing. I'll say good-bye;' and he escaped with a weary conviction that he must devote yet more study to the detested 'Illusion.'

This is only a sample of the petty vexations to which he had exposed himself. He had taken over a business which he did not understand, and naturally found the technicalities troublesome, for though, as has been seen, his own tendencies were literary, he had not soared so high as a philosophical romance, while his scholarship, more brilliant than profound, was not always equal to the 'unseen passages' from out-of-the-way authors with which Holroyd had embellished his chapters.

But a little more care made him feel easier on this score, and then there were many compensations; for one unexpected piece of good fortune, which will be recorded presently, he had mainly to thank his friend's book.

He had met an old acquaintance of his, a certain young Herbert Featherstone, who had on any previous chance encounter seemed affected by a kind of trance, during which his eyes lost all power of vision, but was now completely recovered, so much so indeed as to greet Mark with a quite unexpected warmth.

Was it true that he had written this new book? What was its name—'Delusion' or something? Fellows were saying he had; hadn't read it himself; his mother and sister had; said it was a devilish good book, too. Where was he hanging out now, and what was he doing on the 10th? Could he come to a little dance his people had that night? Very well, then, he should have a card.

Mark was slightly inclined to let the other understand that he knew the worth of this resuscitated friendliness, but he refrained. He knew of the Featherstones as wealthy people, with the reputation of giving the pleasantest entertainments in London. He had his way to make in the world, and could not afford, he thought, to neglect these opportunities. So he went to the dance and, as he happened to dance well, enjoyed himself, in spite of the fact that two of his partners had read 'Illusion,' and knew him as the author of it. They were both pretty and charming girls, but Mark did not enjoy either of those particular valses. In the course of the evening he had a brief conversation with his hostess, and was fortunate enough to produce a favourable impression. Mrs. Featherstone was literary herself, as a reputedly strong-minded lady who had once written two particularly weak-minded novels would necessarily be. She liked to have a few rising young literary men in her train, with whom she might discuss subjects loftier than ordinary society cares to grasp; but she was careful at the same time that her daughter should not share too frequently in these intellectual privileges, for Gilda Featherstone was very handsome, and literary men are as impressionable as other people.

Mark called one Saturday afternoon at the Featherstones' house in Grosvenor Place, as he had been expressly invited to do on the occasion of the dance, and found Mrs. Featherstone at home. It was not her regular day, and she received him alone, though Mark heard voices and laughter now and then from behind the hangings which concealed the end room of the long suite.

'And now let us talk about your delightful "Illusion," Mr. Ernstone,' she said graciously. 'Do you know, I felt when I read your book that some of my innermost thoughts, my highest aspirations, had been put into words—and such words—for me! It was soul speaking to soul, and you get that in so few novels, you know! What a rapture literary creation is! Don't you feel that? I am sure, even in my own poor little way—you must know that I have scribbled once upon a time—even in my own experience, I know what a state of excitement I got into over my own stories. One's characters get to be actual living companions to one; they act by themselves, and all one has to do is just to sit by and look on, and describe.'

This seemed to Mark to prove a vividness of imagination on Mrs. Featherstone's part to which her literary productions had not, so far as he knew, done full credit. But he was equal to the occasion.

'Your characters, Mrs. Featherstone, are companions to many more than their creator. I must confess that I, for one, fell hopelessly in love with your Gwendoline Vane, in "Mammon and Moonshine."' Mark had once read a slashing review of a flabby little novel with a wooden heroine of that name, and turned it to good account now, after his fashion.

'Now, how nice of you to say that,' she said, highly pleased. 'I am very fond of Gwendoline myself—my ideal, you know. I won't quote that about "praise from Sir Hubert," because it's so very trite, but I feel it. But do you really like Gwendoline better than my Magdalen Harwood, in "Strawberries and Cream."'

Here Mark got into deep water once more; but he was no mean conversational swimmer, and reached dry land without any unseemly floundering.

'It has been suggested to me, do you know,' she said when her own works had been at last disposed of, 'that your "Illusion" would make such an admirable play; the central motive really so dramatic. Of course one would have to leave the philosophy out, and all the beautiful reflections, but the story would be left. Have you ever thought of dramatising it yourself, Mr. Ashburn?'

Mark had not. 'Ah, well,' she said, 'if ever I have time again to give to literature, I shall ask your permission to let me see what I can do with it. I have written some little charades for drawing-room theatricals, you know, so I am not quite without experience.'

Mark, wondering inwardly how Holroyd would relish this proposal if he were alive, said that he was sure the story would gain by her treatment; and presently she proposed that they should go to the further room and see 'how the young people were getting on,' which Mark received with an immense relief, and followed her through the portière to the inner room, in which, as will be seen, an unexpected stroke of good fortune was to befall him.

They found the young people, with a married sister of Mrs. Featherstone, sitting round a small table on which was a heap of cartes-de-visite, as they used to be called for no very obvious reason.

Gilda Featherstone, a lively brunette, with the manner of a young lady accustomed to her own way, looked up from the table to welcome Mark. 'You've caught us all at a very frivolous game, Mr. Ashburn. I hope you won't be shocked. We've all had our feelings outraged at least once, so we're going to stop now, while we're still on speaking terms.'

'But what is it?' said Mrs. Featherstone. 'It isn't cards, Gilda dearest, is it?'

'No, mother, not quite; very nearly though. Mr. Caffyn showed it us; he calls it "photo-nap."'

'Let me explain, Mrs. Featherstone,' said Caffyn, who liked to drop in at Grosvenor Place occasionally, where he was on terms of some intimacy. 'I don't know if you're acquainted with the game of "nap"?' Mrs. Featherstone shook her head, not too amiably, for she had been growing alarmed of late by a habit her daughter had acquired of mentioning or quoting this versatile young man whom her husband persisted so blindly in encouraging. 'Ah!' said Caffyn, unabashed. 'Well, anyway, this is modelled on it. We take out a selection of photographs, the oldest preferred, shuffle them, and deal round five photographs to each player, and the ugliest card in each round takes the trick.'

'I call it a most ill-natured game,' said the aunt, who had seen an old and unrecognised portrait of herself and the likenesses of several of her husband's family (a plain one) voted the master-cards.

'Oh, so much must be said for it,' said Caffyn; 'it isn't a game to be played everywhere, of course; but it gives great scope for the emotions. Think of the pleasure of gaining a trick with the portrait of your dearest friend, and then it's such a capital way of ascertaining your own and others' precise positions in the beauty scale, and all the plain people acquire quite a new value as picture-cards.'

He had played his own very cautiously, having found his amusement in watching the various revelations of pique and vanity amongst the others, and so could speak with security.

'My brothers all took tricks,' said one young lady, who had inherited her mother's delicate beauty, while the rest of the family resembled a singularly unhandsome father—which enabled her to speak without very deep resentment.

'So did poor dear papa,' said Gilda, 'but that was the one taken in fancy dress, and he would go as Dante.'

'Nothing could stand against Gurgoyle,' observed Caffyn. 'He was a sure ace every time. He'll be glad to know he was such a success. You must tell him, Miss Featherstone.'

'Now I won't have poor Mr. Gurgoyle made fun of,' said Mrs. Featherstone, but with a considerable return of amiability. 'People always tell me that with all his plainness he's the most amusing young man in town, though I confess I never could see any signs of it myself.'

The fact was that an unlucky epigram by the Mr. Gurgoyle in question at Mrs. Featherstone's expense, which of course had found its way to her, had produced a coolness on her part, as Caffyn was perfectly well aware.

'"Ars est celare artem," as Mr. Bancroft remarks at the Haymarket,' he said lightly. 'Gurgoyle is one of those people who is always put down as witty till he has the indiscretion to try. Then they put him down some other way.'

'But why is he considered witty then, if he isn't?' asked Gilda Featherstone.

'I don't know. I suppose because we like to think Nature makes these compensations sometimes, but Gurgoyle must have put her out of temper at the very beginning. She's done nothing in that way for him.'

Mrs. Featherstone, although aware that the verdict on the absent Gurgoyle was far from being a just one, was not altogether above being pleased by it, and showed it by a manner many degrees more thawed than that she had originally prescribed to herself in dealing with this very ineligible young actor.

'Mr. Ashburn,' said Miss Featherstone, after one or two glances in the direction of Caffyn, who was absorbed in following up the advantage he had gained with her mother, 'will you come and help me to put these photos back? There are lots of Bertie's Cambridge friends here, and you can tell me who those I don't know are.'

So Mark followed her to a side table, and then came the stroke of good fortune which has been spoken of; for, as he was replacing the likenesses in the albums in the order they were given to him, he was given one at the sight of which he could not avoid a slight start. It was a vignette, very delicately and artistically executed, of a girl's head, and as he looked, hardly daring to believe in such a coincidence, he was almost certain that the pure brow, with the tendrils of soft hair curling above it, the deep clear eyes, and the mouth which for all its sweetness had the possibility of disdain in its curves, were those of no other than the girl he had met months ago, and had almost resigned himself never to meet again.

His voice trembled a little with excitement as he said 'May I ask the name of this lady?'

'That is Mabel Langton. I think she's perfectly lovely; don't you? She was to have been at our dance the other night, and then you would have seen her. But she couldn't come at the last moment.'

'I think I have met Miss Langton,' said Mark, beginning to see now all that he had gained by learning this simple surname. 'Hasn't she a little sister called Dorothy?'

'Dolly? Oh yes. Sweetly pretty child—terribly spoilt. I think she will put dear Mabel quite in the shade by the time she comes out; her features are so much more regular. Yes; I see you know our Mabel Langton. And now, do tell me, Mr. Ashburn, because of course you can read people's characters so clearly, you know, what do you think of Mabel, really and truly?'

Miss Featherstone was fond of getting her views on the characters of her friends revised and corrected for her by competent male opinion, but it was sometimes embarrassing to be appealed to in this way, while only a very unsophisticated person would permit himself to be entirely candid, either in praise or detraction.

'Well, really,' said Mark, 'you see, I have only met her once in my life.'

'Oh, but that must be quite enough for you, Mr. Ashburn! And Mabel Langton is always such a puzzle to me. I never can quite make up my mind if she is really as sweet as she seems. Sometimes I fancy I have noticed—and yet I can't be sure—I've heard people say that she's just the least bit, not exactly conceited, perhaps, but too inclined to trust her own opinion about things and snub people who won't agree with her. But she isn't, is she? I always say that is quite a wrong idea about her. Still perhaps— Oh, wouldn't you like to know Mr. Caffyn? He is very clever and amusing, you know, and has just gone on the stage, but he's not as good there as we all thought he would be. He's coming this way now.' Here Caffyn strolled leisurely towards them, and the introduction was made. 'Of course you have heard of Mr. Ashburn's great book, "Illusion"?' Gilda Featherstone said, as she mentioned Mark's name.

'Heard of nothing else lately,' said Caffyn. 'After which I am ashamed to have to own I haven't read it, but it's the disgraceful truth.'

Mark felt the danger of being betrayed by a speech like this into saying something too hideously fatuous, over the memory of which he would grow hot with shame in the night-watches, so he contented himself with an indulgent smile, perhaps, in default of some impossible combination of wit and modesty, his best available resource.

Besides, the new acquaintance made him strangely uneasy; he felt warned to avoid him by one of those odd instincts which (although we scarcely ever obey them) are surely given us for our protection; he could not meet the cold light eyes which seemed to search him through and through.

'Mr. Ashburn and I were just discussing somebody's character,' said Miss Featherstone, by way of ending an awkward pause.

'Poor somebody!' drawled Caffyn, with an easy impertinence which he had induced many girls, and Gilda amongst them, to tolerate, if not admire.

'You need not pity her,' said Gilda, indignantly; 'we were defending her.'

'Ah!' said Caffyn, 'from one another.'

'No, we were not; and if you are going to be cynical, and satirical, and all that, you can go away. Well, sit down, then, and behave yourself. What, must you go, Mr. Ashburn? Good-bye, then. Mr. Caffyn, I want you to tell me what you really think about—'

Mark heard no more than this; he was glad to escape, to get away from Caffyn's scrutiny. 'He looked as if he knew I was a humbug!' he thought afterwards; and also to think at his leisure over this new discovery, and all it meant for him.

He knew her name now; he saw a prospect of meeting her at some time or other in the house he had just left; but perhaps he might not even have to wait for that.

This little girl, whose childish letter he had tossed aside a few days since in his blindness, who else could she be but the owner of the dog after which he had clambered up the railway slope? And he had actually been about to neglect her appeal!

Well, he would write now. Who could say what might not come of it? At all events, she would read his letter.

That letter gave Mark an infinite deal of trouble. After attentively reading the little story to which it referred, he sat down to write, and tore up sheet after sheet in disgust, for he had never given much study to the childish understanding, with its unexpected deeps and shallows, and found the task of writing down to it go much against the grain. But the desire of satisfying a more fastidious critic than Dolly gave him at last a kind of inspiration, and the letter he did send, with some misgiving, could hardly have been better written for the particular purpose.

He was pleasantly reassured as to this a day or two later by another little note from Dolly, asking him to come to tea at Kensington Park Gardens on any afternoon except Monday or Thursday, and adding (evidently by external suggestion) that her mother and sister would be pleased to make his acquaintance.

Mark read this with a thrill of eager joy. What he had longed for had come to pass, then; he was to see her, speak with her, once more. At least he was indebted to 'Illusion' for this result, which a few months since seemed of all things the most unlikely. This time, perhaps, she would not leave him without a word or sign, as when last they met; he might be allowed to come again; even in time to know her intimately.

And he welcomed this piece of good fortune as a happy omen for the future.

CHAPTER XIV

IN THE SPRING

Mark lost no time in obeying Dolly's summons, and it was with an exhilaration a little tempered by a nervousness to which he was not usually subject that he leaped into the dipping and lurching hansom that was to carry him to Kensington Park Gardens.

As Mark drove through the Park across the Serpentine, and saw the black branches of the trees looking as if they had all been sprinkled with a feathery green powder, and noticed the new delicacy in the bright-hued grass, he hailed these signs as fresh confirmation of the approach of summer—a summer that might prove a golden one for him.

But as he drew nearer Notting Hill, his spirits sank again. What if this opportunity were to collapse as hopelessly as the first? Mabel would of course have forgotten him—would she let him drop indifferently as before? He felt far from hopeful as he rang the bell.

He asked for Miss Dorothy Langton, giving his name as 'Mr. Ernstone,' and was shown into a little room filled with the pretty contrivances which the modern young lady collects around her. He found Dolly there alone, in a very stately and self-possessed mood.

'You can bring up tea here, Champion,' she said, 'and some tea-cake—you like tea-cake of course,' she said to Mark, with something of afterthought. 'Mother and Mabel are out, calling or something,' she added, 'so we shall be quite alone. And now sit down there in that chair and tell me everything you know about fairies.'

Mark's heart sank—this was not at all what he had hoped for; but Dolly had thrown herself back in her own chair, with such evident expectation, and a persuasion that she had got hold of an authority on fairy-lore, that he did not dare to expostulate—although in truth his acquaintance with the subject was decidedly limited.

'You can begin now,' said Dolly calmly, as Mark stared blankly into his hat.

'Well,' he said, 'what do you want to know about them?'

'All about them,' said Dolly, with the air of a little person accustomed to instant obedience; Mark's letter had not quite dispelled her doubts, and she wanted to be quite certain that such cases as that of the sugar prince were by no means common.

'Well,' said Mark again, clearing his throat, 'they dance round in rings, you know, and live inside flowers, and play tricks with people—that is,' he added, with a sort of idea that he must not encourage superstition, 'they did once—of course there are no such things now.'

'Then how was it that that little girl you knew—who was not me—ate one up?'

'He was the last one,' said Mark.

'But how did he get turned into sugar? Had he done anything wrong?'

'That's how it was.'

'What was it—he hadn't told a story, had he?'

'It's exactly what he had done,' said Mark, accepting this solution gratefully; 'an awful story!'

'What was the story?' Dolly demanded at this, and Mark floundered on, beginning to consider Dolly, for all her pretty looks and ways, a decided little nuisance.

'He—he said the Queen of the Fairies squinted,' he stammered in his extremity.

'Then it was she who turned him into sugar?'

'Of course it was,' said Mark.

'But you said he was the last fairy left!' persisted the terrible Dolly.

'Did I?' said Mark miserably; 'I mean the last but one—she was the other.'

'Then who was there to tell the story to?' Dolly cross-examined, and Mark quailed, feeling that any more explanation would probably land him in worse difficulties.

'I don't think you know very much about it, after all,' she said with severity. 'I suppose you put all you knew into the story. But you're quite sure there was no fairy inside the figure I ate, aren't you?'

'Oh yes,' said Mark, 'I—I happen to know that.'

'That's all right, then,' said Dolly, with a little sigh of relief. 'Was that the only fairy story you know?'

'Yes,' Mark hastened to explain, in deadly fear lest he might be called upon for another.

'Oh,' said Dolly, 'then we'd better have tea'—for the door had opened.

'It's not Champion after all,' she cried; 'it's Mabel. I never heard you come back, Mabel.'

And Mark turned to realise his dearest hopes and find himself face to face once more with Mabel.

She came in, looking even lovelier, he thought, in her fresh spring toilette than in the winter furs she had worn when he had seen her last, bent down to kiss Dolly, and then glanced at him with the light of recognition coming into her grey eyes.

'This is Mr. Ernstone, Mab,' said Dolly.

The pink in Mabel's cheeks deepened slightly; the author of the book which had stirred her so unusually was the young man who had not thought it worth his while to see any more of them. Probably had he known who had written to him, he would not have been there now, and this gave a certain distance to her manner as she spoke.

'We have met before, Mr. Ernstone,' she said, giving him her ungloved hand. 'Very likely you have forgotten when and how, but I am sure Dolly had not, had you, Dolly?'

But Dolly had, having been too much engrossed with her dog on the day of the breakdown to notice appearances, even of his preserver, very particularly. 'When did I see him before, Mabel?' she whispered.

'Oh, Dolly, ungrateful child! don't you remember who brought Frisk out of the train for you that day in the fog?' But Dolly hung her head and drooped her long lashes, twining her fingers with one of those sudden attacks of awkwardness that sometimes seize the most self-possessed children. 'You never thanked him then, you know,' continued Mabel; 'aren't you going to say a word to him now?'

'Thank you very much for saving my dog,' murmured Dolly, very quickly and without looking at him; when Mabel, seeing that she was not at her ease, suggested that she should run and fetch Frisk to return thanks in person, which Dolly accepted gladly as permission to escape.

Mark had risen, of course, at Mabel's entrance, and was standing at one corner of the curtained mantelpiece; Mabel was at the other, absently smoothing the fringe with delicate curves of her hand and with her eyes bent on the rug at her feet. Both were silent for a few moments. Mark had felt the coldness in her manner. 'She remembers how shabbily she treated me,' he thought, 'and she's too proud to show it.'

'You must forgive Dolly,' said Mabel at last, thinking that if Mark meant to be stiff and disagreeable, there was no need at least for the interview to be made ridiculous. 'Children have short memories—for faces only, I hope, not kindnesses. But if you had cared to be thanked we should have seen you before.'

'Rather cool that,' Mark thought. 'I am only surprised,' he said, 'that you should remember it; you gave me more thanks than I deserved at the time. Still, as I had no opportunity of learning your name or where you lived—if you recollect we parted very suddenly, and you gave me no permission—'

'But I sent a line to you by the guard,' she said; 'I gave you our address and asked you to call and see my mother, and let Dolly thank you properly.'

She was not proud and ungracious after all, then. He felt a great joy at the thought, and shame, too, for having so misjudged her. 'If I had ever received it,' he said, 'I hope you will believe that you would have seen me before this; but I asked for news of you from that burly old impostor of a guard, and he—he gave me no intelligible message' (Mark remembered suddenly the official's extempore effort), 'and certainly nothing in writing.'

Mark's words were evidently sincere, and as she heard them, the coldness and constraint died out of Mabel's face, the slight misunderstanding between them was over.

'After all, you are here, in spite of guards,' she said, with a gay little laugh. 'And now we have even more to be grateful to you for.' And then, simply and frankly, she told him of the pleasure 'Illusion' had given her, while, at her gracious words, Mark felt almost for the first time the full meanness of his fraud, and wished, as he had certainly never wished before, that he had indeed written the book.

But this only made him shrink from the subject; he acknowledged what she said in a few formal words, and attempted to turn the conversation, more abruptly than he had done for some time on such occasions. Mabel was of opinion, and with perfect justice, that even genius itself would scarcely be warranted in treating her approval in this summary fashion, and felt slightly inclined to resent it, even while excusing it to herself as the unintentional gaucherie of an over-modest man.

'I ought to have remembered perhaps,' she said, with a touch of pique in her voice, 'that you must long ago have tired of hearing such things.'

He had indeed, but he saw that his brusqueness had annoyed her, and hastened to explain. 'You must not think that is so,' he said, very earnestly; 'only, there is praise one cannot trust oneself to listen to long—'

'And it really makes you uncomfortable to be talked to about "Illusion"?' said Mabel.

'I will be quite frank, Miss Langton,' said Mark (and he really felt that he must for his own peace of mind convince her of this); 'really it does. Because, you see, I feel all the time—I hope, that is—that I can do much better work in the future.'

'And we have all been admiring in the wrong place? I see,' said Mabel, with apparent innocence, but a rather dangerous gleam in her eyes.

'Oh, I know it sounds conceited,' said Mark, 'but the real truth is, that when I hear such kind things said about a work which—which gave me so very little trouble to produce, it makes me a little uncomfortable sometimes, because (you know how perversely things happen sometimes), because I can't help a sort of fear that my next book, to which I really am giving serious labour, may be utterly unnoticed, or—or worse!'

There was no possibility of mistaking this for mock-modesty, and though Mabel thought such sensitiveness rather overstrained, she liked him for it notwithstanding.

'I think you need not fear that,' she said; 'but you shall not be made uncomfortable any more. And you are writing another book? May I ask you about that, or is that another indiscretion?'

Mark was only too delighted to be able to talk about a book which he really had written; it was at least a change; and he plunged into the subject with much zest. 'It deals with things and men,' he concluded, 'on rather a larger scale than "Illusion" has done. I have tried to keep it clear of all commonplace characters.'

'But then it will not be quite so lifelike, will it?' suggested Mabel; 'and in "Illusion" you made even commonplace characters interesting.'

'That is very well,' he said, a little impatiently, 'for a book which does not aim at the first rank. It is easy enough to register exactly what happens around one. Anybody who keeps a diary can do that. The highest fiction should idealise.'

'I'm afraid I prefer the other fiction, then,' said Mabel. 'I like to sympathise with the characters, and you can't sympathise with an ideal hero and heroine. I hope you will let your heroine have one or two little weaknesses, Mr. Ernstone.'

'Now you are laughing at me,' said Mark, more humbly. 'I must leave you to judge between the two books, and if I can only win your approval, Miss Langton, I shall prize it more than I dare to say.'

'If it is at all like "Illusion—" Oh, I forgot,' Mabel broke off suddenly. 'That is forbidden ground, isn't it? And now, will you come into the drawing-room and be introduced to my mother? We shall find some tea there.'

Mrs. Langton was a little sleepy after a long afternoon of card-leaving and call-paying, but she was sufficiently awake to be gracious when she had quite understood who Mark was.

'So very kind of you to write to my little daughter about such nonsense,' she said. 'Of course I don't mean that the story itself was anything of the kind, but little girls have such silly fancies—at least mine seem to have. You, were just the same at Dolly's age, Mabel.... Now I never recollect worrying myself about such ideas.... I'm sure I don't know how they get it. But I hear it is such a wonderful book you have written, Mr. Ernstone. I've not read it yet. My wretched health, you know. But really, when I think how clever you must be, I feel quite afraid to talk to you. I always consider it must require so much cleverness and—and perseverance—you know, to write any book.'

'Oh, Mabel, only think,' cried Dolly, now quite herself again, from one of the window-seats, 'Frisk has run away again, and been out ever since yesterday morning. I forgot that just now. So Mr. Ernstone can't see him after all!'

And Mabel explained to her mother that they had recognised in the author of 'Illusion' the unknown rescuer of Dolly's dog.

'You mustn't risk such a valuable life as yours is now any more,' said Mrs. Langton, after purring out thanks which were hazily expressed, owing to an imperfect recollection of the circumstances. 'You must be more selfish after this, for other people's sakes.'

'I'm afraid such consideration would not be quite understood,' said Mark, laughing.

'Oh, you must expect to be misunderstood, else there would be no merit in it, would there?' said Mrs. Langton, not too lucidly. 'Dolly, my pet, there's something scratching outside the door. Run and see what it is.'

Mark rose and opened the door, and presently a ridiculous little draggled object, as black as a cinder, its long hair caked and clotted with dried mud, shuffled into the room with the evident intention of sneaking into a warm corner without attracting public notice—an intention promptly foiled by the indignant Dolly.

'O-oh!' she cried; 'it's Frisk. Look at him, everybody—do look at him.'

The unhappy animal backed into the corner by the door with his eyes on Dolly's, and made a conscience-stricken attempt to sit up and wave one paw in deprecation, doubtless prepared with a plausible explanation of his singular appearance, which much resembled that of 'Mr. Dolls' returning to Jenny Wren after a long course of 'three-penn'orths.'

'Aren't you ashamed of yourself?' demanded Dolly. '(Don't laugh, Mr. Ernstone, please—it encourages him so.) Oh, I believe you're the very worst dog in Notting Hill.'

The possessor of that bad eminence sat and shivered, as if engaged in a rough calculation of his chances of a whipping; but Dolly governed him on these occasions chiefly by the moral sanction—an immunity he owed to his condition.

'And this,' said Dolly, scathingly, 'this is the dog you saved from the train, Mr. Ernstone! There's gratitude! The next time he shall be left to be killed—he's not worth saving!'

Either the announcement or the suspense, according as one's estimate of his intellectual powers may vary, made the culprit snuffle dolefully, and after Dolly had made a few further uncomplimentary observations on the general vileness of his conduct and the extreme uncleanliness of his person, which he heard abjectly, he was dismissed with his tail well under him, probably to meditate that if he did not wish to rejoin his race altogether, he really would have to pull up.

Soon after this sounds were heard in the hall, as of a hat being pitched into a corner, and a bag with some heavy objects in it slammed on a table to a whistling accompaniment. 'That's Colin,' said Dolly, confidentially. 'Mother says he ought to be getting more repose of manner, but he hasn't begun yet.'

And soon after Colin himself made his appearance. 'Hullo, Mabel! Hullo, mother! Yes, I've washed my hands and I've brushed my hair. It's all right, really. Well, Dolly. What, Mr. Ashburn here!' he broke off, staring a little as he went up to shake hands with Mark.

'I ought to have explained, perhaps,' said Mark. 'Ernstone is only the name I write under. And I had the pleasure of having your son in my form at St. Peter's for some time. Hadn't I, Colin?'

'Yes, sir,' said Colin, shyly, still rather overcome by so unexpected an apparition, and thinking this would be something to tell 'the fellows' next day.

Mabel laughed merrily. 'Mr. Ashburn, I wonder how many more people you will turn out to be!' she said. 'If you knew how afraid I was of you when I used to help Colin with his Latin exercises, and how angry when you found me out in any mistakes! I pictured you as a very awful personage indeed.'

'So I am,' said Mark, 'officially. I'm sure your brother will agree to that.'

'I don't think he will,' said Mabel. 'He was so sorry when they moved him out of your form, that you can't have been so very bad.'

'I liked being in the Middle Third, sir,' said Colin, regaining confidence. 'It was much better fun than old—I mean Mr. Blatherwick's is. I wish I was back again—for some things,' he qualified conscientiously.

When the time came to take his leave, Mrs. Langton asked for his address, with a view to an invitation at no distant time. A young man, already a sort of celebrity, and quite presentable on other accounts, would be useful at dances, while he might serve to leaven some of her husband's slightly heavy professional dinners.

Mabel gave him her hand at parting with an air of entire friendliness and good understanding which she did not usually display on so short a probation. But she liked this Mr. Ashburn already, who on the last time she had met him had figured as a kind of hero, who was the 'swell' master for whom, without having seen him, she had caught something of Colin's boyish admiration, and who, lastly, had stirred and roused her imagination through the work of his own.

Perhaps, after all, he was a little conceited, but then it was not an offensive conceit, but one born of a confidence in himself which was fairly justified. She had not liked his manner of disparaging his first work, and she rather distrusted his idealising theories; still, she knew that clever people often find it difficult to do justice to their ideas in words. He might produce a work which would take rank with the very greatest, and till then she could admire what he had already accomplished.

And besides he was good-looking—very good-looking; his dark eyes had expressed a very evident satisfaction at being there and talking to her—which of course was in his favour; his manner was bright and pleasant: and so Mabel found it agreeable to listen to her mother's praise of their departed visitor.

'A very charming young man, my dear. You've only to look at him to see he's a true genius; and so unaffected and pleasant with it all. Quite an acquisition, really.'

'I found him, mother,' interrupted Dolly; 'he wouldn't have come but for me. But I'm rather disappointed in him myself; he didn't seem to care to talk to me much; and I don't believe he knows much about fairies.'

'Don't be ungrateful, Dolly,' said Mabel. 'Who saved Frisk for you?'

'Oh, he did; I know all that; but not because he liked Frisk, or me either. It was because—I don't know why it was because.'

'Because he is a good young man, I suppose,' said Mrs. Langton instructively.

'No, it wasn't that; he doesn't look so very good; not so good as poor Vincent did; more good than Harold, though. But he doesn't care about dogs, and he doesn't care about me, and I don't care about him!' concluded Dolly, rather defiantly.

As for Mark, he left the house thoroughly and helplessly in love. As he walked back to his rooms he found a dreamy pleasure in recalling the different stages of the interview. Mabel's slender figure as she stood opposite him by the mantelpiece, her reserve at first, and the manner in which it had thawed to a frank and gracious interest; the suspicion of a critical but not unkindly mockery in her eyes and tone at times—it all came back to him with a vividness that rendered him deaf and blind to his actual surroundings. He saw again the group in the dim, violet-scented drawing-room, the handsome languid woman murmuring her pleasant commonplaces, and the pretty child lecturing the prodigal dog, and still felt the warm light touch of Mabel's hand as it had lain in his for an instant at parting.

This time, too, the parting was not without hope; he might look forward to seeing her again after this. A summer of golden dreams and fancies had indeed begun for him from that day, and as he thought again that he owed these high privileges to 'Illusion,' events seemed more than ever to be justifying an act which was fast becoming as remote and unreproachful as acts will, when the dread of discovery—that great awakener of conscience—is sleeping too.

CHAPTER XV

Harold Caffyn had not found much improvement in his professional prospects since we first made his acquaintance; his disenchantment was in fact becoming complete. He had taken to the stage at first in reliance on the extravagant eulogies of friends, forgetting that the standard for amateurs in any form of art is not a high one, and he was very soon brought to his proper level. A good appearance and complete self-possession were about his sole qualifications, unless we add the voice and manner of a man in good society, which are not by any means the distinctive advantages that they were a few years ago. The general verdict of his fellow-professionals was, 'Clever enough, but no actor,' and he was without the sympathy or imagination to identify himself completely with any character and feelings opposed to his own; he had obtained one distinct success, and one only—at a matinée, when a new comedy was presented in which a part of some consequence had been entrusted to him. He was cast for a cool and cynical adventurer, with a considerable dash of the villain in him, and played it admirably, winning very favourable notices from the press, although the comedy itself resulted as is not infrequent with matinées, in a dismal fiasco. However, the matinée proved for a time of immense service to him in the profession, and even led to his being chosen by his manager to represent the hero of the next production at his own theatre—a poetical drama which had excited great interest before its appearance—and if Caffyn could only have made his mark in it, his position would have been assured from that moment. But the part was one of rather strained sentiment, and he could not, rather than would not, make it effective. In spite of himself, his manner suggested rather than concealed any extravagances in the dialogue, and, worse still, gave the impression that he was himself contemptuously conscious of them; the consequence being that he repelled the sympathies of his audience to a degree that very nearly proved fatal to the play. After that unlucky first night the part was taken from him, and his engagement, which terminated shortly afterwards, was not renewed.

Caffyn was not the man to overcome his deficiencies by hard and patient toil; he had counted upon an easy life with immediate triumphs, and the reality baffled and disheartened him. He might soon have slid into the lounging life of a man about town, with a moderate income, expensive tastes, and no occupation, and from that perhaps even to shady and questionable walks of life. But he had an object still in keeping his head above the social waters, and the object was Mabel Langton.

He had long felt that there was a secret antagonism on her side towards himself, which at first he had found amusement in provoking to an occasional outburst, but was soon piqued into trying to overcome and disarm, and the unexpected difficulty of this had produced in him a state of mind as nearly approaching love as he was capable of.

He longed for the time when his wounded pride would be salved by the consciousness that he had at last obtained the mastery of this wayward nature, when he would be able to pay off the long score of slights and disdains which he had come to exaggerate morbidly; he was resolved to conquer her sooner or later in defiance of all obstacles, and he had found few natures capable of resisting him long after he had set himself seriously to subdue them.

But Mabel had been long in showing any sign of yielding. For some time after the loss of the 'Mangalore' she had been depressed and silent to a degree which persuaded Caffyn that his old jealousy of Holroyd was well-grounded, and when she recovered her spirits somewhat, while she was willing to listen and laugh or talk to him, there was always the suggestion of an armistice in her manner, and any attempt on his part to lead the conversation to something beyond mere badinage was sure to be adroitly parried or severely put down, as her mood varied.

Quite recently, however, there had been a slight change for the better; she had seemed more pleased to see him, and had shown more sympathy and interest in his doings. This was since his one success at the matinée, and he told himself triumphantly that she had at last recognised his power; that the long siege was nearly over.

He would have been much less complacent had he known the truth, which was this. At the matinée Mabel had certainly been at first surprised almost to admiration by an unexpected display of force on Caffyn's part. But as the piece went on, she could not resist an impression that this was not acting, but rather an unconscious revelation of his secret self; the footlights seemed to be bringing out the hidden character of the man as though it had been written on him in sympathetic ink.

As she leaned back in the corner of the box he had sent them, she began to remember little traits of boyish malice and cruelty. Had they worked out of his nature, as such strains sometimes will, or was this stage adventurer, cold-blooded, unscrupulous, with a vein of diabolical humour in his malevolence, the real Harold Caffyn?

And then she had seen the injustice of this and felt almost ashamed of her thoughts, and with the wish to make some sort of reparation, and perhaps the consciousness that she had not given him many opportunities of showing her his better side, her manner towards him had softened appreciably.

Caffyn only saw the effects, and argued favourably from them. 'Now that fellow Holroyd is happily out of the way,' he thought, 'she doesn't care for anybody in particular. I've only to wait.'

There were considerations other than love or pride which made the marriage a desirable one to him. Mabel's father was a rich man, and Mabel herself was entitled independently to a considerable sum on coming of age. He could hardly do better for himself than by making such a match, even from the pecuniary point of view.

And so he looked about him anxiously for some opening more suitable to his talent than the stage-door, for he was quite aware that at present Mabel's father, whatever Mabel herself might think, would scarcely consider him a desirable parti.

Caffyn had been lucky enough to impress a business friend of his with a firm conviction of his talents for business and management, and this had led to a proposal that he should leave the stage and join him, with a prospect of a partnership should the alliance prove a success.

The business was a flourishing one, and the friend a young man who had but recently succeeded to the complete control of it, while Caffyn had succeeded somehow in acquiring a tolerably complete control of him. So the prospect was really an attractive one, and he felt that now at last he might consider the worst obstacles to his success with Mabel were disposed of.

He had plenty of leisure time on his hands at present, and thought he would call at Kensington Park Gardens one afternoon, and try the effect of telling Mabel of his prospects. She had been so cordial and sympathetic of late that it would be strange if she did not express some sort of pleasure, and it would be for him to decide then whether or not his time had come to speak of his hopes.

Mrs. and Miss Langton were out, he was told at the door. 'Miss Dolly was in,' added Champion, to whom Caffyn was well known.

'Then I'll see Miss Dolly,' said Caffyn, thinking that he might be able to pass the time until Mabel's return. 'In the morning-room is she? All right.'

He walked in alone, to find Dolly engaged in tearing off the postage stamp from a letter. 'Hallo, Miss Juggins, what mischief are you up to now?' he began, as he stood in the doorway.

'It's not mischief at all,' said Dolly, hardly deigning to look up from her occupation. 'What have you come in for, Harold?'

'For the pleasure of your conversation,' said Caffyn. 'You know you always enjoy a talk with me, Dolly.' (Dolly made a little mouth at this.) 'But what are you doing with those scissors and that envelope, if I'm not indiscreet in asking?'

Dolly was in a subdued and repentant mood just then, for she had been so unlucky as to offend Colin the day before, and he had not yet forgiven her. It had happened in this way. It had been a half-holiday, and Colin had brought home an especial friend of his to spend the afternoon, to be shown his treasures and, in particular, to give his opinion as an expert on the merits of Colin's collection of foreign postage-stamps.

Unhappily for Colin's purpose, however, Dolly had completely enslaved the friend from the outset. Charmed by his sudden interest in the most unboyish topics, she had carried him off to see her doll's house, and, in spite of Colin's grumbling dissuasion, the base friend had gone meekly. Worse still, he had remained up there listening to Dolly's personal anecdotes and reminiscences and seeing Frisk put through his performances, until it was too late to do anything like justice to the stamp album, over which Colin had been sulkily fuming below, divided between hospitality and impatience.

Dolly had been perfectly guiltless of the least touch of coquetry in thus monopolising the visitor, for she was not precocious in this respect, and was merely delighted to find a boy who, unlike Colin, would condescend to sympathise with her pursuits; but perhaps the boy himself, a susceptible youth, found Dolly's animated face and eager confidences more attractive than the rarest postal issues.

When he had gone, Colin's pent-up indignation burst out on the unsuspecting Dolly. She had done it on purpose. She knew Dickinson major came to see his stamps. What did he care about her rubbishy dolls? And there she had kept him up in the nursery for hours wasting his time! It was too bad of her, and so on, until she wept with grief and penitence.

And now she was seizing the opportunity of purchasing his forgiveness by an act of atonement in kind, in securing what seemed to her to be probably a stamp of some unknown value—to a boy. But she did not tell all this to Caffyn.

'Do you know about stamps—is this a rare one?' she said, and brought the stamp she had removed to Caffyn. The postmark had obliterated the name upon it.

'Let's look at the letter,' said Caffyn; and Dolly put it in his hand.

He took it to the window, and gave a slight start. 'When did this come?' he said sharply.

'Just now,' said Dolly; 'a minute or two before you came. I heard the postman, and I ran out into the hall to see the letters drop in the box, and then I saw this one with the stamp, and the box wasn't locked, so I took it out and tore the stamp off. Why do you look like that, Harold? It's only for Mabel, and she won't mind.'

Caffyn was still at the window; he had just received a highly unpleasant shock, and was trying to get over it and adjust himself to the facts revealed by what he held in his hand.

The letter was from India, bore a Colombo postmark, and was in Vincent Holroyd's hand, which Caffyn happened to know; if further proof were required he had it by pressing the thin paper of the envelope against the inclosure beneath, when several words became distinctly legible, besides those visible already through the gap left by the stamp. Thus he read, 'Shall not write again till you—' and lower down Holroyd's full signature.

And the letter had that moment arrived. He saw no other possible conclusion than that, by some extraordinary chance, Holroyd had escaped the fate which was supposed to have befallen him. He was alive; a more dangerous rival after this than ever. This letter might even contain a proposal!

'No use speaking to Mabel after she has once seen this. Confound the fellow! Why the deuce couldn't he stay in the sea? It's just my infernal luck!'

As he thought of the change this letter would work in his prospects, and his own complete powerlessness to prevent it, the gloom and perplexity on his face deepened. He had been congratulating himself on the removal of this particular man as a providential arrangement made with some regard to his own convenience. And to see him resuscitated, at that time of all others, was hard indeed to bear. And yet what could he do?

As Caffyn stood by the window with Holroyd's letter in his hand, he felt an insane temptation for a moment to destroy or retain it. Time was everything just then, and even without the fragment he had been able to read, he could, from his knowledge of the writer, conclude with tolerable certainty that he would not write again without having received an answer to his first letter. 'If I was only alone with it!' he thought impatiently. But he was a prudent young man, and perfectly aware of the consequences of purloining correspondence; and besides, there was Dolly to be reckoned with—she alone had seen the thing as yet. But then she had seen it, and was not more likely to hold her tongue about that than any other given subject. No, he could do nothing; he must let things take their own course and be hanged to them!

His gloomy face filled Dolly with a sudden fear; she forgot her dislike, and came timidly up to him and touched his arm. 'What's the matter, Harold?' she faltered. 'Mabel won't be angry. I—I haven't done anything wrong, have I, Harold?'

He came out of his reverie to see her upturned face raised to his—and started; his active brain had in that instant decided on a desperate expedient, suggested by the sight of the trouble in her eyes. 'By Jove, I'll try!' he thought; 'it's worth it—she's such a child—I may manage it yet!'

'Wrong!' he said impressively, 'it's worse than that. My poor Dolly, didn't you really know what you were doing?'

'N—no,' said Dolly; 'Harold, don't tease me—don't tell me what isn't true ... it—it frightens me so!'

'My dear child, what can I tell you? Surely you know that what you did was stealing?'

'Stealing!' echoed Dolly, with great surprised eyes. 'Oh, no, Harold—not stealing. Why, of course I shall tell Mabel, and ask her for the stamp afterwards—only if I hadn't torn it off first, she might throw it away before I could ask, you know!'

'I'm afraid it was stealing all the same,' said Caffyn, affecting a sorrowfully compassionate tone; 'nothing can alter that now, Dolly.'

'Mabel won't be angry with me for that, I know,' said Dolly; 'she will see how it was really.'

'If it was only Mabel,' said Caffyn, 'we should have no reason to fear; but Mabel can't do anything for you, poor Dolly! It's the law that punishes these things. You know what law is?—the police, and the judges.'

The piteous change in the child's face, the dark eyes brimming with rising tears, and the little mouth drawn and trembling, might have touched some men; indeed, even Caffyn felt a languid compunction for what he was doing. But his only chance lay in working upon her fears; he could not afford to be sentimental just then, and so he went on, carefully calculating each word.

'Oh, I won't believe it,' cried Dolly, with a last despairing effort to resist the effect his grave pity was producing; 'I can't. Harold, you're trying to frighten me. I'm not frightened a bit. Say you are only in fun!'

But Caffyn turned away in well-feigned distress. 'Do I look as if it was fun, Dolly?' he asked, with an effective quiver in his low voice; he had never acted so well as this before. 'Is that this morning's paper over there?' he asked, with a sudden recollection, as he saw the sheet on a little round wicker table. 'Fetch it, Dolly, will you?'

'I must manage the obstinate little witch somehow,' he thought impatiently, and turned to the police reports, where he remembered that morning to have read the case of an unhappy postman who had stolen stamps from the letters entrusted to him.

He found it now and read it aloud to her. 'If you don't believe me,' he added, 'look for yourself—you can read. Do you see now—those stamps were marked. Well, isn't this one marked?'

'Oh, it is!' cried Dolly, 'marked all over! Yes, I do believe you now, Harold. But what shall I do? I know—I'll tell papa—he won't let me go to prison!'

'Why, papa's a lawyer—you know that,' said Caffyn; 'he has to help the law—not hinder it. Whatever you do, I shouldn't advise you to tell him, or he would be obliged to do his duty. You don't want to be shut up for years all alone in a dark prison, do you, Dolly? And yet, if what you've done is once found out, nothing can help you—not your father, not your mamma—not Mabel herself—the law's too strong for them all!'

This strange and horrible idea of an unknown power into whose clutches she had suddenly fallen, and from which even love and home were unable to shield her, drove the poor child almost frantic; she clung to him convulsively, with her face white as death, terrified beyond tears. 'Harold!' she cried, seizing his hand in both hers, 'you won't let them! I—I can't go to prison, and leave them all. I don't like the dark. I couldn't stay in it till I was grown up, and never see Mabel or Colin or anybody. Tell me what to do—only tell me, and I'll do it!'

Again some quite advanced scoundrels might have hesitated to cast so fearful a shadow over a child's bright life, and the necessity annoyed Caffyn to some extent, but his game was nearly won—there would not be much more of it.

'I mustn't do anything for you,' he said; 'if I did my duty, I should have to give you up to— No, it's all right, Dolly, I should never dream of doing that. But I can do no more. Still, if you choose, you can help yourself—and I promise to say nothing about it.'

'How do you mean?' said Dolly; 'if—if I stuck it together and left it?'

'Do you think that wouldn't be seen? It would, though! No, Dolly, if anyone but you and I catches sight of that letter, it will all be found out—must be!'

'Do you mean?—oh, no, Harold, I couldn't burn it!'

There was a fire in the grate, for the morning, in spite of the season, had been chilly.

'Don't suppose I advise you to burn it,' said Caffyn. 'It's a bad business from beginning to end—it's wrong (at least it isn't right) to burn the letter. Only—there's no other way, if you want to keep out of prison. And if you make up your mind to burn it, Dolly, why you can rely on me to keep the secret. I don't want to see a poor little girl shut up in prison if I can help it, I can tell you. But do as you like about it, Dolly; I mustn't interfere.'

Dolly could bear it no more; she snatched the flimsy foreign paper, tore it across and flung it into the heart of the fire. Then, as the flames began to play round the edges, she repented, and made a wild dart forward to recover the letter. 'It's Mabel's,' she cried; 'I'm afraid to burn it—I'm afraid!'

But Caffyn caught her, and held her little trembling hands fast in his cool grasp, while the letter that Holroyd had written in Ceylon with such wild secret hopes flared away to a speckled grey rag, and floated lightly up the chimney. 'Too late now, Dolly!' he said, with a ring of triumph in his voice. 'You would only have blistered those pretty little fingers of yours, my child. And now,' he said, indicating the scrap of paper which bore the stamp, 'if you'll take my advice, you'll send that thing after the other.'

For the sake of this paltry bit of coloured paper Dolly had done it all, and now that must go!—she had not even purchased Colin's forgiveness by her wrong—and this last drop in her cup was perhaps the bitterest. She dropped the stamp guiltily between two red-hot coals, watched that too as it burnt, and then threw herself into an arm-chair and sobbed in passionate remorse.

'Oh, why did I do it?' she wailed; 'why did you make me do it, Harold?'

'Come, Dolly, I like that,' said Caffyn, who saw the necessity for having this understood at once. 'I made you do nothing, if you please—it was all done before I came in. I may think you were very sensible in getting rid of the letter in that way—I do—but you did it of your own accord—remember that.'

'I was quite good half an hour ago,' moaned the child, 'and now I'm a wicked girl—a—a thief! No one will speak to me any more—they'll send me to prison!'

'Now don't talk nonsense,' said Caffyn, a little alarmed, not having expected a child to have such strong feelings about anything. 'And for goodness' sake don't cry like that—there's nothing to cry about now.... You're perfectly safe as long as you hold your tongue. You don't suppose I shall tell of you, do you?' (and it really was highly improbable). 'There's nothing to show what you've done. And—and you didn't mean to do anything bad, I know that, of course. You needn't make yourself wretched about it. It's only the way the law looks at stealing stamps, you know. Come, I must be off now; can't wait for Mabel any longer. But I must see a smile before I go—just a little one, Juggins—to thank me for helping you out of your scrape, eh?' (Dolly's mouth relaxed in a very faint smile.) 'That's right—now you're feeling jolly again; cheer up, you can trust me, you know.' And he went out, feeling tolerably secure of her silence.

'It's rough on her, poor little thing!' he soliloquised as he walked briskly away; 'but she'll forget all about it soon enough—children do. And what the deuce could I do? No, I'm glad I looked in just then. Our resuscitated friend won't write again for a month or two—and by that time it will be too late. And if this business comes out (which I don't imagine it ever will) I've done nothing anyone could lay hold of. I was very careful about that. I must have it out with Mabel as soon as I can now—there's nothing to be gained by waiting!'

Would Dolly forget all about it? She did not like Harold Caffyn, but it never occurred to her to disbelieve the terrible things he had told her. She was firmly convinced that she had done something which, if known, would cut her off completely from home and sympathy and love; she who had hardly known more than a five minutes' sorrow in her happy innocent little life, believed herself a guilty thing with a secret. Henceforth in the shadows there would lurk something more dreadful even than the bogeys with which some foolish nursemaids people shadows for their charges—the gigantic hand of the law, ready to drag her off at any moment from all she loved. And there seemed no help for her anywhere—for had not Harold said that if her father or anyone were to know, they would be obliged to give her up to punishment.

Perhaps if Caffyn had been capable of fully realising what a deadly poison he had been instilling into this poor child's mind, he might have softened matters a little more (provided his object could have been equally well attained thereby), and that is all that can be said for him. But, as it was, he only saw that he must make as deep an impression as he could for the moment, and never doubted that she would forget his words as soon as he should himself.

But if there was some want of thought in the evil he had done, the want of thought in this case arose from a constitutional want of heart.

CHAPTER XVI

'Well, Jane,' said Mr. Lightowler one evening, when he had invited himself to dine and sleep at the house in Malakoff Terrace, 'I suppose you haven't heard anything of that grand young gentleman of yours yet?'

The Ashburns, with the single exception of Trixie, had remained obstinately indifferent to the celebrity which Mark had so suddenly obtained; it did not occur to most of them indeed that distinction was possible in the course he had taken. Perhaps many of Mahomet's relations thought it a pity that he should abandon his excellent prospects in the caravan business (where he was making himself so much respected), for the precarious and unremunerative career of a prophet.

Trixie, however, had followed the book's career with wondering delight; she had bought a copy for herself, Mark not having found himself equal to sending her one, and she had eagerly collected reviews and allusions of all kinds, and tried hard to induce Martha at least to read the book.

Martha had coldly declined. She had something of her mother's hard, unimaginative nature, and read but little fiction; and besides, having from the first sided strongly against Mark, she would not compromise her dignity now by betraying so much interest in his performances. Cuthbert read the book, but in secret, and as he said nothing to its discredit, it may be presumed that he could find no particular fault with it. Mrs. Ashburn would have felt almost inclined, had she known the book was in the house, to order it to be put away from among them like an evil thing, so strong was her prejudice; and her husband, whatever he felt, expressed no interest or curiosity on the subject.

So at Mr. Lightowler's question, which was put more as a vent for his own outraged feelings than any real desire for information, Mrs. Ashburn's face assumed its grimmest and coldest expression as she replied—'No, Solomon. Mark has chosen his own road—we neither have nor expect to have any news of him. At this very moment he may be bitterly repenting his folly and disobedience somewhere.'

Upon which Cuthbert observed that he considered that extremely probable, and Mr. Ashburn found courage to ask a question. 'I—I suppose he hasn't come or written to you yet, Solomon?' he said.

'No, Matthew,' said his brother-in-law, 'he has not. I'd just like to see him coming to me; he wouldn't come twice, I can tell him! No, I tell you, as I told him, I've done with him. When a young man repays all I've spent on him with base ingratitude like that, I wash my hands of him—I say deliberately—I wash my 'ands. Why, he might have worked on at his law, and I'd a' set him up and put him in the way of making his living in a few years; made him a credit to all connected with him, I would! But he's chosen to turn a low scribbler, and starve in a garret, which he'll come to soon enough, and that's what I get for trying to help a nephew. Well, it will be a lesson to me, I know that. Young men have gone off since my young days; a lazy, selfish, conceited lot they are, all of 'em.'

'Not all, Solomon,' said his sister. 'I'm sure there are young men still who—Cuthbert, how long was it you stayed at the office after hours to make up your books? Of his own free will, too, Solomon! And he's never had anyone to encourage him, or help him on, poor boy!'

Mrs. Ashburn was not without hopes that her brother might be brought to understand in time that the family did not end with Mark, but she might have spared her pains just then.

'Oh,' he said, with a rather contemptuous toss of the head, 'I wasn't hinting. I've nothing partickler against him—he's steady enough, I dessay. One of the other kind's enough in a small family, in all conscience! Ah, Jane, if ever a man was regularly taken in by a boy, I was by his brother Mark—a bright, smart, clever young chap he was as I'd wish to see. Give that feller an education and put him to a profession, thinks I, and he'll be a credit to you some of these days. And see what's come of it!'

'It's very sad—very sad for all of us, I'm sure,' sighed Mrs. Ashburn.

At this, Trixie, who had been listening to it all with hot cheeks and trembling lips, could hold out no longer.

'You talk of Mark—Uncle and all of you,' she said, looking prettier for her indignation, 'as if he was a disgrace to us all! You seem to think he's starving somewhere in a garret, and unknown to everybody. But he's nothing of the sort—he's famous already, whether you believe it or not. You ought to be proud of him.'

'Beatrix, you forget yourself,' said her mother; 'before your uncle, too.'

'I can't help it,' said Trixie; 'there's no one to speak up for poor Mark but me, ma, and I must. And it's all quite true. I hear all about books and things from—at the Art School where I go, and Mark's book is being talked about everywhere! And you needn't be afraid of his coming to you for money, Uncle, for I was told that Mark will be able to get as much money as ever he likes for his next books; he will be quite rich, and all just by writing! And nobody but you here seems to think the worse of him for what he has done! I'll show you what the papers say about him presently. Why, even your paper, ma, the "Weekly Horeb," has a long article praising Mark's book this week, so I should think it can't be so very wicked. Wait a minute, and you shall see!'

And Trixie burst impetuously out of the room to fetch the book in which she had pasted the reviews, leaving the others in a rather crestfallen condition, Uncle Solomon especially looking straight in front of him with a fish-like stare, being engaged in trying to assimilate the very novel ideas of a literary career which had just been put before him.

Mrs. Ashburn muttered something about Trixie being always headstrong and never given to serious things, but even she was a little shaken by the unexpected testimony of her favourite oracle, the 'Horeb.'

'Look here, Uncle,' said Trixie, returning with the book and laying it down open before him. 'See what the — says, and the —; oh, and all of them!'

'I don't want to see 'em,' he said, sulkily pushing the book from him. 'Take the things away, child; who cares what they say? They're all at the same scribbling business themselves; o' course they'd crack up one another.'

But he listened with a dull, glazed look in his eyes, and a grunt now and then, while she read extracts aloud, until by-and-by, in spite of his efforts to repress it, a kind of hard grin of satisfaction began to widen his mouth.

'Where's this precious book to be got?' he said at last.

'Are you so sure he's disgraced you, now, Uncle?' demanded Trixie triumphantly.

'Men's praise is of little value,' said Mrs. Ashburn, harshly. 'Your uncle and we look at what Mark has done from the Christian's standpoint.'

'Well, look here, y' know. Suppose we go into the matter now; let's talk it out a bit,' said Uncle Solomon, coming out of a second brown study. 'What 'ave you got against Mark?'

'What have I got against him, Solomon?' echoed his sister in supreme amazement.

'Yes; what's he done to set you all shaking your heads at?'

'Why, surely there's no need to tell you? Well, first there's his ingratitude to you, after all you've done for him!'

'Put me out of the question!' said Mr. Lightowler, with a magnanimous sweep of his hand, 'I can take care of myself, I should 'ope. What I want to get at is what he's done to you. What do you accuse the boy of doing, Matthew, eh?'

Poor little Mr. Ashburn seemed completely overwhelmed by this sudden demand on him. 'I? oh, I—well, Jane has strong views, you know, Solomon, decided opinions on these subjects, and—and so have I!' he concluded feebly.

'Um,' said Mr. Lightowler, half to himself, 'shouldn't a' thought that was what's the matter with you! Well, Jane, then I come back to you. What's he done? Come, he hasn't robbed a church, or forged a cheque, has he?'

'If you wish me to tell you what you know perfectly well already, he has, in defiance of what he knows I feel on this subject, connected himself with a thing I strongly disapprove of—a light-minded fiction.'

'Now you know, Jane, that's all your confounded—I'm speaking to you as a brother, you know—your confounded narrer-minded nonsense! Supposing he has written a "light-minded fiction," as you call it, where's the harm of it?'

'With the early training you received together with me, Solomon, I wonder you can ask! You know very well what would have been thought of reading, to say nothing of writing, a novel in our young days. And it cuts me to the heart to think that a son of mine should place another stumbling-block in the hands of youth.'

'Stumbling grandmother!' cried Mr. Lightowler. 'In our young days, as you say, we didn't go to playhouses, and only read good and improving books, and a dull time we 'ad of it! I don't read novels myself now, having other things to think about. But the world's gone round since then, Jane. Even chapel-folk read these light-minded fictions nowadays, and don't seem to be stumblin' about more than usual.'

'If they take no harm, their own consciences must be their guide; but I've a right to judge for myself as well as they, I think, Solomon.'

'Exactly, but not for them too—that's what you're doin', Jane. Who the dickens are you, to go about groaning that Mark's a prodigal son, or a lost sheep, or a goat, or one of those uncomplimentary animals, all because he's written a book that everyone else is praising? Why are you to be right and all the rest of the world wrong, I'd like to know? Here you've gone and hunted the lad out of the house, without ever consulting me (who, I think, Jane, I do think, have acted so as to deserve to be considered and consulted in the matter), and all for what?'

'I'm sure, Solomon,' said Mrs. Ashburn, with one or two hard sniffs which were her nearest approach to public emotion; 'I'm sure I never expected this from you, and you were quite as angry with Mark as any of us.'

'Because I didn't know all—I was kep' in the dark. From what you said I didn't know but what he'd written some rubbish which wouldn't keep him in bread and cheese for a fortnight, and leave him as unknown as it found him. Naterally I didn't care about that, when I'd hoped he'd be a credit to me. But it appears he is being a credit to me—he's making his fortune, getting famous, setting the upper circles talking of him. I thought Sir Andrew, up at the Manor House, was a-chaffing me the other day when he began complimenting me on my nephew, and I answered him precious short; but I begin to think now as he meant it, and I went and made a fool of myself! All I ever asked of Mark was to be a credit to me, and so long as he goes and is a credit to me, what do I care how he does it? Not that!'

At sentiments of such unhoped-for breadth, Trixie was so far carried away with delight and gratitude as to throw her arms round her uncle's puffy red neck, and bestow two or three warm kisses upon him. 'Then you won't give him up after all, will you, Uncle?' she cried; 'you don't think him a disgrace to you!'

Uncle Solomon looked round him with the sense that he was coming out uncommonly well. 'There's no narrermindedness about me, Trixie, my girl,' he said; 'I never have said, nor I don't say now, that I have given your brother Mark up; he chose not to take the advantages I offered him, and I don't deny feeling put out by it. But what's done can't be helped. I shall give a look into this book of his, and if I see nothing to disapprove of in it, why I shall let him know he can still look to his old uncle if he wants anything. I don't say more than that at present. But I do think, Jane, that you've been too 'ard on the boy. We can't be all such partickler Baptists as you are, yer know!'

'I'm glad to hear you say that, Solomon,' quavered Mr. Ashburn; 'because I said as much to Jane (if you recollect my mentioning it, my dear?) at the time; but she has decided views, and she thought otherwise.'

The unfortunate Jane, seeing herself deserted on all sides, began to qualify, not sorry in her inmost heart to be able to think more leniently, since the 'Weekly Horeb' sanctioned it, of her son's act of independence.

'I may have acted on imperfect knowledge,' she said; 'I may have been too hasty in concluding that Mark had only written some worldly and frivolous love-tale to keep minds from dwelling on higher subjects. If so, I'm willing to own it, and if Mark was to come to me—'

But Mr. Lightowler did not care to lose his monopoly of magnanimity in this way. 'That comes too late now, Jane,' he said; 'he won't come back to you now, after the way you've treated him. You've taken your line, and you'll have to keep to it. But he shan't lose by that while I live—or afterwards, for that matter—he was always more of a son to me than ever you made of him!'

And when he went to bed, after some elaboration of his views on the question, he left the family, with one exception, to the highly unsatisfactory reflection that they had cut themselves off from all right to feel proud and gratified at Mark's renown, and that the breach between them was too wide now to be bridged.

CHAPTER XVII

IN WHICH MARK MAKES AN ENEMY AND RECOVERS A FRIEND

Mark's fame was still increasing, and he began to have proofs of this in a pleasanter and more substantial form than empty compliment. He was constantly receiving letters from editors or publishers inviting him to write for them, and offering terms which exceeded his highest expectations. Several of these proposals—all the more tempting ones, in fact—he accepted at once; not that he had anything by him in manuscript just then of the kind required from him, but he felt a vague sense of power to turn out something very fine indeed, long before the time appointed for the fulfilment of his promises.

But, so far, he had not done any regular literary work since his defection: he was still at St. Peter's, which occupied most of his time, but somehow, now that he could devote his evenings without scruple to the delights of composition, those delights seemed to have lost their keenness, and besides, he had begun to go out a great deal.

He had plenty of time before him, however, and his prospects were excellent; he was sure of considerable sums under his many agreements as soon as he had leisure to set to work. There could be no greater mistake than for a young writer to flood the market from his inkstand—a reflection which comforted Mark for a rather long and unexpected season of drought.

Chilton and Fladgate had begun to sound him respecting a second book, but Mark could not yet decide whether to make his coup with 'One Fair Daughter' or 'Sweet Bells Jangled.' At first he had been feverishly anxious to get a book out which should be legitimately his own as soon as possible, but now, when the time had come, he hung back.

He did not exactly feel any misgivings as to their merits, but he could not help seeing that with every day it was becoming more and more difficult to put 'Illusion' completely in the shade, and that if he meant to effect this, he could afford to neglect no precautions. New and brilliant ideas, necessitating the entire reconstruction of the plots, were constantly occurring to him, and he set impulsively to work, shifting and interpolating, polishing and repolishing, until he must have invested his work with a dazzling glitter—and yet he could not bring himself to part with it.

He was engaged in this manner one Wednesday afternoon in his rooms, when he heard a slow heavy step coming up the stairs, followed by a sharp rap at the door of his bedroom, which adjoined his sitting-room. He shouted to the stranger to come in, and an old gentleman entered presently by the door connecting the two rooms, in whom he recognised Mr. Lightowler's irascible neighbour. He stood there for a few moments without a word, evidently overcome by anger, which Mark supposed was due to annoyance at having first blundered into the bedroom. 'It's old Humpage,' he thought. 'What can he want with me?' The other found words at last, beginning with a deadly politeness. 'I see I am in the presence of the right person,' he began. 'I have come to ask you a plain question.' Here he took something from his coat-tail pocket, and threw it on the table before Mark—it was a copy of 'Illusion.' 'I am told you are in the best position to give me information on the subject. Will you kindly give me the name—the real name—of the author of this book? I have reasons, valid reasons for requiring it.' And he glared down at Mark, who had a sudden and disagreeable sensation as if his heart had just turned a somersault. Could this terrible old person have detected him, and if so what would become of him?

Instinct rather than reason kept him from betraying himself by words. 'Th-that's a rather extraordinary question, sir,' he gasped faintly.

'Perhaps it is,' said the other; 'but I've asked it, and I want an answer.'

'If the author of the book,' said Mark, 'had wished his real name to be known, I suppose he would have printed it.'

'Have the goodness not to equivocate with me, sir. It's quite useless, as you will understand when I tell you that I happen to know'—(he repeated this with withering scorn)—'I happen to know the name of the real author of this—this precious production. I had it, let me tell you, on very excellent authority.'

'Who told you?' said Mark, and his voice seemed to him to come from down stairs. Had Holroyd made a confidant of this angry old gentleman?

'A gentleman whose relation I think you have the privilege to be, sir. Come, you see I know you, Mr.—Mr. Cyril Ernstone,' he sneered. 'Are you prepared to deny it?'

Mark drew a long sweet breath of relief. What a fright he had had! This old gentleman evidently supposed he had unearthed a great literary secret; but why had it made him so angry?

'Certainly not,' he replied, firm and composed again now. 'I am Mr. Cyril Ernstone. I'm very sorry if it annoys you.'

'It does annoy me, sir. I have a right to be annoyed, and you know the reason well enough!'

'Do you know,' said Mark languidly, 'I'm really afraid I don't.'

'Then I'll tell you, sir. In this novel of yours you've put a character called—wait a bit—ah, yes, called Blackshaw, a retired country solicitor, sir.'

'Very likely,' said Mark, who had been getting rather rusty with 'Illusion' of late.

'I'm a retired country solicitor, sir! You've made him a man of low character; you show him up all through the book as perpetually mixing in petty squabbles, sir; on one occasion you actually allow him to get drunk Now what do you mean by it?'

'Good heavens,' said Mark, with a laugh, 'you don't seriously mean to tell me you consider all this personal?'

'I do very seriously mean to tell you so, young gentleman,' said Mr. Humpage, showing his teeth with a kind of snarl.

'There are people who will see personalities in a proposition of Euclid,' said Mark, now completely himself again, and rather amused by the scene; 'I should think you must be one of them, Mr. Humpage. Will it comfort you if I let you know that I—that this book was written months before I first had the pleasure of seeing you.'

'No, sir, not at all. That only shows me more clearly what I knew already. That there has been another hand at work here. I see that uncle of yours behind your back here.'

'Do you though?' said Mark. 'He's not considered literary as a general rule.'

'Oh, he's quite literary enough to be libellous. Just cast your eye over this copy. Your uncle sent this to me as a present, the first work of his nephew. I thought at first he was trying to be friendly again, till I opened the book! Just look at it, sir!' And the old man fumbled through the leaves with his trembling hands. 'Here's a passage where your solicitor is guilty of a bit of sharp practice—underlined by your precious uncle! And here he sets two parties by the ears—underlined by your uncle, in red ink, sir; and it's like that all through the book. Now what do you say?'

'What can I say?' said Mark, with a shrug. 'You must really go and fight it out with my uncle; if he is foolish enough to insult you, that's not exactly a reason for coming here to roar at me.'

'You're as bad as he is, every bit. I had him up at sessions over that gander, and he hasn't forgotten it. You had a hand in that affair, too, I remember. Your victim, sir, was never the same bird again—you'll be pleased to hear that—never the same bird again!'

'Very much to its credit, I'm sure,' said Mark. 'But oblige me by not calling it my victim. I don't suppose you'll believe me, but the one offence is as imaginary as the other.'

'I don't believe you, sir. I consider that to recommend yourself to your highly respectable uncle, you have deliberately set yourself to blacken my character, which may bear comparison with your own, let me tell you. No words can do justice to such baseness as that!'

'I agree with you. If I had done such a thing no words could; but as I happen to be quite blameless of the least idea of hurting your feelings, I'm beginning to be rather tired of this, you see, Mr. Humpage.'

'I'm going, sir, I'm going. I've nearly said my say. You have not altered my opinion in the least. I'm not blind, and I saw your face change when you saw me. You were afraid of me. You know you were. What reason but one could you have for that?'

Of course Mark could have explained even this rather suspicious appearance, but then he would not have improved matters very much; and so, like many better men, he had to submit to be cruelly misunderstood, when a word might have saved him, although in his case silence was neither quixotic nor heroic.

'I can only say again,' he replied in his haughtiest manner, 'that when this book was written, I had never seen you, nor even heard of your existence. If you don't believe me, I can't help it.'

'You've got your own uncle and your own manner to thank for it if I don't believe you, and I don't. There are ways of juggling with words to make them cover anything, and from all I know of you, you are likely enough to be apt at that sort of thing. I've come here to tell you what I think of you, and I mean to do it before I go. You've abused such talents as you've been gifted with, sir; gone out of your way to attack a man who never did you any harm. You're a hired literary assassin—that's my opinion of you! I'm not going to take any legal proceeding against you—I'm not such a fool. If I was a younger man, I might take the law, in the shape of a stout horse-whip, into my own hands; as it is, I leave you to go your own way, unpunished by me. Only, mark my words—you'll come to no good. There's a rough sort of justice in this world, whatever may be said, and a beginning like yours will bring its own reward. Some day, sir, you'll be found out for what you are! That's what I came to say!'

And he turned on his heel and marched downstairs, leaving Mark with a superstitious fear at his heart at his last words, and some annoyance with Holroyd for having exposed him to this, and even with himself for turning craven at the first panic.

'I must look up that infernal book again!' he thought. 'Holroyd may have libelled half London in it for all I know.'

Now it may be as well to state here that Vincent Holroyd was as guiltless as Mark himself of any intention to portray Mr. Humpage in the pages of 'Illusion'; he had indeed heard of him from the Langtons, but the resemblances in the imaginary solicitor to Dolly's godfather were few and trivial enough, and, like most of such half-unconscious reminiscences, required the aid of a malicious dulness to pass as anything more than mere coincidences.

But the next day, while Mark was thinking apprehensively of 'Illusion' as a perfect mine of personalities, the heavy steps were heard again in the passage and up the staircase; he sighed wearily, thinking that perhaps the outraged Mr. Humpage had remembered something more offensive, and had called again to give him the benefit of it.

However, this time the visitor was Mr. Solomon Lightowler, who stood in the doorway with what he meant to be a reassuring smile on his face—though, owing to a certain want of flexibility in his uncle's features, Mark misunderstood it.

'Oh, it's you, is it?' he said bitterly. 'Come in, Uncle, come in. You undertook when I saw you last never to speak to me again, but I don't mind if you don't. I had a thorough good blackguarding yesterday from your friend Humpage, so I've got my hand in. Will you curse me sitting down or standing? The other one stood!'

'No, no, it ain't that, my boy. I don't want to use 'ard words. I've come to say, let bygones be bygones. Mark, my boy, I'm proud of yer!'

'What, of a literary man! My dear uncle, you can't be well—or you've lost money.'

'I'm much as usual, thanky, and I haven't lost any money that I know of, and—and I mean it, Mark, I've read your book.'

'I know you have—so has Humpage,' said Mark.

Uncle Solomon chuckled. 'You made some smart 'its at 'Umpage,' he said. 'When I first saw there was a country solicitor in the book, I said to myself, "That's goin' to be 'Umpage," and you 'ad him fine, I will say that. I never thought to be so pleased with yer.'

'You need not have shown your pleasure by sending him a marked copy.'

'I was afraid he wouldn't see it if I didn't,' explained Mr. Lightowler, 'and I owed him one over that gander, which he summonsed me for, and got his summons dismissed for his trouble. But I've not forgotten it. P'r'aps it was going rather far to mark the places; but there, I couldn't 'elp it.'

'Well, I suppose you know that amounts to libel?' said Mark, either from too hazy a recollection of the law on the subject of 'publication' or the desire to give his uncle a lesson.

'Libel! Why, I never wrote anything—only underlined a passage 'ere and there. You don't call that libelling!'

'A judge might, and, any way, Uncle, it's deuced unpleasant for me. He was here abusing me all the afternoon—when I never had any idea of putting the hot-headed old idiot into a book. It's too bad—it really is!'

"Umpage won't law me—he's had enough of that. Don't you be afraid, and don't show yourself poor-spirited. You've done me a good turn by showing up 'Umpage as what I believe him to be—what's the good of pretending you never meant it—to me? You don't know how pleased you've made me. It's made a great difference in your prospects, young man, I can tell yer!'

'So you told me at the "Cock,"' said Mark.

'I don't mean that way, this time. I dessay I spoke rather 'asty then; I didn't know what sort of littery line you were going to take up with, but if you go on as you've begun, you're all right. And when I have a nephew that makes people talk about him and shows up them that makes themselves unpleasant as neighbours, why, what I say is, Make the most of him! And that brings me to what I've come about. How are you off in the matter o' money, hey?'

Mark was already beginning to feel rather anxious about his expenses. His uncle's cheque was by this time nearly exhausted, his salary at St. Peter's was not high and, as he had already sent in his resignation, that source of income would dry up very shortly. He had the money paid him for 'Illusion,' but that of course he could not use; he had not sunk low enough for that, though he had no clear ideas what to do with it. He would receive handsome sums for his next two novels, but that would not be for some time, and meanwhile his expenses had increased with his new life to a degree that surprised himself, for Mark was not a young man of provident habits.

So he gave his uncle to understand that, though he expected to be paid some heavy sums in a few months, his purse was somewhat light at present.

'Why didn't you come to me?' cried his uncle; 'you might a' known I shouldn't have stinted you. You've never found me near with you. And now you're getting a big littery pot, and going about among the nobs as I see your name with, why, you must keep up the position you've made—and you shall too! You're quite right to drop the schoolmastering, since you make more money with your scribbling. Your time's valuable now. Set to and scribble away while you're the fashion; make your 'ay while the sun shines, my boy. I'll see yer through it. I want you to do me credit. I want everyone to know that you're not like some of these poor devils, but have got a rich old uncle at your back. You let 'em know that, will yer?'

And, quite in the manner of the traditional stage uncle, he produced his cheque book and wrote a cheque for a handsome sum, intimating that that would be Mark's quarterly allowance while he continued to do him credit, and until he should be independent of it. Mark was almost too astounded for thanks at first by such very unexpected liberality, and something, too, in the old man's coarse satisfaction jarred on him and made him ashamed of himself. But he contrived to express his gratitude at last.

'It's all right,' said Uncle Solomon; 'I don't grudge it yer. You just go on as you've begun.' ('I hope that doesn't mean "making more hits at Humpage,"' thought Mark.) 'You thought you could do without me, but you see you can't; and look here, make a friend of me after this, d'ye hear? Don't do nothing without my advice. I'm a bit older than you are, and p'r'aps I can give you a wrinkle or two, even about littery matters, though you mayn't think it. You needn't a' been afraid your uncle would cast you off, Mark—so long as you're doing well. As I told your mother the other day, there's nothing narrerminded about me, and if you feel you've a call to write, why, I don't think the worse of you for it. I'm not that kind of man.'

And after many more speeches of this kind, in the course of which he fully persuaded himself, and very nearly his nephew, that his views had been of this broad nature from the beginning, and were entirely uninfluenced by events, he left Mark to think over this new turn of fortune's wheel, by which he had provoked a bitter foe and regained a powerful protector, without deserving one more than the other.

He thought lightly enough of the first interview now; it was cheaply bought at the price of the other. 'And after all,' he said to himself, 'what man has no enemies?'

But only those whose past is quite stainless, or quite stained, can afford to hold their enemies in calm indifference, and although Mark never knew how old Mr. Humpage's enmity was destined to affect him, it was not without influence on his fortunes.

CHAPTER XVIII

A DINNER PARTY

Mrs. Langton did not forget Mark; and before many days had gone by since his call, he received an invitation to dine at Kensington Park Gardens on a certain Saturday, to which he counted the days like a schoolboy. The hour came at last, and he found himself in the pretty drawing-room once more. There were people there already; a stout judge and his pretty daughter, a meek but eminent conveyancer with a gorgeous wife, and a distinguished professor with a bland subtle smile, a gentle voice and a dangerous eye. Other guests came in afterwards, but Mark hardly saw them. He talked a little to Mrs. Langton, and Mrs. Langton talked considerably to him during the first few minutes after his entrance, but his thoughts kept wandering, like his eyes, to Mabel as she moved from group to group in her character of supplementary hostess, for Mrs. Langton's health did not allow her to exert herself on these occasions.

Mabel was looking very lovely that evening, in some soft light dress of pale rose, with a trail of pure white buds and flowers at her shoulder. Mark watched her as she went about, now listening with pretty submission to the gorgeous woman in the ruby velvet and the diamond star, who was laying down some 'little new law' of her own, now demurely acknowledging the old judge's semi-paternal compliments, audaciously rallying the learned professor, or laughing brightly at something a spoony-looking, fair-haired youth was saying to her.

Somehow she seemed to Mark to be further removed than ever from him; he was nothing to her amongst all these people; she had not even noticed him yet. He began to be jealous of the judge, and the professor too, and absolutely to hate the spoony youth.

But she came to him at last. Perhaps she had seen him from the first, and felt his dark eyes following her with that pathetic look they had whenever things were not going perfectly well with him. She came now, and was pleased to be gracious to him for a few minutes, till dinner was announced.

Mark heard it with a pang. Now they would be separated, of course; he would be given to the ruby woman, or that tall, keen-faced girl with the pince-nez; he would be lucky if he got two minutes' conversation with Mabel in the drawing-room later on. But he waited for instructions resignedly.

'Didn't papa tell you?' she said; 'you are to take me in—if you will?' If he would! He felt a thrill as her light fingers rested on his arm; he could scarcely believe his own good fortune, even when he found himself seated next to her as the general rustle subsided, and might accept the delightful certainty that she would be there by his side for the next two hours at least.

He forgot to consult his menu; he had no very distinct idea of what he ate or drank, or what was going on around him, at least as long as Mabel talked to him. They were just outside the radius of the big centre lamp, and that and the talk around them produced a sort of semi-privacy.

The spoony young man was at Mabel's right hand, to be sure, but he had been sent in with the keen-faced young lady who came from Girton, where it was well known that the marks she had gained in one of the great Triposes under the old order, would—but for her sex—have placed her very high indeed in the class list. Somebody had told the young man of this, and, as he was from Cambridge too, but had never been placed anywhere except in one or two walking races at Fenner's, it had damped him too much for conversation just yet.

'Have you been down to Chigbourne lately?' Mabel asked Mark suddenly, and her smile and manner showed him that she remembered their first meeting. He took this opportunity of disclaiming all share in the treatment of the unfortunate gander, and was assured that it was quite unnecessary to do so.

'I wish your uncle, Mr. Humpage, thought with you,' he said ruefully, 'but he has quite made up his mind that I am a villain of the deepest dye;' and then, encouraged to confide in her, he told the story of the old gentleman's furious entry and accusation.

Mabel looked rather grave. 'How could he get such an idea into his head?' she said.

'I'm afraid my uncle had something to do with that,' said Mark, and explained Mr. Lightowler's conduct.

'It's very silly of both of them,' she said; 'and then to drag you into the quarrel, too! You know, old Mr. Humpage is not really my uncle—only one of those relations that sound like a prize puzzle when you try to make them out. Dolly always calls him Uncle Anthony—he's her godfather. But I wish you hadn't offended him, Mr. Ashburn, I do really. I've heard he can be a very bitter enemy. He has been a very good friend to papa; I believe he gave him almost the very first brief he ever had; and he's kind to all of us. But it's dangerous to offend him. Perhaps you will meet him here some day,' she added, 'and then we may be able to make him see how mistaken he has been.'

'How kind of you to care about it!' said he, and his eyes spoke his gratitude for the frank interest she had taken in his fortunes.

'Of course I care,' said Mabel, looking down as she spoke. 'I can't bear to see anyone I like and respect—as I do poor Uncle Anthony—persist in misjudging anybody like that.'

Mark had hoped more from the beginning of this speech than the conclusion quite bore out, but it was delightful to hear her talking something more than society nothings to him. However, that was ended for the present by the sudden irruption of the spoony young man into the conversation; he had come out very shattered from a desperate intellectual conflict with the young lady from Girton, to whom he had ventured on a remark which, as he made it, had seemed to him likely to turn out brilliant. 'You know,' he had announced solemnly, 'opinions may differ, but in these things I must say I don't think the exception's always the rule—eh? don't you find that?' And his neighbour replied that she thought he had hit upon a profound philosophical truth, and then spoilt it by laughing. After which the young man, thinking internally 'it sounded all right, wonder if it was such bosh as she seems to think,' had fled to Mabel for sanctuary and plunged into an account of his University disasters.

'I should have floored my "General" all right, you know,' he said, 'only I went in for too much poetry.'

'Poetry?' echoed Mabel, with a slight involuntary accent of surprise.

'Rhymes, you know, not regular poetry!'

'But, Mr. Pidgely, I don't quite see; why can't you floor generals with rhymes which are not regular poetry? Are they so particular in the army?'

'It isn't an army exam.; it's at Cambridge; and the rhymes are all the chief tips done into poetry—like "Paley" rhymes, y' know. Paley rhymes give you, for instance, all the miracles or all the parables right off in about four lines of gibberish, and you learn the gibberish and then you're all right. I got through my Little-go that way, but I couldn't the General. Fact is, my coach gave me too many rhymes!'

'And couldn't you recollect the—the tips without rhymes?'

'Couldn't remember with 'em,' he said. 'I could have corked down the verses all right enough, but the beggars won't take them. I forgot what they were all about, so I had to show up blank papers. And I'd stayed up all one Long too!'

'Working?' asked Mabel, with some sympathy.

'Well—and cricketing,' he said ingenuously. 'I call it a swindle.'

'He talks quite a dialect of his own,' thought Mabel surprised. 'Vincent didn't. I wonder if Mr. Ashburn can.'

Mr. Ashburn, after a short period of enforced silence spent in uncharitable feelings respecting fair-haired Mr. Pidgely, had been suddenly attacked by the lady on his left, a plump lady with queer comic inflections in her voice, the least touch of brogue, and a reputation for daring originality.

'I suppose now,' she began, 'ye've read the new book they're talking so much about—this "Illusion"? And h'wat's your private opinion? I wonder if I'll find a man with the courage to agree with me, for I said when I'd come to the last page, "Well, they may say what they like, but I never read such weary rubbish in all me life," and I never did!'

Mark laughed—he could not help it—but it was a laugh of real enjoyment, without the slightest trace of pique or wounded vanity in it. 'I'll make a confession,' he said. 'I do think myself that the book has been luckier than it deserves—only, as the—the man who wrote it is a—a very old friend of mine—you see, I mustn't join in abusing it.'

Mabel heard this and liked Mark the better for it. 'I suppose he couldn't do anything else very well without making a scene,' she thought, 'but he did it very nicely. I hope that woman will find out who he is though; it will be a lesson to her!' Here Mabel was not quite fair, perhaps, for the lady had a right to her opinion, and anything is better than humbug. But she was very needlessly pitying Mark for having to listen to such unpalatable candour, little dreaming how welcome it was to him, or how grateful he felt to his critic. When Mark was free again, after an animated discussion with his candid neighbour, in which each had amused the other and both were on the way to becoming intimate, he found the spoony youth finishing the description of a new figure he had seen in a cotillon. 'You all sit down on chairs, don't you know,' he was saying, 'and then the rest come through doors;' and Mabel said, with a spice of malice (for she was being excessively bored), that that must be very pretty and original.

Mr. Langton was chatting ponderously at his end of the table, and Mrs. Langton was being interested at hers by an account the judge's lady was giving of a protégé of hers, an imbecile, who made his living by calling neighbours who had to be up early.

'Perhaps it's prejudice,' said Mrs. Langton, 'but I do not think I should like to be called by an idiot; he might turn into a maniac some day. They do quite suddenly at times, don't they?' she added, appealing to the professor, 'and that wouldn't be nice, you know, if he did. What would you do?' she inquired generally.

'Shouldn't get up,' said a rising young barrister.

'I should—under the bed, and scream,' said the lively young lady he had taken down. And so for some minutes that end of the table applied itself zealously to solving the difficult problem of the proper course to take on being called early by a raving maniac.

Meanwhile Mabel had succeeded in dropping poor Mr. Pidgely and resuming conversation with Mark; this time on ordinary topics—pictures, books, theatres, and people (especially people); he talked well, and the sympathy between them increased.

Then as the dessert was being taken round, Dolly and Colin came in. 'I've had ices, Mabel,' said the latter confidentially in her ear as he passed her chair on his way to his mother; but Dolly stole quietly in and sat down by her father's side without a word.

'Do you notice any difference in my sister Dolly?' Mabel asked Mark, with a little anxious line on her forehead.

'She is not looking at all well,' said Mark, following the direction of her glance. There certainly was a change in Dolly; she had lost all her usual animation, and sat there silent and constrained, leaving the delicacies with which her father had loaded her plate untouched, and starting nervously whenever he spoke to her. When good-natured Mr. Pidgely displayed his one accomplishment of fashioning a galloping pig out of orange-peel for her amusement, she seemed almost touched by his offering, instead of slightly offended, as the natural Dolly would have been.

'I don't think she is ill,' said Mabel, 'though I was uneasy about that at first. Fräulein and I fancy she must be worrying herself about something, but we can't get her to say what it is, and I don't like to tease her; very likely she is afraid of being laughed at if she tells anybody. But I do so wish I could find out; children can make themselves so terribly wretched over mere trifles sometimes.'

But the hour of 'bereavement,' as Mr. Du Maurier calls it, had come; gloves were being drawn on, the signal was given. Mr. Pidgely, after first carefully barricading the path on his side of the table with his chair, opened the door, and the men, left to themselves, dropped their hypocritical mask of resigned regret as the handle turned on Mrs. Langton's train, and settled down with something very like relief.

Mark, of course, could not share this, though it is to be feared that even he found some consolation in his cigarette; the sound of Mabel's voice had not ceased to ring in his ears when her father took him by the arm and led him up to be introduced to the professor, who was standing before a picture. The man of science seemed at first a little astonished at having an ordinary young man presented to him in this way, but when his host explained that Mark was the author of the book of which the professor had been speaking so highly, his manner changed, and he overwhelmed him with his courtly compliments, while the other guests gathered gradually nearer, envying the fortunate object of so marked a distinction.

But the object himself was horribly uncomfortable; for it appeared that the professor in reading 'Illusion' had been greatly struck by a brilliant simile drawn from some recent scientific discoveries with which he had had some connection, and had even discovered in some passages what he pronounced to be the germ of a striking theory that had already suggested itself to his own brain, and he was consequently very anxious to find out exactly what was in Mark's mind when he wrote. Before Mark knew where he was, he found himself let in for a scientific discussion with one of the leading authorities on the subject, while nearly everyone was listening with interest for his explanation. His forehead grew damp and cold with the horror of the situation—he almost lost his head, for he knew very little about science. Thanks, however, to his recent industry, he kept some recollection of the passages in question, and without any clear idea of what he was going to say, plunged desperately into a long and complicated explanation. He talked the wildest nonsense, but with such confidence that everyone in the room but the professor was impressed. Mark had the mortification of seeing, as the great man heard him out with a quiet dry smile, and a look in his grey eyes which he did not at all like, that he was found out. But the professor only said at the end, 'Well, that's very interesting, Mr. Ashburn, very interesting indeed—you have given me a really considerable insight into your—ah—mental process.' And for the rest of the evening he talked to his host. As he drove home with his wife that night, however, his disappointment found vent: 'Never been so taken in in my life,' he remarked; 'I did think from his book that that young Ernstone and I would have something in common; but I tried him but got nothing out of him but rubbish; probably got the whole thing up out of some British Association speech and forgotten it! I hate your shallow fellows, and 'pon my word I felt strongly inclined to show him up, only I didn't care to annoy Langton!'

'I'm glad you didn't, dear,' said his wife; 'I don't think dinner-parties are good places to show people up in, and really Mr. Ernstone, or Ashburn, whatever his name is, struck me as being so very charming—perhaps you expected too much from him.'

'H'm, I shall know better another time,' he said.

But the incident, even as it was, left Mark with an uncomfortable feeling that his evening had somehow been spoilt, particularly as he did not succeed in getting any further conversation with Mabel in the drawing-room afterwards to make him forget the unpleasantness. Vincent Holroyd's work was still proving itself in some measure an avenger of his wrongs.

CHAPTER XI

DOLLY'S DELIVERANCE

About a week after the dinner recorded in the last chapter, Mark repaired to the house in Kensington Park Gardens to call as in duty bound, though, as he had not been able to find out on what afternoon he would be sure of finding Mrs. Langton at home, he was obliged to leave this to chance. He was admitted, however—not by the stately Champion, but by Colin, who had seen him from the window and hastened to intercept him.

'Mabel's at home, somewhere,' he said, 'but will you come in and speak to Dolly first? She's crying awfully about something, and she won't tell me what. Perhaps she'd tell you. And do come, sir, please; it's no fun when she's like that, and she's always doing it now!' For Colin had an unlimited belief, founded as he thought on experience, in the persuasive powers of his former master.

Mark had his doubts as to the strict propriety of acceding to this request—at all events until it had been sanctioned by some higher authority than Colin—but then he remembered Mabel's anxiety on the night of the dinner; if he could only set this child's mind at ease, would not that excuse any breach of conventionality—would it not win a word of gratitude from her sister? He could surely take a little risk and trouble for such a reward as that; and so, with his usual easy confidence, he accepted a task which was to cost him dear enough. 'You'd better leave me to manage this, young man,' he said at the door. 'Run off to your sister Mabel and explain things, tell her where I am and why, you know.' And he went into the library alone. Dolly was crouching there in an arm-chair, worn out by sobbing and the weight of a terror she dared not speak of, which had broken her down at last. Mark, who was good-natured enough in his careless way, was touched by the utter abandonment of her grief; for the first time he began to think it must be something graver than a mere childish trouble, and, apart from all personal motives, longed sincerely to do something, if he could, to restore Dolly to her old childish self. He forgot everything but that, and the unselfish sympathy he felt gave him a tact and gentleness with which few who knew him best would have credited him. Gradually, for at first she would say nothing, and turned away in lonely hopelessness, he got her to confess that she was very unhappy; that she had done something which she must never, never tell to anybody.

Then she started up with a flushed face and implored him to go away and leave her. 'Don't make me tell you!' she begged piteously. 'Oh, I know you mean to be kind, I do like you now—only I can't tell you, really. Please, please go away—I'm so afraid of telling you.'

'But why?' said Mark. 'I'm not very good myself, Dolly—you need not be afraid of me.'

'It isn't that,' said Dolly, with a shudder; 'but he said if I told anyone they would have to send me to prison.'

'Who dared to tell you a wicked lie like that?' said Mark indignantly, all the manhood in him roused by the stupid cruelty of it. 'It wasn't Colin, was it, Dolly?'

'No, not Colin; it was Harold—Harold Caffyn. Oh, Mr. Ashburn,' she said, with a sudden gleam of hope, 'wasn't it true? He said papa was a lawyer, and would have to help the law to punish me—'

'The infernal scoundrel!' muttered Mark to himself, but he saw that he was getting to the bottom of the mystery at last. 'So he told you that, did he?' he continued; 'did he say it to tease you, Dolly?'

'I don't know. He often used to tease, but never like that before, and I did do it—only I never never meant it.'

'Now listen to me, Dolly,' said Mark. 'If all you are afraid of is being sent to prison, you needn't think any more about it. You can trust me, can't you? You know I wouldn't deceive you. Well, I tell you that you can't have done anything that you would be sent to prison for—that's all nonsense. Do you understand? Harold Caffyn said that to frighten you. No one in the world would ever dream of sending you to prison, whatever you'd done. Are you satisfied now?'

Rather to Mark's embarrassment, she threw her arms round his neck in a fit of half-hysterical joy and relief. 'Tell me again,' she cried; 'you're sure it's true—they can't send me to prison? Oh, I don't care now. I am so glad you came—so glad. I will tell you all about it now. I want to!'

But some instinct kept Mark from hearing this confession; he had overcome the main difficulty—the rest was better left in more delicate hands than his, he thought. So he said, 'Never mind about telling me, Dolly; I'm sure it wasn't anything very bad. But suppose you go and find Mabel, and tell her; then you'll be quite happy again.'

'Will you come too?' asked Dolly, whose heart was now completely won.

So Mark and she went hand-in-hand to the little boudoir at the back of the house where they had had their first talk about fairies, and found Mabel in her favourite chair by the window; she looked round with a sudden increase of colour as she saw Mark.

'I mustn't stay,' he said, after shaking hands. 'I ought not to come at all, I'm afraid, but I've brought a young lady who has a most tremendous secret to confess, which she's been making herself, and you too, unhappy about all this time. She has come to find out if it's really anything so very awful after all.'

And he left them together. It was hard to go away after seeing so little of Mabel, but it was a sacrifice she was capable of appreciating.

CHAPTER XX

A DECLARATION—OF WAR

On the morning of the day which witnessed Dolly's happy deliverance from the terrors which had haunted her so long, Mabel had received a note from Harold Caffyn. He had something to say to her, he wrote, which could be delayed no longer—he could not be happy until he had spoken. If he were to call some time the next morning, would she see him—alone?

These words she read at first in their most obvious sense, for she had been suspecting for some time that an interview of this kind was coming, and even felt a little sorry for Harold, of whom she was beginning to think more kindly. So she wrote a few carefully worded lines, in which she tried to prepare him as much as possible for the only answer she could give, but before her letter was sent Dolly had told her story of innocent guilt.

Mabel read his note again and tore up her reply with burning cheeks. She must have misunderstood him—it could not be that; he must have felt driven to repair by confession the harm he had done. And she wrote instead—'I shall be very willing to hear anything you may have to say,' and took the note herself to the pillar-box on the hill.

Harold found her answer on returning late that night to his room, and saw nothing in it to justify any alarm. 'It's not precisely gushing,' he said to himself, 'but she couldn't very well say more just yet. I think I am pretty safe.' So the next morning he stepped from his hansom to the Langtons' door, leisurely and coolly enough. Perhaps his heart was beating a little faster, but only with excitement and anticipation of victory, for after Mabel's note he could feel no serious doubts.

He was shown into the little boudoir looking out on the square, but she was not there to receive him—she even allowed him to wait a few minutes, which amused him. 'How like a woman!' he thought. 'She can't resist keeping me on the tenterhooks a little, even now.' There was a light step outside, she had come at last, and he started to his feet as the door opened. 'Mabel!' he cried—he had meant to add 'my darling'—but something in her face warned him not to appear too sure of her yet.

She was standing at some distance from him, with one hand lightly resting on a little table; her face was paler than usual, she seemed rather to avoid looking at him, while she did not offer to take his outstretched hand. Still he was not precisely alarmed by all this. Whatever she felt, she was not the girl to throw herself at any fellow's head; she was proud and he must be humble—for the present.

'You had something to say to me—Harold?' With what a pretty shy hesitation she spoke his name now, he thought, with none of the sisterly frankness he had found so tantalising; and how delicious she was as she stood there in her fresh white morning dress. There was a delightful piquancy in this assumed coldness of hers—a woman's dainty device to delay and heighten the moment of surrender! He longed to sweep away all her pretty defences, to take her to his arms and make her own that she was his for ever. But somehow he felt a little afraid of her; he must proceed with caution. 'Yes,' he said, 'there is something I must say to you—you will give me a hearing, Mabel, won't you?'

'I told you I would hear you. I hope you will say something to make me think of you differently.'

He did not understand this exactly, but it did not sound precisely encouraging.

'I hoped you didn't think me a very bad sort of fellow,' he said. And then, as she made no answer, he plunged at once into his declaration. He was a cold lover on the stage, but practice had at least given him fluency, and now he was very much in earnest—he had never known till then all that she was to him: there was real passion in his voice, and a restrained power which might have moved her once.

But Mabel heard him to the end only because she felt unable to stop him without losing control over herself. She felt the influence of his will, but it made her the more thankful that she had so powerful a safeguard against it.

He finished and she still made no response, and he began to feel decidedly awkward; but when at last she turned her face to him, although her eyes were bright, it was not with the passion he had hoped to read there.

'And it really was that, after all!' she said bitterly. 'Do you know, I expected something very different.'

'I said what I feel. I might have said it better perhaps,' he retorted, 'but at least tell me what you expected me to say, and I will say that.'

'Yes, I will tell you. I expected an explanation.'

'An explanation!' he repeated blankly; 'of what?'

'Is there nothing you can remember which might call for some excuse if you found I had heard of it? I will give you every chance, Harold. Think—is there nothing?'

Caffyn had forgotten the stamp episode as soon as possible, as a disagreeable expedient to which he had been obliged to resort, and which had served its end, and so he honestly misunderstood this question.

'Upon my soul, no,' he said earnestly. 'I don't pretend to have been any better than my neighbours, but since I began to think of you, I never cared about any other woman. If you've been told any silly gossip—'

Mabel laughed, but not merrily. 'Oh, it is not that—really it did not occur to me to be jealous at any time—especially now. Harold, Dolly has told me everything about that letter,' she added, as he still looked doubtful.

He understood now at all events, and took a step back as if to avoid a blow. Everything! his brain seemed dulled for an instant by those words; he thought that he had said enough to prevent the child from breathing a syllable about that unlucky letter, and now Mabel knew 'everything!'

But he recovered his power of thought almost directly, feeling that this was no time to lose his head. 'I suppose I'm expected to show some emotion,' he said lightly; 'it's evidently something quite too terrible. But I'm afraid I want an explanation this time.'

'I think not, but you shall have it. I know that you came in and found that poor child tearing off the stamp from some old envelope of mine, and had the wickedness to tell her she had been stealing. Do you deny it?'

'Some old envelope!' The worst of Caffyn's fear vanished when he heard that. She did not know that it contained an unread letter then; she did not guess—how could she, when Dolly herself did not know it—where the letter had come from. He might appease her yet!

Caffyn's first inference, it may be said, was correct; in Dolly's mind her guilt had consisted in stealing a marked stamp, and her hurried and confused confession had, quite innocently and unconsciously, left Mabel ignorant of the real extent and importance of what seemed to her a quite imaginary offence.

'Deny it!' he said, 'of course not; I remember joking her a little over something of the sort. Is that all this tremendous indignation is about—a joke?'

'A joke!' she said indignantly; 'you will not make anyone but yourself merry over jokes like that. You set to work deliberately to frighten her; you did it so thoroughly that she has been wretched for days and days, ill and miserable with the dread of being sent to prison. You did threaten her with a prison, Harold; you told her she must even be afraid of her own father—of all of us.... Who can tell what she has been suffering, all alone, my poor little Dolly! And you dare to call that a joke!'

'I never thought she would take it all so literally,' he said.

'Oh, you are not stupid, Harold; only a cruel fool could have thought he was doing no harm. And you have seen her since again and again; you must have noticed how changed she was, and yet you had no pity on her! Can't you really see what a thing you have been doing? Do you often amuse yourself in that way, and with children?'

'Hang it, Mabel,' said Caffyn uneasily, 'you're very hard on me!'

'Why were you hard on my darling Dolly?' Mabel demanded. 'What had she done to you—how could you find pleasure in torturing her? Do you hate children—or only Dolly?'

He made a little gesture of impatient helplessness. 'Oh, if you mean to go on asking questions like that—' he said, 'of course I don't hate your poor little sister. I tell you I'm sorry she took it seriously—very sorry. And—and, if there's anything I can do to make it up to her somehow; any—any amends, you know—'

The hardship, as he felt at the time, of his peculiar position was that it obliged him to offer such a lame excuse for his treatment of Dolly. Without the motive he had had for his conduct, it must seem dictated by some morbid impulse of cruelty—whereas, of course, he had acted quite dispassionately, under the pressure of a necessity—which, however, it was impossible to explain to Mabel.

'I suppose "amends" mean caramels or chocolates,' said Mabel; 'chocolates to compensate for making a child shrink for days from those who loved her! She was fretting herself ill, and we could do nothing for her: a very little more and it might have killed her. Perhaps your sense of humour would have been satisfied by that? If it had not been for a friend—almost a stranger—who was able to see what we were all blind to, that a coward had been practising on her fears, we might never have guessed the truth till— till it was too late!'

'I see now,' he said; 'I thought there must be someone at the bottom of this; someone who, for purposes of his own, has contrived to put things in the worst light for me. If you can condescend to listen to slanderers, Mabel, I shall certainly not condescend to defend myself.'

'Oh, I will tell you his name,' she said, 'and then even you will have to own that he had no motive for doing what he did but natural goodness and kindness. I doubt even if he has ever met you in his life; the man who rescued our Dolly from what you had made her is Mr. Mark Ashburn, the author of 'Illusion' (her expression softened slightly, from the gratitude she felt, as she spoke his name, and Caffyn noted it). 'If you think he would stoop to slander you— But what is the use of talking like that? You have owned it all. No slander could make it any worse than it is!'

'If you think as badly of me as that,' said Caffyn, who had grown deadly pale, 'we can meet no more, even as acquaintances.'

'That would be my own wish,' she replied.

'Do you mean,' he asked huskily, 'that—that everything is to be over between us? Has it really come to that, Mabel?'

'I did not know that there ever was anything between us, as you call it,' she said. 'But of course, after this, friendship is impossible. We cannot help meeting. I shall not even tell my mother of this, for Dolly's sake, and so this house will still be open to you. But if you force me to protect Dolly or myself, you will come here no more.'

Her scornful indifference only filled him with a more furious desire to triumph over it; he had felt so secure of her that morning, and now she had placed this immeasurable distance between them. He had never felt the full power of her beauty till then, as she stood there with that haughty pose of the head and the calm contempt in her eyes; he had seen her in most moods—playfully perverse, coldly civil, and unaffectedly gracious and gentle—and in none of them had she made his heart ache with the mad passion that mastered him now.

'It shall not end like this!' he said violently; 'I won't let you make a mountain of a molehill in this way, Mabel, because it suits you to do so. You have no right to judge me by what a child chooses to imagine I said!'

'I judge you by the effects of what you did say. I can remember very well that you had a cruel tongue as a boy—you are quite able to torture a child with it still.'

'It is your tongue that is cruel!' he retorted; 'but you shall be just to me. I love you, Mabel—whether you like it or not—you shall not throw me off like this. Do you hear? You liked me well enough before all this! I will force you to think better of me; you shall own it one day. No, I'm mad to talk like this—I only ask you to forgive me—to let me hope still!'

He came forward as he spoke and tried to take her hands, but she put them quickly behind her. 'Don't dare to come nearer!' she said; 'I thought I had made you feel something of what I think of you. What can I say more? Hope! do you think I could ever trust a man capable of such deliberate wickedness as you have shown by that single action?—a kind of malice that I hardly think can be human. No, you had better not hope for that. As for forgiving you, I can't even do that now; some day, perhaps, when Dolly has quite forgotten, I may be able to forget too, but not till then. Have I made you understand yet? Is that enough?'

Caffyn was still standing where she had checked his advance; his face was very grey and drawn, and his eyes were fixed on the Eastern rug at his feet. He gave a short savage laugh. 'Well, yes,' he said, 'I think perhaps I have had enough at last. You have been kind enough to put your remarks very plainly. I hope, for your own sake, I may never have a chance of making you any return for all this.'

'I hope so too,' she said; 'I think you would use it.'

'Thanks for your good opinion,' he said, as he went to the door. 'I shall do my best, if the time comes, to deserve it.'

She had never faltered during the whole of this interview. A righteous anger had given her courage to declare all the scorn and indignation she felt. But now, as the front door closed upon him, the strength that had sustained her so long gave way all at once; she sank trembling into one of the low cushioned chairs, and presently the reaction completed itself in tears, which she had not quite repressed when Dolly came in to look for her.

'Has he gone?' she began; and then, as she saw her sister's face, 'Mabel! Harold hasn't been bullying you?'

'No, darling, no,' said Mabel, putting her arms round Dolly's waist. 'It's silly of me to cry, isn't it? for Harold will not trouble either of us again after this.'

Meanwhile Harold was striding furiously down the other side of the hill in the direction of Kensal Green, paying very little heed where his steps might be leading him, in the dull rage which made his brain whirl.

Mabel's soft and musical voice, for it had not ceased to be that, even when her indignation was at its highest, rang still in his ears. He could not forget her bitter scornful speeches; they were lashing and stinging him to the soul.

He had indeed been hoist with his own petard; the very adroitness with which he had contrived to get rid of an inconvenient rival had only served to destroy his own chances for ever.

He knew that never again would Mabel suffer him to approach her on the old friendly footing—it would be much if she could bring herself to treat him with ordinary civility—he had lost her for ever, and hated her accordingly from the bottom of his heart. 'If I can ever humble you as you have humbled me to-day, God help you, my charming Mabel!' he said to himself. 'To think that that little fool of a child should have let out everything, at the very moment when I had the game in my own hands! I have to thank that distinguished novelist, Mr. Mark Ashburn, for that, though; he must trouble himself to put his spoke in my wheel, must he? I shan't forget it. I owe you one for that, my illustrious friend, and you're the sort of creditor I generally do pay in the long run.'

Only one thing gave him a gleam—not of comfort, precisely, but gloomy satisfaction; his manoeuvre with the letter had at least succeeded in keeping Holroyd apart from Mabel. 'He's just the fellow to think he's jilted, and give her up without another line,' he thought; 'shouldn't wonder if he married out there. Miss Mabel won't have everything her own way!'

He walked on, past the huge gasometers and furnaces of the Gas Company, and over the railway and canal bridges, to the Harrow Road, when he turned mechanically to the right. His eyes saw nothing—neither the sluggish barges gliding through the greasy black stream on his right, nor the doleful string of hearses and mourning coaches which passed him on their way to or from the cemetery. It was with some surprise that, as he began to take note of his surroundings again, he found himself in Bayswater, and not far from his own rooms. He thought he might as well return to them as not, and as he reached the terrace in which he had taken lodgings, he saw a figure coming towards him that seemed familiar, and in whom, as he drew nearer, he recognised his uncle, Mr. Antony Humpage. He was in no mood to talk about indifferent topics just then, and if his respected uncle had only had his back instead of his face towards him, Caffyn would have made no great effort to attract his attention. As it was, he gave him the heartiest and most dutiful of welcomes. 'You don't mean to say you've actually been looking me up?' he began; 'how lucky that I came up just then—another second or two and I should have missed you. Come in, and let me give you some lunch?'

'No, my boy, I can't stay long. I was in the neighbourhood on business, and I thought I'd see if you were at home. I won't come up again now, I must get back to my station. I waited for some time in those luxurious apartments of yours, you see, thinking you might come in. Suppose you walk a little way back with me, eh? if you've no better engagement.'

'Couldn't have a better one,' said Caffyn, inwardly chafing; but he always made a point of obliging his uncle, and for once he had no reason to consider his time thrown away. For, as they walked on together in the direction of the Edgware Road, where the old gentleman intended to take the Underground to King's Cross, Mr. Humpage, after some desultory conversation on various subjects, said suddenly, 'By the way, you know a good many of these writing fellows, Harold—have you ever come across one called Mark Ashburn?'

'I've met him once,' said Caffyn, and his brows contracted. 'Wrote this new book, "Illusion," didn't he?'

'Yes, he did—confound him!' said the other warmly, and then launched into the history of his wrongs. 'Perhaps I oughtn't to say it at my age,' he concluded, 'but I hate that fellow!'

'Do you though?' said Caffyn with a laugh; 'it's a singular coincidence, but so do I.'

'There's something wrong about him, too,' continued the old man; 'he's got a secret.'

('So have most of us!' thought his nephew.) 'But what makes you think so?' he asked aloud, and waited for the answer with some interest.

'I saw it in the fellow's face; no young man with a clear record ever has such a look as he had when I came in. He was green with fear, sir; perfectly green!'

'Is that all?' and Caffyn was slightly disappointed. 'You know, I don't think much of that. He might have taken you for a dun, or an indignant parent, or something of that sort; he may be one of those nervous fellows who start at anything, and you came there on purpose to give him a rowing, didn't you?'

'Don't talk to me,' said the old man impatiently; 'there's not much nervousness about him—he's as cool and impudent a rascal as ever I saw when he's nothing to fear. It was guilt, sir, guilt. You remember that picture of the Railway Station, and the look on the forger's face when the detectives lay hold of him at the carriage door? I saw that very look on young Ashburn's face before I'd spoken a dozen words.'

'What were the words?' said Caffyn. 'Proceed, good uncle, as we say in our profession; you interest me much!'

'I'm sure I forget what I said—I was out of temper, I remember that. I think I began by asking him for the real name of the author of the book.'

Again Caffyn was disappointed. 'Of course he was in a funk then; he knew he had put you into it. So you say at least; I've not read the book myself.'

'It wasn't that at all, I tell you,' persisted the old man obstinately; 'you weren't there, and I was. D'ye think I don't know better than you? He's not the man to care for that. When he found what I'd really come about he was cool enough. No, no, he's robbed, or forged, or something, at some time or other, take my word for it—and I only hope I shall live to see it brought home to him!'

'I hope it will find him at home when it is,' said Caffyn; 'these things generally find the culprits "out" in more senses than one, to use an old Joe Miller. He would look extremely well in the Old Bailey dock. But this is Utopian, Uncle.'

'Well—we shall see. I turn off here, so good-bye. If you meet that libelling scoundrel again, you remember what I've told you.'

'Yes, I will,' thought Caffyn as he walked back alone. 'I must know more of my dear Ashburn; and if there happens to be a screw loose anywhere in my dear Ashburn's past, I shall do my humble best to give it a turn or two. It's a charming amusement to unmask the perfidious villain, as I suppose I must call myself after to-day, but it was hardly safe to do it if he has his reasons for wearing a domino himself. If I could only think that excellent uncle of mine had not found a mare's nest! And if I can only put that screw on!'

CHAPTER XXI

A PARLEY WITH THE ENEMY

Mr. Fladgate was one of those domestically inclined bachelors who are never really at ease in rooms or chambers, and whose tastes lead them, as soon as they possess the necessary means, to set up a substantial and well-regulated household of their own. He had a large old-fashioned house in the neighbourhood of Russell Square, where he entertained rather frequently in a solid unpretentious fashion. At his Sunday dinners especially, one or two of the minor celebrities of the day were generally to be met, and it was to one of these gatherings that Mark was invited, as one of the natural consequences of the success of 'Illusion.' He found himself, on arriving, in company with several faces familiar to him from photographs, and heard names announced which were already common property. There were some there who had been famous once and were already beginning to be forgotten, others now obscure who were destined to be famous some day, and a few, and these by no means the least gifted, who neither had been nor would be famous at any time. There were two or three constellations of some magnitude on this occasion, surrounded by a kind of 'milky way' of minor stars, amongst which the bar, the studios, and the stage were all more or less represented.

Mark, as a rising man who had yet to justify a first success, occupied a position somewhere between the greater and lesser division, and Mr. Fladgate took care to make him known to many of the leading men in the room, by whom he found himself welcomed with cordial encouragement.

Presently, when he had shifted for a moment out of the nearest focus of conversation, his host, who had been 'distributing himself,' as the French say, amongst the various knots of talkers, came bustling up to him. 'Er—Mr. Ashburn,' he began, 'I want you to know a very clever young fellow here—known him from a boy—he's on the stage now, and going to surprise us all some of these days. You'll like him. Come along and I'll introduce him to you; he's very anxious to know you.' And when Mark had followed him as he threaded his way across the room, he found himself hurriedly introduced to the man with the cold light eyes whom he had met at the Featherstones' on the day when he had recognised Mabel Langton's portrait. Mr. Fladgate had already bustled away again, and the two were left together in a corner of the room. Dolly's revelations of the terrorism this man had exercised over her had strengthened the prejudice and dislike Mark had felt on their first meeting; he felt angry and a little uncomfortable now, at being forced to come in contact with him, but there was no way of avoiding it just then, and Caffyn himself was perfectly at his ease.

'I think we have met before—at Grosvenor Place,' he began blandly; 'but I dare say you have forgotten.'

'No,' said Mark, 'I remember you very well; and besides,' he added, with a significance that he hoped would not be thrown away, 'I have been hearing a good deal about you lately from the Langtons—from Miss Langton, that is.'

'Ah!' said Caffyn; 'that would be flattering to most men, but when one has the bad luck, like myself, to displease such a very impulsive young lady as Miss Langton, the less she mentions you the better.'

'I may as well say,' returned Mark coldly, 'that, as to that particular affair in which you were concerned, whatever my opinions are, I formed them without assistance.'

'And you don't care to have them unsettled again by any plea for the defence? That's very natural. Well, with Miss Langton's remarks to guide me, I think I can guess what your own opinion of me is likely to be just now. And I'm going to ask you, as a mere matter of fair play, to hear my side of the question. You think that's very ridiculous, of course?'

'I think we can do no good by discussing it any farther,' said Mark; 'we had better let the matter drop.'

'But you see,' urged Caffyn, 'as it is, the matter has dropped—on me, and really I do think that you, who I understand were the means—of course from the best possible motives—of exposing me as a designing villain, might give me an opportunity of defending myself. I took the liberty of getting Fladgate to bring us together, expressly because I can't be comfortable while I know you have your present impressions of me. I don't expect to persuade Miss Langton to have a little charity—she's a woman; but I hoped you at least would give me a hearing.'

Mark felt some of his prejudice leaving him already; Caffyn had not the air of a man who had been detected in a course of secret tyranny. There was something flattering, too, in his evident wish to recover Mark's good opinion; he certainly ought to hear both sides before judging so harshly. Perhaps, after all, they had been making a little too much of this business. 'Well,' he said at last, 'I should be very glad if I could think things were not as bad as they seem. I will hear anything you would like to say about it.'

'Quite the high moral censor,' thought the other savagely. 'Confound his condescension!'

'I was sure you would give me a chance of putting myself right,' he said, 'but I can't do it now. They're going down to dinner; we will talk it over afterwards.'

At dinner conversation was lively and well sustained, though perhaps not quite so sparkling as might have been expected from such an assembly. As a rule, those who talked most and best were the men who still had their reputation to make, and many of the great men there seemed content to expose themselves to such brilliancy as there was around them, as if silently absorbing it for future reproduction, by some process analogous to the action of luminous paint.

Caffyn was placed at some distance from Mark, and as, after dinner, he was entreated to sit down to the piano, which stood in a corner of the room to which they had adjourned for cigars and coffee, it was some time before their conversation was resumed.

Caffyn was at his best as he sat there rippling out snatches of operatic morceaux, and turning round with a smile to know if they were recognised. His performance was not remarkable for accuracy, as he had never troubled himself to study music, or anything else, seriously, but it was effective enough with a non-critical audience; his voice, too, when he sang, though scarcely strong enough to fill a room of much larger size, was pleasant and not untrained, and it was some time before he was permitted to leave the music-stool.

He rattled off a rollicking hunting song, full of gaiety and verve, and followed it up with a little pathetic ballad, sung with an accent of real feeling (he could throw more emotion into his singing than his acting), while, although it was after dinner, the room was hushed until the last notes had died away, and when he rose at length with a laughing plea of exhaustion, he was instantly surrounded by a buzz of genuine gratitude. Mark heard all this, and the last remnants of his dislike and distrust vanished; it seemed impossible that this man, with the sympathetic voice, and the personal charm which was felt by most of those present, could be capable of finding pleasure in working on a child's terrors. So that when Caffyn, disengaging himself at length from the rest, made his way to where Mark was sitting, the latter felt this almost as a distinction, and made room for him with cordiality. Somebody was at the piano again, but as all around were talking, the most confidential conversations could be carried on in perfect security, and Caffyn, seating himself next to Mark, set himself to remove all prejudices.

He put his case very well, without obsequiousness or temper, appealing to Mark as a fellow man-of-the-world against a girl's rash judgment. 'You know,' he said, in the course of his arguments, 'I'm not really an incarnate fiend in private life. Miss Langton is quite convinced I am. I believe I saw her looking suspiciously at my boots the other day; but then she's a trifle hard on me. My worst fault is that I don't happen to understand children. I'd got into a way of saying extravagant things; you know the way one does talk rubbish to children; well, of joking in that sort of way with little What's-her-name. She always seemed to understand it well enough, and I should have thought she was old enough to see the simpler kind of joke, at all events. One day I chanced to chaff her about a stamp she took off some envelope. Well, I daresay I said something about stealing and prisons, all in fun, of course, never dreaming she would think any more about it. A fortnight afterwards, suddenly there's a tremendous hullabaloo. You began it. Oh, I know it was natural enough, but you did begin it. You see the child looking pale and seedy, and say at once, "something on her mind." Well, I don't know, and she might have been such a little idiot as to take a chance word au grand sérieux; it might have been something else on her mind; or she mightn't have had anything on her mind at all. Anyway, she tells you a long story about prisons, and how one Harold Caffyn had told her she would go there, and so on, and you, with that vivid imagination of yours, conjure up a tearful picture of a diabolical young man (me, you know) coldly gloating over the terrors of a poor little innocent ignorant child, eh? (Miss Dolly's nearly ten, and anything but backward for her age; but that's of no consequence.) Well, then you go and impart some of your generous indignation to Miss Langton; she takes it in a very aggravated form, and gives it to me. Upon my word, I think I've had rather hard lines!'

Mark really felt a little remorseful just then, but he made one more attempt to maintain his high ground. 'I don't know that I should have thought so much of the joke itself,' he said, 'but you carried it on so long; you saw her brooding over it and getting worse and worse, and yet you never said a word to undeceive the poor child!'

'Now, you know, with all respect to you, Ashburn,' said Caffyn, who was gradually losing all ceremony, 'that about seeing her brooding is rubbish—pure rubbish! I saw the child, I suppose, now and again; but I didn't notice her particularly, and if I had, I don't exactly know how to detect the signs of brooding. How do you tell it from indigestion? and how are you to guess what the brooding is about? I tell you I'd forgotten the whole thing. And that was what all your righteous wrath was based upon, was it? Well, it's very delightful, no doubt, to figure as a knight-errant, or a champion, and all that kind of thing—particularly when you make your own dragon—but when you come prancing down and spit some unlucky lizard, it's rather a cheap triumph. But there, I forgive you. You've made a little mistake which has played the very deuce with me at Kensington Park Gardens. It's too late to alter that now, and if I can only make you see that there has been a mistake, and I'm not one of the venomous sort of reptiles after all, why, I suppose I must be content with that!'

He succeeded in giving Mark an uneasy impression that he had made a fool of himself. He had quite lost the feeling of superiority under the tone of half-humorous, half-bitter remonstrance which Caffyn had chosen to take, and was chiefly anxious now to make the other forget his share in the matter. 'Perhaps I was too ready to put the worst construction on what I heard,' he said apologetically, 'but after what you've told me, why—'

'Well, we'll say no more about it,' said Caffyn; 'you understand me now, and that's all I cared about.' ('You may be a great genius, my friend,' he was thinking, 'but it's not so very difficult to get round you, after all!') 'Look here,' he continued, 'will you come and see me one of these days—it would be a great kindness to me. I've got rooms in Kremlin Road, Bayswater, No. 72.'

Mark changed countenance very slightly as he heard the address—it had been Holroyd's. There was nothing in that to alarm him, and yet he could not resist a superstitious terror at the coincidence. Caffyn noticed the effect directly. 'Do you know Kremlin Road?' he said.

Something made Mark anxious to explain the emotion he felt he had given way to. 'Yes,' he said, 'a—a very old friend of mine had lodgings at that very house. He was lost at sea, so when you mentioned the place I—'

'I see,' said Caffyn. 'Of course. Was your friend Vincent Holroyd, I wonder?'

'You knew him?' cried Mark; 'you!'

('Got the Railway Station effect that time!' thought Caffyn. 'I begin to believe my dear uncle touched a weak spot after all. If he has a secret, it's ten to one Holroyd knew it—knows it, by Jove!')

'Oh, yes, I knew poor old Holroyd,' he said; 'that's how I came to take his rooms. Sad thing, his going down like that, wasn't it? It must have been a great shock for you—I can see you haven't got over it even yet.'

'No,' stammered Mark, 'no—yes, I felt it a great deal. I—I didn't know you were a friend of his, too; did—did you know him well?'

'Very well; in fact I don't fancy he had any secrets from me.'

Like lightning the thought flashed across Mark's mind, what if Caffyn had been entrusted with Holroyd's literary projects? But he remembered the next moment that Holroyd had expressly said that he had never told a soul of his cherished work until that last evening in Rotten Row. Caffyn had lied, but with a purpose, and as the result confirmed his suspicions he changed the subject, and was amused at Mark's evident relief.

Towards the end of the evening Mr. Fladgate came up in his amiable way and laid his hand jocularly on Caffyn's shoulder. 'Let me give you a word of advice,' he said laughing; 'don't talk to Mr. Ashburn here about his book.'

'Shouldn't presume to,' said Caffyn. 'But do you come down so heavily on ignorant admiration, Ashburn, eh?'

'Oh, it isn't that,' said Mr. Fladgate; 'it's his confounded modesty. I shall be afraid to tell him when we think about bringing out another edition. I really believe he'd like never to hear of it again!'

Mark felt himself flush. 'Come,' he said, with a nervous laugh, 'I'm not so bad as all that!'

'Oh, you're beginning to stand fire better. But (it's such a good story you must let me tell it, Mr. Ashburn, particularly as it only does you credit). Well, he was so ashamed of having it known that he was the author of "Illusion," that he actually took the trouble to get the manuscript all copied out in a different hand! Thought he'd take me in that way, but he didn't. No, no, as you young fellows say, I "spotted" him directly; eh, Mr. Ashburn?'

'I'm afraid it's time for me to be off,' said Mark, dreading further revelations, and too nervous to see that they could do him no possible harm. But the fact was, Caffyn's presence filled him with a vague alarm which he could not shake off.

Good-natured Mr. Fladgate was afraid he had offended him. 'I do hope you weren't annoyed at my mentioning that about the manuscript?' he said, as he accompanied Mark to the door. 'It struck me as so curious, considering the success the book has had, that I really couldn't resist telling it.'

'No, no,' said Mark, 'it's all right; I didn't mind in the least. I—I'm not ashamed of it!'

'Why, of course not,' said his host; 'it will be something for your biographer to record, eh? You won't have another cigar to take you home? Well, good-night.'

'Good-night,' said Mark, and added some words of thanks for a pleasant evening.

Had he had such a pleasant evening? he asked himself, as he walked home alone in the warm night air. He had been well treated by everybody, and there had been men present whose attention was a distinction in itself, and yet he felt an uneasiness which he found it difficult to trace back to any particular cause. He decided at last that he was annoyed to find that the casual mention of Holroyd's name should still have power to discompose him—that was a weakness which he must set himself to overcome.

At the same time no one could possibly discover his secret; there was no harm done. And before he reached his lodgings, he decided that the evening had been pleasant enough.

CHAPTER XXII

STRIKING THE TRAIL

It was Sunday once more—a bright morning in June—and Caffyn was sitting over his late breakfast and the 'Observer' in his rooms at Bayswater. He was in a somewhat gloomy and despondent frame of mind, for nothing seemed to have gone well with him since his disastrous reception in Mabel's boudoir. His magnificent prospects in commerce had suddenly melted away into thin air, for his confiding friend and intending partner had very inconsiderately developed symptoms of a premature insanity, and was now 'under restraint.' He himself was in debt to a considerable extent; his father had firmly refused to increase what in his opinion was a handsome allowance; and Caffyn had been obliged to go to a theatrical agent with a view of returning to the boards, while no opening he thought it worth his while to accept had as yet presented itself.

Mabel had not relented in the least. He had met her once or twice at the Featherstones' and, although she had not treated him with any open coolness, he felt that henceforth there must be an impassable barrier between them. Now and then, even while she forced herself in public to listen to him, the invincible horror and repugnance she felt would be suddenly revealed by a chance look or intonation— and he saw it and writhed in secret. And yet he went everywhere that there was a possibility of meeting her, with a restless impulse of self-torture, while his hate grew more intense day by day.

And all this he owed to Mark Ashburn—a fact which Harold Caffyn was not the man to forget. He had been careful to cultivate him, had found out his address and paid him one or two visits, in which he had managed to increase the intimacy between them.

Mark was now entirely at his ease with him. His air of superiority had been finally dropped on the evening of Mr. Fladgate's dinner, and he seemed flattered by the assiduity with which Caffyn courted his society. Still, if he had a secret, it was his own still. Caffyn watched in vain for the look of sudden terror which he had once succeeded in surprising. At times he began to fear that it was some involuntary nervous contraction from which his own hopes had led him to infer the worst, for he was aware that countenances are not always to be depended upon; that a nervous temperament will sometimes betray all the signs of guilt from the mere consciousness that guilt is suspected. If that was the case here, he felt himself powerless. It is only in melodramas that a well-conducted person can be steeped in crime, and he did not see his way very clearly to accomplishing that difficult and dangerous feat with Mark Ashburn.

So he hated Mark more intensely at the thought that, after all, his past might be a blameless one. But even if this were not so, and he had a secret after all, it might be long enough before some fortunate chance gave Caffyn the necessary clue to it. Well, he would wait and watch as patiently as he might till then, and however long the opportunity might be in coming, when it came at last it should not find him too indifferent or reluctant to make use of it.

While he thought out his position somewhat to this effect, his landlady appeared to clear away the breakfast things; she was a landlady of the better class, a motherly old soul who prided herself upon making her lodgers comfortable, and had higher views than many of her kind on the subjects of cookery and attendance. She had come to entertain a great respect for Caffyn, although at first, when she had discovered that he was 'one of them play-actors,' she had not been able to refrain from misgivings. Her notions of actors were chiefly drawn from the ramping and roaring performers at minor theatres, and the seedy blue-chinned individuals she had observed hanging about their stage-doors; and the modern comedian was altogether beyond her experience.

So when she found that her new lodger was 'quite the gentleman, and that partickler about his linen, and always civil and pleasant-spoken, and going about as neat as a new pin, and yet with a way about him as you could see he wouldn't stand no nonsense,' her prejudices were entirely conquered.

'Good morning, Mr. Caffyn, sir,' she began; 'I come up to clear away your breakfast, if you're quite done. Sarah Ann she's gone to chapel, which she's a Primitive Methodist, she says, though she can't never tell me so much as the text when she come back, and I tell her, "My good gal," I ses to her, "what do you go to chapel for?" and it's my belief that as often as not she don't go near it. But there, Mr. Caffyn, if a gal does her work about the 'ouse of a week, as I will say for Sarah Ann—'

Caffyn groaned. Good Mrs. Binney had a way of coming in to discourse on things in general, and it was always extremely difficult to get rid of her. She did not run down on this occasion until after an exhaustive catalogue, à la Mrs. Lirriper, of the manners and customs of a whole dynasty of maids-of-all-work, when she began to clear his breakfast-table. He was congratulating himself on her final departure, when she returned with a bundle of papers in her hand. 'I've been meanin' to speak to you about these, this ever such a time,' she said. 'Binney, he said as I'd better, seeing as you've got his very rooms, and me not liking to burn 'em, and the maids that careless about papers and that, and not a line from him since he left.'

'It would certainly be better not to burn the rooms, unless they're insured, Mrs. Binney, and I should be inclined to prefer their not being burnt while I'm in them, unless you make a point of it,' said Caffyn mildly.

'Lor, Mr. Caffyn, who was talking of burnin' rooms? You do talk so ridiklus. It's these loose papers of Mr. 'Olroyd's as I came to speak to you about, you bein' a friend of his, and they lyin' a burden on my mind for many a day, and litterin' up all the place, and so afraid I am as Sarah Ann'll take and light the fire with 'em one of these mornings, and who knows whether they're not of value, and if so what should I say if he came and asked me for 'em back again?'

'Well, he won't do that, Mrs. Binney, if it's true that he was drowned in the "Mangalore," will he?'

'Drowned! and me never to hear it till this day. It's quite took me aback. Poor dear gentleman, what an end for him—to go out all that way only to be drowned! I do seem to be told of nothing but deaths and dying this morning, for Binney's just 'eard that poor old Mr. Tapling, at No. 5 opposite, was took off at last quite sudden late last night, and he'd had a dropsy for years, and swell up he would into all manner o' shapes as I've seen him doin' of it myself!'

'Well, I'll look over the papers for you, Mrs. Binney,' interrupted Caffyn. 'I don't suppose there's anything of much importance, but I can tell you what ought to be kept.' He would have solved her difficulties by advising her to burn the whole of them, but for some vague idea that he might be able to discover something amongst all these documents which would throw some light upon Holroyd's relations with Mark.

So when Mrs. Binney was at last prevailed on to leave him in peace, he sat down with the sheaf of miscellaneous papers she had left him, and began to examine them without much hope of discovering anything to the purpose.

They seemed to be the accumulations of some years. There were rough drafts of Latin and Greek verses, outlines for essays, and hasty jottings of University and Temple lectures—memorials of Holroyd's undergraduate and law-student days. Then came notes scribbled down in court with a blunt corroded quill on borrowed scraps of paper, and elaborate analyses of leading cases and Acts of Parliament, which belonged to the period of zeal which had followed his call to the Bar.

He turned all these over carelessly enough, until he came upon some sheets fastened together with a metal clip. 'This does not look like law,' he said half aloud. '"Glamour—romance by Vincent Beauchamp." Beauchamp was his second name, I think. So he wrote romances, did he, poor devil! This looks like the scaffolding for one, anyway; let's have a look at it. List of characters: Beaumelle Marston; I've come across that name somewhere lately, I know; Lieutenant-Colonel Duncombe; why, I know that gentleman, too! Was this ever published? Here's the argument.' He read and re-read it carefully, and then went to a bookshelf and took down a book with the Grosvenor Library label; it was a copy of 'Illusion,' by Cyril Ernstone.

With that by his side he turned over the rest of Holroyd's papers, and found more traces of some projected literary work; skeleton scenes, headings for chapters, and even a few of the opening pages, with some marginal alterations in red ink, all of which he eagerly compared with the printed work before him.

Then he rose and paced excitedly up and down his room. 'Is this his secret?' he thought. 'If I could only be sure of it! It seems too good to be true ... they might have collaborated, or the other might have made him a present of a plot, or even borrowed some notions from him.... And yet there are some things that look uncommonly suspicious. Why should he look so odd at the mere mention of Holroyd's name? Why did he get the manuscript recopied? Was it modesty—or something else? And why does one name only appear on the title-page, and our dear friend take all the credit to himself? There's something fishy about it all, and I mean to get at it. Job was perfectly correct. It is rash for an enemy to put his name to a book—especially some other fellow's book. Mr. Mark Ashburn and I must have a little private conversation together, in which I shall see how much I remember of the action of the common pump.'

He sat down and wrote a genial little note, asking Mark, if he had no better engagement, to come round and dine quietly with him at the house in Kremlin Road that evening, gave it to his landlord with directions to take a cab to Mark's rooms, and if he could, bring back an answer, after which he waited patiently for his messenger's return.

Binney returned in the course of an hour or so, having found Mark in, and brought a note which Caffyn tore open impatiently. 'I have a friend coming to dinner to-night, Mr. Binney,' he said, turning round with his pleasant smile when he had read the answer. 'It's Sunday, I know, but Mrs. Binney won't mind for once, and tell her she must do her very best; I want to give my friend a little surprise.'

CHAPTER XXIII

PIANO PRACTICE

Caffyn was conscious of a certain excitement that Sunday evening as he waited for Mark Ashburn's arrival. He felt that he might be standing on the threshold of a chamber containing the secret of the other's life—the key of which that very evening might deliver into his hands. He was too cautious to jump at hasty conclusions; he wished before deciding upon any plan of action to be practically certain of his facts; a little skilful manipulation, however, would most probably settle the question one way or the other, and if the result verified his suspicions he thought he would know how to make use of his advantage. There is a passage in the 'Autocrat of the Breakfast Table' where the author, in talking of the key to the side-door by which every person's feelings may be entered, goes on to say, 'If nature or accident has put one of these keys into the hands of a person who has the torturing instinct, I can only solemnly pronounce the words that justice utters over its doomed victims, "The Lord have mercy on your soul!"' There, it is true, the key in question unlocks the delicate instrument of the nervous system, and not necessarily a Bluebeard's chamber of guilt; but where the latter is also the case to some extent the remark by no means loses in significance, and if any man had the torturing instinct to perfection, Caffyn might be said to be that individual. There was nothing he would enjoy more than practising upon a human piano and putting it hopelessly out of tune; but pleasant as this was, he felt he might have to exercise some self-denial here, at all events for the present, lest his instrument should become restive and escape before he had quite made up his mind what air he could best play upon it.

In the meantime Mark was preparing to keep the appointment in the pleasantest and most unsuspecting frame of mind. After answering Caffyn's note he had met the Langtons as they came out of church and returned with them to lunch. Dolly was herself again now, her haunting fears forgotten with the happy ease of childhood, and Mabel had made Mark feel something of the gratitude she felt to him for his share in bringing this about. He had gone on to one or two other houses, and had been kindly received everywhere, and now he was looking forward to a quiet little dinner with the full expectation of a worthy finish to a pleasant day. Even when he mounted the stairs of the house which had been once familiar to him, and stood in Holroyd's old rooms, he was scarcely affected by any unpleasant associations. For one thing, he was beginning to have his conscience tolerably well in hand; for another, the interior of the rooms was completely transformed since he had seen them last.

Then they were simply the furnished apartments of a man who cared but little for his personal well-being; now, when he passed round the handsome Japanese screen by the door, he saw an interior marked by a studied elegance and luxury. The common lodging-house fireplace was concealed by an elaborate oak over-mantel, with brass plaques and blue china; the walls were covered with a delicate blue-green paper and hung with expensive etchings and autotype drawings of an æsthetically erotic character; small tables and deep luxurious chairs were scattered about, and near the screen stood a piano and a low stand with peacock's feathers arranged in a pale blue crackle jar. In spite of the pipes and riding-whips on the racks, the place was more like a woman's boudoir than a man's room, and there were traces in its arrangements of an eye to effect which gave it the air of a well-staged scene in a modern comedy.

It looked very attractive, softly lit as it was by shaded candles in sconces and a porcelain lamp with a crimson shade, which was placed on the small oval table near the fern-filled fireplace; and as Mark placed himself in a low steamer chair and waited for his host to make his appearance, he felt as if he was going to enjoy himself.

'I shall have my rooms done up something in this way,' he thought, 'when my book comes out.' The blinds were half drawn and the windows opened wide to the sultry air, and while he waited he could hear the bells from neighbouring steeples calling in every tone, from harsh command to persuasive invitation, to the evening services.

Presently Caffyn lounged in through the hangings which protected his bedroom door. 'Sorry you found me unready,' he said; 'I got in late from the club somehow, but they'll bring us up some dinner presently. Looking at that thing, eh?' he asked, as he saw Mark's eye rest on a small high-heeled satin slipper in a glass case which stood on a bracket near him. 'That was Kitty Bessborough's once—you remember Kitty Bessborough, of course? She gave it to me just before she went out on that American tour, and got killed in some big railway smash somewhere, poor little woman! I'll tell you some day how she came to make me a present of it. Here's Binney with the soup now.'

Mrs. Binney sent up a perfect dinner, at which her husband assisted in a swallow-tailed coat and white tie, a concession he would not have made for every lodger, and Caffyn played the host to perfection, though with every course he asked himself inwardly, 'Shall I open fire on him yet?' and still he delayed.

At last he judged that his time had come; Binney had brought up coffee and left them alone. 'You sit down there and make yourself at home,' said Caffyn genially, thrusting Mark down into a big saddle-bag arm-chair ('where I can see your confounded face,' he added inwardly). 'Try one of these cigars—they're not bad; and now we can talk comfortably. I tell you what I want to talk about,' he said presently, and a queer smile flitted across his face; 'I want to talk about that book of yours. Oh, I know you want to fight shy of it, but I don't care. It isn't often I have a celebrated author to dine with me, and if you didn't wish to hear it talked about you shouldn't have written it, you know. I want you to tell me a few facts I can retail to people on the best authority, don't you know; so you must just make up your mind to conquer that modesty of yours for once, old fellow, and gratify my impertinent curiosity.'

Mark was feeling so much at ease with himself and Caffyn that even this proposition was not very terrible to him just then. 'All right,' he said lazily; 'what do you want to know first?'

'That's right. Well, first, I must tell you I've read the book. I'd like to say how much I was struck by it if I might.'

'I'm very glad you liked it,' said Mark.

'Like it?' echoed Caffyn; 'my dear fellow, I haven't been so moved by anything for years. The thought you've crammed into that book, the learning, the passion and feeling of the thing! I envy you for being able to feel you have produced it all.' ('That ought to fetch him,' he thought.)

'Oh, as for that,' said Mark with a shrug, and left his remark unfinished, but without, as the other noticed, betraying any particular discomposure.

'Do you remember, now,' pursued Caffyn, 'how the central idea first occurred to you?'

But here again he drew a blank, for Mark had long ago found it expedient to concoct a circumstantial account of how and when the central idea had first occurred to him.

'Well, I'll tell you,' he said. 'It shows how oddly these things are brought about. I was walking down Palace Gardens one afternoon....' and he told the history of the conception of 'Illusion' in his best manner, until Caffyn raged internally.

'You brazen humbug!' he thought; 'to sit there and tell that string of lies to me!' When it was finished he remarked, 'Well, that's very interesting; and I have your permission to tell that again, eh?'

'Certainly, my dear fellow,' said Mark, with a wave of his hand. His cigar was a really excellent one, and he thought he would try another presently.

('We must try him again,' thought Caffyn; 'he's deeper than I gave him credit for being.')

'I'll tell you an odd criticism I heard the other day. I was talking to little Mrs. Bismuth—you know Mrs. Bismuth by name? Some fellow has just taken the "Charivari" for her. Well, she goes in for letters a little as well as the drama, reads no end of light literature since she gave up tights for drawing-room comedy, and she would have it that she seemed to recognise two distinct styles in the book, as if two pens had been at work on it.'

('Now I may find out if that really was the case after all,' he was thinking.) 'I thought you'd be amused with that,' he added, after a pause. Mark really did seem amused; he laughed a little.

'Mrs. Bismuth is a charming actress,' he said, 'but she'd better read either a little more or a little less light literature before she goes in for tracing differences in style. You can tell her, with my compliments, that a good many pens were at work on it, but only one brain. Where is it your matches live?'

'I can't draw him,' thought Caffyn. 'What an actor the fellow is! And yet, if it was all aboveboard, he wouldn't have said that! and I've got Holroyd's handwriting, which is pretty strong evidence against him. But I want more, and I'll have it.'

He strolled up to the mantelpiece to light a cigarette, for which purpose he removed the shade from one of the candles, throwing a stronger light on his friend's face, and then, pausing with the cigarette still unlighted between his fingers, he asked suddenly: 'By the way, Fladgate said some other fellow wrote the book for you the other day!' That shot at least told; every vestige of colour left Mark's face, he half rose from his chair, and then sat down again as he retorted sharply: 'Fladgate said that! What the devil are you talking about...? What fellow?'

'Why, you were there when he said it. Some amanuensis you gave the manuscript to.'

The colour came back in rather an increased quantity to Mark's cheeks. What a nervous fool he was! 'Oh, ah—that fellow!' he said; 'I remember now. Yes, I was absurdly anxious to remain unknown, you see, in those days, and—and I rather wanted to put something in the way of a poor fellow who got his living by copying manuscripts; and so, you see—'

'I see,' said Caffyn. 'What was his name?'

'His name?' repeated Mark, who had not expected this and had no name ready for such immediate use. 'Let me see; I almost forget. It began with a B I know; Brown—Brune—something like that—I really don't recollect just now. But the fact is,' he added with a desperate recourse to detail, 'the first time I saw the beggar he looked so hard up, dressed in—' ('Buckram!' thought Caffyn, but he said nothing)—'in rags, you know, that I felt it would be quite a charity to employ him.'

'So it is,' agreed Caffyn. 'Did he write a good hand? I might be able to give him some work myself in copying out parts.'

'Oh, he'd be useless for that!' put in Mark with some alarm; 'he wrote a wretched hand.'

'Well, but in the cause of charity, you know,' rejoined Caffyn, with inward delight. 'Hang it, Ashburn, why shouldn't I do an unselfish thing as well as you? What's the fellow's address?'

'He—he's emigrated,' said Mark; 'you'd find it rather difficult to come across him now.'

'Should I?' Caffyn returned; 'well, I daresay I should.'

And Mark rose and went to one of the windows for some air. He remained there for a short time looking idly down the darkening street. A chapel opposite was just discharging its congregation, and he found entertainment in watching the long lighted ground-glass windows, as a string of grotesque silhouettes filed slowly across them, like a shadow pantomime turned serious.

When he was tired of that and turned away from the blue-grey dusk, the luxurious comfort of the room struck him afresh. 'You've made yourself uncommonly comfortable here,' he said appreciatively, as he settled down again in his velvet-pile chair.

'Well, I flatter myself I've improved the look of the place since you saw it last. Poor Holroyd, you see, never cared to go in for this kind of thing. Queer reserved fellow, wasn't he?'

'Very,' said Mark; and then, with the perverse impulse which drives us to test dangerous ice, he added: 'Didn't you say, though, the other evening that he had no secrets from you?' ('Trying to pump me, are you?' thought the other; 'but you don't!') 'Did I?' he answered, 'sometimes I fancy, now and then, that I knew less of him than I thought I did. For instance, he was very busy for a long time before he left England over something or other, but he never told me what it was. I used to catch him writing notes and making extracts and so on.... You were a great friend of his, Ashburn, weren't you? Do you happen to know whether he was engaged on some work which would account for that, now? Did he ever mention to you that he was writing a book, for instance?'

'Never,' said Mark; 'did he—did he hint that to you?'

'Never got a word out of him; but I daresay you, who knew him best, will laugh when I tell you this, I always had my suspicions that he was writing a novel.'

'A novel?' echoed Mark; 'Holroyd! Excuse me, my dear fellow, I really can't help laughing—it does seem such a comic idea.'

And he laughed boisterously, overcome by the humour of the notion, until Caffyn said: 'Well, I didn't know him as well as you did, I suppose, but I shouldn't have thought it was so devilish funny as all that!' For Caffyn was a little irritated that the other should believe him to be duped by all this, and that he could not venture as yet to undeceive him. It made him viciously inclined to jerk the string harder yet, and watch Mark's contortions.

'He wasn't that sort of man,' said Mark, when he had had his laugh out; 'poor dear old fellow, he'd have been as amused at the idea as I am.'

'But this success of yours would have pleased him, wouldn't it?' said Caffyn.

For a moment Mark was cut as deeply by this as the speaker intended; he could give no other answer than a sigh, which was perfectly genuine. Caffyn affected to take this as an expression of incredulity. 'Surely you don't doubt that!' he said; 'why, Holroyd would have been as glad as if he had written the book himself. If he could come back to us again, you would see that I am right. What a meeting it would be, if one could only bring it about!'

'It's no use talking like that,' said Mark rather sharply. 'Holroyd's dead, poor fellow, at the bottom of the Indian Ocean somewhere. We shall never meet again.'

'But,' said Caffyn, with his eyes greedily watching Mark's face, 'even these things happen sometimes; he may come back to congratulate you still.'

'How do you mean? He's drowned, I tell you ... the dead never come back!'

'The dead don't,' returned Caffyn significantly.

'Do you—you don't mean to tell me he's alive!'

'If I were to say yes?' said Caffyn, 'I wonder how you would take it.'

If he had any doubts still remaining, the manner in which Mark received these words removed them. He fell back in his seat with a gasp and turned a ghastly lead colour; then, with an evident effort, he leaned forward again, clutching the arms of the chair, and his voice was hoarse and choked when he was able to make use of it. 'You have heard something,' he said. 'What is it? Why can't you tell it? Out with it, man! For God's sake, don't—don't play with me like this!'

Caffyn felt a wild exultation he had the greatest difficulty in repressing. He could not resist enjoying Mark's evident agony a little longer. 'Don't excite yourself, my dear fellow,' he said calmly. 'I oughtn't to have said anything about it.'

'I'm not excited,' said Mark; 'see—I'm quite cool ... tell me—all you know. He—he's alive then ... you have heard from him? I—I can bear it.'

'No, no,' said Caffyn; 'you're deceiving yourself. You mustn't let yourself hope, Ashburn. I have never heard from him from that day to this. You know yourself that he was not in any of the boats; there's no real chance of his having survived.'

For it was not his policy to alarm Mark too far, and least of all to show his hand so early. His experiment had been successful; he now knew all he wanted, and was satisfied with that. Mark's face relaxed into an expression of supreme relief; then it became suspicious again as he asked, almost in a whisper, 'I thought that—but then, why did you say all that about the dead—about coming back?'

'You mustn't be angry if I tell you. I didn't know you cared so much about him, or I wouldn't have done it. You know what some literary fellow—is it Tennyson?—says somewhere about our showing a precious cold shoulder to the dead if they were injudicious enough to turn up again; those aren't the exact words, but that's the idea. Well, I was thinking whether, if a fellow like poor Holroyd were to come back now, he'd find anyone to care a pin about him, and, as you were his closest friend, I thought I'd try how you took it. It was thoughtless, I know. I never dreamed it would affect you in this way; you're as white as chalk still—it's quite knocked you over. I'm really very sorry!'

'It was not a friendly thing to do,' said Mark, recovering himself. 'It was not kind, when one has known a man so long, and believed him dead, and then to be made to believe that he is still alive, it—it—. You can't wonder if I look rather shaken.'

'I don't,' said Caffyn; 'I quite understand. He is not quite forgotten after all, then? He still has a faithful friend in you to remember him; and he's been dead six months? How many of us can hope for that? You must have been very fond of him.'

'Very,' said Mark, with a sad self-loathing as he spoke the lie. 'I shall never see anyone like him—never!'

('How well he does it, after all!' thought Caffyn. 'I shall have plenty of sport with him.') 'Would it give you any comfort to talk about him now and then,' he suggested, 'with one who knew him, too, though not as well perhaps as you did?'

'Thanks!' said Mark, 'I think it would some day, but not yet. I don't feel quite up to it at present.'

'Well,' said the other, with a wholly private grin, 'I won't distress you by talking of him till you introduce the subject; and you quite forgive me for saying what I did, don't you?'

'Quite,' said Mark. 'And now I think I'll say good-night!'

The horror of those few moments in which he had seen detection staring him in the face still clung to him as he walked back to his lodgings. He cursed his folly in ever having exposed himself to such tremendous risks, until he remembered that, after all, his situation remained the same. He had merely been frightened with false fire. If he had not been very sure that the dead would never rise to denounce him, he would not have done what he had done. How could Vincent Holroyd have escaped? Still, it was an ugly thought, and it followed him to his pillow that night and gave him fearful dreams. He was in a large gathering, and Mabel was there, too; he could see her at the other end of an immense hall, and through the crowd Holroyd was slowly, steadily making his way to her side, and Mark knew his object; it was to denounce him. If he could only reach him first, he felt that somehow he could prevent him from attaining his end, and he made frantic efforts to do so; but always the crowd hedged him in and blocked his way with a stupid impassibility, and he struggled madly, but all in vain. Holroyd drew nearer and nearer Mabel, with that stern set purpose in his face, while Mark himself was powerless to move or speak. And so the dream dragged itself on all through the night.

He had some thoughts, on waking, of setting his fears to rest for ever by making some further inquiries, but when he read once more the various accounts he had preserved of the shipwreck, he convinced himself willingly enough that nothing of the kind was necessary. He could dismiss the matter from his mind once for all, and by breakfast-time he was himself again.

Caffyn, now that his wildest hopes of revenge were realised, and he saw himself in a position to make terrible reprisals for the injury Mark Ashburn had done him, revelled in a delicious sense of power, the only drawback to his complete enjoyment of the situation being his uncertainty as to the precise way of turning his knowledge to the best account.

Should he turn upon Mark suddenly with the intimation that he had found him out, without mentioning as yet that Holroyd was in the land of the living? There would be exquisite pleasure in that, and what a field for the utmost ingenuity of malice in constant reminders of the hold he possessed, in veiled threats, and vague mocking promises of secrecy! Could any enemy desire a more poignant retribution? He longed to do all this, and no one could have done it better; but he was habitually inclined to mistrust his first impulses, and he feared lest his victim might grow weary of writhing; he might be driven to despair, to premature confession, flight—suicide, perhaps. He was just the man to die by his own hand

and leave a letter cursing him as his torturer, to be read at the inquest and get into all the papers. No, he would not go too far; for the present he decided to leave Mark in happy ignorance of the ruin tottering above him. He would wait until he was even more prosperous, more celebrated, before taking any decisive steps. There was little fear that he would see his revenge some day, and meanwhile he must be content with such satisfaction as he could enjoy in secret.

'I must put up with the fellow a little longer,' he thought. 'We will go on mourning our dear lost friend together until I can arrange a meeting somehow. A telegram or letter to the Ceylon plantation will fetch him at any time, and I don't care about doing my charming Mabel such a good turn as bringing him back to her just yet. I wonder how my worthy plagiarist is feeling after last night. I think I will go round and have a look at him.'

CHAPTER XXIV

A MEETING IN GERMANY

The summer went by, and Mark's anticipations of happiness were as nearly borne out as such anticipations ever are. He and Mabel met constantly. He saw her in the Row with her father and Dolly— and sometimes had the bliss of exchanging a few words across the railings—at dances and tennis-parties, and in most of the less exclusive events of the season, while every interview left him more deeply infatuated. She seemed always glad to see and talk with him, allowing herself to express a decided interest in his doings, and never once throwing on him the burden of a conversational deadlift in the manner with which a girl knows how to discourage all but the dullest of bores. Now and then, indeed, when Mark's conversation showed symptoms of the occasional inanity common to most men who talk much, she did not spare him; but this was due to a jealous anxiety on her part that he should keep up to his own standard, and if she had not liked him she would not have taken the trouble. He took her light shafts so patiently and good-humouredly, too, that he was generally seized by a contrition which expressed itself in renewed graciousness. Already she had come to notice his arrival on lawns or in drawing-rooms, and caught herself remembering his looks and words after their meeting.

He was still busy with 'Sweet Bells Jangled,' for he had now decided to make his coup with that, but in other respects he was unproductive. He had begun several little things in pursuance of his engagements, but somehow he did not get on with them, and had to lay them aside until the intellectual thaw he expected. Pecuniarily his position was much improved; his uncle had kept his word, and put an allowance at his disposal which made him tolerably easy about his future. He removed to more fashionable quarters in South Audley Street, and led the easy existence there he had long coveted. Still Mr. Lightowler was an unpleasantly constant bluebottle in his ointment. He came up regularly from Chigbourne to inspect him, generally with literary advice and the latest scandal about his detested neighbour, which he thought might be 'worked up into something.' He had discovered the Row as an afternoon lounge where his nephew ought to show himself 'among the swells,' and he insisted, in spite of all Mark's attempts at evasion, in walking him about there. Mark was not perhaps exactly ashamed of the man whose favours he was accepting, at least he did not own as much even to himself, but there were times when, as he met the surprised glances of people he knew slightly, he could have wished that his loud-voiced and unpresentable relative had not got quite such a tight hold of his arm.

At a hint from Trixie he had tendered the olive-branch to his family, which they accepted rather as if it had been something he had asked them to hold for him, and without the slightest approach to anything like a scene. Trixie had, of course, been in communication with him from the first, and kept her satisfaction to herself; Mr. Ashburn was too timid, and his wife too majestic, to betray emotion, while the other two were slightly disappointed. The virtuous members of a family are not always best pleased to see the prodigal at any time, and it is particularly disconcerting to find that the supposed outcast has been living on veal instead of husks during his absence, and associating rather with lions than swine. Mark was not offended at his reception, however, he felt himself independent now; but his easy temper made him anxious to be at peace with them, and if they were not exactly effusive, they made no further pretence of disapproval, and the reconciliation was perfectly genuine as far as it went.

'I am going to see you to the gate, Mark,' Trixie announced, as he rose to go. It was not a long or a perilous journey, but she had an object in accompanying him down the little flagged path. 'I've got something to tell you,' she said, as they stood by the iron gate in the hot August night. 'I wish I knew how to begin.... Mark—how would you like a—a new brother, because I'm going to give you one?'

'Thanks very much, Trixie,' said Mark, 'but I think I can get along without another of them.'

'Ah, but Jack would be a nice one,' said Trixie.

Mark remembered then that he had noticed a decided improvement in her dress and appearance. 'And who is this Jack whom you're so disinterestedly going to make me a present of?' he asked.

'Jack is one of the masters at the Art School,' said Trixie; 'he's awfully handsome—not in your style, but fair, with a longer moustache, and he's too clever almost to live. He had one picture in the Grosvenor this year, in the little room, down by the bottom somewhere, but he hasn't sold it. And when I first went to the School all the girls declared he came round to me twice as much as he did to them, and they made themselves perfectly horrid about it; so I had to ask him not to come so often, and he didn't—for a time. Then one day he asked me if I would rather he never came to me at all, and—and I couldn't say yes, and so somehow we got engaged. Ma's furious about it, and so is Martha; but then, ma has never seen Jack—'

'And Martha has? I see!' put in Mark.

'Jack knows a lot about literature; he admires "Illusion" immensely, Mark,' added Trixie, thinking in her innocence that this would enlist his sympathy at once. 'He wants to know you dreadfully.'

'Well, Trixie,' said Mark paternally, 'you must bring him to see me. We mustn't have you doing anything imprudent, you know. Let me see what I think of him. I hope he's a good fellow?'

'Oh, he is,' said Trixie; 'if you could only see some of his sketches!'

A day or two later, Mark had an opportunity of meeting his intending brother-in-law, of whom he found no particular reason to disapprove, though he secretly thought him a slightly commonplace young man, and too inclined to be familiar with himself; and shortly after he started for the Black Forest, whither Caffyn had prevailed upon him to be his companion. He thought it would be amusing and serve to keep his vengeance alive to have his intended victim always at hand, but the result did not quite come up to his hopes. Mark had so lulled his fears to rest that the most artfully planned introduction of Holroyd's name failed to disturb him. He thought chiefly during their wanderings of Mabel, and her smile and words at parting, and in this occupation he was so pleasantly absorbed that it was impossible to rouse him by any means short of the rudest awakening. And by-and-by a curious change took place in Caffyn's feelings towards him; in spite of himself the virulence of his hatred began to abate. Time and change of scene were proving more powerful than he had anticipated; away from Mabel, his hatred, even of her, flagged more and more with every day, and he was disarmed as against Mark by the evident pleasure the latter took in his society, for the most objectionable persons become more bearable when we discover that they have a high opinion of us—it is such a redeeming touch in their nature. And besides, with all the reason Caffyn had for cherishing a grudge against Mark, somehow, as they became more intimate, he slid gradually into a half-contemptuous and half-affectionate tolerance. He began to think that he would find satisfaction in standing by and letting events work themselves out; he would let this poor fellow enjoy his fool's paradise as long as might be. No doubt, the luxury of secretively enjoying the situation had a great deal to do with this generosity of his, but the fact remains that, for some reason, he was passing from an enemy to a neutral, and might on occasion even become an ally, if nothing occurred to fan his hatred to flame in the meanwhile.

Towards the end of their tour, they arrived at Triberg late one Saturday evening, and on the Sunday, Caffyn, having risen late and finding that Mark had breakfasted and gone out alone, was climbing the path by the waterfall, when, on one of the bridges which span the cascade, he saw a girl's figure leaning listlessly over the rough rail. It was Gilda Featherstone, and he thought he could detect an additional tinge in her cheeks and a light in her eyes as he came towards her. Her father and mother were in one of the shelters above, and Mrs. Featherstone's greeting when she recognised him was the reverse of cordial. This young man might not have followed them there, but it looked extremely like it, and if she could not order him out of the Black Forest as if she had taken it for the summer, she would at least give him no encouragement to stay.

Unfortunately, her husband behaved with an irritating effusiveness; he liked Caffyn, and besides, had not seen an Englishman to talk to familiarly for some days. They were going home next day, he had better come with them. Well, if he could not do that (Mrs. Featherstone having interposed icily, 'Mr. Caffyn has just told you, Robert, that he is with a friend!') he must come to them the moment he returned to England, and they would give him some shooting. Mrs. Featherstone had to hear this invitation and Caffyn's instant acceptance of it with what philosophy she might. It was useless to remonstrate with her husband on his blindness, he had democratic views which might even bear a practical test, and she could only trust to chance and her mother-wit to prevent any calamity; but she was unusually silent as they walked down the winding path back to the hotel where they were all staying.

There was a midday table d'hôte, where the proprietor, a most imposing and almost pontifical personage, officiated as at a religious ceremonial, solemnly ladling out the soup to devout waiters as if he were blessing each portion, after which he stood by and contented himself with lending his countenance (at a rather high rate of interest) to the meal. Caffyn's chair was placed next to Gilda's, and they kept up a continuous flow of conversation. Mark saw them both looking at him at one time, and wondered at the sudden change in Caffyn's face, which (unless his fancy misled him) had a frown on it that was almost threatening. But he was not allowed much time to speculate on the causes, for Mrs. Featherstone (perhaps to emphasise her disapproval of his companion) distinguished Mark by engrossing his entire attention.

That afternoon Mark was sitting outside the hotel, taking his coffee at one of the little round iron tables, by the inevitable trio of scrubby orange trees in green tubs, when Caffyn, whom he had not seen since leaving the table, came up and sat down beside him without a word.

'Have you come out for some coffee?' asked Mark.

'No,' said Caffyn shortly, 'I came out to have a few words with you.'

The Featherstones had all gone off to attend the English afternoon service; there was no one very near them, though in the one broad street there was a certain gentle animation, of townspeople promenading up and down in Sunday array, spectacled young officers, with slender waists and neat uniforms, swaggering about; a portly and gorgeous crier in a green uniform, ringing his bell over a departed purse; little old walnut-faced women, sitting patiently by their fruitstalls, and a band of local firemen in very baggy tunics, the smallest men of whom had crept inside the biggest silver helmets, preparing to execute a selection of airs.

'You look uncommonly serious about something, old fellow,' said Mark, laughing lightly; 'what is it?'

'This,' said Caffyn, with a smouldering fire in his voice and eyes; 'I've just been told that you—you are engaged to Mabel Langton. Is it true?'

Mark was not displeased. This coupling of Mabel's name with his, even though by a mere rumour, sent a delicious thrill through him; it seemed to bring his sweetest hopes nearer realisation. The gay little street vanished for an instant, and he was holding Mabel's hand in the violet-scented drawing-room, but he came to himself almost directly with a start.

'Who told you that?' he said, flushing slightly.

'Never mind who told me. Is it true? I—I warn you not to trifle with me.'

'What on earth is the matter with you?' said Mark. 'No, it's not true; as far as I know at present, there is not the remotest possibility of such a thing coming to pass.'

'But you would make it possible if you could, eh?' asked Caffyn.

'I don't want to hurt your feelings, Caffyn,' said Mark, 'but really you're going a little too far. And even if I had been engaged to Miss Langton (which is very far from the case), I don't exactly see what right you have, after—under the circumstances, you know—to go in for the fire-eating business.'

'You mean I'm out of the running, whoever wins?' said Caffyn. 'I daresay you're right; I'm not aware that I ever entered for the prize. But never mind that. She has taken a dislike to me, but I may be allowed to feel an interest in her still, I suppose. I should like to see her happy, and if you could tell me that you were the man, why then—'

'Well?' said Mark, as the other paused with a curious smile.

'Why, then I should feel at ease about her, don't you know,' he said gently.

'I only wish I could ease your mind for you in that way,' said Mark, 'but it's too soon for that yet.'

'You do mean to ask her, then?' said Caffyn, with his eyes on the little brown-and-yellow imperial postwagen which had just rattled up to the hotel, and the driver of which, in his very unbecoming glazed billycock hat with the featherbrush plume, was then cumbrously descending from his box. Mark had not meant to confide in Caffyn at all; he had only known him a short time, and, although their intimacy had grown so rapidly, with a little more reflection he might have shrunk from talking of Mabel to one whom, rightly or wrongly, she held in abhorrence. But then Caffyn was so sympathetic, so subdued; the temptation to talk of his love to somebody was so strong, that he did not try to resist it.

'Yes, I do,' he said, and his dark eyes were soft and dreamy as he spoke, 'some day ... if I dare. And if she says what I hope she will say, I shall come to you, old fellow, for congratulations.'

He looked round, but Caffyn had started up abruptly and he was alone. 'Very odd of him,' thought Mark, until he saw him meeting the Featherstones on their way back from the service.

Some minutes later, as Gilda and Caffyn were in a corner of the exhibition of carved work at the lower end of the town, she took advantage of the blaring of two big orchestral Black Forest organs, each performing a different overture, and of the innumerable cuckoo cries from the serried rows of clocks on the walls, to go back to their conversation at the table d'hôte. 'Have you asked him yet? Mabel is not engaged to him after all?' (her face fell as she gathered this). 'It is all a mistake, then? Of course it was a great relief to you to hear that?'

'Was it?' was Caffyn's rejoinder; 'why?'

'Why? Because—oh, of course you would be relieved to hear it!' and Gilda made a little attempt to laugh.

'Shall I tell you something?' he said gravely. 'Do you know that I've just begun to think nothing would give me greater satisfaction now than to hear that the rumour you told me of was an accomplished fact.'

'And that Mabel was engaged to Mr. Ashburn? Do you really mean it?' cried Gilda, and her face cleared again.

'I really mean it,' said Caffyn smiling; and it is just possible that he really did.

'Gilda, you're not helping me in the least!' said Mrs. Featherstone, coming up at this juncture; 'and there's your father threatening to get that big clock with a horrid cuckoo in it for the hall at the Grange. Come and tell him, if he must have one, to buy one of the long plain ones.' And Gilda went obediently, for she could feel an interest in clocks and carvings now.

CHAPTER XXV

MABEL'S ANSWER

The wet autumn had merged into a premature season of fog and slush, while a violent gale had stripped off the leaves long before their time. Winter was at hand, and already one or two of the hardier Christmas annuals, fresh from editorial forcing-houses, had blossomed on the bookstalls, and a few masks and Roman candles, misled by appearances, had stolen into humble shop-fronts long before November had begun. All the workers (except the junior clerks in offices, who were now receiving permission to enjoy their annual fortnight) were returning, and even idlers, who had no country-house hospitality to give or receive, were glad to escape some of their burden amongst the mild distractions of a winter in town. Mrs. Langton, who detested the country, had persuaded her husband to let their place 'Glenthorne' for the last two winters, and she and her daughter had already returned to Kensington Park Gardens after a round of visits, leaving Mr. Langton to enjoy a little more shooting before the Courts reopened.

Caffyn was now away at the Featherstones' country seat, somewhere in the Midlands, and Mark, who remained in town after their return from Germany, had taken the earliest opportunity of calling on the Langtons, when Mabel seemed more frankly glad to see him than he had dared to hope, and in one short half-hour the understanding between them had advanced several months. She showed the greatest interest in his wanderings, and he described the various petty adventures in his most effective manner, until even Mrs. Langton was roused to a little indulgent laughter. When Dolly came in later, Mark was embraced enthusiastically. 'I was so afraid you wouldn't be back in time for my party,' she said. 'You will come—now won't you? It's to-morrow week; my birthday, you know.' And of course Mark was delighted to promise to come, as Mabel seconded the invitation.

'We're quite at a loss to know how to amuse the children,' she said a little later. 'Perhaps you can help us to an idea?'

'We could have the Performing Pigmies,' said Mrs. Langton, 'but the boys might tread on them, and that would be so expensive, you know.'

'Don't have any performing things, mother,' pleaded Dolly; 'have only dancing.'

'Most of the boys hate dancing,' said Mabel.

'Some of them don't a bit,' urged Dolly, 'and those who do can stay away; I don't want them. But don't have entertainments; they always leave a horrid mess that takes hours to clear away after them.'

'It's all very well for you, Dolly,' said Mabel, laughing, 'but I shall have to keep the boys in order; and last time they played at robbers, tramping about all over the house, and when everyone had gone there was one of them left behind upstairs, Mr. Ashburn, howling to be let out of the cupboard!'

'Bobby Fraser, that was,' said Dolly; 'stupid little duffer. We won't have him this time. And, mother darling, I want to dance all the time; and it's my own party. Dancing is enough—it is really,' she pleaded in a pretty frenzy of impatience. And Dolly got her own way as usual.

Mabel was a little surprised at her own pleasure in seeing Mark again. She had looked forward to meeting him, but without being prepared for the wild joy that sprang up in her heart as he pressed her hand, and with that unmistakable delight in his eyes at being in her presence. 'Do I care for him as much as that?' she asked herself, and the question answered itself as such questions do.

Mark was his own master now, for he had given up his appointment at St. Peter's, although Mr. Shelford strongly advised him to go in for some regular profession besides literature.

'There'll come a day,' he told him, 'when you've played out all your tunes and your barrel is worn smooth, and no one will throw you any more coppers. Then you'll want a regular employment to fall back upon. Why don't you get called?'

'Because I don't want to be tied down,' said Mark. 'I want to go about and study character. I want to enjoy my life while I can.'

'So did the grasshopper,' said Mr. Shelford.

'You don't believe in me, I know,' said Mark. 'You think I shall never do anything like "Illusion" again. Well, I believe in myself. I think my tunes will last out my life at all events. I really work uncommonly hard. I have two novels ready for the press at this moment, which is pretty well for a mere grasshopper.'

'But wearing for a mere barrel-organ,' said the old gentleman. 'Be careful; don't write too much. The public never forgive a disappointment. Whatever you do, give them of your best.'

And shortly after this conversation Mark left his novel, 'Sweet Bells Jangled,' with Chilton and Fladgate, mentioning terms which even to himself seemed slightly exorbitant. He had a note from the firm in the course of a day or two, appointing an interview, and on going up to the publishing office found both of the partners waiting to receive him. Mr. Chilton was a spare angular man, who confined himself chiefly to the purely financial department.

'We have decided to accept your terms, subject to a few modifications which we can discuss presently,' he said.

'You think the book is likely to be a success?' asked Mark, unable to control his anxiety.

'Any work by the author of "Illusion" is sure to command attention,' said Mr. Chilton.

'But you like the subject?' pursued Mark.

Mr. Chilton coughed. 'I can express no opinion,' he said. 'I don't profess to be a judge of these matters. Fladgate has read the book; he will tell you what he thinks about it.'

But Mr. Fladgate remained silent, and Mark, much as he longed to press him, was too proud to do so. However, as the firm demanded a rather considerable reduction of the original terms, Mr. Fladgate, in explanation, admitted at length that he did not consider 'Sweet Bells Jangled' altogether up to the standard of Mark's first work, and intimated that it would not be advisable to risk bringing it out before the spring season.

'I see,' said Mark, nettled; 'you are not particularly hopeful about it?'

'Oh,' said Mr. Fladgate, with a wave of his hand, 'I wouldn't say that. Chance has a good deal to do with these affairs—a good deal to do. I confess I miss some of the qualities that charmed me in your

"Illusion." It reads to me, if I may say so, like an earlier effort, a much earlier effort; but it may hit the popular taste for all that; and it is certainly in quite a different vein.'

Mark came away rather depressed, but he soon persuaded himself that a publisher was a not infallible judge of literary merit; and then, the firm had every object in depreciating the work whilst negotiations were proceeding. For all that he felt uncomfortable now and then, and he had not wholly got rid of his depression by the time of Dolly's birthday party.

On his arrival, he found that Dolly's wish had been gratified. Dancing was the main attraction, and in the principal room were the usual iron-fisted pianist and red-faced cornet-player, who should be such profound moralists with all their nightly experiences; and dainty little girls were whirling round with the fortunate boys who had elder sisters at home to bully them into acquiring the mysteries of the valse, while the less favoured stood in doorways gibing with the scornfulness of envy.

The least observing might trace the course of several naïve preferences and innocent flirtations during the earlier part of the evening. Big bright-faced boys in devoted attendance on shy and unconscious small maidens many years their juniors, and, en revanche, determined little ladies triumphantly towing about smaller boys, who seemed sometimes elated, but mostly resigned, while one youthful misogynist openly rebelled and fled to Mabel for protection, declaring ungallantly that he would rather be 'at home in bed than bothered like that any longer.'

Dolly was enjoying herself amazingly, dancing chiefly, however, with her dearest girl friend for the time being, since none of the boys danced well enough to please either of them. And besides, boys rather bored Dolly, to whom dancing, as yet, was merely a particularly delightful form of exercise, and who had no precocious tendencies to coquetry. She deigned to dance once with Mark, after which he did his duty by trotting out a succession of calm and self-possessed little girls, who were as unchildlike as if they had been out for a season or two. Then he thought he might reward himself by going to look for Mabel, whom he found in one of the lower rooms endeavouring to amuse the smaller and non-dancing members of the company. She was standing under the centre lamp, flushed and laughing, with two or three children clinging to her dress, and met his amused and admiring eyes with a little gesture of comic despair.

'We've played all the games that were ever invented,' she said; 'and now some of them are getting rough and the rest cross, and there's half an hour before supper, and I don't in the least know what to do with them till then.'

'Shall I see what I can do with them?' said Mark rather rashly.

'Oh, if you would it would be so kind of you. I'm afraid you don't know what you are exposing yourself to.'

Mark, not being devoted to children, felt more than a little dubious himself; but he wanted to be associated with her in something, and volunteered manfully.

'Look here,' he began, as they all stood about staring at him, 'Miss Langton's a little tired. I—I am going to play with you a little now. What shall we have, eh? Blind man's buff?'

But they had had that, and presently one small boy, bolder than the rest, said, 'Play at being Jumbo'—a proposal which seemed generally popular.

'Then may I leave you here?' said Mabel. 'I must go and speak to mother about something. Don't let them be too tiresome.'

This was by no means what Mark had bargained for; but he found himself deserted and reduced to 'play at being Jumbo' with the best possible grace. It was a simple but severe game, consisting in the performer of the principal rôle—who was Mark himself on this occasion—going down on his hands and knees and staggering about the carpet, while everyone else who could find room climbed on his back and thumped him on the head. At last, in self-defence, he was obliged to get rid of them by intimating that he had gone mad, when he had to justify his words by careering round the room trumpeting fiercely, while the children scuttled away before him in an ecstasy of sham terror. At first Mark was profoundly miserable, and even glad that Mabel had not remained to witness his humiliation; but by-and-by he began to enter into the spirit of the thing, and had entirely forgotten his dignity by the time Mabel reappeared. Caffyn (who had now returned from the Featherstones', and had received an invitation from Mrs. Langton in Mabel's absence: 'We've known him from a boy, my dear,' the former had said in justification, 'and he can recite some things to keep the children quiet, you know') stood in the doorway behind her, and looked on with a smile of pity, but she saw nothing ridiculous in Mark just then (and, as he was probably aware, he could stand such tests better than most men). She only thought that his willingness to sacrifice himself for others was a pleasant trait in his character.

'Don't get up, Ashburn; it's delightful to see you making yourself so hot, my dear fellow,' said Caffyn. 'One doesn't get the chance of seeing a successful author ramping about on all fours every day.'

'I can't get up,' said Mark; and in fact a small but unpleasantly sturdy boy had pounced on him as he paused for breath, and, with the sense that he was doing something courageous, was in course of taming the elephant with a hearth-brush.

'What a shame!' cried Mabel. 'Tommy, you horrid boy, you're hurting Mr. Ashburn.' And the hearth-brush was certainly coming down with considerable vigour on the small of the amateur elephant's back.

'I think myself,' gasped Mark, 'that I could bear being shipped off to America now.'

'Yes, indeed,' she said compassionately; 'you mustn't be tormented any more. Tommy, let the poor elephant alone; you've tamed him very nicely.'

'Jumbo had his hind legs tied,' urged Tommy, who had a taste for realism.

'I don't think that will be necessary,' objected Mark. 'I'm beautifully tame now, Master Tommy; observe the mildness of my eye.'

'The game's over now,' said Mabel with decision. 'There, Mr. Ashburn, your elephant life is over. Tommy, come and button my glove for me, like a dear fellow. How dreadfully hot you are! And now Mr. Caffyn is going to recite something; come upstairs, all of you, and listen.'

For Mrs. Langton had begged him to do something to amuse the children. 'I don't want them to dance too much,' she had said. 'If you could manage to cool them down before supper.'

'I'll cool them down!' said Caffyn to himself, with one of his peculiar impulses to safe and secret malevolence. 'If you will get them all together, dear Mrs. Langton,' he replied, 'I'll see what I can do.' And accordingly he entertained them with a harrowing little poem about a poor child dying of starvation in a garret, and dreaming of wealthier and happier children enjoying themselves at parties, which made all the children uncomfortable, and some of the less stolid ones cry. And then he told them a ghost story, crammed with ingenious horrors, which followed most of them home to bed.

Mabel listened in burning indignation; she would have liked to stop him, but grown-up persons were beginning to filter in, and she was afraid of making anything like a scene by interfering. However, when he came up blandly after the performance she let him see her opinion of it.

'Oh, they like to have their flesh creep,' he said with a shrug; 'it's one of the luxuries of youth.'

'It isn't a wholesome one,' said she; 'but I know you have your own theories of the proper way to amuse a child.' She felt a revival of her disgust for the sly treachery he had revealed once before. He gave her a cold keen glance, and the lines round his mouth tightened for an instant.

'You haven't forgiven me, then?' he said.

'I can't forget,' she answered in a low voice.

'We both have good memories, it seems,' he retorted with a short laugh as he held up a curtain for her to pass, and turned away.

It was after supper, and most of the children had been weeded out to be replaced by children of a larger growth. Mark came up to Mabel as she stood by the doorway while the musicians were playing the first few bars of a waltz, and each couple was waiting for some other to begin before them. 'You promised me a dance,' he said, 'in reward for my agility as an elephant. Aren't your duties over now?'

'I think everybody knows everybody now, and no one is sitting out,' said Mabel. 'But really I would rather not dance just yet; I'm a little tired.' For the Fräulein was still away with her family in Germany, and most of the work had fallen upon Mabel, who was feeling some need of a rest. Mark did not try to persuade her.

'You must be,' he agreed. 'Will you—do you mind sitting this dance out with me?'

She made no objection, and they were presently sitting together under the soft light of the ribbed Chinese lanterns in a fernery at the back of the rooms.

'When we go back,' said Mabel, 'I want to introduce you to a Miss Torrington, a great admirer of your book. But you don't care for such things, do you?'

'I wish with all my soul I might never hear of the book again,' said Mark gloomily. 'I—I beg your pardon! It sounds ungrateful. And yet—if you knew—if you only knew!' He was in one of his despondent moods just then, when his skeleton came out of the cupboard and gibbered at him. What right had he, with this fraud on his soul, to be admitted even to the ordinary friendship of a sweet and noble girl? What would she say to him if she knew? And for a moment he felt a mad impulse to tell her.

'I wish you would tell me,' she said gently, as if answering the impulse. But the suggestion, put into words, sobered him. She would despise him; she must. He could not bear to see his shame reflected in her eyes. So he told her half-truths only.

'It is only that I am so tired of being tied to a book,' he said passionately. 'Tied? I am a book. Everyone I meet sees in me, not a man to be judged and liked for himself, but something to criticise and flatter and compare with the nature he revealed in print.'

Half truth as this was, it was more sincere than such confidences are apt to be.

'Your book is you, or a part of you,' said Mabel. 'It seems so absurd that you should be jealous of it.'

'I am,' he said. 'Not so much with others, but when I am with you it tortures me. When you show me any kindness I think, "She would not say that, she would not do this, if I were not the author of 'Illusion.' She honours the book, not you—only the book!"'

'How unjust!' said Mabel. She could not think it a perverted form of diseased vanity. He plainly undervalued his work himself, and its popularity was a real vexation to him. She could only be sorry for him.

'But I see proof of it in others every now and then,' continued Mark, 'people who do not connect me at first with "Cyril Ernstone." Only the other day some of them went so far as to apologise for having snubbed me "before they knew who I was." I don't complain of that, of course—I'm not such an idiot; but it does make me doubtful of the other extreme. And I cannot bear the doubt in your case!'

His eyes were raised pleadingly to hers. He seemed longing, and yet dreading, to speak more plainly. Mabel's heart beat quicker; there was a subtle, delicious flattery in such self-abasement before her of a man she admired so much. Would he say more then, or would he wait? As far as she knew her own mind, she hoped he would wait a little longer. She said nothing, being perhaps afraid of saying too much. 'Yet I know it will be so,' said Mark; 'the book will be forgotten with the next literary sensation, and I shall drop under with it. You will see me about less often, till one day you pass me in the street and wonder who I am, and if you ever met me at all.'

'I don't think I ever gave you the right to say that,' she said, wounded at his tone, 'and you ought to know that I should not do anything of the sort.'

'Will you tell me this,' he said, and his voice trembled with anxiety, 'if—if I had not written this book which was happy enough to give you some pleasure—if I had met you simply as Mark Ashburn, a man who had never written a line in his life, would you have been the same to me? Would you have felt even such interest in me as I like to think sometimes you do feel? Try to give me an answer.... You don't know how much it will mean to me.'

Mabel took refuge in the impersonal. 'Of course,' she said, 'one often likes a person one never saw very much for something he has done; but I think if you ever do meet him and then don't like him for himself, you dislike him all the more for disappointing you. It's a kind of reaction, I suppose.'

'Tell me this too,' Mark entreated, 'is—is that my case?'

'If it had been,' she said softly, 'do you think I should have said that?'

Something in her tone gave Mark courage to dare everything.

'Then you do care for me a little?' he cried. 'Mabel, I can speak now. I loved you ever since I first saw you in that old country church. I never meant to tell you so soon, but I can't help it. I want you—I can't live without you! Will you come to me, Mabel?'

She put both hands trustfully in his as she said, 'Yes, Mark,' and without any more words just then on either side, their troth was plighted. He was still holding the hands she had resigned to him, hardly daring as yet to believe in this realisation of his dearest hopes, when someone stepped quickly in through the light curtains. It was Caffyn, and he put up his eyeglass to conceal a slight start as he saw who were there.

'Sent to look for somebody's fan; told it was left on the folding chair. Ah, sorry to trouble you, Ashburn; that's it behind you; I won't say I found you sitting on it.' And he went out with his prize.

'I think, after that,' said Mabel, with a little laugh, though she was annoyed too, 'you had better take me back again.'

And Mark obeyed, feeling that the unromantic interruption had effectually broken the spell. Fortunately it had happened after, and not before his fate had been decided.

The evening was over, and he was waiting to recover his hat and overcoat when he was joined by Caffyn. 'Umbrella missing?' began the latter; 'mine is, like the departed Christians on the tombstones, you know, "not lost—but gone before." Are you going my way? Come on then.'

When they were outside in the moonlight, he took Mark's arm and said, 'You've got something to tell me, haven't you?'

'I told you I should come to you for congratulations when we were at Triberg,' said Mark, 'but I never hoped to be able to come so soon. She has said "Yes," old fellow. I can't trust myself to talk about it just yet, but I can't help telling you that.'

Caffyn clapped him on the back with a shout of rather wild laughter. 'What a fortunate beggar you are!' he said; 'fame, fortune—and now a charming girl to crown it all. You'll be rousing the envy of the gods soon, you know—unless you're careful!'

CHAPTER XXVI

VISITS OF CEREMONY

Mr. Langton, on being informed that Mark Ashburn proposed to become his son-in-law, took a painfully prosaic view of the matter: 'I can quite understand the fascination of a literary career to a young man,' he had observed to Mark in the course of a trying interview; 'indeed, when I was younger I was frequently suspected myself of contributing to "Punch;" but I always saw where that would lead me, and, as a matter of fact, I never did indulge my inclinations in that direction,' he added, with the complacency of a St. Anthony. 'And the fact is, I wish my son-in-law to have a more assured position: you see, at present you have only written one book—oh, I am quite aware that "Illusion" was well received—remarkably so, indeed; but then it remains to be proved whether you can follow up your success, and—and, in short, while that is uncertain I can't consent to any engagement; you really must not ask me to do so.' And in this determination he was firm for some time, even though secretly impressed on hearing of the sum for which Mark had already disposed of his forthcoming novel, and which represented, indeed, a very fair year's income. It was Uncle Solomon, after all, that proved the heavy piece of ordnance which turned the position at the crisis; he was flattered when his nephew took him into his confidence, and pleased that he should have 'looked so high,' which motives combined to induce him to offer his influence. It was a somewhat desperate remedy, and Mark had his doubts of the impression likely to be produced by such a relative, but it worked unexpectedly well. Mr. Lightowler was too cautious to commit himself to any definite promise, but he made it abundantly clear that he was a 'warm' man, and that Mark was his favourite nephew, for whom he was doing something as it was, and might do more if he continued to behave himself. After the interview in which this was ascertained, Mr. Langton began to think that his daughter might do worse than marry this young Ashburn after all. Mrs. Langton had liked Mark from the first in her languid way, and the fact that he had 'expectations' decided her to support his cause; he was not a brilliant parti, of course, but at least he was more eligible than the young men who had been exciting her maternal alarm of late. And under her grandfather's will Mabel would be entitled on her marriage or coming of age to a sum which would keep her in comfort whatever happened.

All these considerations had their effect, and Mr. Langton, seeing how deeply his daughter's heart was concerned, withdrew his opposition, and even allowed himself to be persuaded that there was no reason for a long engagement, and that the marriage might be fixed to take place early in the following spring. He only made two stipulations: one, that Mark should insure his life in the usual manner; and the other, that he should abandon his nom de plume at once, and in the next edition of "Illusion," and in all future writings, use the name which was his by birth. 'I don't like aliases,' he said; 'if you win a reputation, it seems to me your wife and family should have the benefit of it;' and Mark agreed to both conditions with equal cheerfulness.

Mr. Humpage, as may be imagined, was not best pleased to hear of the engagement; he wrote a letter of solemn warning to Mabel and her father, and, this being disregarded, he nursed his resentment in offended silence. If Harold Caffyn was polite enough when in his uncle's company to affect to share his indignation to the full, elsewhere he accepted Mark's good fortune with cheerful indifference; he could meet Mabel with perfect equanimity, and listen to her mother's somewhat discursive eulogies of her future son-in-law with patience, if not entire assent. Since his autumn visit to the Featherstones, there had been changes in his position which may have been enough to account for his philosophy; he had gained the merchant's good opinion to such an extent that the latter, in defiance of his wife's cautions, had taken the unusual step of proposing that the young actor should give up the stage and occupy a recently vacated desk in Mr. Featherstone's own palatial City offices. Even if his stage ambition had not cooled long since, Caffyn was not the man to neglect such a chance as this; he accepted gratefully, and already the merchant saw his selection, unlikely as it had seemed at first, beginning to be justified by his protégé's clear head and command of languages, while Gilda's satisfaction at the change was at least equal to her father's. And so, whether Harold was softened by his own prosperity, and whether other hopes or distractions came between him and his former passion for revenge, he remained impassive throughout all the preparations for a marriage which he could have prevented had he chosen. At Triberg the thought that Mark (who had, as he considered, been the chief means of ruining his hopes of Mabel) was to be his successful rival had for an instant revived the old spirit; but now he could face the fact with positive contentment, and his feeling towards Mark was rather one of contemptuous amusement than of any actual hostility.

Mark's introduction of Mabel to his family had not been altogether a success; he regretted that he had carelessly forgotten to prepare them for his visit as soon as he pulled the bell-handle by the gate, and caught a glimpse of scared faces at one or two of the windows, followed by sounds from within of wild scurry and confusion—'like a lot of confounded rabbits!' he thought to himself in disgust. Then they had been kept waiting in a chilly little drawing-room, containing an assortment of atrocities in glass, china, worsted, and wax, until Mark moved restlessly about in his nervous irritation, and Mabel felt her heart sink in spite of her love; she had not expected to find Mark's people in luxurious surroundings, but she was unprepared for anything quite so hideous as that room. When Mrs. Ashburn, who had felt that this was an occasion for some attention to toilette, made her appearance, it was hardly a reassuring one: she was not exactly vulgar perhaps, but she was hard, Mabel thought, narrow and ungenial; but the fact was that the consciousness of having been taken unawares robbed her welcome of any cordiality which it might otherwise have possessed. She inferred from her first glance at Mabel's pretty walking costume a fondness for dress and extravagance, which branded her at once as a 'worldling,' between whom and herself there could be nothing in common—in which last opinion she was most probably right, as all Mabel's efforts to sustain a conversation could not save it from frequent lapses. Martha, from shyness as much as stiffness, sat by in almost complete silence; and though Trixie, the only other member of the family who appeared, was evidently won at once by Mabel's appearance, and did all she could to cover the others' shortcomings, she was not sufficiently at her ease to break the chill; and Mark, angry and ashamed as he was, felt paralysed himself under its influence.

On the way back he was unusually silent, from a fear of the impression such an ordeal as she had gone through must have left upon Mabel; and the fact that she did not refer to the interview herself did not reassure him. He need not have been afraid, however; she was not in the least deterred by what she had seen. The sight of the home in which he had been brought up had filled her with a loving pity, suggesting as it did the petty constraints and miseries, the unloveliness of all surroundings, and the total want of appreciation which he must have endured there. And yet all this had not soured him; in spite of it he had produced a great book, strong, yet refined and tender, and free from any taint of narrowness or cynicism. As she thought of this and glanced at Mark's handsome face, so bright and animated in general, but clouded now with the melancholy which his fine eyes could express at times, she longed to say something to relieve it, and yet shrank from being the first to speak in her fear of jarring him.

Mark spoke at last. 'Well, Mabel,' he said, looking down at her with a rather doubtful smile, 'I told you that my mother was a—a little peculiar.'

'Yes,' said Mabel frankly; 'we didn't quite get on together, did we, Mark? We shall some day, perhaps; and even if not—I shall have you!' And she laid her hand on his sleeve with a look of perfect understanding and contentment which, little as he deserved it, chased away all his fears.

CHAPTER XXVII

CLEAR SKY—AND A THUNDERBOLT

'Has any one,' asks George Eliot, in 'Middlemarch,' 'ever pinched into its pilulous smallness the cobweb of pre-matrimonial acquaintance?' And, to press the metaphor, the cobweb, as far as Mark and Mabel were concerned, brilliantly as it shone in all its silken iridescence, would have rolled up into a particularly small pill. Mark was anxious that his engagement should be as short as possible, chiefly from an uneasy fear that his great happiness might elude him after all. The idea of losing Mabel became day by day, as he knew her better, a more intolerable torture, and he could not rest until all danger of that was at an end. Mabel had no fears of a future in which Mark would be by her side; and if she was not blind to some little weaknesses in his character, they did not affect her love and admiration in the least—she was well content that her hero should not be unpleasantly perfect. And the weeks slipped by, until Easter, which fell early that year, had come and gone; the arrangements for the wedding were all completed, and Mark began to breathe more freely as he saw his suspense drawing to a happy end.

It was a bleak day towards the end of March, and Mark was walking across the Park and Gardens from his rooms in South Audley Street to Malakoff Terrace, charged with a little note from Mabel to Trixie, to which he was to bring back an answer; for, although Mabel had not made much progress in the affections of the rest of the Ashburn household, a warm friendship had sprung up already between herself and Mark's youngest sister—the only one of them who seemed to appreciate and love him as he deserved. He felt buoyant and happy as he walked briskly on, with the blustering north-easter at his back seeming to clear his horizon of the last clouds which had darkened it. A very few days more and Mabel would be his own—beyond the power of man to sunder! and soon, too, he would be able to salve the wound which still rankled in his conscience—he would have a book of his own. 'Sweet Bells Jangled' was to appear almost immediately, and he had come to have high hopes of it; it looked most imposing in proof—it was so much longer than 'Illusion;' he had worked up a series of such overwhelming effects in it; its pages contained matter to please every variety of taste—flippancy and learning, sensation and sentiment, careful dissection of character and audacious definition and epigram—failure seemed to him almost impossible. And when he could feel able to lay claim legitimately to the title of genius, surely then the memory of his fraud would cease to reproach him—the means would be justified by the result. He amused himself by composing various critiques on the book (all of course highly eulogistic), and thus pleasantly occupied the way until he gained the cheerful Kensington High Street, the first half of which seems to belong to some bright little market town many miles further from Charing Cross. In the road by the kerbstone he passed a street singer, a poor old creature in a sun-bonnet, with sharp features that had been handsome once, and brilliant dark eyes, who was standing there unregarded, singing some long-forgotten song with the remnants of a voice. Mark's happiness impelled him to put some silver into her hand, and he felt a half-superstitious satisfaction as he heard the blessing she called down on him—as if she might have influence.

No one was at home at Malakoff Terrace but Trixie, whom he found busily engaged in copying an immense plaster nose. 'Jack says I must practise harder at features before I try the antique,' she explained, 'and so he gave me this nose; it's his first present, and considered a very fine cast, Jack says.'

'Never saw a finer nose anywhere,' said Mark—'looks as if it had been forced, eh, Trixie?'

'Mark, don't!' cried Trixie, shocked at this irreverence; 'it's David's—Michael Angelo's David!' He gave her Mabel's note. 'I can't write back because my hands are all charcoaly,' she explained; 'but you can say, "My love, and I will if I possibly can;" and, oh yes, tell her I had a letter from him this morning.'

'Meaning Jack?' said Mark. 'All right, and—oh, I say, Trixie, why won't the governor and mater come to my wedding?'

'It's all ma,' said Trixie; 'she says she should only feel herself out of place at a fashionable wedding, and she's better away.'

'It's to be a very quiet affair, though, thank Heaven!' observed Mark.

'Yes, but don't you see what she really wants is to be able to feel injured by being out of it all—if she can, she'll persuade herself in time that she never was invited at all; you know what dear ma is!'

'Well,' said Mark, with considerable resignation, 'she must do as she pleases, of course. Have you got anything else to tell me, Trixie, because I shall have to be going soon?'

'You mustn't go till I've given you something that came for you—oh, a long time ago, when ma was ill. You see, it was like this: ma had her breakfast in bed, and there was a tray put down on the slab where it was, and it was sticky underneath or something, and so it stuck to the bottom, and the tray wasn't wanted again, and Ann, of course, didn't choose to wash it, so she only found it yesterday and brought it to me.'

'Trixie,' said Mark, 'I can't follow all those "its." I gather that I'm entitled to something sticky, but I haven't a notion what. Hadn't you better get it, whatever it happens to be?'

'Why, it's a letter of course, goose!' said Trixie. 'I told you that the very first thing: wait here, and I'll bring it to you.'

So Mark waited patiently in the homely little back parlour, where he had prepared his work as a schoolboy in the old days, where he had smoked his first cigar in his first Cambridge vacation. He smiled as he thought how purely intellectual his enjoyment of that cigar had been, and how for the first time he had appreciated the meaning of 'the bitter end;' he was smiling still when Trixie returned.

'Whom do you know in India, Mark?' she said curiously; 'perhaps it's some admirer who's read the book. I hope it's nothing really important; if it is, it wasn't our fault that—Mark, you're not ill, are you?'

'No,' said Mark, placing himself with his back to the light, and stuffing the letter, after one hasty glance at the direction, unopened into his pocket. 'Of course not—why should I be?'

'Is there anything in the letter to worry you?' persisted Trixie. 'It can't be a bill, can it?'

'Never mind what it is,' said Mark; 'have you got the keys? I—I should like a glass of wine.'

'Ma left the keys in the cupboard,' said Trixie; 'how lucky! port or sherry, Mark?'

'Brandy, if there is any,' he said, with an effort.

'Brandy! oh, Mark, have you taken to drinking spirits, and so early in the morning?' she asked, with an anxious misgiving that perhaps that was de rigueur with all literary men.

'No, no, don't be absurd. I want some just now, and quick, do you hear? I caught a chill walking across,' he explained.

'You had better try to eat something with it, then,' she advised; 'have some cake?'

'Do you want to make me ill in earnest?' he retorted peevishly, thrusting away the brown cake, with a stale flavour of cupboard about it, with which Trixie tried to tempt him; 'there, it's all right—there's nothing the matter, I tell you.' And he poured out the brandy and drank it. There was a kind of comfort, or rather distraction, in the mere physical sensation to his palate; he thought he understood why some men took to drinking. 'Ha!' and he made a melancholy attempt at the sigh of satisfaction which some people think expected of them after spirits. 'Now I'm a man again, Trixie; that has driven off the chill. I'll be off now.'

'Are you sure you're quite well again?' she said anxiously. 'Very well, then I shan't see you again till you're in church next Tuesday; and oh, Mark, I do so hope you'll be very, very happy!' He was on the door-step by this time, and made no reply, while he kept his face turned from her.

'Good-bye, then,' she said; 'you won't forget my message to Mabel, will you?'

'Let me see, what was it?' he said. 'Ah, I remember; your love, and you will if you can, eh?'

'Yes, and say I've had a letter from him this morning,' she added.

He gave a strange laugh, and then, as he turned, she saw how ghastly and drawn his face looked.

'Have you though?' he said wildly; 'so have I, Trixie, so have I!' And before she could ask any further questions he was gone.

He walked blindly up the little street and into the main road again, unable at first to think with any clearness: he had not read the letter; the stamp and handwriting on the envelope were enough for him. The bolt had fallen from a clear sky, the thing he had only thought of as a nightmare had really happened—the sea had given up its dead! He went on; there was the same old woman in the sun-bonnet, still crooning the same song; he laughed bitterly to think of the difference in his own life since he had last seen her—only a short half-hour ago. He passed the parish church, from which a wedding party was just driving, while the bells clashed merrily under the graceful spire—no wedding bells would ever clash for him now. But he must read that letter and know the worst. Holroyd was alive—that he knew; but had he found him out? did that envelope contain bitter denunciations of his treachery? Perhaps he had already exposed him! he could not rest until he knew how this might be, and yet he dared not read his letter in the street. He thought he would find out a quiet spot in Kensington Gardens and read it there; alone—quite alone. He hurried on, with a dull irritation that the High Street should be so long and so crowded, and that everybody should make such a point of getting in the way; the shock had affected his body as well as his mind; he was cold to the bones, and felt a dull numbing pressure on the top of his head; and yet he welcomed these symptoms, too, with an odd satisfaction; they seemed to entitle him to some sympathy. He reached the Gardens at last, but when he had turned in at the little postern door near the 'King's Arms,' he could not prevail upon himself to open the letter—he tore it half open and put it back irresolutely; he must find a seat and sit down. He struck up the hill, with the wind in his teeth now, until he came to the Round Pond, where there was quite a miniature sea breaking on the southwestern rim of the basin; a small boy was watching a solitary ship labouring far out in the centre, and Mark stood and watched it too, mechanically, till he turned away at last with a nervous start of impatience. Once he had sailed ships on those waters; what would he not give if those days could come back to him again, or if even he could go back these past few months to the time when his conscience was clear and he feared no man! But the past was irrevocable; he had been guilty of this reckless, foolish fraud, and now the consequences were upon him! He walked restlessly on under the bare tossing branches, looking through the black trunks and across the paths glimmering white in the blue-grey distance for a seat where he might be safe from interruption, until at last he discovered a clumsy wooden bench, scored and slashed with the sand-ingrained initials of a quarter of a century's idleness, a seat of the old uncomfortable pattern gradually dying out from the walks. He could wait no longer, and was hurrying forward to secure it, when he was hailed by some one approaching by one of the Bayswater paths, and found that he had been recognised by Harold Caffyn.

CHAPTER XXVIII

MARK KNOWS THE WORST

To avoid Caffyn was out of the question, and so Mark waited for him with as much self-control as he could muster, as he strolled leisurely up. Caffyn's quick eye saw at once that something unusual had happened, and he resolved to find out what that was before they parted. 'Thought it must be you,' he began; 'so you've come out here to meditate on your coming happiness, have you? Come along and pour out some of your raptures, it will do you good; and you don't know what a listener I can be.'

'Not now,' said Mark uneasily; 'I—I think I would rather be alone.'

'Nonsense!' said Caffyn briskly; 'you don't really mean that, I know. Why, I'm going away to-morrow to the lakes. I must have a little talk with you before I go.'

'What are you going there for?' said Mark, without much show of interest.

'My health, my boy; old Featherstone has let me out for a fortnight's run, and I'm going to see what mountain air can do for me.'

'And where are you going now?' asked Mark.

'Now? Well, I was going across to see if the Featherstones would give me some lunch, but I'm in no hurry. I'll go wherever you want to go.'

'Thanks,' said Mark, 'but—but I won't take you out of your way.'

'It's not taking me out of my way a bit. I assure you, my boy, and we haven't had a talk together for ages, so come along.'

'I can't,' said Mark, more uncomfortably still. 'I have some—some business which I must see to alone.'

'Odd sort of place this for business! No, no, Master Mark, it won't do; I've got you, and I mean to stick to you; you know what a tactless beggar I can be when I like. Seriously, do you think I can't see there's something wrong? I'm hanged if I think it's safe to let you go about alone while you're looking like this; it isn't any—any hitch at Kensington Park Gardens, is it?' and there was a real anxiety in his tone as he asked this.

'No,' said Mark shortly, 'it's not that.'

'Have you got into any trouble, then, any scrape you don't see your way out of? You might do worse than tell me all about it.'

'There's nothing to tell,' said Mark, goaded past prudence by this persistence; 'it's only a letter, a rather important letter, which I brought out here to read quietly.'

'Why the deuce couldn't you say so before?' cried Caffyn. 'I won't interrupt you; read your letter by all means, and I'll walk up and down here till you're ready for me—only don't make me think you want to cut me; you might wait till you're married for that, and you ought to know very well (if you don't) why I've been obliged, as it is, to decline the invitation to the marriage feast.'

Mark saw that for some reason Caffyn did not mean to be shaken off just then, and, as he could bear the suspense no longer, and knew that to walk about with Caffyn and talk indifferently of his coming happiness with that letter unread in his pocket would drive him mad, he had no choice but to accept the compromise. So he went to the bench and began to open the letter with trembling hands, while Caffyn paced up and down at a discreet distance. 'I see what it is now,' he thought, as he noticed the foreign envelope, 'I'm uncommonly glad I came up just then. Will he go through with it after this? Will he tell me anything, I wonder? Very little, I fancy, of what I know already. We shall see.'

This was the letter which Mark read, while the northeast wind roared through the boughs overhead, driving the gritty shell-dust in his face, and making the thin paper in his fingers flap with its vicious jerks:—

'Talipot Bungalow, Newera Ellia, Ceylon.

'MY DEAR MARK,—I am not going to reproach you for your long silence, as I dare say you waited for me to write first. I have been intending to write again and again, and have been continually prevented, but I hardly expected to hear from you unless you had anything of importance to tell me. Something, however, has just come to my knowledge here which makes me fancy that you might have other reasons for not writing.' ('What does he mean by that?' thought Mark, in sudden terror, and for a moment dared not read on.) 'Have you by some strange chance been led to believe that I was on board the unfortunate "Mangalore" at the time of the disaster? because I see, on looking over some old Indian papers at the club here, that my name appears on the list of missing. As a matter of fact, I left the ship at Bombay. I had arranged to spend a day or two with some people, old friends of my father's, who have a villa on the Malabar Hill, but on my arrival there found a telegram from Ceylon, warning me to lose no time if I wished to see my father alive. The "Mangalore" was to stop several more days at Bombay, and I decided to go on at once overland to Madras and take my chance there of a steamer for Colombo, leaving my hosts to send down word to the ship of my change of plan. I can only suppose that there was some misunderstanding about this, and even then I cannot understand how the steward could have returned me as on board under the circumstances; but if only the mistake has given you no distress it is not of much consequence, as I wrote since my arrival here to the only other quarter in which the report might have caused alarm. To continue my story, I was fortunate enough to catch a boat at Madras, and so reached Colombo some time before the "Mangalore" was due there, and as I went on at once to Yatagalla, it is not to be wondered at if in that remote part of the country—up in Oudapusilava, in the hill district—it was long before I even heard of the wreck. There was not much society there, as you may imagine, the neighbouring estates being mostly held by native planters or managers, with whom my father had never, even when well, been at all intimate. Well, my poor father rallied a little and lingered for some time after my arrival. His condition required my constant care, and I hope I was able to be of some comfort to him. When he died I thought it best to do what I could, with the overseer's assistance, to carry on the plantation until there was a good opportunity of disposing of it, and for a time it did seem as if my efforts were going to be rewarded—the life was hard and lonely enough, but it had its charms for a solitary man like myself. Then everything seemed to go wrong at once. We had a bad season to begin with, and next fungus suddenly showed itself on the estate, and soon spread to such an extent that as a coffee plantation the place is quite worthless now, though I dare say they will be able to grow tea or cinchona on it. I have done with Yatagalla myself, having just succeeded in getting rid of it; naturally, not for a very large price per acre, but still I shall have enough altogether to live upon if I decide to carry on my old profession, or to start me fairly in some other line. But I am coming home first. (I can't call this island, lovely as most of it is, home.) There is nothing to keep me here any longer except my health, which has been anything but good for the last few months. I have been down with fever after fever; and this place, which I was ordered to as a health resort, is too damp and chilly to get really well in. So I shall make an effort to leave in about a fortnight by the P. and O. "Coromandel," which they tell me is a comfortable boat. After my experience of the "Mangalore" I prefer to trust this time to the regular "liners." I write this chiefly to ask you to do me a kindness if you possibly can. I have a sort of longing to see a friendly face on landing, and lately I have come to persuade myself that after all you may have good news to meet me with. Can you come? I have no time-tables here, but I calculate that the ship will reach Plymouth some time during the Easter holidays, so that, even if you are still at St. Peter's, your school duties will not prevent your coming. You can easily get the exact time we arrive by inquiring at the P. and O. offices in Leadenhall Street. We shall meet so soon now that I need write no more. As it is there is another letter I must write—if I can, for you would hardly believe how difficult I find it to write at all in my present state, though a sea voyage will set me up again.'

The letter ended rather abruptly, the writing becoming almost illegible towards the close, as if the writer's strength had gradually failed him. Mark came to the end with a feeling that was almost relief; his chief dread had been to hear that he was found out, and that his exposure might be made public before he could make Mabel his own. It was terrible to know that the man he had injured was alive, but still it was something that he was still unaware of his injury; it was a respite, and, to a man of Mark's temperament, that was much. Even if Holroyd were strong enough to take his passage by the 'Coromandel,' he could hardly be in England for at least another fortnight, and long before he arrived at Plymouth the wedding would have taken place. And in a fortnight he might be able to hit upon something to soften some of the worst aspects of his fraud; the change in the title of the book, in the nom de plume, and even the alterations of the text might be explained; but then there was that fatal concession of allowing his real name to appear: it was, he knew, to be placed on the title-page of the latest edition—would there be time to suppress that? This occurred to him but vaguely, for it seemed just then as if, when Mabel were once his wife, no calamity could have power to harm him, and now nothing Holroyd could do would prevent the marriage. After that the Deluge!

So he was almost his usual self as he rose and came towards Caffyn; his hand, however, still trembled a little, causing him to bungle in replacing the letter and drop the envelope, which the other obligingly picked up and restored to him.

'Ashburn, my dear fellow,' he began, as they walked on together, 'I hope you won't think me impertinent, but I couldn't help seeing the writing on that envelope, and it seems to me I knew it once, and yet—do you mind telling me if it's from any one I know?'

Mark would of course have preferred to say nothing, but it seemed best on the whole to avoid suspicion by telling the truth. Caffyn, as a friend of Vincent's, would hear it before long; it might look odd if he made any secret of it now, and so he told the tale of the escape much as the letter had given it. His companion was delighted, he laughed with pleasure, and congratulated Mark on the joy he supposed him to feel, until the latter could hardly bear it.

'Who would have hoped for this,' he said, 'when we were talking about the dead coming to life some time ago, eh? and yet it's happened—poor, dear old Vincent! And did you say he is coming home soon?'

'Very soon; in about a fortnight,' said Mark; 'he—he wants me to go down to Plymouth and meet him, but of course I can't do that.'

'A fortnight!' cried Caffyn. 'Capital! But how do you make it out, though?'

'Easily,' said Mark; 'he talks of coming by the "Coromandel" and starting about a fortnight after he wrote—so—'

'I see,' said Caffyn; 'I suppose you've looked at the date? No? Then let me—look here, it's more than five weeks old—look at the postmark—why, it's been in England nearly a fortnight!'

'It was delayed at my people's,' said Mark, not seeing the importance of this at first, 'that's how it was.'

'But—but don't you see?' Caffyn said, excitedly for him, 'if he really has sailed by this "Coromandel," he must be very near now. He might even be in Plymouth by this time.'

'Good God!' groaned Mark, losing all control as the truth flashed upon him while the grey grass heaved under his unstable feet.

Caffyn was watching him, with a certain curiosity which was not without a malicious amusement. 'You didn't expect that,' he said. 'It's capital, isn't it?'

'Capital!' murmured Mark.

'He'll be in time for your wedding,' pursued Caffyn.

'Yes,' said Mark heavily, 'he'll be in time for that now.'

Yes, his doom was advancing upon him fast, and he must wait patiently for it to fall; he was tied down, without possibility of escape, unless he abandoned all hope of Mabel. Perhaps he might as well do that first as last.

'Well,' said Caffyn, 'what are you going to do about it?'

'Do?' echoed Mark. 'What can I do? I shall see him soon enough, I suppose.'

'That's a composed way of expecting a long-lost friend certainly,' said Caffyn, laughing.

'Can't you understand,' retorted Mark, 'that—that, situated as I am ... coming at such a time as this ... even a man's dearest friend might be—might be—'

'Rather in the way? Why, of course, I never thought of that—shows how dull I'm getting! He will be in the way—deucedly in the way, if he comes! After all, though, he may not come!'

'Let us find out,' said Mark; 'surely there's some way of finding out.'

'Oh yes,' said Caffyn. 'I dare say they can tell us at the offices. We'll have a cab and drive there now, and then we shall know what to do. Leadenhall Street, isn't it?'

They walked sharply across to the Bayswater Road, where they could get a hansom; and as they drove along towards the City, Mark's hopes began to rise. Perhaps Holroyd was not on board the 'Coromandel'—and then he tried to prepare himself for the contrary. How should he receive Vincent when he came? for of course he would seek him out at once. The desperate idea of throwing himself on his friend's mercy occurred to him; if he could be the first to tell Holroyd the truth, surely he would consent to arrange the matter without any open scandal! He would not wish to ruin him so long as he received his own again. Both Caffyn and Mark were very silent during that long and wearisome drive, with its frequent blocks in the crowded City thoroughfares; and when they arrived at last at the courtyard in front of the offices, Mark said to his companion, 'You manage this, will you?' for he felt quite unequal to the task himself.

They had to wait some time at a broad mahogany counter before a clerk was at liberty to attend to them, for the office was full of people making various inquiries or paying passage money. Mark cursed the deliberation with which the man before them was choosing his berth on the cabin plan submitted to him; but at last the precautions against the screw and the engines and the kitchens were all taken, and the clerk proceeded to answer Caffyn's questions in the fullest and most obliging manner. He went with them to the telegram boards by the doors, and after consulting a despatch announcing the 'Coromandel's' departure from Gibraltar, said that she would probably be at Plymouth by the next evening, or early on the following morning.

'Now find out if he's on board her,' said Mark; and his heart almost stopped when the clerk came back with a list of passengers and ran his finger down the names.

'V. B. Holroyd—is that your friend? If you think of meeting him at Plymouth, you have only to see our agents there, and they will let you know when the tender goes out to take the passengers ashore.'

After that Mark made his way out blindly, followed by Caffyn. 'Let us talk here; it's quieter,' said the latter when they were in the courtyard again.

'What's the good of talking?' said Mark.

'Don't you think you ought to go down to Plymouth?' suggested Caffyn.

'No,' said Mark, 'I don't. How can I, now?'

'Oh, I know you're wanted for exhibition, and all that, but you could plead business for one day.'

'What is the use?' said Mark. 'He will come to me as soon as he gets to town.'

'No, he won't, my boy,' said Caffyn; 'he will go and see the Langtons even before such a devoted friend as you are. Didn't you know he was like one of the family there?'

'I have heard them mention him,' said the unhappy Mark, on whom a dreadful vision had flashed of Holroyd learning the truth by some innocent remark of Mabel's. 'I—I didn't know they were intimate.'

'Oh, yes,' said Caffyn; 'they'll make a tremendous fuss over him. Now look here, my dear fellow, let's talk this over without any confounded sentiment. Here's your wedding at hand, and here's a long-lost intimate friend about to turn up in the midst of it. You'd very much prefer him to stay away; there's nothing to be ashamed of in that. I should myself if I were in your shoes. No fellow cares about playing second fiddle at his own wedding. Now, I've got a little suggestion to make. I was going down to Wastwater to-morrow, but I wouldn't much mind waiting another day if I could only get a fellow to come with me. I always liked Holroyd, you know—capital good chap he is, and if you leave me to manage him, I believe I could get him to come. I own I rather funk Wastwater all alone at this time of year.'

'He wouldn't go,' said Mark hopelessly.

'He would go there as readily as anywhere else, if you left it to me. I tell you what,' he added, as if the idea had just occurred to him, 'suppose I go down to Plymouth and catch him there? I don't mind the journey a bit.'

'No,' said Mark; 'I am going to meet him. I must be the first to see him. After that, if he likes to go away with you, he can.'

'Then you are going down after all?' said Caffyn. 'What are you going to say to him?'

'That is my affair,' said Mark.

'Oh, I beg pardon! I only meant that if you say anything to him about this wedding, or even let him think the Langtons are in town, I may as well give up any idea of getting him to come away with me. Look here! you might do me a good turn, particularly when you know you won't be sorry to get him off your hands yourself. Tell him you're going abroad in a day or two (that's true; you're going to Switzerland for your honeymoon, you know), and let him think the Langtons are away somewhere on the Continent. It's all for his good; he'll want mountain air and a cheerful companion like me to put him right again. He'll be the first to laugh at an innocent little deception like that.'

But Mark had done with deceptions, as he told himself. 'I shall tell him what I think he ought to know,' he said firmly, and Caffyn, with all his keenness, mistook the purpose in his mind.

'I'll take that for an answer,' he said, 'and I shan't leave town to-morrow on the chance of his being able to go.' And so they parted.

'Ought I to have let him see that I knew?' Caffyn was thinking when he was alone again. 'No, I don't want to frighten him. I think he will play my game without it.'

Mark went back to the Langtons and dined there. Afterwards he told Mabel privately that he would be obliged to leave town for a day or two on pressing business. There was no mistaking his extreme reluctance to go, and she understood that only the sternest necessity took him away at such a time, trusting him too entirely to ask any questions.

But as they parted she said, 'It's only for two days, Mark, isn't it?'

'Only for two days,' he answered.

'And soon we shall be together—you and I—for all our lives,' she said softly, with a great happiness in her low tones. 'I ought to be able to give you up for just two days, Mark!'

Before those two days were over, he thought, she might give him up for ever! and the thought that this was possible made it difficult for him to part as if all were well. He went back and passed a sleepless night, thinking over the humiliating task he had set himself. His only chance of keeping Mabel now lay in making a full confession to Holroyd of his perfidy; he would offer a complete restitution in time. He would plead so earnestly that his friend must forgive him, or at least consent to stay his hand for the present. He would humble himself to any extent, if that would keep him from losing Mabel altogether—anything but that. If he lost her now, the thought of the happiness he had missed so narrowly would drive him mad.

It was a miserably cold day when he left Paddington, and he shivered under his rug as he sat in the train. He could hardly bear the cheerful talk of meeting or parting friends at the various stations at which the train stopped. He would have welcomed a collision which would deal him a swift and painless death, and free him from the misery he had brought upon himself. He would have been glad, like the lover in 'The Last Ride Together'—although for very different reasons—if the world could end that day, and his guilt be swallowed up in the sum of iniquity. But no collision occurred, and (as it is perhaps unnecessary to add) the universe did not gratify him by dissolving on that occasion. The train brought him safely to the Plymouth platform, and left him there to face his difficulty alone. It was about six o'clock in the evening, and he lost no time in inquiring at his hotel for the P. and O. agents, and in making his way to their offices up the stony streets and along a quiet lane over the hill by Hoegate. He was received with courtesy and told all that he wished to know. The 'Coromandel' was not in yet; would not be in now until after dark—if then. They would send him word if the tender was to go out the next morning, said the agent as he wrote him the necessary order to go on board her. After that Mark went back to the hotel and dined—or rather attempted to dine—in the big coffee-room by the side of a blazing fire that was powerless to thaw the cold about his heart, and then he retired to the smoking-room, which he had all to himself, and where he sat staring grimly at the leather benches and cold marble-topped tables around him, while he could hear muffled music and applause from the theatre hard by, varied by the click of the balls in the billiard-room at the end of the corridor. Presently the waiter announced a messenger for him, and on going out into the hall he found a man of seafaring appearance, who brought him a card stating that the tender would leave the Millbay Pier at six the next morning, by which time the 'Coromandel' would most probably be in. Mark went up to his bedroom that night as to a condemned cell; he dreaded another night of sleepless tossing. Sleep came to him, however, merciful and dreamless, as it will sometimes to those in desperate case, but he yielded to it with terror as he felt it coming upon him—for it brought the morning nearer.

CHAPTER XXIX

ON BOARD THE 'COROMANDEL'

It was quite dark the next morning when the hammering of the 'boots' outside the door roused Mark to a miserable sense of the unwelcome duty before him. He dressed by candlelight, and, groping his way down the silent staircase, hunted about in the shuttered coffee-room for the coat and hat he had left there, and went shivering out into the main street, from which he turned up the hill towards the Hoe. The day had dawned by that time, and the sky was a gloomy grey, varied towards the horizon by stormy gleams of yellow; the prim clean streets were deserted, save by an occasional workman going to his labours with a heavy tramp echoing on the wet flags. Mark went along by terraces of lodging-houses, where the placards of 'apartments' had an especially forlorn and futile look against the drawn blinds, and from the areas of which the exhalations, confined during the night, rose in perceptible contrast with the fresh morning air. Then he found himself upon the Hoe, with its broad asphalt promenades and rows of hotels and terraces, rain-washed, silent, and cold, and descending the winding series of steps, he made his way to the Millbay Pier, and entered the Custom House gates. Waiting about the wharf was a little knot of people, apparently bound on much the same errand as himself—although in far higher spirits. Their cheerfulness (probably a trifle aggravated by the consciousness of being up so early) jarred upon him, and he went on past them to the place where two small steamers were lying.

'One of 'em's a-goin' out to the "Coromandel" presently,' said a sailor in answer to his question; 'you'd better wait till the agent's down, or you may be took out to the wrong ship—for there's two expected, but they ain't neither of 'em in yet. Ah!' as a gun was heard outside, 'that'll be the "Coromandel" signallin' now.'

'That ain't her,' said another man, who was leaning over the side of one of the tenders, 'that's the t'other one—the "Emu;" the "Coromandel's" a three-master, she is.'

'Tom knows the "Coromandel,"—don't ye, Tom? Let Tom alone for knowing the "Coromandel!"' said the first sailor—a remark which apparently was rich in hidden suggestion, for they both laughed very heartily.

Presently the agent appeared, and Mark, having satisfied himself that there was no danger of being taken out to the wrong vessel (for, much as he dreaded meeting Holroyd, he dreaded missing him even more), went on board one of the tenders, which soon after began to move out into the dull green water. Now that he was committed to the ordeal his terrors rose again; he almost wished that he had made a mistake after all, and was being taken out to meet the wrong P. and O. The horrible fear possessed him that Holroyd might in some way have learned his secret on the voyage home. Suppose, for instance, a fellow-passenger possessed a copy of 'Illusion,' and chanced to lend it to him—what should he do if his friend were to meet him with a stern and contemptuous repulse, rendering all conciliation out of the question? Tortured by speculations like these, he kept nervously away from the others on board, and paced restlessly up and down near the bows; he saw nothing consciously then, but afterwards every detail of those terrible ten minutes came back to him vividly, down to the lights still hanging in the rigging of the vessels in harbour, and the hoarse cries of the men in a brown-sailed lugger gliding past them out to sea. Out by the bar there was a light haze, in the midst of which lay the long black hull of the 'Coromandel,' and to this the tender worked round in a tedious curve preparatory to lying alongside. As they passed under the stern Mark nerved himself to look amongst the few figures at the gangway for the face he feared—but Holroyd was not amongst them. After several unsuccessful attempts of a Lascar to catch the rope thrown from the tender, accompanied by some remarks in a foreign language on his part which may have been offered in polite excuse for his awkwardness, the rope was secured at length, the tender brought against the vessel's side, and the gangway lashed across. Then followed a short delay, during which the P. and O. captain, in rough-weather costume, conversed with the agent across the rails with a certain condescension.

'Thick as a hedge outside,' Mark heard him say; 'haven't turned in all night. What are we all waiting for now? Here, quartermaster, just ask the doctor to step forward, will you?'

Somehow, at the mention of the doctor, Holroyd's allusions to his illness recurred to Mark's mind, and hopes he dared not confess even to himself, so base and vile were they, rose in his heart.

'Here's the doctor; clean bill of health, eh, doctor?' asked the agent—and Mark held his breath for the answer.

'All well on board.'

'Tumble in, then;' and there was an instant rush across the gangway. Mark followed some of the crowd down into the saloon, where the steward was laying breakfast, but he could not see Holroyd there either, and for a few minutes was pent up in a corner in the general bustle which prevailed. There were glad greetings going on all around him, confused questions and answers, rapid directions to which no one had time to attend, and now and then an angry exclamation over the eagerly read letters: 'And where's mother living now?' 'We've lost that 7.40 express all through that infernal tender!' 'Look here, don't take that bag up on deck to get wet, d'ye hear?' 'Jolly to be back in the old place again, eh?' 'I wish I'd never left it—that d—d scoundrel has gone and thrown all those six houses into Chancery!' and so on, those of the passengers who were not talking or reading being engaged in filling up the telegraph forms brought on board for their convenience. Mark extricated himself from the hubbub as soon as he could, and got hold of the steward. There was a gentleman on board of the name of Holroyd; he seemed well enough, as far as the steward knew, though a bit poorly when he first came aboard, to be sure; he was in his berth just then getting his things together to go ashore, but he'd be up on deck directly. Half sick and half glad at this additional delay, Mark left the saloon and lingered listlessly about above, watching the Lascars hauling up baggage from the hold—they would have been interesting enough to him at any other time, with their seamed bilious complexions of every degree of swarthiness, set off by the touches of colour in their sashes and head coverings, their strange cries and still more uncouth jocularity—but he soon tired of them, and wandered aft, where the steamer-chairs, their usefulness at an end for that voyage, were huddled together dripping and forlorn on the damp red deck. He was still standing by them, idly turning over the labels attached to their backs, and reading the names thereon without the slightest real curiosity, when he heard a well-remembered voice behind him crying, 'Mark, my dear old fellow, so you've come after all! I was half afraid you wouldn't think it worth your while. I can't tell you how glad I am to see you!' And he turned with a guilty start to face the man he had wronged.

'Evidently,' thought Mark, 'he knows nothing yet, or he wouldn't meet me like this!' and he gripped the cordial hand held out to him with convulsive force; his face was white and his lips trembled, he could not speak.

Such unexpected emotion on his part touched and gratified Holroyd, who patted him on the shoulder affectionately. 'It's all right, old boy, I understand,' he said; 'so you did think I was gone after all? Well, this is a greater pleasure to me than ever it can be to you.'

'I never expected to see you again,' said Mark, as soon as he could speak; 'even now I can hardly believe it.'

'I'm quite real, however,' said Holroyd, laughing; 'there's more of me now than when they carried me on board from Colombo; don't look so alarmed—the voyage has brought me round again, I'm my old self again.'

As a matter of fact there was a great change in him; his bearded face, still burnt by the Ceylon sun, was lined and wasted, his expression had lost its old dreaminess, and when he did not smile, was sterner and more set than it had been; his manner, as Mark noticed later, had a new firmness and decision; he looked a man who could be mercilessly severe in a just cause, and even his evident affection was powerless to reassure Mark.

The hatches had by this time been closed over the hold again and the crane unshipped, the warning bell was ringing for the departure of the tender, though the passengers still lingered till the last minute, as if a little reluctant, after all, to desert the good ship that had been their whole world of late; the reigning beauty of the voyage, who was to remain with the vessel until her arrival at Gravesend, was receiving her last compliments during prolonged and complicated leave-takings, in which, however, the exhilaration of most of her courtiers—now that their leave or furlough was really about to begin—was too irrepressible for sentiment. A last delay at the gangway, where the captain and ship's officers were being overwhelmed with thanks and friendly good-byes, and then the deck was cleared at last, the gangway taken in and the rail refastened, and, as the tender steamed off, all the jokes and allusions which formed the accumulated wit of the voyage flashed out with a brief and final brilliancy, until the hearty cheering given and returned drowned them for ever.

On the tender, such acquaintances as Holroyd had made during the voyage gave Mark no chance of private conversation with him, and even when they had landed and cleared the Custom House, Mark made no use of his opportunity; he knew he must speak soon, but he could not tell him just then, and accordingly put off the evil hour by affecting an intense interest in the minor incidents of the voyage, and in Vincent's experiences of a planter's life. It was the same in the hotel coffee-room, where some of the 'Coromandel's' passengers were breakfasting near them, and the conversation became general; after breakfast, however, Mark proposed to spend some time in seeing the place, an arrangement which he thought would lead the way to confession. But Holroyd would not hear of this; he seemed possessed by a feverish impatience to get to London without delay, and very soon they were pacing the Plymouth railway platform together, waiting for the up train, Mark oppressed by the gloomy conviction that if he did not speak soon, the favourable moment would pass away, never to return.

'Where do you think of going to first when you get in?' he asked, in dread of the answer.

'I don't know,' said Holroyd; 'the Great Western, I suppose—it's the nearest.'

'You mustn't go to an hotel,' said Mark; 'won't you come to my rooms? I don't live with my people any longer, you know, and I can easily put you up.' He was thinking that this arrangement would give him a little more time for his confession.

'Thanks,' said Holroyd gratefully; 'it's very kind of you to think of that, old fellow; I will come to you, then—but there is a house I must go to as soon as we get in: you won't mind if I run away for an hour or two, will you?'

Mark remembered what Caffyn had said. 'There will be plenty of time for that to-morrow, won't there?' he said nervously.

'No,' said Holroyd impatiently; 'I can't wait. I daren't. I have let so much time go by already—you will understand when I tell you all about it, Mark. I can't rest till I know whether there is still a chance of happiness left for me, or—or whether I have come too late and the dream is over.'

In that letter which had fallen into Caffyn's hands Holroyd had told Mabel the love he had concealed so long; he had begged her not to decide too hastily; he would wait any time for her answer, he said, if she did not feel able to give it at once; and in the meantime she should be troubled by no further importunities on his part. This was not, perhaps, the most judicious promise to make; he had given it from an impulse of consideration for her, being well aware that she had never looked upon him as a possible lover, and that his declaration would come upon her with a certain shock. Perhaps, too, he wanted to leave himself a margin of hope as long as possible to make his exile endurable; since for months, if no answer came back to him, he could cheat himself with the thought that such silence was favourable in itself; but even when he came to regret his promise, he shrank from risking all by breaking it. Then came his long illness, and the discovery at Newera Ellia; for the first time he thought that there might be other explanations of the delay, and while he was writing the letter which had come to Mark, he resolved to make one more appeal to Mabel, since it might be that his first by some evil chance had failed to reach her. That second appeal, however, was never made. Before he could do more than begin it, the fever he had never wholly shaken off seized him again and laid him helpless, until, when he was able to write once more, he was already on his way to plead for himself. But the dread lest his own punctilious folly and timidity had closed the way to his heart's desire had grown deeper and deeper, and he felt an impulse now which was stronger than his natural reserve to speak of it to some one.

'Yes,' he continued, 'she may have thought I was drowned, as you did; perhaps she has never dreamed how much she is to me: if I could only hope to tell her that even now!'

'Do you mind telling me her name?' said Mark, with a deadly foreboding of what was coming.

'Did I never speak of the Langtons to you?' said Holroyd. 'I think I must have done so. She is a Miss Langton. Mabel, her name is' (he dwelt on the name with a lover's tenderness). 'Some day if—if it is all well, you may see her, I hope. Oddly enough, I believe she has heard your name rather often; she has a small brother who used to be in your form at St. Peter's; did I never tell you?'

'Never,' said Mark. He felt that fate was too hard for him; he had honestly meant to confess all up to that moment, he had thought to found his strongest plea for forbearance on his approaching marriage. How could he do that now? what mercy could he expect from a rival? He was lost if he was mad enough to arm Holroyd with such a weapon; he was lost in any case, for it was certain that the weapon would not lie hidden long; there were four days still before the wedding—time enough for the mine to explode! What could he do? how could he keep the other in the dark, or get rid of him, before he could do any harm? And then Caffyn's suggestions came back to him. Was it possible to make use of Caffyn's desire for a travelling companion, and turn it to his own purpose? If Caffyn was so anxious to have Holroyd with him in the Lakes, why not let him? It was a desperate chance enough, but it was the only one left to him; if it failed, it would ruin him, but that would certainly happen if he let things take their course; if it succeeded, Mabel would at least be his. His resolution was taken in an instant, and carried out with a strategy that gave him a miserable surprise at finding himself so thorough a Judas. 'By the way,' he said, 'I've just thought of something. Harold Caffyn is a friend of mine. I know he wants to see you again, and he could tell you all you want to hear about—about the Langtons, I've heard him mention them often enough; you see you don't even know where they are yet. I'll wire and ask him to meet us at my rooms, shall I?'

'That's a capital idea!' cried Holroyd. 'Caffyn is sure to know; do it at once, like a good fellow.'

'You stay here then, and look out for the train,' said Mark, as he hurried to the telegraph office, leaving Holroyd thinking how thoughtful and considerate his once selfish friend had become. Mark sent the telegram, which ended, 'He knows nothing as yet. I leave him to you.'

When he returned he found that Holroyd had secured an empty compartment in the train which was preparing to start, and Mark got in with a heavy apprehension of the danger of a long journey alone with Holroyd. He tried to avoid conversation by sheltering himself behind a local journal, while at every stoppage he prayed that a stranger might come to his rescue. He read nothing until a paragraph, copied from a London literary paper, caught his eye. 'We understand,' the paragraph ran, 'that the new novel by the author of "Illusion," Mr. Cyril Ernstone (or rather Mr. Mark Ashburn, as he has now declared himself), will be published early in the present spring, and it is rumoured that the second work will show a marked advance on its predecessor.' It was merely the usual puff preliminary, though Mark took it as a prediction, and at any other time would have glowed with anticipated triumph. Now it only struck him with terror. Was it in Holroyd's paper too? Suppose he asked to look at Mark's, and saw it there, and questioned him, as of course he would! What should he say? Thinking to avoid this as far as possible, he crumpled up the tell-tale paper and hurled it out of window; but his act had precisely the opposite effect, for Holroyd took it as an indication that his companion was ready for conversation, and put down the paper he had been pretending to read.

'Mark,' he began with a slight hesitation, and with his first words Mark knew that the question was coming which he dreaded more than anything; he had no notion how he should reply to it, beyond a general impression that he would have to lie, and lie hard.

'Mark,' said Holroyd again, 'I didn't like to worry you about it before, I thought perhaps you would speak of it first; but—but have you never heard anything more of that ambitious attempt of mine at a novel? You needn't mind telling me.'

'I—I can't tell you,' Mark said, looking away out of the window.

'I don't expect anything good,' said Holroyd; 'I never thought—why should I be such a humbug! I did think sometimes—more lately perhaps—that it wouldn't be an utter failure. I see I was wrong. Well, if I was ambitious, it was rather for her than myself; and if she cares for me, what else matters to either of us? Tell me all about it.'

'You—you remember what happened to the first volume of the "French Revolution"?' began Mark.

'Go on,' said Holroyd.

'It—the book—yours, I mean,' said Mark (he could not remember the original title), 'was burnt.'

'Where? at the office? Did they write and tell you so? had they read it?'

Mark felt he was among pitfalls.

'Not at the office,' he said; 'at my rooms—my old rooms.'

'It came back, then?'

'Yes, it came back. There—there was no letter with it; the girl at the lodgings found the manuscript lying about. She—she burnt it.'

The lies sprang in ready succession from his brain at the critical moment, without any other preparation than the emergency—as lies did with Mark Ashburn; till lately he had hoped that the truth might come, and he loathed himself now for this fresh piece of treachery, but it had saved him for the present, and he could not abandon it.

'I thought it would at least have been safe with you,' said Holroyd, 'if you—no, my dear fellow, I didn't mean to reproach you. I can see how cut up you are about it; and, after all, it—it was only a rejected manuscript—the girl only hastened its course a little. Carlyle rewrote his work; but then I'm not Carlyle. We won't say anything any more about it, eh, old fellow? It's only one dream over.'

Mark was seized with a remorse which almost drove him to confess all and take the consequences; but Holroyd had sunk back to his position by the window again, and there was a fixed frown on his face which, although it only arose from painful thought, effectually deterred Mark from speaking. He felt now that everything depended on Caffyn. He sat looking furtively at the other now and then, and thinking what terrible reproaches those firm lips might utter; how differently the sad, kind eyes might regard him before long, and once more he longed for a railroad crash which would set him free from his tangled life. The journey ended at last, and they drove to South Audley Street. Vincent was very silent; in spite of his philosophical bearing, he felt the blow deeply. He had come back with ideas of a possible literary career before him, and it was hard to resign them all at once. It was rather late in the afternoon when they arrived, and Caffyn was there to receive them; he was delighted to welcome Holroyd, and his cordiality restored the other to cheerfulness; it is so pleasant to find that one is not forgotten—and so rare. When Vincent had gone upstairs to see his sleeping-room, Caffyn turned to Mark: there was a kind of grin on his face, and yet a certain admiration too.

'I got your telegram,' he said. 'So—so you've brought yourself to part with him after all?'

'I thought over what you said,' returned Mark, 'and—and he told me something which would make it very awkward and—and painful for him, and for myself too, if he remained.'

'You haven't told him anything, then, still?'

'Nothing,' said Mark.

'Then,' said Caffyn, 'I think I shall not be alone at Wastwater after all, if you'll only let me manage.'

Was Mark at all surprised at the languid Harold Caffyn exerting himself in this way? If he was, he was too grateful for the phenomenon to care very much about seeking to explain it. Caffyn was a friend of his, he had divined that Holroyd's return was inconvenient: very likely he had known of Vincent's hopeless attachment for Mabel, and he was plainly anxious to get a companion at the Lakes; anyone of these was motive enough. Soon after, Holroyd joined them in the sitting-room. Caffyn, after more warm congratulations and eager questioning, broached the Wastwater scheme. 'You may as well,' he concluded, 'London's beastly at this time of year. You're looking as if the voyage hadn't done you much good, too, and it will be grand on the mountains just now; come with me by the early train to-morrow, you've no packing to do. I'm sure we shall pull together all right.'

'I'm sure, of that,' said Vincent; 'and if I had nothing to keep me in town—but I've not seen the Langtons yet, you know. And, by-the-bye, you can tell me where I shall find them now. I suppose they have not moved?'

'Now I've got you!' laughed Caffyn; 'if the Langtons are the only obstacle, you can't go and see them, for the very good reason that they're away—abroad somewhere!'

'Are they all there?'

'Every one of 'em; even the father, I fancy, just now.'

'Do you know when they're likely to be back?'

'Haven't heard,' said Caffyn calmly; 'they must come back soon, you see, for the lovely Mabel's wedding.'

Mark held his breath as he listened; what was Caffyn going to say next? Vincent's face altered suddenly.

'Then Mabel—Miss Langton, is going to be married?' he asked in a curiously quiet tone.

'Rather,' said Caffyn; 'brilliant match in its way, I understand. Not much money on his side, but one of the coming literary fellows, and all that kind of thing, you know; just the man for that sort of girl. Didn't you know about it?'

'No,' said Holroyd uneasily; he was standing with his elbow on the mantelpiece, with his face turned from the other two; 'I didn't know—what is his name?'

'Upon my soul I forget—heard it somewhere.—Ashburn, you don't happen to know it, do you?'

'I!' cried Mark, shrinking; 'no, I—I haven't heard.'

'Well,' continued Caffyn, 'it isn't of much consequence, is it? I shall hit upon it soon, I dare say. They say she's deucedly fond of him, though. Can't fancy disdainful Miss Mabel condescending to be deucedly fond of any one—but so they tell me. And I say, Holroyd, to come back to the point, is there any reason why you should stay in town?'

'None,' said Holroyd, with pain ringing in his voice, 'none in the world why I should stay anywhere now.'

'Well, won't you come with me? I start the first thing to-morrow—it will do you good.'

'It's kind of you to ask,' said Vincent, 'but I can't desert Ashburn in that way after he took the trouble to come down and meet me; we've not seen one another for so long,—have we, Mark?'

Caffyn smiled in spite of himself. 'Why, didn't he tell you?' he said; 'he's arranged to go abroad himself in a day or two.'

Vincent glanced round at Mark, who stood there the personification of embarrassment and shame. 'I see,' he said, with a change in his voice, 'I shall only be in the way here, then.' Mark said nothing—he could not. 'Well, Caffyn, I'll come with you; the Lakes will do as well as any other place for the short time I shall be in England.'

'Then you haven't come home for good?' inquired Caffyn.

'For good? no—not exactly,' he replied bitterly; 'plantation life has unsettled me, you see. I shall have to go back to it.'

'To Ceylon!' cried Mark, with hopes that had grown quite suddenly. Was it, could it be possible that the threatened storm was going to pass away—not for a time, but altogether?

'Anywhere,' said Holroyd! 'what does it matter?'

'There's a man I know,' observed Caffyn, 'who's going out to a coffee estate somewhere in Southern India, the Annamalli Hills, I think he said; he was wanting some one with a little experience to go out with him the other day. He's a rattling good fellow too—Gilroy, his name is. I don't know if you'd care to meet him. You might think it good enough to join him, at all events for a trial.'

'Yes,' said Holroyd, listlessly, 'I may as well see him.'

'Well,' said Caffyn, 'he's at Liverpool just now, I believe. I can write to him and tell him about you, and ask him to come over and meet us somewhere, and then you could settle all about it, you know, if you liked the look of him.'

'It's very good of you to take all this trouble,' said Vincent gratefully.

'Bosh!' said Caffyn, using that modern form for polite repudiation of gratitude—'no trouble at all; looks rather as if I wanted to get rid of you, don't you know—Gilroy's going out so very soon.'

'Is he?' said Vincent. He had no suspicions; Mabel's engagement seemed only too probable, and he knew that he had never had any claim upon her; but for all that, he had no intention of taking the fact entirely upon trust; he would not leave England till he had seen her and learned from her own lips that he must give up hope for ever; after that the sooner he went the better.

'You needn't go out with him unless you want to—you might join him later there; but of course you wouldn't take anything for granted, nothing. Still, if you did care to go out at once, I suppose you've nothing in the way of preparations to hinder you, eh?'

'No,' said Vincent; 'it would only be transferring my trunks from one ship to another; but I—I don't feel well enough to go out just yet.'

'Of course not,' said Caffyn; 'you must have a week or two of mountain air first, then you'll be ready to go anywhere; but I must have you at Wastwater,' he added, with a laughing look of intelligence at Mark, whose soul rose against all this duplicity—and subsided again.

How wonderfully everything was working out! Unless some fatality interposed between then and the next morning, the man he dreaded would be safely buried in the wildest part of the Lake District—he might even go off to India again and never learn the wrong he had suffered! At all events, Mark was saved for a time. He was thankful, deeply thankful now that he had resisted that mad impulse to confession.

Vincent had dropped into an arm-chair with his back to the window, brooding over his shattered ambitions; all his proud self-confidence in his ability to win fame for the woman he loved was gone now; he felt that he had neither the strength nor the motive to try again. If—if this he had heard was true, he must be an exile, with lower aims and a blanker life than those he had once hoped for.

All at once Mark, as he stood at the window with Caffyn, stepped back with a look of helpless terror.

'What the deuce is it now?' said the other under his breath.

Mark caught Caffyn's elbow with a fierce grip; a carriage had driven up; they could see it plainly still in the afternoon light, which had only just begun to fade.

'Do you see?' muttered Mark thickly. 'She's in it; she looked up—and saw me!'

Caffyn himself was evidently disturbed. 'Not, not Mabel?' he whispered. 'Worse! it's Dolly—and she'll come up. She'll see him!'

The two stood there staring blankly at each other, while Holroyd was still too absorbed to have the least suspicion that the future happiness or misery of himself and others was trembling just then in the balance.

CHAPTER XXX

THE WAY OF TRANSGRESSORS

Dolly's mere appearance in the room would lead Vincent to suspect that he had been deceived; her first words would almost inevitably expose the fraud. She was coming up, nevertheless, and Mark felt powerless to prevent her—he could only indulge himself in inwardly cursing Caffyn's ingenuity and his own weakness for having brought him to such a pass as this. Caffyn was shaken for the moment, but he soon recovered himself. 'Keep cool, will you,' he whispered (he might have shouted, for Vincent saw and heard nothing just then): 'you stay here and keep him amused—don't let him go near the window!' Then he added aloud, 'I'll go and see if I can find that Bradshaw. Almost certain I didn't bring it with me; but if you saw it there, why'—and he was gone.

Mark caught up a paper with a rapid, 'Oh! I say, Vincent, did you see this correspondence about competitive examinations? Of course you haven't, though—just listen then, it's rather amusing!' and he began to read with desperate animation a string of letters on a subject which, in the absence of worthier sport, was just then being trailed before the public. The newspaper hid his face, and while he read he could strain his ears for the first sign of Dolly's approach. She had seen him, he was sure, and she would insist upon coming up—she was so fond of him! He wished now he had gone down himself instead of leaving it to Caffyn.

Meanwhile the latter had rushed down in time to wave back the maid who was coming to the door, and which he opened himself. Dolly was standing there alone on the doorsteps. She had prepared a polite little formula for the servant, and was therefore disappointed to see Caffyn.

'Why, it's you!' she said, in rather an injured tone.

'You never expected such luck as that, did you?' said Caffyn. 'Is there anything I can do for your ladyship?'

'Mabel asked me to drive round this way and ask if Mark has come back. There's Fräulein in the carriage too, but I wanted to ask all by myself.'

'Pray step this way,' said Caffyn, leading the way with mock politeness to a little sitting-room on the ground floor.

'I can't stay long,' said Dolly. 'Mark isn't here—I saw his face at the window upstairs. Mabel told me to see if he was quite well, and I want to ask him how he is and where he's been.'

'Afraid you can't see him just now,' said Caffyn, 'he's got some one with him he hasn't seen for a long time—we mustn't disturb him; tell Mabel he'll come to-morrow and he's quite well.'

Dolly was preparing to go, when she discovered some portmanteaus and boxes in a corner. 'What a funny box, with all those red tickets on it!' she said. 'Oh, and a big white helmet—it's green inside. Is Mark going to be married in that thing, Harold?'—all at once she stopped short in her examination. 'Why—why, they've got poor Vincent's name on them! they have—look!' And Caffyn realised that he had been too ingenious: he had forgotten all about this luggage in showing Dolly to that room, in his fear lest her voice should be too audible in the passage.

'There, there—you're keeping Fräulein waiting all this time. Never mind about the luggage,' he said hurriedly. 'Good-bye, Dolly; sorry you can't stop.'

'But I can stop,' objected Dolly, who was not easily got rid of at the best of times. 'Harold, I'm sure that dear Vincent has come alive again—he's the somebody Mark hasn't seen for a long time.... Oh, if it really is ... I must go and see!'

Caffyn saw his best course now was the hazardous one of telling the truth. 'Well,' he said, 'as it happens, you're right. Vincent was not drowned, and he is here—but I don't advise you to go to see him for all that.'

'Why?' said Dolly, with her joy suddenly checked—she scarcely knew why.

'He's in a fearful rage with you just now,' said Caffyn; 'he's found out about that letter—that letter you burnt.'

'Mabel said I was never to worry about that horrid letter any more—and I'm not going to—so it's no use your trying to make me,' said Dolly defiantly. And then, as her fears grew, she added, 'What about that letter?'

'Well,' said Caffyn, 'it appears that the letter you tore the stamp off was from Vincent (it had a foreign stamp, I remember), and it was very important. He never got an answer, and he found out somehow that it was because you burnt it—and then—my goodness, Dolly, what a rage he was in!'

'I don't care,' said Dolly. 'Mabel will tell Vincent how it was—she knows.'

'Ah, but you see she don't know,' said Caffyn. 'Do you suppose if she had known who the letter was from and what it was about she would have taken it so quietly? Why, she thinks it was only an old envelope you burnt—I heard her say so—you know she still believes Vincent is dead. She doesn't know the truth yet, but Vincent will tell her. Are you coming up to see him?'

'No,' said Dolly, trembling; 'I—I think I won't—not to-day.'

'Wise child!' said Caffyn, approvingly. 'Between ourselves, Dolly, poor Vincent has come back in such a queer state that he's not fit to see anyone just yet, and we're dreadfully afraid of his meeting Mabel and frightening her.'

'Oh, don't let him come—don't!' cried terrified Dolly.

'Well, I tell you what we've done—I got Mark to agree to it—we haven't told him that you're any of you at home at all; he thinks you're all away, and he's coming with me into the country to-morrow; so, unless you tell Mabel you've seen him—'

'Oh, but I won't; I don't want her to know—not now!' said Dolly. 'Oh, and I was so glad when I first heard of it! Is he—is he very angry, Harold?'

'I don't advise you to come near him just yet,' he said. 'You won't tell Fräulein, of course? I'll see you to the carriage ... how do, Fräulein? Home, I suppose?' And the last thing he saw was Dolly's frightened glance up at the window as the carriage drove off. 'She won't tell this time,' he said to himself.

And indeed poor Dolly was silent enough all the way home, and met Fräulein Moser's placid stream of talk with short and absent answers. That evening, however, in the schoolroom, she roused herself to express a sudden interest in Colin's stamp album, which she coaxed him to show her.

As he was turning over the pages, one by one, she stopped him suddenly. 'What is that one?' she said, pointing out a green-coloured stamp amongst the colonial varieties.

'Can't you read?' said Colin, a little contemptuously, even while regarding this healthy interest as a decided sign of grace in a girl: 'there's "Ceylon Postage" on the top, isn't there? It isn't rare, though—twenty-four cents—I gave twopence for it; but I've had much more expensive ones, only I swopped them. If you want to see a rare one, here's a Virgin Islands down here—'

'I think I'll see the rest another time, Colin, thanks,' said Dolly; 'I'm tired now.'

'I mayn't have time to show you another day,' said Colin, 'so you'd better—' But Dolly had gone—her passion for information having flickered out as suddenly as it rose. She knew that English-looking green stamp well enough; there had been dreadful days once when it had seemed always floating before her eyes, the thing which might send her to prison; she was much older now, of course, and knew better; but, for all that, it had not quite lost its power to plague her yet.

For, this time at least, she was sure that Harold had not been teasing; she had burnt the letter, and it came from Ceylon; Vincent must have written it, and he had come back and meant to scold her—she had cried so when she heard he was drowned, and now she was afraid to see him—a shadow she dared not speak of had once more fallen across her life!

Caffyn came up with a Bradshaw in his hand. 'Had a hunt after it, I can tell you,' he said; 'and then your old landlady and I had a little chat—I couldn't get away from her. Aren't you fellows ready for some dinner?' And the relief with which Mark had seen the carriage roll away below had really given him something of an appetite.

Before dinner, however, Mark took Caffyn up into his bedroom under the pretence of washing his hands, but with the real object of preventing a hideous possibility which—for his fears quickened his foresight—had just occurred to him. 'If you don't mind,' he began awkwardly, 'I—I'd rather you didn't mention that I had written—I mean, that you didn't say anything about "Illusion," you know.'

Caffyn's face remained unchanged. 'Certainly, if you wish it,' he said; 'but why? Is this more of your modesty?'

'No,' said Mark, weakly, 'no; not exactly modesty; but, the fact is, I find that Holroyd has been going in for the same sort of thing himself, and—and not successfully; and so I shouldn't like to—'

'Quite so,' agreed Caffyn. 'Now, really, that's very nice and considerate of you to think of that, Ashburn. I like to see that sort of thing in a fellow, you know; shows he isn't spoilt by success! Well, you can rely on me—I won't breathe a word to suggest your being in any way connected with pen and ink.'

'Thanks,' said Mark, gratefully; 'I know you won't,' and they went down.

Mark could not but feel degraded in his own eyes by all this hypocrisy; but it was so necessary, and was answering its purpose so well, that his mental suffering was less than might have been expected.

At dinner he felt himself able, now that his fears were removed, to encourage conversation, and drew from Holroyd particulars of his Ceylon life, which supplied them with topics for that evening, and prevented the meal from becoming absolutely dull, even though it was at no time remarkable for festivity.

'I tell you what I can't quite understand,' said Caffyn on one occasion. 'Why did you let us all go on believing that you were drowned on the "Mangalore" when a letter or two would have put it all right?'

'I did write one letter home,' said Holroyd, with a faint red tingeing his brown cheeks. 'I might have written to Mark, I know; but I waited to hear from him first, and then one thing after another prevented me. It was only when I sent down to Colombo, months afterwards, for my heavy baggage, that I heard what had happened to the ship.'

'Well,' observed Caffyn, 'you might have written then.'

'I know that,' said Holroyd: 'the fact is, though, that I never thought it possible, after going off the ship, as I did at Bombay, that I could be reported amongst the missing. As soon as I discovered that that was so, I wrote. No doubt I ought to have written before; still, when you have a large estate on your hands, and you feel your health gradually going, and failure coming closer and closer, you don't feel a strong inclination for correspondence.'

He fell back into a moody silence again. Perhaps, after all, his silence had arisen from other causes still; perhaps, as his health declined, he had come to find a morbid satisfaction in the idea that he was alone—forgotten by those he cared for—until his very isolation had become dear to him. He had been a fool—he knew that now—his two friends had mourned him sincerely, and would have been overjoyed to hear that he was alive. He had wronged them—what if he had wronged Mabel too? Another had won her, but had not his own false delicacy and perverted pride caused him to miss the happiness he hungered for? 'At all events,' he thought, 'I won't whine about it. Before I go out again I will know the worst. If the other man is a good fellow, and will make her happy, I can bear it.' But deep down in his heart a spark of hope glimmered still.

'Well, I must be going,' said Caffyn, breaking in on his reverie. 'I've got to pack before I go to bed. Look here, Vincent' (and he consulted the Bradshaw as he spoke), 'there's a train at ten in the morning, from Euston; gets in to Drigg late at night; we can sleep there, and drive over to Wastwater next day. Will that do you?'

'It's rather sudden,' said Holroyd, hesitating.

'Oh, come, old fellow, you're not going to back out of it now. I've stayed over a day on the chance of bringing you; you promised to come just now; there's nothing to keep you, and I've set my heart on having you.'

'Then I'll come,' said Holroyd. 'We'll meet on the platform to-morrow.'

Mark breathed more freely again. He accompanied Caffyn down to the front door, and then, as they stood for a moment in the little passage dimly lighted by a feeble kerosene lamp on a bracket, each looked at the other strangely.

'Well,' said Caffyn, with a light laugh, 'I hope you are satisfied: he'll be well out of the way for at least a fortnight, and, if this Gilroy business comes off, he may be taken off your hands altogether before you come back.'

'I know,' said Mark, 'you've been awfully kind about it; the—the only thing I can't understand is, why you're taking all this trouble.' For this was beginning to exercise his mind at last.

'Oh,' said Caffyn, 'is that it? Well, I don't mind telling you—I like you, my boy, and if anything I can do will save you a little worry and give me a companion in my loneliness into the bargain (mind, I don't say that hasn't something to do with it), why, I'm delighted to do it. But if you'd rather see some more of him before he goes out again, there's no hurry. Gilroy will wait, and I won't say any more about it.'

'It—it seems a good opening,' said Mark hastily, not without shame at himself; 'perhaps the sooner it is arranged the better, don't you think?'

Caffyn laughed again. 'You old humbug!' he said. 'Why don't you tell the truth? You've found out he's a defeated rival, and you don't care about having him sitting sighing on the door-step of that little house in—where is it?—on Campden Hill! Well, don't be alarmed; I think he'll go, and I promise you I won't try to prevent him if he's keen on it.'

He laughed aloud once or twice as he walked home. Mark's tender solicitude for his friend's future tickled his sense of humour. 'And the funniest thing about it is,' he thought, 'that I'm going to help the humbug!'

Mark was up early the next morning, and hurried Holroyd over his breakfast as much as he dared. He had a ghastly fear of missing the train, in consequence of which they arrived at Euston at least half an hour before the time of starting. Caffyn was not on the platform, and Mark began to dread his being too late. 'And then,' he thought with a shudder, 'I shall have him on my hands for another whole day. Another day of this would drive me mad! And I must see Mabel this morning.' The luggage had been duly labelled, and there was nothing to do but to wander up and down the platform, Mark feeling oppressed by a sinking premonition of disaster whenever he loosed his hold of Holroyd's arm for a moment. He was waiting while the latter bought a paper at the bookstall, when suddenly he felt himself slapped heavily on the back by some one behind him, and heard a voice at whose well-known accents he very nearly fell down with horror. It was his terrible uncle!

"Ullo, you know, this won't do, young fellow; what's all this?' he began, too evidently bursting with the badinage which every Benedick must endure. 'Why, you ain't going for your honeymoon before the wedding?—that's suspicious-lookin', that is!'

'No, no, it's all right,' said Mark, trembling; 'how do you do, uncle? I—I'd rather you didn't talk about—about that here—not quite so loud!'

'Well, I don't know what there is in that to be ashamed of,' said his uncle; 'and if I mayn't be allowed to talk about a wedding—which but for me, mind yer, would a' been long enough in coming about—p'raps you'll tell me who is; and, as to talking loud, I'm not aware that I'm any louder than usual. What are you looking like that for? Hang me if I don't think there's something in this I ought to see to!' he broke out, with a sudden change of face, as his shrewd little eyes fell on Holroyd's rug, which Mark was carrying for the moment. 'Mark, for all your cleverness, you're a slippery feller—I always felt that about you. You're up to something now—you're meaning to play a trick on one that trusts you, and I won't have it—do you hear me?—I tell you I won't have it!'

'What do you mean?' faltered Mark. For the instant he thought himself detected, and did not pause to think how improbable this was.

'You know what I mean. I'm not going to stand by and see you ruin yourself. You shan't set a foot in the train if I have to knock you down and set on you myself! If' (and his voice shook here)—'if you've got into any mess—and it's money—I'll clear you this time, whatever it costs me, but you shan't run away from that dear girl that you're promised to—I'm d—d if you do!'

Mark laughed naturally and easily enough.

'Did you think I was going to run away then—from Mabel?'

'You tell me what you're doing 'ere at this time o' day, then,' said his uncle, only partially reassured. 'What's that you're carrying?'

'This? My friend's rug. I'm seeing a friend off—that's all. If you do not believe me, I'll show you the friend.' As he looked back at the bookstall he saw something which stiffened him once more with helpless horror: the man at the stall was trying to persuade Holroyd to buy a book for the journey—he was just dusting one now, a volume in a greenish cover with bold crimson lettering, before recommending it; and the book was a copy of the latest edition of 'Illusion,' the edition which bore Mark's name on the title-page! In his despair Mark did the very last thing he would otherwise have done—he rushed up to Holroyd and caught his arm. 'I say, old fellow, don't let them talk you into buying any of that rubbish. Look here, I—I want to introduce you to my uncle!'

'I wasn't asking the gentleman to buy no rubbish,' said the man at the bookstall, resenting the imputation. 'This is a book which is 'aving a large sale just now: we've sold as many as'—but here Mark succeeded in getting Vincent away and bringing him up to Mr. Lightowler.

'How are you, sir?' began that gentleman, with a touch of condescension in his manner. 'So it's only you that's goin' off? Well, that's a relief to my mind, I can tell yer; for when I saw Mark 'ere with that rug, I somehow got it into my mind that he was goin' to make a run for it. And there 'ud be a pretty thing for all parties—hey?'

'Your nephew very kindly came to see me off, that's all,' said Holroyd.

'Oh,' said Uncle Solomon, with a tolerant wave of his hand, 'I don't object to that, yer know, I've no objections to that—not that I don't think (between ourselves, mind yer) that he mightn't p'raps he better employed just now;' and here, to Mark's horror, he winked with much humorous suggestiveness at both of them.

'That is very likely,' said Holroyd.

'What I mean by saying he might be "better employed,"' continued Uncle Solomon, 'is that when—'

'Yes, yes, uncle,' Mark hastened to interpose, 'but on special occasions like these one can leave one's duties for a while.'

'Now there I think you make your mistake—you make too sure, Mark. I tell you (and I think your friend 'ere will bear me out in this) that, in your situation, it don't do to go leaving 'em in the lurch too often—it don't do!' Mark could stand no more of this.

'A lurch now,' he said—'what an odd expression that is! Do you know, I've often tried to picture to myself what kind of a thing a lurch may be. I always fancy it must be a sort of a deep hole. Have you any idea, Vincent?' Mark would have been too thankful to have been able to drop his uncle down a lurch of that description occasionally, particularly when he chose, as he did on this occasion, to take offence at his nephew's levity.

'Lurch is a good old English word, let me tell yer, Mr. Schoolmaster that was,' he broke in; 'and if I'd done as many a man in my position would, and left you in the lurch a few months ago, where would you ha' been?—that's what I'd like to know! For I must tell yer, Mr. Holroyd, that that feller came to me with a precious long face, and says he, "Uncle," he says, "I want you to—"'

Mark felt that in another moment the whole story of his uncle's intervention at Kensington Park Gardens would burst upon Holroyd with the force of a revelation, and he was at the end of his resources. Where was Caffyn all this time? How could he be so careless as to be late?

'I—I don't think it's quite fair to tell all that,' he expostulated weakly.

'Fair!' said Uncle Solomon. 'I made no secrecy over it. I did nothing to be ashamed of and hush up, and it's no disgrace to you that I can see to be helped by an uncle that can afford it. Well, as I was saying, Mark came to me—'

Here a small Juggernaut car in the shape of a high-piled truck came rolling down on them with a shout of, 'By your leave there, by your leave!' from the unseen porter behind. Mark drew Vincent sharply aside, and then saw Caffyn coming quickly towards them through the crowd, and forgot the torpedo his uncle was doing his best to launch: he felt that with Caffyn came safety. Caffyn, who had evidently been hurrying, gave a sharp glance at the clock: 'Sorry to be late,' he said, as he shook hands. 'Binny fetched me a hansom with a wobbling old animal in it that ran down like a top when we'd got half-way; and of course the main road was up for the last mile—however, I've just done it. Come along, Holroyd, I've got a carriage.' And the three men went off together, leaving Mr. Lightowler behind in a decidedly huffy frame of mind.

'Good-bye, Mark,' said Vincent affectionately before he got in. 'We've not had time to see much of one another, have we? I can't say how glad I am, though, even to have had that. I shall try not to leave England without seeing you once more; but, if we don't meet again, then good-bye and God bless you, old boy! Write to me from abroad, and tell me where you are. We mustn't lose touch of one another again—eh?'

'Good-bye,' said Caffyn, in a hurried voice before he followed. 'I've got your Swiss address, haven't I? and if—if anything happens, you shall hear from me.'

The next minute Mark stood back, and as the long line of chocolate-and-white carriages rolled gently past he caught his last sight of Vincent's face, with the look on it that he could not hope to see again. He saw Caffyn too, who gave him a cool side-jerk of the head at parting, with a smile which, when Mark recollected it later, seemed to account for some of the uneasiness he felt. But, after all, this desperate plan had prospered, thanks to Caffyn's unconscious assistance. If Vincent had been gagged and bound and kept in a dungeon cell till the wedding was over, he could hardly be more harmless than he would be at Wastwater. Two more days—only two more—and the calamity he dreaded even more than exposure would be averted for ever—none but he would call Mabel Langton his wife! Thinking this as he left the platform, he ran up against his uncle, whom he had completely forgotten: he was harmless now as a safety match bereft of its box, and Mark need fear him no longer. 'Why, there you are, uncle—eh?' he said, with much innocent satisfaction. 'I couldn't think where you'd got to.'

'Oh, I dessay,' growled Mr. Lightowler, 'and your friend nearly lost the train lookin' for me, didn't he? I'm not to be got over by soft speakin', Mark, and I'm sharp enough to see where I'm not wanted. I must say, though, that that feller, if he's one of your friends, might a' shown me a little more common respect, knowing 'oo I was, instead o' bolting away while I was talkin' to him, for all the world as if he wanted to get rid of me.'

Mark saw that his uncle was seriously annoyed, and hastened to soothe his ruffled dignity—a task which was by no means easy.

'It isn't as if I needed to talk to him either,' he persisted. 'I've a friend of my own to see off, that's why I'm here at this time (Liverpool he's goin' to),' he added, with some obscure sense of superiority implied in this fact; 'and let me tell you, he's a man that's looked up to by every one there, is Budkin, and'll be mayor before he dies! And another thing let me say to you, Mark. In the course of my life I've picked up, 'ere and there, some slight knowledge of human character, and I read faces as easy as print. Now I don't like the look of that friend of yours.'

'Do you mean Caffyn?' asked Mark.

'I don't know him; no, I mean that down-lookin' chap you introduced to me—'Olroyd, isn't it? Well, don't you have too much to do with him—there's something in his eye I don't fancy; he ain't to be trusted, and you mind what I say.'

'Well,' said Mark, 'I can promise you that I shall see no more of him than I can help in future, if that's any relief to your mind.'

'You stick to that then, and—'ullo, there is Budkin come at last! You come along with me and I'll introduce you (he's not what you call a refined sort of feller, yer know,' he explained forbearingly, 'but still we've always been friends in a way); you can't stop? Must go back to Miss Mabel, hey? Well, well, I won't keep yer; good-bye till the day after to-morrow then, and don't you forgit what you'd 'a been if you'd been thrown on the world without an uncle—there'd be no pretty Miss Mabel for you then, whatever you may think about it, young chap!'

When Mark made his appearance at Kensington Park Gardens again, Dolly watched his face anxiously, longing to ask if Vincent had really gone at last, but somehow she was afraid. And so, as the time went by, and no Vincent Holroyd came to the door to denounce her, she took comfort and never knew how her fears were shared by her new brother-in-law.

CHAPTER XXXI

AGAG

At a certain point between Basle and Schaffhausen, the Rhine, after winding in wide curves through low green meadows fringed with poplars, suddenly finds itself contracted to a narrow and precipitous channel, down which it foams with a continuous musical roar. On the rocks forming this channel, connected by a quaint old bridge, stand the twin towns, Gross and Klein Laufingen. Of the two there can be no question which has the superior dignity, for, while Klein Laufingen (which belongs to Baden) is all comprised in a single narrow street ending in a massive gatehouse, Gross Laufingen, which stands in Swiss territory, boasts at least two streets and a half, besides the advantages of a public platz that can scarcely be smaller than an average London back garden, a church with a handsome cupola and blue and gold-faced clock, and the ruins of what was once an Austrian stronghold crowning the hill around which the roofs are clustered, with a withered tree on the ragged top of its solitary tall grey tower. Gross Laufingen has seen more stirring times than at present: it was a thriving post town once, a halting-place for all the diligences. Napoleon passed through it, too, on his way to Moscow, and on the roof of an old tower outside the gate is still to be seen a grotesque metal profile, riddled with the bullets of French conscripts, who made a target of it in sport or insult, when a halt was called. Now the place is sleepy and quiet enough: there are no diligences to rattle and lumber over the stones, and the most warlike spectacle there is provided by the Swiss militiamen as they march in periodically from the neighbouring villages to have their arms inspected, singing choruses all the way. There is a railway, it is true, on the Klein Laufingen bank, but a railway where the little station and mouth of the tunnel have been so ornamentally treated that at a slight distance a train coming in irresistibly suggests one of those working models set in motion by either a dropped penny or the fraudulent action of the human breath, as conscience permits. So innocent an affair is powerless to corrupt Laufingen, and has brought as yet but few foreigners to its gates. English, Russian, and American tourists may perhaps exclaim admiringly as the trains stop, affording a momentary view of the little town grouped compactly on the rocks with the blue-green cataract rushing by—but they are bound for Schaffhausen or the Black Forest or Constance, and cannot break the journey—so the hosts of personally conducted ones pass Laufingen by, and Laufingen seems upon the whole resigned to its obscurity. But Mark Ashburn, at least, had felt its gentle attractions, having come upon it almost by accident, as he returned alone from the Black Forest after the tour with Caffyn. His thoughts were constantly of Mabel Langton at that time, and he found a dreamy pleasure in the idea of coming to Laufingen some day when she should be his companion, which made him look upon everything he saw merely as a background for her fair face. It had seemed a very hopeless dream then, and yet a few months more and the dream had come to pass. He was at Laufingen once again, and Mabel was by his side.

The long nightmare of those days before the wedding was over at last. He had not dared to feel secure, even in the church, so strong was his presentiment of evil. But nothing had happened, the words were spoken which made Mabel his own, and neither man nor angel intervened. And now a week had gone by, during which nothing from without had threatened his happiness; and for a time, as he resolutely shut his eyes to all but the present, he had been supremely happy. Then by degrees the fox revived and began to gnaw once more. His soul sickened as he remembered in what a Fool's Paradise he was living. Unless Holroyd decided to leave England at once with this young Gilroy of whom Caffyn had spoken—a stranger—he would certainly learn how he had been tricked with regard to Mabel's marriage, and this would lead him on to the full discovery of his wrongs. In his mad determination to win her at all costs, Mark had disregarded everything but the immediate future. If shame and misery were to come upon him, he had told himself, he would at least have the memory of a period of perfect bliss to console him—he might lose all else, but Mabel could not be taken from him. But now, as she took no pains to hide the content which filled her heart, he would scarcely bear to meet her sweet grey eyes for the thought that soon the love he read in them would change to aversion and cold contempt, and each dainty caress was charged for him with a ferocious irony. He knew at last his miserable selfishness in having linked her lot with his, and there were times when in his torture he longed for courage to tell her all, and put an end with his own hand to a happiness which was to him the bitterest of delusions. But he dared not; he had had such marvellous escapes already that he clung to the hope that some miracle might save him yet.

And this was Mark's condition on the morning when this chapter finds him. There is a certain retreat which the town would seem to have provided for the express benefit of lovers—a rustic arbour on a little mount near the railway station overlooking the Rhine Fall. The surly, red-bearded signalman who watched over the striped barrier at the level crossing by the tunnel had understood the case from the first, and (not altogether from disinterested motives, perhaps) would hasten to the station as soon as he saw the young couple crossing the bridge and fetch the key of the little wooden gate which kept off all unlicensed intruders.

It was on this mount that Mark stood now with Mabel by his side, looking down on the scene below. Spring had only just set in, and the stunted acacia trees along the road to the bridge were still bare, and had the appearance of distorted candelabra; the poplars showed only the mistiest green as yet, the elms were leafless, and the horse-chestnuts had not unfolded a single one of their crumpled claws. But the day was warm and bright, the sky a faint blue, with a few pinkish-white clouds shaded with dove colour near the horizon, pigeons were fluttering round the lichened piers of the old bridge, which cast a broad band of purple on the bright green water, and the cuckoo was calling incessantly from the distant woods. Opposite were the tall houses, tinted in faint pink and grey and cream colour, with their crazy wooden balconies overhanging the rocks, and above the high-pitched brown roofs rose the church and the square tree-crowned ruin, behind which was a background of pine-covered hills, where the snow still lay amongst the trunks in a silver graining on the dark red soil. Such life as the little place could boast was in full stir; every now and then an ox-cart or a little hooded gig would pass along the bridge, and townsmen in brown straw hats would meet half-way with elaborate salutations and linger long to gossip, and bare-headed girls with long plaited pigtails present their baskets and bundles to be peered into or prodded suspiciously by the customs officer stationed at the Baden frontier-post, striped in brilliant crimson and yellow, like a giant sugarstick. Over on the little Laufenplatz children were playing about amongst the big iron salmon cages, and old people were sitting in the sunshine on the seats by the fountain, where from time to time a woman would fill her shining tin pails, or a man come to rinse out a tall wooden funnel before strapping it on his back. Down on the rocks below, in a little green cradle swinging over the torrent, sat a man busy with his pipe and newspaper, which he occasionally left to haul up and examine the big salmon nets by the aid of the complicated rigging of masts and yards at his side.

'How charming it all is!' said Mabel, turning her bright face to Mark. 'I am so glad we didn't let ourselves be talked into going anywhere else. Mamma thought we were mad to come here so early in the year. I think she fancied it was somewhere in the heart of the Alps, though, and I never expected anything like this myself?'

'How would you like to stay out here more than a month, Mabel—all the summer, perhaps?' he asked.

'It would be delightful, for some things,' she said, 'but I think I shall be willing to go back when the end of the month comes, Mark; we must, you know; our house will be ready for us, and then there is your work waiting for you, you know you would never write a line here, you are so disgracefully idle!'

'I—I was only joking,' he said (although his expression was far from jocular); 'we will enjoy all this while we can, and when—when the end comes we can remember how happy we were!'

'When the end of this comes we shall only be beginning to be very happy in another way at home in our own pretty house, Mark. I'm not in the least afraid of the future. Are you?'

He drew her slight form towards him and pressed her to his heart with a fervour in which there was despair as well as love.

'Do you think I could be afraid of any future, so long as you were part of it, my darling?' he said. 'It is only the fear of losing you that comes over me sometimes!'

'You silly boy!' said Mabel, looking up at his overcast face with a little tender laugh. 'I never knew you could be so sentimental. I am quite well, and I don't mean to die as long as you want me to take care of you!'

He dreaded to lose her by a parting far bitterer than death; but he had said too much already, and only smiled sadly to himself at the thought of the ghastly mockery which the memory of her words now might have for him in a day or two. She was daintily rearranging the violets in his buttonhole, and he caught the slender white hands in his, and, lifting them to his lips, kissed them with a passionate humility. A little while, perhaps, and those dear hands would never again thrill warm in his grasp as he felt them now!

'I'm afraid,' said Mabel a little later, 'you're letting yourself be worried still by something. Is it the new book? Are you getting impatient to hear about it?'

'I did expect some letters before this,' replied Mark (he was indeed fast growing desperate at Caffyn's silence); 'but I dare say everything is going on well.'

'The train from Basle came in just as we got here,' said Mabel. 'See, there is the postman crossing the bridge now; I'm getting anxious too, Mark, I can't think why I have had no letters from home lately. I hope it is nothing to do with Dolly. She was looking quite ill when we went away, almost as she did—oh, Mark, if I thought Harold had dared to frighten her again!'

Mark remembered that afternoon in South Audley Street. He had never sought to know why Dolly had gone away so obediently, but now he felt a new uneasiness; he had never meant her to be frightened; he would see into it if he ever came home again.

'I don't think he would do such a thing now,' he said, and tried to believe so himself. 'I always thought, you know, Mabel, you were rather hard on him about that affair.'

'I can never change my mind about it,' said Mabel.

'When you are angry, do you never forgive?' asked Mark.

'I could never forgive treachery,' she said. 'Dolly believed every word he said, and he knew it and played on her trust in him for some horrible pleasure I suppose he found in it. No, I can never forgive him for that, Mark, never!'

He turned away with a spasm of conscience. If Caffyn had been a traitor, what was he?

He was roused from a gloomy reverie by Mabel's light touch on his arm. 'Look, Mark,' she cried, 'there is something you wanted to see—there's a timber raft coming down the river.'

For within the last few days the Rhine had risen sufficiently to make it possible to send the timber down the stream, instead of by the long and costly transport overland, and as she spoke the compact mass of pine trunks lashed together came slowly round the bend of the river, gradually increasing in pace until it shot the arch of the bridge and plunged through the boiling white rapids, while the raft broke up with a dull thunder followed by sharp reports as the more slender trunks snapped with the strain.

Mark looked on with a sombre fascination, as if the raft typified his life's happiness, till it was all over, and some of the trunks, carried by a cross current into a little creek, had been pulled in to the shore with long hooks, and the rest had floated on again in placid procession, their scraped wet edges gleaming in the sunlight.

As he turned towards the town again, he saw the porter of their hotel crossing the bridge, with the director's little son, a sturdy flaxen-haired boy of about four, running by his side. They passed through the covered part of the bridge and were hidden for an instant, and then turned up the road towards the station.

'They are coming this way,' said Mabel. 'I do believe little Max is bringing me a letter, the darling! I'll run down to the gate and give him a kiss for it.'

For the child's stolid shyness had soon given way to Mabel's advances, and now he would run along the hotel corridors after her like a little dog, and his greatest delight was to be allowed to take her letters to her. They were close to the mount now, the porter in his green baize apron and official flat cap, and little Max in his speckled blue blouse, trotting along to keep up, and waving the envelope he held in his brown fist. Mark could see from where he stood that it was not a letter that the child was carrying.

'It's a telegram, Mabel,' he said, disturbed, though there was no particular cause as yet for being so.

Mabel instantly concluded the worst. 'I knew it,' she said, and the colour left her cheeks and she caught at the rough wooden rail for support. 'Dolly is ill.... Go down and see what it is.... I'm afraid!'

Mark ran down to the gate, and took the telegram away from little Max, whose mouth trembled piteously at not being allowed to deliver it in person to the pretty English lady, and—scarcely waiting to hear the porter's explanation that as he had to come up to the station he had brought the message with him, knowing that he would probably find the English couple in their favourite retreat—he tore open the envelope as he went up the winding path. The first thing that met him was the heading: From H. Caffyn,

Pillar Hotel, Wastwater, and he dared not go on. Something very serious must have happened, since Caffyn had sent a telegram! Before he could read further Mabel came down to meet him.

'It is Dolly, then!' she cried as she saw Mark's face. 'Oh, let us go back at once, Mark, let us go back!'

'It's not from home,' said Mark: 'it's private; go up again, Mabel, I will come to you presently.'

Mabel turned without a word, wounded that he should have troubles which she might not share with him.

When Mark read the telegram he could scarcely believe his eyes at first. Could it really be that the miracle had happened? For the words ran, 'H. of his own accord decided to leave England without further delay. Started yesterday.' That could only mean one thing after what Caffyn had said when they met last. Vincent had gone with Gilroy. In India he would be comparatively harmless; it would be even possible now to carry out some scheme by which the book could be restored without scandal. At last the danger was past! He crumpled up the telegram and threw it away, and then sprang up to rejoin Mabel, whose fears vanished as she met his radiant look. 'I hope I didn't frighten you, darling,' he said. 'It was a business telegram, about which I was getting anxious. I was really afraid to read it for a time; but it's all right, it's good news, Mabel. You don't know what a relief it is to me! And now what shall we do? I feel as if I couldn't stay up here any longer. Shall we go and explore the surrounding country? It won't tire you?'

Mabel was ready to agree to anything in her delight at seeing Mark his old self again, and they went up the narrow street of Klein Laufingen, and through the gatehouse out upon the long white tree-bordered main road, from which they struck into a narrow path which led through the woods to the villages scattered here and there on the distant green slopes.

Mark felt an exquisite happiness as they walked on; the black veil which clouded the landscape was rent. Nature had abandoned her irony. As he walked through the pine-woods and saw the solemn cathedral dimness suddenly chased away as the sunbeams stole down the stately aisles, dappling the red trunks with golden patches and lighting the brilliant emeralds of the moss below, he almost felt it as intended in delicate allusion to the dissipation of his own gloom. Mabel was by his side, and he need tremble no longer at the thought of resigning the sweet companionship, he could listen while she confided her plans and hopes for the future, with no inward foreboding that a day would scatter them to the winds! His old careless gaiety came back as they sat at lunch together in the long low room of an old village inn, while Mabel herself forgot her anxiety about Dolly and caught the infection of his high spirits. They walked back through little groups of low white houses, where the air was sweet with the smell of pine and cattle, and the men were splitting firewood and women gossiping at the doors, and then across the fields, where the peasants looked up to mutter a gruffly civil 'G'n Abend' as they turned the ox-plough at the end of the furrow. Now and then they came upon one of the large crucifixes common in the district, and stopped to examine the curious collection of painted wooden emblems grouped around the central figure, or passed a wayside shrine like a large alcove, with a woman or child kneeling before the gaudily coloured images, but not too absorbed in prayer to cast a glance in the direction of the footsteps.

The sun had set when they reached the old gatehouse again, and saw through its archway the narrow little street with its irregular outlines in bold relief against a pale-green evening sky.

'I haven't tired you, have I?' said Mark, as they drew near the striped frontier post at the entrance to the bridge.

'No, indeed,' she said; 'it has been only too delightful. Why,' she exclaimed suddenly, 'I thought we were the only English people in Laufingen. Mark, surely that's a fellow-countryman?'

'Where?' said Mark. The light was beginning to fade a little, and at first he only saw a stout little man with important pursed lips trimming the oil-lamp which lit up the covered way over the bridge.

'Straight in front; in the angle there,' said Mabel; and even at that distance he recognised the man whose face he had hoped to see no more. His back was turned to them just then, but Mark could not mistake the figure and dress. They were Vincent Holroyd's!

In one horrible moment the joyous security he had felt only the moment before became a distant memory. He stopped short in an agony of irresolution. What could he do? If he went on and Holroyd saw them, as he must, his first words would tell Mabel everything. Yet he must face him soon; there was no escape, no other way but across that bridge. At least, he thought, the words which ruined him should not be spoken in his hearing; he could not stand by and see Mabel's face change as the shameful truth first burst upon her mind.

His nerves were just sufficiently under his control to allow him to invent a hurried pretext for leaving her. He had forgotten to buy some tobacco in a shop they had just passed, he said; he would go back for it now, she must walk on slowly and he would overtake her directly; and so he turned and left her to meet Vincent Holroyd alone.

CHAPTER XXXII

AT WASTWATER

In a little private sitting-room of the rambling old whitewashed building, half farmhouse, half country inn, known to tourists as the Pillar Hotel, Wastwater, Holroyd and Caffyn were sitting one evening, nearly a week after their first arrival in the Lake district. Both were somewhat silent, but the silence was not that contented one which comes of a perfect mutual understanding, as appeared by the conscious manner in which they endeavoured to break it now and then, without much success. By this time, indeed, each was becoming heartily tired of the other, and whatever cordiality there had been between them was fast disappearing on a closer acquaintance. During the day they kept apart by unspoken consent, as Caffyn's natural indolence was enough of itself to prevent him from being Vincent's companion in the long mountain walks by which he tried to weary out his aching sense of failure; but at night, as the hotel was empty at that season, they were necessarily thrown together, and found it a sufficient infliction.

Every day Holroyd determined that he would put an end to it as soon as he could with decency, as a nameless something in Caffyn's manner jarred on him more and more, while nothing but policy restrained Caffyn himself from provoking an open rupture. And so Holroyd was gazing absently into the fire, where the peat and ling crackled noisily as it fell into fantastic peaks and caves, and Caffyn was idly turning over the tattered leaves of a visitors' book, which bore the usual eloquent testimony to the stimulating influence of scenery upon the human intellect. When he came to the last entry, in which, while the size of the mountains was mentioned with some approval, the saltness of the hotel butter was made the subject of severe comment, he shut the book up with a yawn.

'I shall miss the life and stir of all this,' he observed, 'when I get back to town again.' Holroyd did not appear to have heard him, and, as Caffyn had intended a covert sting, the absence of all response did not improve his temper. 'I can't think why the devil they don't send me the paper,' he went on irritably. 'I ordered it to be sent down here regularly, but it never turns up by any chance. I should think even you must be getting anxious to know what's become of the world outside this happy valley?'

'I can't say I am particularly,' said Holroyd; 'I'm so used to being without papers now.'

'Ah,' said Caffyn, with the slightest of sneers, 'you've got one of those minds which can be converted into pocket kingdoms on an emergency. I haven't, you know. I'm a poor creature, and I confess I do like to know who of my friends have been the last to die, or burst up, or bolt, or marry—just now the last particularly. I wonder what's going on in the kitchen, eh?' he added, as now and then shouts and laughter came from that direction. 'Hallo, Jennie, Polly, whatever your name is,' he said to the red-cheeked waiting-maid who entered that instant, 'we didn't ring, but never mind; you just come in time to tell us the cause of these unwonted festivities—who've you got in your kitchen?'

'It's t' hoons,' said the girl.

'Hounds, is it? jolly dogs, rather, I should say.'

'Ay, they've killed near here, and they're soopin' now. Postman's coom over fra' Drigg wi' a letter—will it be for wan of ye?' and she held out an eccentrically shaped and tinted envelope; 'there's a bonny smell on it,' she observed.

'It's all right,' said Caffyn, 'it's mine; no newspapers, eh? Well, perhaps this will do as well!' and as the door closed upon the maid he tore open the letter with some eagerness. 'From the magnificent Miss Featherstone—I must say there's no stiffness about her style, though! What should you say when a letter begins like this— I forgot, though,' he said, stopping himself, 'you're the kind of man who gets no love-letters to speak of.'

'None at all,' said Vincent; 'certainly not to speak of.'

'Well, it's best to keep out of that sort of thing, I dare say, if you can. Gilda tells me that she's been officiating as bridesmaid—full list of costumes and presents—"sure it will interest me," is she? Well, perhaps she's right. Do you know, Holroyd, I rather think I shall go in and see how the jovial huntsmen are getting on in there. You don't mind my leaving you?'

'Not in the least,' said Holroyd; 'I shall be very comfortable here.'

'I don't quite like leaving you in here with nothing to occupy your powerful mind, though,' and he left the room. He came back almost directly, however, with a copy of some paper in his hand: 'Just remembered it as I was shutting the door,' he said; 'it's only a stale old Review I happened to have in my portmanteau; but you may not have seen it, so I ran up and brought it down for you.'

'It's awfully good of you to think of it, really,' said Vincent, much more cordially than he had spoken of late. He had been allowing himself to dislike the other more and more, and this slight mark of thoughtfulness gave him a pang of self-reproach.

'Well, it may amuse you to run through it,' said Caffyn, 'so I got it for you.'

'Thanks,' said Holroyd, without offering to open the paper. 'I'll look at it presently.'

'Don't make a favour of it, you know,' said Caffyn; 'perhaps you prefer something heavier (you've mental resources of your own, I know); but there it is if you care to look at it.'

'I'd give anything to see him read it!' he thought when he was outside; 'but it really wouldn't be safe. I don't want him to suspect my share in the business.' So he went on to the kitchen and was almost instantly on the best of terms with the worthy farmers and innkeepers, who had been tracking the fox on foot all day across the mountains. Vincent shivered as he sat over the fire; he had overwalked himself and caught a chill trudging home in the rain that afternoon over the squelching rushy turf of Ennerdale, and now he was feeling too languid and ill to rouse himself. There was a letter that must be written to Mabel, but he felt himself unequal to attempting it just then, and was rather glad than otherwise that the hotel inkstand, containing as it did a deposit of black mud and a brace of pre-Adamite pens, decided the matter for him. He took up the Review Caffyn had so considerately provided for his entertainment and began to turn over the pages, more from a sense of obligation than anything else. For some time he could not keep his attention upon what he read.

He had dreamy lapses, in which he stood again on the mountain top he had climbed that day, and looked down on the ridges of the neighbouring ranges, which rose up all around like the curved spines of couching monsters asleep there in the solemn stillness—and then he came to himself with a start as the wind moaned along the winding passages of the inn, stealthily lifting the latch of the primitive sitting-room door, and swelling the carpet in a highly uncanny fashion.

After one of these recoveries he made some effort to fix his thoughts, and presently he found himself reading a passage which had a strangely familiar ring in it—he thought at first it was merely that passing impression of a vague sameness in things which would vanish on analysis—but, as he read on, the impression grew stronger at every line. He turned to the beginning of the article, a notice on a recent book, and read it from beginning to end with eager care. Was he dreaming still, or mad? or how was it that in this work, with a different title and by a strange writer, he seemed to recognise the creation of his own brain? He was sure of it; this book 'Illusion' was practically the same in plot and character—even in names—as the manuscript he had entrusted to Mark Ashburn, and believed a hopeless failure. If this was really his book, one of his most cherished ambitions had not failed after all; it was noticed in a spirit of warm and generous praise, the critic wrote of it as having even then obtained a marked success—could it be that life had possibilities for him beyond his wildest hopes?

The excitement of the discovery blinded Vincent just then to all matters of detail: he was too dazzled to think calmly, and only realised that he could not rest until he had found out whether he was deceiving himself or not. Obviously he could learn nothing where he was, and he resolved to go up to town immediately. He would see Mark there, if he was still in London, and from him he would probably get information on which he might act—for, as yet, it did not even occur to Vincent that his friend could have played a treacherous part. Should he confide in Caffyn before he went? Somehow he felt reluctant to do that; he thought that Caffyn would feel no interest in such things (though here, as we know, he did him an injustice), and he decided to tell him no more than might seem absolutely necessary.

He rang and ordered the dog-cart to take him to Drigg next day in time to meet the morning train, and, after packing such things as he would want, lay awake for some time in a sleeplessness which was not irksome, and then lost himself in dreams of a fantastically brilliant future.

When Caffyn had had enough of the huntsmen he returned to the sitting-room, and was disgusted to find that Holroyd had retired and left the Review. 'I shall hear all about it to-morrow,' he said to himself; 'and if he knows nothing—I shall have to enlighten him myself!'

But not being an early riser at any time, he overslept himself even more than usual next day, ignoring occasional noises at his door, the consequence being that, when he came down to breakfast, it was only to find a note from Vincent on his plate: 'I find myself obliged to go to town at once on important business,' he had written. 'I tried to wake you and explain matters, but could not make you hear. I would not go off in this way if I could help it; but I don't suppose you will very much mind.'

Caffyn felt a keen disappointment, for he had been looking forward to the pleasure of observing the way in which Vincent would take the discovery; but he consoled himself: 'After all, it doesn't matter,' he thought; 'there's only one thing that could start him off like that! What he doesn't know he'll pick up as he goes on. When he knows all, what will he do? Shouldn't wonder if he went straight for Mark. Somehow I'm rather sorry for that poor devil of a Mark—he did me a bad turn once, but I've really almost forgiven him, and—but for Mabel—I think I should have shipped dear Vincent off in perfect ignorance—dear Vincent did bore me so! But I want to be quits with charming, scornful Mabel, and, when she discovers that she's tied for life to a sham, I do think it will make her slightly uncomfortable— especially if I can tell her she's indebted to me for it all! Well, in a day or two there will be an excellent performance of the cottage-act from the "Lady of Lyons" over there, and I only wish I could have got a seat for it. She'll be magnificent. I do pity that miserable beggar, upon my soul, I do—it's some comfort to think that I never did him any harm; he lost me Mabel—and I kept him from losing her. I can tell him that if he tries any reproaches!'

Meanwhile Vincent was spinning along in the dog-cart on his way to Drigg. There had been a fall of snow during the night, and the mountains across the lake seemed grander and more awful, their rugged points showing sharp and black against the blue-tinted snow which lay in the drifts and hollows, and their peaks rising in glittering silver against a pale-blue sky. The air was keen and bracing, and his spirits rose as they drove past the grey-green lake, and through the plantations of bright young larches and sombre fir. He arrived at Drigg in good time for the London train, and, as soon as it stopped at a station of importance, seized the opportunity of procuring a copy of 'Illusion' (one of the earlier editions), which he was fortunate enough to find on the bookstall there. He began to read it at once with a painful interest, for he dreaded lest he had deluded himself in some strange way, but he had not read very far before he became convinced that this was indeed his book—his very own. Here and there, it was true, there were passages which he did not remember having written, some even so obviously foreign to the whole spirit of the book that he grew hot with anger as he read them—but for the most part each line brought back vivid recollections of the very mood and place in which it had been composed. And now he observed something which he had not noticed in first reading the Review—namely, that 'Illusion' was published by the very firm to which he had sent his own manuscript. Had not Mark given him to understand that Chilton and Fladgate had rejected it? How could he reconcile this and the story that the manuscript had afterwards been accidentally destroyed, with the fact of its publication in its present form? And why was the title changed? Who was this Cyril Ernstone, who had dared to interfere with the text? The name seemed to be one he had met before in some connection—but where? Had not Mark shown him long ago a short article of his own which had been published in some magazine over that or some very similar signature? Terrible suspicions flashed across him when these and many other similar circumstances occurred to him. He fought hard against them, however, and succeeded in dismissing them as unworthy of himself and his friend: he shrank from wronging Mark, even in thought, by believing him capable of such treachery as was implied in these doubts. He felt sure of his honour, and that he had only to meet him to receive a perfectly satisfactory explanation of his conduct in the matter, and then Mark and he would hunt down this impostor, Cyril Ernstone, together, and clear up all that was mysterious enough at present. In the meantime he would try to banish it from his mind altogether, and dwell only on the new prospects which had opened so suddenly before him; and in this he found abundant occupation for the remainder of his journey.

He reached Euston too late to do anything that night, and the next morning his first act, even before going in search of Mark, was to drive to Kensington Park Gardens with some faint hope of finding that Mabel had returned. But the windows were blank, and even the front door, as he stood there knocking and ringing repeatedly, had an air of dust and neglect about it which prepared him for the worst. After considerable delay a journeyman plumber unfastened the door and explained that the caretaker had just stepped out, while he himself had been employed on a job with the cistern at the back of the house. He was not able to give Vincent much information. The family were all away; they might be abroad, but he did not know for certain; so Vincent had to leave, with the questions he longed to put unasked. At South Audley Street he was again disappointed. The servant there had not been long in the place, but knew that Mr. Ashburn, the last lodger, had gone away for good, and had left no address, saying he would write or call for his letters. Holroyd could not be at ease until he had satisfied himself that his friend had been true to him. He almost hated himself for feeling any doubt on the subject, and yet Mark had certainly behaved very strangely; in any case he must try to find out who this Cyril Ernstone might be, and he went on to the City and called at Messrs. Chilton and Fladgate's offices with that intention.

Mr. Fladgate himself came down to receive him in the little room in which Mark Ashburn had once waited. 'You wished to speak to me?' he began.

'You have published a book called "Illusion,"' said Vincent, going straight to the point in his impatience. 'I want to know if you feel at liberty to give me any information as to its author?' Mr. Fladgate's eyebrows went up, and the vertical fold between them deepened.

'Information,' he repeated. 'Oh, dear me, no; it is not our practice, really. But you can put your question of course, if you like, and I will tell you if we should be justified in answering you,' he added, as he saw nothing offensive in his visitor's manner.

'Thank you,' said Vincent. 'I will, then. Would you be justified in telling me if the name of "Cyril Ernstone" is a real or assumed one?'

'A few days ago I should have said certainly not; as it is—I presume you are anxious to meet Mr. Ernstone?'

'I am,' said Vincent: 'very much so.'

'Ah, just so; well, it happens that you need not have given yourself the trouble to come here to ask that question. As you are here, however, I can gratify your curiosity without the slightest breach of confidence. There is our later edition of the book on that table; the title-page will tell you all you want to know.'

Vincent's hand trembled as he took the book. Then he opened it, and the title-page did tell him all. His worst suspicions were more than verified. He had been meanly betrayed by the man he had trusted—the man whom he had thought his dearest friend! The shock stunned him almost as if it had found him totally unprepared. 'It was Mark, then,' he said only half aloud, as he put the book down again very gently.

'Ah, so you know him?' said Mr. Fladgate, who stood by smiling.

'He was one of my oldest friends,' replied Vincent, still in a low voice.

'And you suspected him, eh?' continued the publisher, who was not the most observant of men.

'He took some pains to put me off the scent,' said Vincent.

'Yes; he kept his secret very well, didn't he? Now, you see, he feels quite safe in declaring himself—a very brilliant young man, sir. I congratulate you in finding an old friend in him.'

'I am very fortunate, I know,' said Vincent, grimly.

'Oh, and it will be a pleasant surprise for him too!' said Mr. Fladgate, 'very pleasant on both sides. Success hasn't spoilt him in the least—you won't find him at all stuck up!'

'No,' agreed Vincent, 'I don't think I shall. And now perhaps you will have no objection to give me his present address, and then I need trouble you no longer at present.'

'I see—you would naturally like to congratulate him!'

'I should like to let him know what I think about it,' said Holroyd.

'Exactly—well, let me see, I ought to have his address somewhere. I had a letter from him only the other day—did I put it on my file? no, here it is—yes. "Hotel Rheinfall, Gross Laufingen, Switzerland,"—if you write to your friend any time this month, it will find him there.'

Vincent took the address down in his notebook and turned to go.

'Good day,' said Mr. Fladgate, 'delighted to have been of any service to you—by the way, I suppose you saw your friend's'—but before he could allude to Mark Ashburn's marriage he found himself alone, Vincent having already taken a somewhat abrupt departure.

He could not trust himself to hear Mark talked of in this pleasant vein any longer. It had required some effort on his part to restrain himself when he first knew the truth, and only the consciousness that his unsupported assertions would do no good had kept him silent. He would wait to make his claim until he could bring evidence that could not be disregarded—he would go to Mark Ashburn and force him to give him an acknowledgment which would carry conviction to every mind.

He would go at once. Mark had evidently gone to this place, Gross Laufingen, with the idea of avoiding him—he would follow him there! He lost no time in making inquiries, and soon learnt that Gross Laufingen was about two hours' journey from Basle, and that by leaving London next morning he would catch the fast train through from Calais to Basle, and arrive there early on the following day. He made all necessary arrangements for starting, and wrote to Caffyn to say that he was going abroad, though he did not enter into further details, and on receiving this letter Caffyn took the opportunity of gratifying his malicious sense of humour by despatching (at considerable trouble and expense to himself, for Wastwater is far enough from any telegraph poles) the message Mark had received from little Max's hand on the mount.

Vincent set out on his journey with a fierce impatience for the end, when he would find himself face to face with this man whom he had thought his friend, whose affectionate emotion had touched and cheered him when they met at Plymouth, and who had been deliberately deceiving him from the first.

All the night through he pictured the meeting to himself, with a stern joy at the thought of seeing Mark's handsome false face change with terror at the sight of him—would he beg for mercy, or try to defend himself? would he dare to persist in his fraud? At the bare thought of this last possibility a wave of mad passion swept over his brain—he felt that in such a case he could not answer for what he might say or do.

But with the morning calmer thoughts came: he did not want revenge—only justice. Mark should restore everything in full—it was his own fault if he had placed himself in such a position that he could not do that without confessing his own infamy. If there was any way of recovering his own and sparing Mark to some extent in the eyes of the world, he would agree to it for the sake of their old friendship, which had been strong and sincere on his own side at least; but no sentimental considerations should stand between him and his right.

Basle was reached in the early morning, and the pretty city was flushed with rose, and the newly risen sun was sparkling on the variegated roofs and cupolas as he drove across the bridge to the Baden station. He felt jaded and ill after a journey in which he had slept but little, and, finding that he would not be able to go on to Laufingen for some time, was obliged to recruit himself by a few hours' sleep at an hotel.

It was past midday when he awoke, and the next train, which started late in the afternoon, brought him to Laufingen, just as the last sunset rays were reddening the old grey ruin on the hill, and the towns and river below showed themselves in an enchanted atmosphere of violet haze.

Leaving his luggage at the station until he should have found a place to stay at for the night, Vincent walked down to the bridge, intending to go to the Rheinfall Hotel and inquire for Mark. There is a point where the covered portion of the bridge ends, and the structure is supported by a massive stone pier, whose angles, facing up and down the river and protected by a broad parapet, form recesses on either side of the roadway. Here he stopped for a moment, fascinated by the charm of the scene, and, leaning upon the ledge, watched the last touches of scarlet fading out of the slate-coloured cloud-masses in the west. He was roused from this occupation by a voice which called his name in a low tremulous tone which sent the blood rushing back to his heart, and as he turned to see a graceful figure just passing out from under the arched roof towards him, he recognised Mabel Langton.

The dying light fell full on her face, which had an expression half of awe, half of incredulous joy—she came towards him, holding out two eager hands, and the awe vanished, but the joy grew more assured.

'Vincent!' she cried. 'Is it really you? you have come back to us—or am I dreaming?'

He had met her at last, and in this place to which he had come anticipating nothing but pain and contest ... she had not forgotten him—the glad shining in her sweet eyes told him that, and a great and glorious hope sprang up within him.

In her presence he forgot his wrongs, he forgot the very object of a journey which had thus led him to her side, all his past feelings seemed petty and ignoble, and fame itself a matter of little worth; he took her small gloved hands and stood there, resting his eyes on the dear face which had haunted his thoughts through all his weary exile. 'Thank God,' he murmured, 'it is no dream—this time!'

CHAPTER XXXIII

IN SUSPENSE

Mark, as he left his wife with that hastily invented excuse of the forgotten tobacco, turned back with a blind instinct of escape; he went to the foot of the hilly little street down which Mabel and he had lately passed, and halted there undecidedly; then he saw a flight of rough steps by a stone fountain and climbed them, clutching the wooden rail hard as he went up; they led to a little row of cabins, barricaded by stacks of pine-wood, and further on there was another short flight of steps, which brought him out upon a little terrace in front of a primitive stucco church. Here he paused to recover breath and think, if thought was possible. Above the irregular line of high-pitched brown roofs at his feet he could just catch a glimpse of the rushing green Rhine, with the end of the covered way on the bridge and the little recess beyond. It was light enough still for him to see clearly the pair that stood in that recess: Vincent's broad figure leaning earnestly towards that other one—he was drawing closer—now he drew back again as if to watch the effect of his words. Mark knew well what she must be hearing down there. He strained his eyes as the dusk shrouded the two more and more; he thought that, even there, he would be able to see a change when the blow fell. 'Mabel, my darling—my innocent darling!' he groaned aloud, 'have pity on me—do not give me up!' From the opposite side he could hear the faint strains of a street organ which was playing a lively popular air; it had come in that morning, and he and Mabel had been amused at the excitement it produced amongst the unsophisticated inhabitants; it had exhausted its répertoire over and over again, but its popularity seemed yet undiminished.

As he leaned there on the rough stone parapet his panic gradually abated, and the suspense became intolerable; he could not stay there. By this time too the worst must have happened; it was useless to try to avoid the inevitable; he would go down and face his doom, without giving her further cause to despise him. The idea of denying the charge never occurred to him for a moment; he knew that face to face with his accuser such audacity was beyond his powers; he had nothing to say in defence, but he must hear his sentence.

And so, in a sort of despairing apathy, he went steadily down again to the street level, and, with a self-command for which he had not dared to hope, passed with a firm tread along the covered way across the bridge.

After the first surprise of meeting, Vincent had had to explain, in answer to Mabel's eager questions, the manner in which he had escaped being a victim to the 'Mangalore' disaster; the explanation was commonplace enough, and when it was given she exclaimed reproachfully, 'But why did you lead us all to believe that the worst had happened? You must have known how it would grieve us; it was not like you, Vincent.'

'But I wrote,' he rejoined; 'surely you got my letter, Mabel?'

'You did write, then?' she said. 'I am glad of that. But the letter never came. I never dreamed that there was the slightest hope till I saw you here. I hardly dared to speak to you at first. And how do you come to be here at all? You have not told me that yet.'

'I was on my way to punish a scoundrel,' he said abruptly, 'but I had almost forgotten all that. Never mind about me, Mabel; tell me about yourself now. You don't know how I have been longing for the very smallest news of you!'

'What am I to tell you?' said Mabel smiling. 'Where shall I begin, Vincent?'

'Well, first, your own question back again,' he said. 'How do you come to be here, and all alone? Are your people at the hotel? Am I to see them to-night?'

'My people are all at Glenthorne just now,' said Mabel with some natural surprise, which, however, only made Vincent conclude she must be travelling with friends. Were they her future parents-in-law, he wondered jealously. He could not rest till he knew how that was.

'Mabel,' he said earnestly, 'they told me you were engaged; is it true?'

She had not yet grown quite accustomed to her new dignity as a wife, and felt a certain shyness in having to announce it to Vincent.

'It was,' she said, looking down; 'it is not true now. Haven't you really heard that, Vincent?'

But, instead of reading her embarrassment aright, he saw in it an intimation that his worst fears were without foundation. He had not come too late. She was free—there was hope for him yet. But even then he did not dare to express the wild joy he felt.

'Do you mean,' he said—and his voice betrayed nothing—'that it is broken off?'

'Broken off!' she repeated, with a little touch of bewilderment. 'Why—oh, Vincent, what a dreadful thing to ask! I thought you would understand, and you don't a bit. I am not engaged now, because—because this is my wedding journey!'

If Vincent had been slow to understand before, he understood now. It was all over; this was final, irrevocable. The radiant prospect which had seemed to open a moment before to his dazzled eyes had closed for ever. For a moment or two he did not speak. If he had made any sound it would have been a cry of pain; but he repressed it. That must be his secret now, and he would keep it till death. He kept it well then at least, for there was no faltering in his voice as he said slowly, 'I did not know. You will let me congratulate you, Mabel, and—and wish you every happiness.'

'Thank you, Vincent,' said Mabel not too warmly, thinking that, from so old a friend as Vincent, these felicitations were cold and conventional.

'You are happy, are you not?' he asked anxiously.

'Happier than I ever thought possible,' she said softly. 'When you see my—my husband' (she spoke the word with a pretty, shy pride), 'and know how good he is, Vincent, you will understand.' If she had ever suspected the place she filled in Vincent's heart she would have spared him this; as it was she treated him as an affectionate elder brother, who needed to be convinced that she had chosen wisely; and it was in some degree his own fault that she did so; he had never given her reason to think otherwise.

'I wish he would come; I can't think where he can be all this time,' continued Mabel. 'I want you to know one another. I am sure you will like Mark, Vincent, when you know him.'

Vincent started now unmistakably; not all his self-control could prevent that. Till that moment it had not occurred to him that Mabel's presence there, in the town where he had expected to come upon Mark, was more than a coincidence. He had been led to believe that Mark and she were not even acquainted, and even the discovery that she was married did not prepare him for something more overwhelming still.

'Mark!' he cried. 'Did you say Mark? Is that your husband's name? Not—not Mark Ashburn?'

'How that seems to astonish you,' said Mabel. 'But I forgot; how stupid of me! Why, you are a friend of his, are you not?'

Holroyd's anger came back to him all at once, with a deadly force that turned his heart to stone.

'I used to be,' he answered coldly, not caring very much just then in his bitterness if the scorn he felt betrayed itself or not. But Mabel took his answer literally.

'Why, of course,' she said. 'I remember we came upon your portrait once at home, and he asked if it was not you, and said you were one of his oldest friends.'

'I thought he would have forgotten that,' was all Vincent's answer.

'I am quite sure he will be very glad to welcome you back again,' said Mabel, 'and you will be glad to hear that since you saw him he has become famous. You have been so long away that you may not have heard of the great book he has written, "Illusion."'

'I have read it,' said Vincent shortly. 'I did not know he wrote it.'

'He did write it,' said Mabel. 'But for that we might never have known one another. He has to admit that, even though he does try to run down his work sometimes, and insist that it has been very much overrated!'

'He says so, does he?' Vincent replied. 'Yes, I can quite understand that.'

Some intonation in his voice struck Mabel's ear. 'Perhaps you agree with him?' she retorted jealously.

Holroyd laughed harshly. 'No, indeed,' he said, 'I should be the last man in the world to do that. I only meant I could understand your husband taking that view. I read the book with intense interest, I assure you.'

'You don't speak as if you quite meant me to believe that,' she said. 'I'm afraid the book was not practical enough to please you, Vincent. Ceylon seems to have hardened you.'

'Very possibly,' he replied; and then followed a short silence, during which Mabel was thinking that he had certainly altered—hardly for the better, and Holroyd was wondering how much longer he would have to bear this. He was afraid of himself, feeling the danger of a violent outburst which might reveal her delusion with a too brutal plainness. She must know all some time, but not there—not then.

He had finally mastered any rebellious impulses, however, as Mabel, who had been anxiously watching the bridge for some time, went to meet someone with a glad cry of relief. He heard her making some rapid explanations, and then she returned, followed by Mark Ashburn.

Mabel's greeting told the wretched Mark that the blow had not fallen yet. Vincent evidently was determined to spare neither of them. Let him strike now, then; the less delay the better.

He walked up to the man who was his executioner with a dull, dogged expectation of what was coming. He tried to keep himself straight, but he felt that his head was shaking as if with palsy, and he was grateful that the dusk hid his face. 'Here is Mark, at last,' said Mabel. 'He will tell you himself that he at least has not forgotten.'

But Mark said nothing; he did not even put out his hand. He stood silently waiting for the other to speak. Vincent was silent, too, for a time, looking at him fixedly. This was how they had met, then. He had pictured that meeting many times lately, but it had never been anything like the reality. And Mabel still suspected nothing. There was a touch of comedy of a ghastly kind in the situation, which gave Vincent a grim amusement, and he felt a savage pleasure, of which he was justly ashamed later, in developing it.

'I have been trying to explain to your wife,' he said at last, 'that I have been away so long that I could hardly hope you would remember the relations between us.'

Mark made some reply to this; he did not know what.

'At least,' Vincent continued calmly, 'I may congratulate you upon the success of your book. I should have done so when we met the other day if I had understood then that you were the author. Your modesty did not allow you to mention it, and so I discover it later.'

Mark said nothing, though his dry lips moved.

'When you met!' cried Mabel in wonder. 'Did you know Vincent was alive then, Mark? And you never told me!'

'He naturally did not think it would interest you, you see,' said Vincent.

'No,' said Mabel, turning to Mark, 'you couldn't know that Vincent had once been almost one of the family; I forgot that. If you had only thought of telling me!'

The two men were silent again, and Mabel felt hurt and disappointed at Vincent's want of cordiality. He seemed to take it for granted that he had been forgotten. He would thaw presently, and she did her best to bring this about by all the means in her power, in her anxiety that the man she respected should do justice to the man she loved.

That conversation was, as far as Mark was concerned, like the one described in 'Aurora Leigh'—

'Every common word
Seemed tangled with the thunder at one end,
And ready to pull down upon their heads
A terror out of sight.'

The terror was close at hand when Mabel said, in the course of her well-meant efforts to bring them into conversation, 'It was quite by accident, do you know, Mark, that Vincent should have met us here at all; he was on his way to find some man who has— I forget what you said he had done, Vincent.'

'I don't think I went into particulars,' he replied. 'I described him generally as a scoundrel. And he is.'

'I hope you were able to find that out before he could do you any injury?' said Mabel.

'Unfortunately, no,' he said. 'When I found out, the worst was done.'

'Would you rather not talk about it,' she continued, 'or do you mind telling us how you were treated?'

Vincent hesitated; just then the sense of his wrong, the sight of the man who had deceived him, made him hard as adamant. Could he desire a fuller satisfaction than was offered him now?

'It's rather a long story,' he said; 'perhaps this is not quite the place to tell it. You might find it interesting, though, from the literary point of view,' he added, turning suddenly on Mark, who did not attempt to meet his eyes.

'Tell it by all means, then,' said the latter, without moving his head.

'No; you shall hear it another time,' said Holroyd. 'Put shortly, Mabel, it's this: I trusted the other man; he deceived me. Nothing very original in that, is there?'

'I'm afraid not,' said Mabel. 'Did he rob you, Vincent? Have you lost much?'

'Much more than money! Yes, he robbed me first and paid me the compliment of a highly artistic chain of lies afterwards. That was a needless waste; the ordinary sort of lie would have been quite enough for me—from him.'

Mark heard all this with a savage inclination at first to cut the scene short, and say to Mabel, 'He means Me. I robbed him! I lied to him! I am the scoundrel—it's all true! I own it—now let me go!'

But he let Holroyd take his own course in the end, with an apathetic acknowledgment that he had the right to revenge himself to the very utmost.

The house at the nearer end of the bridge had a small projecting gallery, where he remembered having seen a tame fox run out when he was there in the autumn before. He caught himself vaguely speculating whether the fox was there still, or if it had died; and yet he heard every word that Vincent was saying.

'And what do you mean to do with him when you meet?' asked Mabel.

'Ah,' said Vincent, 'I have thought over that a good deal. I have often wondered whether I could keep calm enough to say what I mean to say. I think I shall; in these civilised days we have to repress ourselves now and then, but that won't, of course, prevent me from punishing him as he deserves; and, when those nearest and dearest to him know him as he really is, and turn from him, even he will feel that a punishment!' (He turned to Mark again) 'Don't you agree with me?' he asked.

Mark moistened his lips before answering. 'I think you will find it very easy to punish him,' he said.

'Is he—is he married?' asked Mabel.

'Oh, yes,' said Vincent; 'I was told that his wife believes in him still.'

'And you are going to undeceive her?' she said.

'She must know the truth. That is part of his punishment,' replied Vincent.

'But it will be so terrible for her, poor thing!' said Mabel, with an infinite compassion in her voice. 'What if the truth were to kill her?'

'Better that,' he said bitterly, 'than to go on loving a lie! Whatever happens her husband is responsible, not I. That is the correct view, Ashburn, I think?'

'Quite correct,' said Mark.

'It may be correct,' cried Mabel indignantly, 'but it is very cruel! I didn't think you could be so harsh, either of you. Of course, I don't know what the man has done; perhaps if I did I might be "correct" too. But, Vincent, I do ask you to think a little of his poor wife. She, at least, has done you no harm! Is there no way—no way at all—to get back something of what you have lost; even to punish the man, if you must, and yet spare his wife?'

'If there were,' he cried passionately, 'do you suppose I would not take it? Is it my fault that this man has done me such a wrong that he can only make amends for it by exposing himself? What can I do?'

'I suppose there is no help for it, then,' agreed Mabel reluctantly, 'but I wish she had not to suffer too. Only think what it must be to have to give up believing in one's husband!' and as she spoke she slid a confiding hand through Mark's arm.

There was another silence, and, as it seemed plain now that the interview was not likely to be a success, she made haste to end it. 'We must say good-bye now, Vincent,' she said. 'I hope you are not so harsh as your words.'

'I don't know. I feel considerably harsher just now, I think,' he said. 'Good-bye then, Mabel. By the way, Ashburn,' he added in a slightly lowered tone, 'there is something I have to say to you.'

'I know,' muttered Mark doggedly. 'Are you going to say it now?'

'No, not now,' he answered; 'you must meet me—where shall we say? I don't know this place—here? No, on that little terrace over there, by the fountain; it will be quieter. Be there at nine.—I am going to tell your husband the details of that story, Mabel,' he continued aloud, 'and then we shall decide what to do. You will spare him to me for half an hour?'

'Oh, yes,' said Mabel, cheerfully. She thought this looked as if they were going to arrive at a better understanding. Mark looked at Vincent, but his face was impenetrable in the dim light as he added, again in an undertone, 'You are to say nothing until I give you leave. If you are not at the place by nine, remember, I shall come to you.'

'Oh, I will be there,' said Mark recklessly; and they parted.

As Mabel and Mark were walking back, she said suddenly, 'I suppose, when you met Vincent last, you told him that you were going to marry me, Mark?'

'Didn't he say so?' he answered, prevaricating even then.

'I thought you must have done so,' she said, and was silent.

Vincent had known then. He had deliberately kept away from them all. He had pretended to ignore the marriage when they met; that was his way of resenting it. She had not thought of this till then, and it confirmed her in the idea that Ceylon had sadly changed him.

They dined alone together in the large bare Speise-Saal, for the handsome hotel was scarcely ever occupied even in the season. Now they had it all to themselves, and the waiters almost fought with one another for the privilege of attending upon them. The 'Director' himself—a lively, talkative little German, who felt his managerial talents wasted in this wilderness—came in to superintend their meals, partly to refresh himself by the contemplation of two real guests, but chiefly to extend his English vocabulary.

Hitherto Mark had considered him a nuisance, but he was glad that evening when the host followed the fish in with his customary greeting. 'Good-night! You haf made a goot valk? Guten appetit—yes?' and proceeded to invite them to a grand concert, which was to take place in the hotel the following Sunday.

'Zere vill pe ze pandt from Klein-Laufingen; it is all brass, and it is better as you vill not go too near. Zey blow vair strong ven zey go off, but a laty from hier vill gambole peautifully after zem on ze piano. You vill come—yes?'

When he had gone at last little Max came in and stood by Mabel, with his mouth gaping like a young bird's for chance fragments of dessert. Mark was grateful to him, too, for diverting her attention from himself. He grew more and more silent as the long Black Forest clock by the shining porcelain stove ticked slowly on towards the hour. It was time to go, and he rose with a shiver.

'You will not be very long away, will you, dear?' said Mabel, looking up from the orange she was peeling for the child. 'And you will do what you can for the poor woman, I know.'

'Yes, yes,' he said as he reached the door. 'Good-bye, Mabel!'

'Good-bye,' she said, nodding to him brightly. 'Max, say "Good-evening, Herr Mark; a pleasant walk,"' but Max backed away behind the stove, declining to commit himself to an unknown tongue. Mark took a last look at her laughing gaily there in the lamplight. Would he ever hear her laugh like that again? How would he ever find courage to tell her? There was little need just then of Holroyd's prohibition.

He went down to the hotel steps to the little open space where the two streets unite, and where the oil lamp suspended above by cords dropped a shadow like a huge spider on the pale patch of lighted ground below. The night was warm and rather dark; no one was about at that hour; the only sound was the gurgle of the fountain in the corner, where the water-jets gleamed out of the blackness like rods of twisted crystal. He entered the narrow street, or rather alley, leading to the bridge. In the state of blank misery he was in his eye seized upon the smallest objects as if to distract his mind, and he observed—as he might not have done had he been happy—that in the lighted upper room of the corner house they had trained growing ivy along the low raftered ceiling.

So, too, as he went on he noticed details in each dim small-paned shop-front he passed. The tobacconist's big wooden negro, sitting with bundles of Hamburg cigars in his lap and filling up the whole of the window; the two rows of dangling silver watches at the watchmaker's; the butcher's unglazed slab, with its strong iron bars, behind which one small and solitary joint was caged like something dangerous to society; even the grotesque forms in which the jugs and vases at the china shop were shadowed on the opposite wall.

He looked up at a quaint metal inn-sign, an ancient ship, which swung from a wrought-iron bracket overhead. 'When next I pass under that!' he thought.

He came to the end of the street at last, when his way to the place of meeting lay straight on, but he turned to his right instead, past the Zoll-Verein—where the chief was busy writing by the window under his linen-shaded oil-lamp—and on to the bridge as if some irresistible attraction were drawing him.

When he reached the recess opposite to that in which Mabel had met Vincent he stopped mechanically and looked around; the towns were perfectly still, save for the prolonged organ note of the falls, which soon ceases to strike the ear. On either bank the houses gleamed pale under a low sky, where the greenish moonlight struggled through a rack of angry black clouds. While he stood there the clock under the church cupola above struck the quarters and clanged out the hour, followed, after a becoming pause, by the gatehouse clock across the river, and such others as the twin towns possessed.

It was nine o'clock. Vincent Holroyd was waiting there on the terrace, stern and pitiless.

Mark made a movement as if to leave the recess, and then stopped short. It was no use; he could not face Holroyd. He looked over the side, down on the water swirling by, in which the few house lights were reflected in a dull and broken glimmer. Was there any escape for him there?

It would only be a plunge down into that swollen rushing torrent, and he would be past all rescue. An instant of suffocating pain, then singing in his ears, sparks in his eyes, unconsciousness—annihilation perhaps—who knew? Just then any other world, any other penalty, seemed preferable to life and Mabel's contempt!

From the recess he could see an angle of the hotel, and one of the windows of their room. It was lighted; Mabel was sitting there in the arm-chair, perhaps waiting for him. If he went back he must tell her. If he went back!

Whether he lived or died, she was equally lost to him now. His life would bring her only misery and humiliation—at least he could leave her free!

Vincent would speak and think less hardly of him then, and, if not, would it matter?

His mind was made up—he would do it! He looked towards Mabel's window with a wild, despairing gaze. 'Forgive me!' he cried with a hoarse sob, as if she could hear, and then he threw off his hat and sprang upon the broad parapet.

CHAPTER XXXIV

ON THE LAUFENPLATZ

Vincent had left the Gasthaus zur Post, the old-fashioned inn outside Klein-Laufingen, at which he had taken up his quarters for the night, a little before nine, and walked down the street, with his mind finally made up as to the course he meant to take, although he shrank from the coming interview almost as intensely as Mark himself. He passed under the covered way of the bridge, and had nearly reached the open part, when he recognised the man he was coming to meet standing in one of the recesses. He noticed him look round in evident fear of observation—he did not seem, however, to have seen or heard Vincent, and presently the latter saw him throw his hat away, as if in preparation for action of some sort. Vincent guessed at once what he was intending to do; it darted across his mind that this might be the best solution of the difficulty—he had only to keep silent for a few seconds. Was it certain even now that he could prevent this self-destruction if he would? But such inhumanity was impossible to him. Instinctively he rushed forward out of the shadow and, seizing Mark by the arm as he sprang upon the parapet, dragged him roughly back. 'You coward!' he cried, 'you fool! This is the way you keep your appointment, is it? You can do that afterwards if you like—just now you will come with me.'

Tragic as a rash act, such as Mark was contemplating, is when successful, an interruption brings with it an inevitable bathos; when he first felt that grasp on his arm, he thought himself in the power of a German policeman, and, prepared as he was a moment before to face a sudden death, he quailed before the prospect of some degrading and complicated official process; it was almost a relief to see instead his bitterest enemy!

He made no attempt at resistance or escape—perhaps life seemed more tolerable after all now he had been brought back to it; he went meekly back with Vincent, who still held his arm firmly, and they reached the Laufenplatz without another word.

The little terrace above the Rhine was almost dark, the only light came in a reflected form from a street lamp round the corner, and they had to pick their way round the octagonal stone fountain and between the big iron salmon cages, to some seats under the five bare elms by the railings. There Vincent sat down to recover breath, for the scene he had just gone through was beginning to tell upon him, and he was overcome by a feeling of faintness which made him unable to speak for some moments. Meanwhile Mark stood opposite by the railings waiting sullenly, until Vincent rose at last and came to his side; he spoke low and with difficulty, but, in spite of the torrent roaring over the rocks below, Mark heard every word.

'I suppose,' Vincent began, 'I need not tell you why I wished to see you?'

'No,' said Mark; 'I know.'

'From your manner on the bridge just now,' continued Holroyd, relentlessly, 'it looked almost as if you wished to avoid a meeting—why should you? I told you I wished my authorship to be kept a secret, and you sheltered it with your own name. Very few friends would have done that!'

'You have the right to indulge in this kind of pleasantry,' said the tortured Mark; 'I know that—only be moderate if you can. Cut the sneers and the reproaches short, and give me the finishing stroke; do you suppose I don't feel what I am?'

'Reproaches are ungenerous, of course,' retorted Holroyd; 'I am coming to the "finishing stroke," as you call it, in my own time; but first, though you may consider it bad taste on my part, I want to know a little more about all this. If it's painful to you, I'm sorry—but you scarcely have the right to be sensitive.'

'Oh, I have no rights!' said Mark, bitterly.

'I'll try not to abuse mine,' said Vincent, more calmly, 'but I can't understand why you did this—you could write books for yourself, what made you covet mine?'

'I'll tell you all there is to tell,' said Mark: 'I didn't covet your book—it was like this; my own novels had both been rejected. I knew I had no chance, as things were, of ever getting a publisher to look at them. I felt I only wanted a fair start. Then Fladgate got it into his head that I was the author of that manuscript of yours. I did tell him how it really was, but he wouldn't believe me, and then—upon my soul, Holroyd, I thought you were dead!'

'And had no rights!' concluded the other drily; 'I see—go on.'

'I was mad, I suppose,' continued Mark; 'I let him think he was right. And then I met Mabel ... by that time everybody knew me as the author of "Illusion." I—I could not tell her I was not.... Then we were engaged, and, four days before the wedding, you came back—you know all the rest.'

'Yes, I know the rest,' cried Vincent, passionately; 'you came to meet me—how overcome you were! I thought it was joy, and thanked Heaven, like the fool I was, that I had anyone in the world to care so much about me! And you let me tell you about—about her; and you and Caffyn between you kept me in the dark till you could get me safely out of the way. It was a clever scheme—you managed it admirably. You need not have stolen from anyone with such powers of constructing a plot of your own! There is just one thing, though, I should like to have explained. I wrote Mabel a letter—I know now that she never received it—why?'

'How can I tell?' said Mark. 'Good God! Holroyd, you don't suspect me of that!'

'Are you so far above suspicion?' asked Vincent; 'it would only be a very few more pages!'

'Well, I deserve it,' said Mark, 'but whether you believe me or not, I never saw a letter of yours until the other day. I never imagined you were alive even till I read your letter to me.'

'That must have been a delightful surprise for you,' said Vincent; 'you kept your head though—you did not let it interfere with your arrangements. You have married her—you—of all the men in the world! Nothing can ever undo that now—nothing!'

'I have married her,' said Mark; 'God forgive me for it! But at least she cares for no one else, Holroyd. She loves me—whatever I am!'

'You need not tell me that,' interrupted Vincent; 'I know it. I have seen it for myself—you have been clever even in that!'

'What do you mean?' asked Mark.

'Do you know what that book of mine was to me?' continued Vincent, without troubling to answer; 'I put all that was best of myself into it, I thought it might plead for me some day, perhaps, to a heart I hoped to touch; and I come back to find that you have won the heart, and not even left me my book!'

'As for the book,' said Mark, 'that will be yours again now.'

'I meant to make it so when I came here,' Vincent answered. 'I meant to force you to own my rights, whatever the acknowledgment cost you.... But I know now that I must give that up. I abandon all claim to the book; you have chosen to take it—you can keep it!'

The revulsion of feeling caused by so unexpected an announcement almost turned Mark's head for the moment; he caught Vincent by the arm in his excitement. 'What,' he cried, 'is this a trick—are you in earnest—you will spare me after all? You must not, Vincent, I can't have it—I don't deserve it!'

Vincent drew back coldly: 'Did I say you deserved it?' he asked, with a contempt that stung Mark.

'Then I won't accept it, do you hear?' he persisted; 'you shall not make this sacrifice for me!'

Holroyd laughed grimly enough: 'For you!' he repeated; 'you don't suppose I should tamely give up everything for you, do you?'

'Then,' faltered Mark, 'why—why—?'

'Why am I going to let you alone? Do you remember what I told you on that platform at Plymouth?—that is why. If I had only known then, I would have fought my hardest to expose you, if it was necessary to save her in that way—for her sake, not mine. I don't suppose there ever was much hope for me. As it is, you have been clever enough to choose the one shield through which I can't strike you—if I ever thought more of that wretched book than of her happiness, it was only for a moment—she knows nothing as yet, and she must never know!'

'She will know it some day,' said Mark, heavily.

'Why should she know?' demanded Vincent, impatiently; 'you don't mean that that infernal Caffyn knows?'

'No, no,' replied Mark, in all sincerity; 'Caffyn doesn't know—how could he? But you can't hide these things: you—you may have talked about it yourself already!'

'I have not talked about it!' said Vincent, sharply; 'perhaps I was not too proud of having been gulled so easily. Can't you understand? This secret rests between you and me at present, and I shall never breathe a word of it—you can feel perfectly safe—you are Mabel's husband!'

It is to be feared that Vincent's manner was far enough from the sublime and heroic; he gave up his book and his fame from the conviction that he could not do otherwise; but it was not easy for all that, and he did not try to disguise the bitter contempt he felt for the cause.

Mark could not endure the humiliation of such a pardon—his spirit rose in revolt against it.

'Do you think I will be forgiven like this?' he cried, recklessly. 'I don't want your mercy! I won't take it! If you won't speak, I shall!'

Vincent had not expected any resistance from Mark, and this outburst, which was genuine enough, showed that he was not utterly beneath contempt, even then.

Holroyd's manner was less harsh and contemptuous when he next spoke:

'It's no use, Ashburn,' he said firmly; 'it's too late for all that now—you must accept it!'

'I shall not,' said Mark again. 'I've been a scoundrel, I know, but I'll be one no longer; I'll tell the truth and give you back your own. I will do what's right at last!'

'Not in that way,' said Vincent; 'I forbid it. I have the right to be obeyed in this, and you shall obey me. Listen to me, Ashburn; you can't do this—you forget Mabel. You have made her love you and trust her happiness to your keeping; your honour is hers now. Can't you see what shame and misery you will plunge her in by such a confession? It may clear your conscience, but it must darken her life—and that's too heavy a price to pay for such a mere luxury as peace of mind.'

'How can I go on deceiving her?' groaned Mark; 'it will drive me mad!'

'It will do nothing of the sort!' retorted Holroyd, his anger returning; 'I know you better—in a couple of days it won't even affect your appetite! Why, if I had not come over here, if I had gone out again to India as you hoped I should, you were prepared to go on deceiving her—your mind kept its balance well enough then!'

Mark knew this was true, and held his tongue.

'Think of me as safe in India, then,' Vincent continued more quietly. 'I shall trouble you quite as little. But this secret is mine as well as yours—and I will not have it told. If you denounce yourself now, who will be the better for it? Think what it will cost Mabel.... You do love her, don't you?' he asked, with a fierce anxiety; 'you—you have not married her for other reasons?'

'You think I am too bad even to love honestly,' said Mark, bitterly; 'but I do.'

'Prove it then,' said Vincent. 'You heard her pleading on the bridge for the woman who would suffer by her husband's shame; she was pleading for herself then—and not to me only, to you! Have pity on her; she is so young to lose all her faith and love and hope at once. You can never let her know what you have been; you can only try to become all she believes you to be.'

In his heart, perhaps, Mark was not sorry to be convinced that what he had resolved to do was impossible. The high-strung mood in which he had been ready to proclaim his wrong-doing was already passing away. Vincent had gained his point.

'You are right,' Mark said slowly; 'I will keep it from her if I can.'

'Very well,' Vincent answered, 'that is settled then. If she asks you what has passed between us, you can say that I have told you my story, but that you are not at liberty to speak of it. Mabel will not try to know more. Stay, I will write a line' (and he went to the corner of the street and wrote a few words on a leaf from his notebook). 'Give that to her,' he said as he returned. 'And now I think we've nothing more to say.'

'Only one other thing,' stammered Mark; 'I must do this.... When they—they published your book they paid me.... I never touched the money. I have brought it with me to-night; you must take it!' and he held out a small packet of notes.

Vincent turned haughtily away. 'Excuse me,' he said, 'it is not mine; I will have nothing to do with it. Under the circumstances, you can't expect me to touch that money. Keep it; do what you choose with it.'

'I choose this, then!' said Mark, violently, and tearing the notes up, he flung them over the railings to drift down on the rocks or into the tossing grey foam beyond.

'You need not have done that,' said Holroyd, coldly; 'there were the poor. But just as you please!' and he made a movement as if to go.

Mark stopped him with a gesture.

'Are you going like this?' he said, and his voice trembled. 'If you knew all I felt, even you might pity me a little! Can't you forgive?'

Vincent turned. 'No,' he said, shortly, 'I can't. I put temptation in your way, and though I never dreamed then that it could be a temptation to you, I could have forgiven you for giving way to it when you believed me dead. But I came back, and you went on with it; you lied to me—more, you dared to marry her, without a care for the shame and sorrow, which was all you had to bring her. If I said I forgave you for that, it would be a mockery. I don't, and I can't!'

'I see,' said Mark. 'When we meet again we are to be strangers, then?'

'No,' said Vincent; 'if we meet we must do so as ordinary acquaintances—for Mabel's sake. But there are no appearances to keep up here. Can't you see I want to be left to myself?' he asked, with a sudden burst of nervous irritation.

'Have your way then?' said Mark, and left him there by the railings.

Mark's first feelings as he walked slowly back up the little street where the little shops were all shuttered and dark now, were by no means enviable; he felt infinitely mean and small in his own eyes, and shrank from entering Mabel's presence while his nerves were still crawling under the scorching contempt of Vincent's dismissal. If, during the interview, there had been moments when he was deeply contrite and touched at the clemency so unexpectedly shown him, the manner of his pardon seemed to release him from all obligations to gratitude—he had only been forgiven for another's sake; and for a time he almost loathed so disgraceful an immunity, and felt the deep humiliation of a sentence that condemned him 'to pay the price of lies by being constrained to lie on still.' But by degrees, even in that short walk, his elastic temperament began to assert itself; after all, it might have been worse. He might by now have been drifting, dead and disfigured, down the river to Basle; he might have been going back to Mabel with the fearful necessity upon him of telling her all that night. One person knew him, and despised him for what he was; but that person would never tell his secret. That painful scene which had just passed would never have to be gone through again; he could think of it as a horrible dream. Yes, he was safe now, really safe this time. His position was far more secure than when he had read that telegram of Caffyn's; and here he wondered, for the first time, whether Caffyn had been deliberately misled or only mistaken in sending such a delusive message. But that did not very much matter now, and he soon abandoned speculation on the subject. He had much to be thankful for; his future was free from all danger. He had had a severe lesson, and he would profit by it; henceforth (with the one necessary reservation) he would be honest and true—Mabel should never repent her trust in him. 'Sweet Bells Jangled' would be before the world by the time they returned, and after that he feared nothing. And so, though he was subdued and silent on his return, there was no other trace in his manner of what he had suffered during the last hour. He found Mabel by the window of their sitting-room, looking out at the houses across the river, which were now palely clear in the cold moonlight, their lights extinguished, and only a pane glittering here and there in some high dormer window, while the irregular wooden, galleries and hanging outhouses were all thrown up vividly by the intense shadows.

'What a very long time you have been away!' she said; 'but I know Vincent can be very pleasant and interesting if he likes.'

'Very,' said Mark, and gave her Holroyd's note.

'I leave here early to-morrow for Italy,' she read, 'and may not see you again for some little time. I have told your husband my story, but, on consideration, have thought it best to pledge him to tell no one—not even you. But the man who injured me shall be safe for your sake.'

'You did persuade him, then!' she said, looking up gratefully to Mark. 'Oh, I am glad! How good you are, and how well you must have spoken, dear, to make him give up his idea of punishing the man! So Vincent is going away at once. Do you know I am afraid I am rather glad?'

And Mark made no answer; what was there to say?

Vincent stood there by the railings on the Laufenplatz for some time after Mark had left him; he was feeling the reaction both in mind and body from his recent conflict. 'How will it all end?' he asked himself wearily. 'Can any good come from letting this deceit go on? Is he strong enough to carry out his part? If not, the truth will only come at last, and be even more cruel when it does come.' Yet he had done what still seemed the obvious and only thing to do, if Mabel's happiness was considered. He was ashamed even that he had not seen it earlier, and trembled as he remembered that only a providential chance had restrained him from some fatal disclosure to Mabel that afternoon on the bridge. But at least he had acted for the best, and he would hope for it.

Thinking thus, he recrossed the river to Klein-Laufingen, where a mounted German officer, many sizes too big for the little street, was rousing it from its first slumber as he clattered along, with his horse's hoofs striking sparks from the rough cobbles, and passed under the old gateway, where his accoutrements gleamed for an instant in the lamplight before horse and rider vanished in the darkness beyond. Vincent passed out, too, out on the broad white road, and down the hill to his homely Gasthaus. He felt weak and very lonely—lonelier even than when he had parted from Mabel long ago on the eve of his Ceylon voyage. He could hope then; now he had lost her for ever! Still, one of his wishes had been granted—he had been able to be of service to her, to make some sacrifice for her dear sake. She would never know either of his love or his sacrifice, and though he could not pretend that there was no bitterness in that, he felt that it was better thus. 'After all,' he thought, 'she loves that fellow. She would never have cared for me.' And there was truth in this last conclusion. Even if Mabel and Mark had never met, and she could have known Vincent as he was, the knowledge might not have taught her to love. A woman cannot give her heart as a prix Montyon, or there might be more bachelors than there are.

CHAPTER XXXV

MISSED FIRE!

It was an evening early in May, and Harold Caffyn was waiting at Victoria for the arrival of the Dover train, which was bringing back Mark and Mabel from the Continent. This delicate attention on his part was the result of a painful uncertainty which had been vexing him ever since the morning on which he read Vincent's farewell note at Wastwater. 'It is a poor tale,' as Mrs. Poyser might say, to throw your bomb and never have the satisfaction of hearing it explode—and yet that was his position; he had 'shot his arrow into the air,' like Longfellow; but, less fortunate than the poet, he was anything but sure that his humble effort had reached 'the heart of a friend.' Now he was going to know. One thing he had ascertained from the Langtons—Vincent Holroyd had certainly followed the couple to Laufingen, and they had seen him there—Harold had found Mrs. Langton full of the wonderful news of the return of the dead. But nothing had come of it as yet; if there was a sensation in store for the literary world, Mabel's letters apparently contained no hint of it, and for a time Caffyn felt unpleasantly apprehensive that there might have been a hitch somehow in his admirable arrangements. Then he reflected that Mabel would naturally spare her mother as long as possible; he would not believe that after all the trouble he had taken, after Holroyd had actually hunted down the culprit, the secret could have been kept from her any longer. No, she must know the real truth, though she might be proud enough to mask her sufferings while she could. But still he longed for some visible assurance that his revenge had not unaccountably failed; and, as he had ascertained that they were to return on this particular evening, and were not to be met except by the Langton carriage, it occurred to him that here would be an excellent opportunity of observing Mabel at a time when she would not imagine it necessary to wear a mask. He would take care to remain unseen himself; a single glance would tell him all he needed to know, and he promised himself enjoyment of a refined and spiritual kind in reading the effects of his revenge on the vivid face he had loved once, and hated now with such malignant intensity. The train came in with a fringe of expectant porters hanging on the footboards, and as the doors flew open to discharge a crowd, flurried but energetic, like stirred ants, even Caffyn's well-regulated pulse beat faster.

He had noticed Champion waiting on the platform and kept his eye upon him in the bustle that followed; he was going up to a compartment now—that must be Mark he was touching his hat to as he received directions; Caffyn could not see Mark's face yet as his back was towards him, but he could see Mabel's as she stepped lightly out on the platform—there was a bright smile on her face as she acknowledged the footman's salute, and seemed to be asking eager questions. Caffyn felt uncomfortable, for there was nothing forced about her smile, no constraint in her eyes as she turned to Mark when they were alone again, and seemed to be expressing her eager delight at being home again. And Mark, too, had the face of a man without a care in the world—something must have gone wrong, terribly wrong, it was clear! They were coming towards him; he had meant to avoid them at first, but now his curiosity would not allow this, and he threw himself in their way, affecting an artless surprise and pleasure at being the first to welcome them back. Mark did not appear at all disconcerted to see him, and Mabel could not be frigid to anybody just then in the flush of happy expectation, which she did not try to conceal; altogether it was a bitter disappointment to Caffyn.

He quite gasped when Mark said, with a frank unconsciousness, and without waiting for the subject to be introduced by him, 'Oh, I say, Caffyn, what on earth made you think poor old Vincent was going back to India at once? He's not going to do anything of the kind; he's wandering about the Continent. We knocked up against him at Laufingen!'

Caffyn gave a searching look at Mabel's sweet, tranquil face, then at Mark's, which bore no sign of guilt or confusion. 'Knocked up against you!' he repeated; 'why—why, didn't he expect to find you there, then?'

Mabel answered this: 'It was quite an accident that he stopped at Laufingen at all,' she said; 'he was going on to Italy.'

Caffyn did not give up even then—he tried one last probe: 'Of course,' he said; 'I forgot, your husband kept him so completely in the dark about it all—eh, Mark? Why, when you got him to come down to Wastwater with me, he had no idea what festivities were in preparation—had he?'

'No, my boy,' said Mark, with a perfectly natural and artistic laugh; 'I really don't believe he had—you mustn't be shocked, darling,' he added to Mabel; 'it was all for his good, poor fellow. I must tell you some day about our little conspiracy. It's all very well for you, though,' he turned to Caffyn again, 'to put it all on to me—you had more to do with it than I—it was your own idea, you know!'

'Oh!' said Caffyn; 'well, if you like to put it in that way—.' He lost his self-possession completely—there was something in all this he could not at all understand.

The fact was that Mark felt himself able now to face the whole world with equanimity; the knowledge that no one would ever detect him made him a consummate actor. He had long made up his mind how he would greet Caffyn when they met again, and he was delighted to find himself so composed and equal to the occasion.

Caffyn stood looking after the carriage as it drove away with them; he had quite lost his bearings: the paper in Holroyd's hand, Mark's own behaviour in so many instances, Vincent's rapid pursuit, had all seemed to point so clearly to one conclusion—yet what was he to think now? He began for the first time to distrust his own penetration; he very much feared that his elaborate scheme of revenge was a failure, that he must choose some other means of humbling Mabel, and must begin all over again, which was a distressing thought to a young man in his situation. He was glad now that he had never talked of his suspicions, and had done nothing openly compromising. He would not give up even yet, until he had seen Holroyd, and been able to pump him judiciously; until then he must bear the dismal suspicion that he had overreached himself.

One of his shafts at least had not fallen altogether wide, for as Mark and Mabel were being driven home across the Park, she said suddenly: 'So Harold knew that Vincent was alive, then?'

'Yes,' said Mark, 'he knew,' and he looked out of the window at the sunset as he spoke.

'And you and Harold kept him from hearing of our wedding?' she said. 'Mark, I thought you said that you had told him?'

'Oh, no,' said Mark; 'you misunderstood—there—there were reasons.'

'Tell me them,' said Mabel.

'Well,' said Mark, 'Vincent was ill—anyone could see that what he wanted was rest, and that the fatigue and—and—the excitement of a wedding would be too much for him—Caffyn wanted a companion up at Wastwater, and begged me to say nothing about our marriage just then, and leave it to him to tell him quietly later on—that's all, darling.'

'I don't like it, dear,' said Mabel; 'I don't like your joining Harold in a thing like that. I know you did it all for the best, but I don't see why you could not have told him; if he was not well enough to come to the wedding we should have understood it!'

'Perhaps you're right,' said Mark, easily, 'but, at all events, no harm has come of it to anybody. How they are thinning the trees along here, aren't they? Just look down that avenue!'

And Mabel let him turn the conversation from a subject she was glad enough to forget.

CHAPTER XXXVI

LITTLE RIFTS

One bright morning in May, not long after the return from the Continent, Mabel was sitting in her own room at the back of the small house which had been taken on Campden Hill; she was writing at a table by the raised window, when the door opened suddenly, and Mark burst in, in a state of suppressed but very evident excitement. 'I have brought you something!' he said, and threw down three peacock-blue volumes upon her open blotting-case; the title, 'Sweet Bells Jangled,' ran in sprawling silver letters from corner to corner of the covers, through a medley of cracked bells and withered hyacinths in dull gold; the general effect being more bold than pleasing. Mabel was just about to exclaim sympathetically, 'What a frightful binding they've given you, dear;' when Mark informed her, with some complacency, that it was his own design. 'Nowadays, you see,' he explained, 'you want something to catch the eye, or you won't be read!' Inwardly Mabel could not help wondering that he could condescend to such a device, or think it necessary in his own case. 'Look at the fly-leaf,' he said, and she opened the first volume, and read the printed dedication, 'To My Wife.' 'I thought that must bring me luck,' he said; 'and now, darling, do you know what you are going to do? You are going to put away all those confounded letters and sit down here, and read the opening chapters carefully, and tell me what you think of them.' For till then he had made continual excuses for not showing her any portion of his new work, either in manuscript or proof, from mixed motives of vanity and diffidence.

Mabel laughed with affectionate pride at his anxiety: 'This is what comes of marrying a great author!' she said; 'go away and let me begin at once, and tell you at lunch how I enjoyed it.'

'No,' said Mark despotically, 'I'm going to stay here—or you might try to skip.'

'But I can't allow that,' she protested; 'suppose I find I'm obliged to skip—suppose it's a terrible disappointment? No, you ridiculous Mark, I didn't mean it—stay if you like, I'm not afraid of being disappointed—though I really would enjoy it best in solitude!'

Mark insisted; he felt that at last he was about to be reinstated in his own opinion, he could wait no longer for the assurance of triumph; when he saw with his own eyes the effect of his genius upon Mabel, when he read the startled delight and growing admiration in her face, then at last he would know that he was not actually an impostor!

There are many methods of self-torture, but perhaps few more ingenious and protracted than submitting the result of one's brain-work to a person whose good opinion we covet, and watching the effect. Mark imposed it on himself, nevertheless, chiefly because in his heart he had very little fear of the result. He took a rocking-chair and sat down opposite Mabel, trying to read the paper; by-and-by, as she read on in silence, his heart began to beat and he rocked himself nervously, while his eyes kept wandering from the columns to the pretty hands supporting the volume which hid Mabel's face. Hands reveal many things, and Mabel's could be expressive enough at times—but they told him nothing then; he watched them turn a leaf from time to time, they always did so deliberately, almost caressingly, he thought, but with no eagerness—although the opening was full of incident. He calculated that she must be at a place where there was a brilliant piece of humorous description; she had a fair share of humour—why didn't she laugh?

'Have you got to that first appearance of the Curate on the tennis-ground?' he asked at last.

She laid down the volume for an instant, and he saw her eyes—they were calm and critical. 'Past that! I am beginning Chapter Three,' she said.

The second chapter had contained some of his most sparkling and rollicking writing—and it had not even moved her to smile! He consoled himself with the reflection that the robuster humour never does appeal to women. He had begun his third chapter with a ludicrous anecdote which, though it bordered on the profane, he had considered too good to be lost, but now he had misgivings.

'I'm afraid,' he ventured dubiously, 'you won't quite like that bit about the bishop, darling?'

'I'm afraid I don't quite,' she replied from behind the book. The story had no real harm in it, even in Mabel's eyes; the only pity was that in any part of 'Illusion' it would have been an obvious blot—and that it did not seem out of keeping in the pages she was reading now.

She had sat down to read with such high hopes, so sure an anticipation of real enjoyment, that it was hard to find that the spell was broken; she tried to believe that she read on because she was interested—her real reason was a dread of some pause, when she would be asked to give her opinion. What should she say?

Perhaps it should be explained at once that the book was not a foolish one; Mark, whatever else he was, could scarcely be called a fool, and had a certain share of the literary faculty; it was full of smart and florid passages that had evidently been industriously polished, and had something of the perishable brilliancy of varnish. There is a kind of vulgarity of mind so subtle as to resist every test but ink, and the cheap and flashy element in Mark's nature had formed a deposit, slight, perhaps, but perceptible in more than one page of 'Sweet Bells Jangled.' Mabel felt her heart grow heavier as she read. Why had he chosen to deliberately lower his level like this? Where were the strong and masterly touch, the tenderness and the dignity of his first book? That had faults, too, even faults of taste—but here the faults had almost overgrown the taste! Surely if she read on, she would find the style attain the old distinction, and the tone grow noble and tender once again—but she read on, and the style was always the same, and the tone, if anything, rather worse!

Mark had long since moved to a spot where he could command her face; her fine eyebrows were slightly drawn, her long lashes lowered, and her mouth compressed as if with pain—somehow the sight did not encourage him. She was becoming conscious that her expression was being closely watched, which seldom adds a charm to reading, and at last she could persevere no longer, and shut the book with a faint sigh.

'Well,' said Mark, desperately; he felt as if his fate hung on her answer.

'I—I—have read so little yet,' she said; 'let me tell you what I think at the end!'

'Tell me what you think of it so far,' said Mark.

'Must I?' she said, almost imploringly.

'Yes,' said Mark, with a grating attempt at a laugh; 'put me out of my misery!'

She loved him too well to make some flattering or evasive reply—she was jealous for his reputation, and could not see him peril it without a protest. 'Oh, Mark,' she cried, locking her hands and pressing them tight together, 'you must feel yourself—it is not your best—you have done such great work—you will again, I know, dear—but this, it is not worthy of you—it is not worthy of "Illusion"!'

He knew too well that it was his best, that it was not in him to do better; if the world's verdict agreed with hers, he was a failure indeed. He had been persuading himself that, after all, he was not a common impostor, that he had genius of his own which would be acknowledged far above his friend's talent; now all at once the conviction began to crumble.

He turned upon her with a white face and a look of anger and mortification in his eyes. 'The first is always the best, of course,' he said bitterly; 'that is the regulation verdict. If "Sweet Bells" had come first, and "Illusion" second, you would have seen this sad falling off in the second book. I did not think you would be the first to take up that silly old cry, Mabel—I thought I could always come to my wife for encouragement and appreciation; it seems I was mistaken!'

Mabel bit her lip, and her eyes were dazzled for a moment: 'You asked me what I thought,' she said in a low voice; 'do you think it was pleasant to tell you? When you ask me again, I shall know better how you expect to be answered!'

He felt all at once what he had done, and hastened to show his penitence; she forgave, and did not let him see how deeply she had been wounded—only from that day some of the poetry of her life had turned to prose. Of 'Sweet Bells Jangled' she never spoke again, and he did not know whether she ever read it to the end or not.

They had finished breakfast one Saturday morning, and Mark was leisurely cutting the weekly reviews, when he suddenly sheltered himself behind the paper he had been skimming—'Sweet Bells' was honoured with a long notice. His head swam as he took in the effect with some effort. The critic was not one of those fallen angels of literature who rejoice over an unexpected recruit; he wrote with a kindly recollection of 'Illusion,' and his condemnation was sincerely reluctant; still, it was unmixed condemnation, and ended with an exhortation to the author to return to the 'higher and more artistic aims' of his first work. Mark's hand shook till the paper rustled when he came to that; he was so long silent that Mabel looked up from reading her letters, and asked if the new book was reviewed yet.

'Reviewed yet!' said Mark from behind the article; 'why, it hasn't been out a fortnight.'

'I know,' said Mabel, 'but I thought perhaps that, after "Illusion"—'

'Every book has to wait its turn!' said Mark, as he saved himself with all the reviews, and locked himself in the little study where he sketched out the stories to which he had not as yet found appropriate endings.

There was another notice amongst the reviews, but in that the critic was relentless in pointing out that the whilom idol had feet of clay—and enormous ones; after a very severe elaboration of the faults, the critic concluded: 'It almost seems as though the author, weary of the laudation which accompanied the considerable (if, in some degree, accidental) success of his first book, had taken this very effectual method of rebuking the enthusiasm. However this may be, one more such grotesque and ill-considered production as that under review, and we can promise him an instant cessation of all the inconveniences of popularity.'

Mark crumpled up the paper and pitched it to the other end of the room in a fury—it was a conspiracy, they were writing him down—oh, the malice and cowardice of it! He destroyed both reviews lest Mabel should see her opinion confirmed, and her faith in him should be shaken.

However, sundry copies of the reviews in question were forwarded to him by good-natured people who thought it might amuse him to see them, and one was even sent to Mabel with red chalk crosses in thoughtful indication of the more unpleasant passages; she saw the date, and remembered it as the day on which Mark had fenced himself in at breakfast. She came in with the paper as he sat in his study, and putting one hand on his shoulder, bent over him with a loving reproach in her eyes: 'Someone has just sent me this,' she said; 'you have seen it I know. Why didn't you trust me, dear? Why have you let this come from others? Never try to hide things from me again, Mark—not even for my good! and—and after this let us share everything—sorrow and all—together!' She kissed him once on the forehead, and left him there to his own thoughts.

Why, thought Mabel, was he not strong enough to disregard criticism if he was satisfied with his own work, as he evidently was? She hated to think of his having tried to keep their notices from her in that weak, almost underhand, way; she knew that the motive was not consideration for her feelings, and had to admit sadly that her hero was painfully human after all.

Still 'Illusion' had revealed a nature the nobility of which no weaknesses could obscure, and if his daily life did not quite bear out such indications, he was Mark Ashburn, and she loved him. Nothing could alter that.

Some weeks later Vincent returned from Italy, and one of the first persons he met was Harold Caffyn. It was in the City, where Vincent had had business, and he attempted at first to pass the other by with the curtest possible recognition; he had never understood his conduct in the Wastwater episode, and still resented it. But Caffyn would not allow himself to be cut, and his greeting was blandly affectionate as he accused his friend of abandoning him up in the Lake district; he was determined, if he could, to convince Holroyd that his silence as to Mabel's impending marriage had been due solely to consideration for his feelings, and then, when confidence was restored, he could sound him upon the result of his journey to Laufingen. But Vincent, from a vague feeling of distrust, was on his guard. Caffyn got nothing out of him, even by the most ingenious pumping; he gathered that he had met Mark at Laufingen; but with all his efforts he was not able to discover if that meeting had really been by accident or design. He spoke casually of 'Illusion,' but Vincent showed no particular emotion.

'I suppose you don't know,' he added, 'that Mrs. Featherstone has done it the honour of making a play of it—it's going to be done at the end of the season at their house, before a select party of distinguished sufferers.'

Holroyd had not heard that.

'I've been let in for it,' Caffyn continued; 'I'm playing that stick of a poet, "Julian," the beggar's name is; it's my last appearance on the boards, till I come out as Benedick—but that won't interest you, and it's a sort of secret at present.'

Vincent was not curious, and asked no questions.

'Who do you think is to be the Beaumelle, though?' said Caffyn; 'the author's own wife! Romantic that, eh? She's not half bad at rehearsals; you must come and see us, my boy!'

'Perhaps I shall,' said Vincent, mechanically, and left him, as much at fault as ever, but resolved to have patience still.

Caffyn's was a nature that liked tortuous ways for their own sake; he had kept his suspicions to himself hitherto, he was averse to taking any direct action until he was quite sure of his ground. He had those papers in Holroyd's writing, it was true, but he had begun to feel that they were not evidence enough to act on. If by some extraordinary chance they were quite compatible with Mark's innocence, then if he brought a charge against him, or if any slanderous insinuations were traced to him, he would be placed in an extremely awkward and invidious position. 'If I'm right,' he thought, 'Master Vincent's playing some deep game of his own—it may be mine for all I know; at all events I'll lie low till I can find out where the cards are, and whether an ace or two has got up my sleeve.'

Vincent had been able to speak with perfect calmness of his lost book, because he had almost brought himself to a philosophic indifference regarding it, the more easily as he had had consoling indications lately that his creative power had not been exhausted with that one effort, and that with returning health he might yet do good work in the world.

But now, as he walked on after leaving Caffyn, this indifference suddenly vanished; his heart beat with a secret and exquisite bliss, as he thought of this play in which Mabel was to represent his own heroine. To hear that his work was to receive the rather moderate distinction which can be conferred by its dramatisation on a private stage would scarcely have elated him under ordinary circumstances; it was no longer any concern of his at all. Still he could not resist the subtle flattery in the knowledge that his conception was about to be realised in a manner for which few authors would dare to hope—the woman who had inspired it would lend it all her own grace and beauty and tenderness to fill the faint outline he had traced with such loving pains. All the banality of private theatricals could not spoil that— she need not even act, she had only to be her own sweet self to give life and charm to the poorest play, and the most incompetent of performances. And then, as he thought of it, a wild longing came over him to be there and see her; there might be something grotesque, and, under the circumstances, almost undignified in such a longing now, but it possessed him nevertheless. He would not betray himself or Mark, but this one gratification he hungered for, and neither pride nor prudence had power to restrain him.

He had meant to see as little as possible of Mabel on his return, but he broke this resolution now. He would not keep away, he thought; surely he could trust himself to bear the sight of her happiness; it ought to reconcile him more fully to all he had endured to secure it, and then he would be able to find out from her if this, which he had heard from Caffyn, was really true.

And so, having procured the address from Mrs. Langton, he went on that same afternoon to Campden Hill, not knowing, nor indeed greatly caring just then, that this was not the way to deaden the pain at his heart.

CHAPTER XXXVII

MARK ACCEPTS A DISAGREEABLE DUTY

Vincent had his misgivings, as he walked towards Campden Hill, that at such a period of the London season his journey would most probably be a fruitless one. But as he approached the house he found one or two carriages waiting outside, the horses troubling the hot afternoon stillness with the sharp clinking of harness as they tossed their impatient heads; and by the time he had reached the gate the clatter of china and the sustained chorus of female voices coming through the open windows made it plain enough that Mabel was 'at home,' in a sense that was only one degree less disappointing than what he had dreaded.

He was almost inclined to turn back or pass on, for he was feeling ill and weak—the heat had brought on a slight tendency to the faintness which still reminded him occasionally of his long prostration in Ceylon, and he had a nervous disinclination just then to meet a host of strangers. The desire to see Mabel again prevailed, however, and he went in. The pretty double drawing-room was full of people, and as everyone seemed to be talking at once, Vincent's name was merely an unimportant contribution to the general hubbub. He saw no one he knew, he was almost the only man there, and for a time found himself penned up in a corner, reduced to wait patiently until Mabel should discover him in the cool half-light which filtered through the lowered sunblinds.

He followed her graceful figure with his eyes as often as it became visible through the crowd. It was easy to see that she was happy—her smile was as frank and gay as ever. The knowledge of this should have consoled him, he had expected it to do so, and yet, to tell the truth, it was not without its bitterness. Mabel had been his ideal of women, his fair and peerless queen, and it pained him—as it has pained unsuccessful lovers before—to think that she could contentedly accept pinchbeck for gold. It was inconsistent on his part, since he had sacrificed much for the very object of concealing from her the baseness of Mark's metal. He forgot, too, the alchemy of love.

But one cannot be always consistent, and this inconsistency of Vincent's was of that involuntary and mental kind which is not translated into action.

She saw him at last and welcomed him with an eager impulsiveness—for she knew now that she had been unjust to him at Laufingen. They talked for some minutes, until Vincent said at last, 'I hear you are going to play Beaumelle?'

'Oh, yes,' said Mabel. 'Isn't it presumption? But Mrs. Featherstone (you've met her once or twice at our house, you know)—Mrs. Featherstone would not hear of my refusing. Mark, I believe, thinks the part hardly suited to me, but I mean to try and astonish him, even though I may not carry out his own idea. I love Beaumelle in the book so much that I ought not to be quite a failure in the play.'

'No, you will not fail,' said Vincent, and dared not say more on that point. 'I—I should like very much to see this play,' he said, a little awkwardly. 'Could it be managed?'

'I will try,' said Mabel. 'I am sure Mrs. Featherstone will give me a card for you if she can. But I warn you, Vincent, it's not a good play. There's one strong scene in the third act, and the rest is a long succession of tête-à-tête—like a society "Punch and Judy." It will bore you.'

'I think not,' said Vincent, 'and you won't forget, will you?'

'Of course not,' she replied. 'There is Mrs. Featherstone coming in now. I will ask her at once.'

But Mrs. Featherstone had an air of suppressed flurry and annoyance which was discouraging, and Gilda's handsome face was dark and a little defiant, as she followed her mother into the room.

'Can you get away from all these people for two minutes?' said Mrs. Featherstone, after the first greetings; 'I've something to tell you.'

Mabel took her through the rooms out upon a balcony overlooking the garden and screened from the sun by a canvas awning. 'We shall be quiet here,' she said.

Mrs. Featherstone did not speak for some moments. At last she said: 'Oh, my dear, I don't know how to tell you—I can't talk about it with ordinary patience yet—only think, our foolish, self-willed Gilda told us this morning that that Mr. Caffyn had proposed to her and she had accepted him—after all the offers she has refused—isn't it too shocking to think of? And she won't listen to a word against him, the silly child is perfectly infatuated!'

'What does Mr. Featherstone say?' asked Mabel, to whom the news was scarcely a surprise.

'My dear, he knows very well it is all his fault, and that if he hadn't taken the young man up in that ridiculous way all this would never have happened—so, of course, he pretends not to see anything so very unsuitable about the affair—but he doesn't like it, really. How can he? Gilda might have married into the peerage—and now she is going to do this! I'm almost afraid these theatricals have brought it on.'

Mabel was sincerely sorry. She was fond of Gilda, and thought her far too good for Harold. 'It may come to nothing after all,' she said, as the only form of consolation she could think of.

'If I could hope so!' sighed the distressed mother, 'but she is so headstrong. Still, he's not in a position to marry at present—unless Robert is insane enough to advance him to one. Would you speak to her? It would be so sweet of you if you only would!'

But Mabel felt obliged to decline so delicate a mission, and excused herself. Then, as they re-entered the room she mentioned Holroyd's petition. Mrs. Featherstone recollected him faintly, and was rather flattered by his anxiety to see her play; but then he was quite a nonentity, and she was determined to have as brilliant and representative an audience as possible for the performance.

'My dear,' she said, 'I would if I could, but it's quite out of the question; my list is overfull as it is, and I haven't an idea where we shall put all the people who will come; there's so much talk about it everywhere that we have had next to no refusals. But if he's only anxious to see the play, and doesn't mind not being seen at it, he could get some idea of the treatment next Friday if he cares to come to the dress rehearsal. You know we arranged to run right through it for the first time. We thought of a small impromptu dance after the rehearsal, so if Mr. Holroyd would like to come a little earlier I shall be charmed to see him.'

So Vincent was brought up to the lady, who repeated the invitation to the rehearsal, which he accepted, as it practically gave him the opportunity he had desired.

Meanwhile Gilda had drawn Mabel aside towards one of the windows. 'Well,' she said, 'so you have been told the great news?'

Mabel admitted this, and added something as nearly approaching to congratulation as her conscience allowed.

'Ah,' said Gilda, 'you're on mamma's side.'

'I am on no side,' said Mabel, 'provided he makes you happy.'

'Which you think rather doubtful?' replied Gilda, with a jarring little laugh. 'Really, Mabel, I do think you might resign him a little more gracefully!'

'I'm afraid I don't understand you,' said Mabel, proudly.

'No?' said Gilda. 'You are very innocent, dear. I can't undertake to explain—only I am not altogether blind.'

'I hope not,' said Mabel, and left her. She was afraid that if she stayed she might be tempted to say what could do no possible good now.

Mrs. Featherstone had gone, with a gracious reminder to Vincent of his promise to come to the rehearsal. It was late in the afternoon, and everyone seemed suddenly alarmed at the idea of being the last to go, the consequence being that the rooms were cleared in an astonishingly short time. Mabel stopped Vincent as he too was preparing to take his leave. 'You must stay till Mark comes back, Vincent. He has taken Dolly to the Academy, really, I believe, to get away from all this. You haven't seen Dolly since you came back, and she's staying with me for a few days. You won't go away without seeing her?'

Vincent had been disappointed at not seeing her at the Langtons' the day before, and waited willingly enough now. It would be some comfort to know that the child had not forgotten him, and would be glad to see him. He had not long to wait. A hansom drove up, and the next minute Dolly came into the room with all her old impetuosity. 'I've come back, Mab,' she announced, to prevent any mistake on that head. 'We drove home all the way in a black cab with yellow wheels—didn't you see it? Oh, and in the Academy there was a little girl with a dog just like Frisk, and I saw a lot of people I knew, and—'

'Don't you see someone you used to know?' said Mabel, breaking in on her stream of reminiscences.

'Have you forgotten me, Dolly?' said Vincent, coming forward out of the shade. His voice was a little harsh from emotion.

The change in the child's face as she saw him was instantaneous and striking; all the light died out of her face, she flushed vividly, and then turned deadly pale.

'You knew Vincent wasn't dead really, Dolly?' said Mabel.

'Yes,' whispered Dolly, still shrinking from him, however.

'And is this all you have to say to me, Dolly?' said Vincent, who was cut to the heart by this reception. Nothing was the same—not even the love of this child.

Dolly had not been long in recovering from the effect of Caffyn's last act of terrorism; for a day or two she had trembled, but later, when she heard of Vincent as away in Italy, she could feel safe from his anger, and so in time forgot. Now it all revived again; he had sprung suddenly from nowhere—he was demanding what she had to say for herself—what should she do?

She clung to Mabel for protection. 'Don't you be cross too!' she cried. 'Promise me you won't and I'll tell you all about it ... you don't know.... Harold said you didn't. And I never meant to burn Vincent's letter. Don't let him be angry!'

Vincent was naturally completely bewildered. 'What is she talking about?' he asked helplessly.

'I can guess,' said Mabel. 'Come away with me, Dolly, and you shall tell me all about it upstairs;' and as Dolly was not unwilling to unburden herself this time, they left Vincent with Mark, who had just joined them. Mark was uncomfortable and silent for some time when they were alone, but at last he said: 'I suppose you have been told of the—the theatricals? I—I couldn't very well help it, you know. I hope you don't mind?'

'Mind!' said Vincent. 'Why should I mind? What is it to me—now? I thought that was finally settled at Laufingen.'

'I felt I must explain it, that's all,' said Mark, 'and—and I've a great deal to bear just now, Holroyd. Life isn't all roses with me, I assure you. If you could remember that now and then, you might think less hardly of me!'

'I will try,' Vincent had said, and was about to say more, when Mabel returned alone. Her eyes were brilliant with anger. Children can occasionally put the feats of the best constructed phonograph completely in the shade; everything that Caffyn had told her about that unfortunate burnt letter Dolly had just reproduced with absolute fidelity.

'I know what happened to your letter now, Vincent,' Mabel said. 'Mark, you never would see anything so very bad in the trick Harold played Dolly about that wretched stamp—see if this doesn't alter your opinion.' And she told them the whole story, as it has been already described, except that the motives for so much chicanery were necessarily dark to her. A little comparison of dates made it clear beyond a doubt that an envelope with the Ceylon stamp had been burnt just when Vincent's letter should in the ordinary course have arrived.

'And Dolly says he told her himself it was your letter!' concluded Mabel.

'Ah,' said Vincent, 'not that that proves it. But I think this time he has spoken truth; only why has he done all this? Why suppress my letter and turn Dolly against me?'

'Malice and spite, I suppose,' said Mabel. 'He has some grudge against you, probably; but go up now, Vincent, and comfort Dolly—you'll find her in my little writing-room, quite broken-hearted at the idea that you should be angry with her.'

Vincent went up at once, and was soon able to regain Dolly's complete confidence. When he had gone, Mabel said to Mark: 'Harold has been here very often lately, dear. I tried to think better of him when I saw you wished it—but I can't go on after this, you see that yourself, don't you?'

Mark was angry himself at what he had heard. Now he knew how Harold had contrived to get rid of Dolly that afternoon in South Audley Street, it made him hot and ashamed to think that he had profited by such a device. He certainly had, from motives he did not care to analyse himself, persuaded Mabel to tolerate Caffyn as a guest, but lately even Mark could no longer pretend that his visits were not far more frequent than welcome.

Something of the old uneasiness in Caffyn's presence had begun to return, though Mark did not know why. At times before his marriage he had had moments of panic or mistrust, but he always succeeded in forgetting the incidents which had aroused them. If Caffyn suspected anything about 'Illusion' he would have spoken long before, he told himself. After the interview with Holroyd at Laufingen, he had ceased to think about the matter—he was safe now. What harm could anyone's mere suspicion do him? And yet, for all that, he was not sorry to free himself from further intrusions of a visitor in whose glance he sometimes surprised a subtle mockery, almost as if his friend had actually detected his secret and was cynically enjoying the humour of the thing. It was only imagination on his own part, but it was not a pleasant fancy.

'He's an infernal scoundrel!' he said, with an indignation that was only very slightly exaggerated. 'You are right, darling, you shall not have to see any more of him.'

'But can't he be punished, Mark?' asked Mabel, and her eyes shone.

Mark coughed. If this affair were brought to light, some of its later stages might not appear entirely to his own credit.

'I don't quite see what he could be punished for,' he said.

'Not for stealing a letter?' she asked. 'It was no less.'

'Rather difficult to bring home to him,' he said: 'couldn't be done without a frightful amount of—of scandal and unpleasantness.'

'No,' said Mabel, thoughtfully, 'I suppose nothing can be done—and yet, poor Gilda! Do you know she is actually engaged to him? It's dreadful to think of that now. At least he shall never come here again, and mother must be told too when I take Dolly back. You will tell him, Mark, when you meet him that he must not call himself a friend of ours any longer. You will make him understand that, won't you?'

'Can't you tell him yourself at one of the rehearsals?' asked Mark.

'I would rather you told him, dear,' she said, 'and there are no rehearsals till Friday.'

'Oh,' said Mark, 'very well, darling, I will—of course I will!'

He was already beginning to feel that the interview might not be altogether agreeable.

CHAPTER XXXVIII

HAROLD CAFFYN MAKES A PALPABLE HIT

As Mabel had said, she did not meet Harold Caffyn again until both were dining at Mrs. Featherstone's on the evening of the first rehearsal to which Vincent had been favoured with an invitation. The instant he saw her he felt that some change had taken place in their relations, that the toleration he had met with since her marriage had given place to the old suspicion and dislike. It was an early and informal dinner, the guests being a few of those who were to take part in the acting later on. Mrs. Featherstone had contrived that Caffyn, notwithstanding his position as accepted suitor, should not sit next to Gilda, and on taking his place he found Mabel on his other hand and his fiancée opposite. As often as he could, he tried to open a conversation with the former, but she met him coldly and shortly, and with each attempt he fell back baffled. He might have persevered but for the consciousness that Gilda's eyes were upon them, for she had been growing very exacting since the engagement had been formally declared. But just before the ladies rose he found an opportunity to say, 'Mabel—Mrs. Ashburn—am I unfortunate enough to have displeased you lately?'

'Displeased is not the right word,' she said: 'you have done far more than that.'

'And am I not to be told my offence?' he said, looking at her keenly.

'Not here,' she replied. 'You can ask my husband, if you like.'

'Really?' he said. 'You refer me to him, then? We must try and come to an understanding together, I suppose.'

'When you have heard him,' she said, 'there is one thing I shall have to say to you myself.'

'May I come and hear it later?' asked Caffyn, and Mabel gave a little sign of assent as she left the table.

'I shall send down for you when we're ready,' said Mrs. Featherstone at the door. 'Will those who have any changes to make mind coming now—it's so late, and we must get in the way of being punctual.'

One or two who were playing servants or character-parts left the table immediately; the others remained, and Harold, whose dressing would not take him long, found himself next to Mark, and rather apart from the men, at the host's end of the table.

'You're the very man I wanted to have a little talk with!' he began in an easy conversational manner. 'Your wife seems deucedly annoyed with me for some reason—she says you can explain. Now, just tell me quietly without any nonsense—what's it all about, eh?'

Now that Mark had seen the other's conduct in its true light he was really indignant: Caffyn seemed more undesirable an associate than ever. He would have been justified in taking a high standpoint from which to deal with him—since whatever his own errors had been, they would never be revealed now—but somehow, he adopted an almost conciliatory tone.

'The fact is,' he replied, with an embarrassed cough, 'it's about that letter of Holroyd's.'

Caffyn's face slightly changed.

'The devil it is!' he said. 'Thought I'd heard the last of that long ago!'

'You're likely to hear a good deal more about it, I'm afraid,' said Mark. 'It has only just come out that it was his, and unopened—you will find it awkward to contradict.'

Caffyn was silent for a time. Dolly must have spoken again. What a fool he had been to trust a child a second time!—and yet he had had no choice. 'Well,' he said at last, 'and what are you going to do about it?'

Mark's throat grew huskier. It was odd, for there was really no reason for being afraid of the man. 'Well, I—in short, I may as well tell you plainly, my wife thinks it is better we should not see any more of you in future.'

There was a dangerous look in Caffyn's eye which Mark did not at all like. 'Ah, well, of course you mean to talk her out of that?' he said lightly.

Was there a concealed menace in his tone? If so, Mark thought, he probably considered that his services connected with Vincent's sudden return gave him a claim. Well, he must disabuse him of that idea at once.

'It would be of no use if I tried to talk her out of it; but, to be quite candid, I—I don't intend to do anything of the kind.... I know we've been friends and all that sort of thing, and till I knew this I always said what I could for you; but—but this suppressing a letter is very different. I can't feel the same myself for you after that, it is better to tell you so distinctly. And then—there is poor little Dolly—she is my sister now—it seems you have been frightening her a second time.'

'On whose account—eh, Ashburn?' asked Caffyn.

Mark had expected this. 'I'm sorry to say on mine,' he replied; 'but if I had known, do you suppose that for one moment— I don't deny that, as I told you at the time, I was glad to see Holroyd leave town just then; but it was—was not so important as all that! Still you did me a service, and I'm sorry to have to do this, but I can't help myself. You will find others harder on you than I am!'

'Does that mean that Mrs. Langton has been told this precious story with all the latest improvements?' asked Caffyn.

'Not yet,' said Mark, 'but she must know before long.'

'And as for yourself, you consider me such an utterly irreclaimable blackguard that you can't afford to be seen with me any longer?' pursued Caffyn.

'My dear fellow,' protested Mark, 'I don't want to judge you. But, as far as the conclusion goes, I'm afraid it comes to that!'

'Perhaps, it has not quite come to that yet,' said Caffyn, as he drew his chair closer to Mark's, and, resting one arm on the back, looked him full in the face with searching intensity. 'Are you sure you have the right to be so very exclusive?'

If Mark could have controlled his nerves then, he might have been able to parry a thrust which, had he only known it, was something of an experiment. As it was, the unexpectedness of it took him off his guard, just when he thought he was proof against all surprises. The ghastly change in him told Caffyn that he had struck the right chord after all, and a diabolical joy lit his eyes as he leaned forward and touched his arm affectionately.

'You infernal hypocrite!' he said very softly. 'I know all about it. Do you hear?'

'About what?' gasped the miserable man, and then with a flickering effort at defiance, 'What do you mean?' he asked, 'tell me what you are hinting at?'

'Keep quiet,' said Caffyn, 'don't excite yourself: they'll notice something presently if you look like that! Here are some fellows coming round with the coffee, wait till they have gone, and I'll tell you.'

Mark had to wait while one man brought him his cup with the milk and sugar, and another followed with the coffee. His hands shook and upset the cream as he tried to take up a lump of sugar.

'I wouldn't take milk if I were you,' advised Caffyn. 'Try a liqueur brandy'—a recommendation to which Mark paid no attention.

It seemed an eternity till the men had gone; all the time Mark tried to believe this was one of the old dreams which had not visited him for so long, or, if he was really awake, that Caffyn must have got hold of something else—not that; he had had false alarms like this before, and nothing had come of them.

Caffyn seemed to have forgotten their recent conversation as he deliberately sipped his coffee and took a cigarette; he offered Mark one and it was declined. 'What do you suspect me of having done?' demanded Mark. 'Oh, my dear fellow, I don't suspect you,' replied Caffyn, 'I know. You can't play the moralist with me, you high-minded old paragon!' He spoke with a kind of savage jocularity. 'I tell you I know that you got your fame and fortune, and even that charming Mabel of yours, by a meaner trick than I, who don't pretend to be particular, should care to dirty my hands with. I may have helped a child to burn a letter—I don't remember that I ever stole a book. I've been an ass in my time, I dare say, but not quite such an ass as to go about in a lion's skin!' Mark sat there dumb and terror-stricken. His buried secret had risen after all—it was all over. He could only say in his despair—

'Has Holroyd told you?'

Caffyn knew all he wanted when he heard that. 'We won't go into that,' he said. 'It's quite enough for you that I know. Do you feel quite such a virtuous horror of continuing my acquaintance now? Couldn't you bring yourself to overlook my little shortcomings this time? Must you really close your respectable door on me?'

Mark only looked at him.

'You fool,' said Caffyn, 'to give yourself airs with me. I've done you more than one good turn. I believe I rather liked you—you did the thing so well that I'm hanged if I should have had the heart to show you up. And now you will go and make an enemy of me—is it quite prudent?'

'What do you want me to do?' asked Mark, with his hand shielding his eyes from the shaded candles near him.

'Now you're getting sensible!' said Caffyn. 'We shall hit it off yet! You've got some authority over your wife, I suppose? Use it. Stop this cackle about the letter: make her shut her mouth; I can't afford to lose the entrée to two houses like your father-in-law's and your own, just now. I can be discreet too—it shall be mouth for mouth. If you don't—if you stand by and let your wife and her mother go about spreading this story until I daren't show my face anywhere, why, I shall take care to come to grief in good company! Mabel can smash me if you like to let her, but if you do, by — it shall bring my sting out! Is it a bargain?'

Mark hesitated. As they sat there he heard the sounds outside of arriving carriages and entering footsteps; people were coming in for this rehearsal. How he loathed the thought of it now! How was he to go through it?

'We shall have to go presently,' said Caffyn. 'I am waiting for my answer—yes or no?'

'No,' said Mark. 'I see no use in playing mouse to your cat. Do you think I don't know that it would come out sooner or later—if not from you, from him? As to forcing my wife to receive you as a friend, I'm not quite rascal enough for that yet. Do whatever you please!'

It was despair more than anything that drove him to defiance, for his knowledge of Mabel showed him that the bargain proposed, apart from its rascality, was an impossible one.

'Well,' said Caffyn, with a shrug, 'you leave me no choice, so in the course of a day or two, my friend, look out for squally weather! Whether I sink or swim myself, I shall see you go to the bottom!'

Mr. Featherstone, who was getting slightly tired of the enthusiastic young amateurs at his end of the table, here suggested an adjournment to the music-room.

'You'll come and look on, sir, won't you?' said his son.

But the merchant shook his head.

'I think I can hold on till the night itself, Bertie, my boy!' with a cleverly fielded yawn. 'I hear all about it from your mother. You'll find me in the billiard-room if you want me, you know!'

Mark rose from the table to which he had sat down with so light a heart. Black disgrace was before him, the Laufingen crisis had come again, and this time nothing could save him. He lingered behind the other men as they mounted the broad staircase, and as he lingered was overtaken by Vincent, who had just left his hat and overcoat below, and was about to go upstairs.

'Stop!' cried Mark. 'Don't go up yet, I want to speak to you. Come in here!' and he almost forced him into the library, which was empty, and where a lamp was burning.

'So we're on a level after all, are we?' he said savagely, as he shut the door.

Holroyd simply asked him what he meant.

'You know!' said Mark. 'All that generosity at Laufingen was a sham, was it—a blind? It didn't suit you that I should give myself up of my own free will, and so soon, so you put me off my guard! And now'— his voice was thick with passion as he spoke—'now you have set that villain, that d—d Caffyn, on me! Chivalrous that, isn't it? I've fallen into good hands between you!'

Vincent was hardly less angry. 'You think every one is like yourself!' he said. 'If it is any comfort to you to believe that I can break my word and betray those who trusted it, believe it—it's not worth my while to set you right?'

No one who saw his face could doubt that he, at least, was no traitor; and Mark felt lower than ever as he realised his mistake.

'Forgive me!' he stammered. 'I see, I ought to have known better. I hardly know what I am saying or doing just now—but Caffyn has found out everything, and—and who could have told him?'

'If any one betrayed you, it must have been yourself!' said Vincent. 'Look here, Ashburn, don't give it up like this—keep your head, man! He can't really know this, it must be all guesswork. Did he mention my name?'

'Yes,' said Mark.

'Well, I must have it out with him, then. What does it matter what he says if we both contradict him? I think I shall be able to manage him; only, for Heaven's sake, keep cool, leave everything to me, try to be your usual self. Where is this rehearsal going on? Let us go there at once—you'll be wanted!'

Mark said no more just then; he led the way to the music-room, and then went himself to the part which was screened off as a green-room.

The music-room was a long high gallery, at one end of which the stage had been set up. There was a small audience of a dozen or so, who were mostly related to the performers, and admitted only because it had not been found practicable to keep them out. The rehearsal had just begun as Vincent entered.

It was much like most rehearsals, and would hardly lose its tediousness in description. There were constant interruptions and repetitions, and most of the characters wore the air of people who had been induced to play a game they thought silly, but who were resolved to maintain their self-respect as long as possible; this appearance might be due to an artistic reserve of force in some cases, in others to nervousness, in nearly all to a limited knowledge of the lines they had to deliver, and all these causes would certainly be removed 'on the night,' because the actors said so themselves. Still, on that particular evening, they prevented the play from being seen to the best advantage.

It was not a good play, and as a dramatisation of 'Illusion' was worse than the most sanguine of Mrs. Featherstone's acquaintances could have foreseen; and yet, as Vincent stood and looked on from the background, he felt strangely stirred when Mabel was on the stage. She, at least, had too intense a sympathy with her part to be able to walk through it, even at a rehearsal, though it would have been absurd to exert her full powers under the circumstances.

But there were moments in the later scenes (which even Mrs. Featherstone had not been able to deprive of all power or pathos) when Mabel was carried away by the emotion she had to represent, and the anguish in her face and low ringing tones went to Vincent's heart, as he thought how soon it might become a terrible reality.

He could scarcely bear to see her there simulating a sorrow which was nothing to that which might be coming upon her, and from which all his devotion might not save her this time. He was impatient to meet Caffyn and find out what he knew, and how he might be silenced; but Caffyn was on the stage continually, in his capacity of stage manager, and Vincent was forced to wait until his opportunity should present itself.

It was a relief to him when the rehearsal, after dragging on through three long acts, came to a premature close, owing to the lateness of the hour and a decided preference on the part of the younger members of the company for the dancing which had been promised later as a bribe, and which they had no intention of sacrificing to a fourth act—for art must not be too long with amateurs.

The room was being cleared accordingly, when Vincent saw his hostess coming with Caffyn in his direction, and heard her say, 'Well, I will ask Mr. Holroyd then if you wish it!' She seemed excited and annoyed, and he thought Caffyn's face bore an odd expression of triumph. He waited for the question with a heavy anticipation.

'Mr. Caffyn tells me you're quite an authority,' began Mrs. Featherstone (she had not yet found herself able to mention him as 'Harold'). 'You heard our little discussion about the close of that third act, just now? Now do tell me, how did it strike you?'

This appeal was an unexpected relief to him; he protested that he was not qualified to express any opinion.

'Now really,' said Caffyn, 'that won't quite do; we know how interested you are in the book.'

'We are so grateful for the least little hint,' simpered Mrs. Featherstone, 'and it is so useful to know how a scene strikes just the ordinary observer, you know; so if you did notice anything, don't, please, be afraid to mention it!'

Vincent had told himself that in going there he would be able to put away all personal association with the play; he had given the book up once and for all, he only desired to see Mabel once as his lost heroine. But nature had proved too strong for him after all: the feebleness of this dramatic version had vexed his instincts as creator more than he was willing to believe, and when in this very closing scene the strongest situation in the book had been ruined by the long and highly unnecessary tirade which had been assigned to the hero, Vincent's philosophy had been severely shaken.

And so at this, some impulse, too strong for all other considerations, possessed him to do what he could to remove that particular blemish at least—it was not wise, but it was absolutely disinterested.

He suggested that a shorter and simpler sentence at the critical moment might prove more effective than a long set speech.

Mrs. Featherstone smiled an annoyed little smile. 'You don't quite understand the point,' she said. 'There was no question about the text—I had no idea of altering that: we are merely in doubt as to the various positions at the fall of the curtain!'

'I'm afraid I've no suggestions to make, then,' said Vincent, not without some inward heat.

'Oh, but,' put in Caffyn, and his lip curled with malicious enjoyment, 'give us an idea of the short simple sentence you would substitute—it's easy enough to make a general criticism of that sort.'

'Yes, indeed,' said Mrs. Featherstone. 'That is only fair, Mr. Holroyd!'

If he had been cooler he might have resisted what was obviously a challenge from the enemy, but just then he had lost some of his usual self-control. 'Something of this kind,' he said, and gave the line he had originally written.

'Now that is very funny,' said Mrs. Featherstone, icily. 'Really. Why, do you know, my dear Mr. Holroyd, that the speech you find such fault with happens to be just the one I took entire from the book itself!' And it was in fact one of Mark's improvements.

Vincent then saw for the first time that Mabel had joined the group, and he was angry with himself for his folly.

'Where has Ashburn got to? We must tell him that!' cried Caffyn. 'That distinguished man has been keeping out of the way all the evening. There he is over there in the corner!' and he gave him a sign that he was wanted. No one had seen Mark for some little time, and he had interfered very little during the rehearsal. Now as he came towards them he looked shaken and ill.

'My dear fellow,' said Caffyn, 'this presumptuous man here has been suggesting that your immortal dialogue wants cutting badly. Crush him!'

'He has every right to his opinion,' said Mark, with an effort.

'Ah,' said Caffyn with a keen appreciation of the situation, 'but just explain your views to him, Holroyd. He may think there's something in them!'

'It is a pity,' said Mabel, 'that Mark's book should have been without the advantage of Mr. Holroyd's assistance so long!'

She was the more angry with Vincent because she felt that he was right.

'I don't think I quite deserved that,' said Vincent, sadly. 'If my opinion had not been asked I should not have ventured to criticise; and, now that I know that I have the book against me, of course I have nothing more to say. You seem to have misunderstood me a little,' he added, looking straight at Caffyn. 'If you can give me a minute I could easily explain all I meant.'

Caffyn understood. 'In private, I suppose?' he suggested softly, as he drew Vincent a little aside. 'I thought as much,' said Caffyn, as the other assented; 'they're going to dance here. Come up on the stage: it's clear now, and the rag's down.'

He led the way up the wooden steps by the proscenium, pushed aside the gold-and-crimson hangings, and they were in comparative darkness and absolute privacy immediately.

'Now,' began Vincent, 'you had some object in saying what you did down there. What was it?'

Caffyn had seated himself on the edge of a table which had been rolled into a corner with some other stage furniture. He smiled with much sweetness as he replied, 'I say, you know, we'd better come to the point. I know all about it!'

Only the pressing need of discovering the full extent of the other's information kept Vincent from some outburst.

'What do you know?' he demanded.

'Well,' said Caffyn, 'I know that you are the real pig, so to speak, and that miserable humbug Ashburn's only the squeak.'

'You mean you think you know that—what is your authority?'

'Now,' protested Caffyn, in a tone of injury, 'do you think I should venture on a bold statement like that without anything to back my opinion?'

'And if Ashburn and I both deny your bold statement—what becomes of it?'

'Ashburn has not denied it, and if he did I could put my hand on some written evidence which would go a long way to settle the question.'

'I should like to see your evidence,' said Vincent.

'I was sure you would,' said Caffyn, 'but I don't happen to have it here; in fact, the papers which contain it are in the charge of a very dear friend of mine, who chanced to discover them.'

Vincent did not believe him.

'Perhaps you can describe them?' he asked quickly.

'Aha!' said Caffyn, 'I've made you sit up, as they say across the water. Oh, I'll give you every information. Those papers are of interest to the collector of literary curiosities as being beyond a doubt the original rough draft of that remarkable work "Illusion," then better known as—let me see, was it "Glow-worms"? no—something like it, "Glamour!" They were found in your late rooms, and one needn't be an expert to recognise that peculiar fist of yours. Are you satisfied?'

Vincent had not expected this, having fancied that his loose papers had all been destroyed, as he had certainly intended them to be on leaving England. He was silent for some seconds, then he said: 'You must get those papers for me: they are mine.'

'But, my dear fellow,' argued Caffyn, 'what earthly use can they be to you?'

'What business is that of yours?' retorted Vincent. 'I want them—I mean to have them.'

'You won't do any good by taking that tone with me, you know. Just listen to reason: if you produce these papers yourself, you'll only be laughed at for your pains. You must let some one else manage the business for you. You can't smash Ashburn alone—you can't indeed!'

'And who told you,' said Vincent, 'that I want to smash Ashburn?'

'For Heaven's sake don't you turn hypocrite!' drawled Caffyn. 'You can speak out now—if you've got anything inside you but sawdust, of course you want to smash Ashburn! I saw your game long ago.'

'Did you?' said Vincent, who began to have the greatest difficulty in keeping his temper. 'And what was my game?'

'Why,' explained Caffyn, 'you knew well enough that if you set up a claim like that on your mere word, you wouldn't find many to believe you, and you didn't feel up to such a fight as you would have before you; so you've very prudently been lying low till you could get Master Mark off his guard, or till something turned up to help you. Now's your time. I'll help you!'

'Then, once more, get me those papers,' said Vincent.

'To think,' observed Caffyn, with pity, 'that the man who could write "Illusion" should be so dense. Don't I tell you you must keep in the background? You leave it all to me. There's a literary fellow I know who's on lots of journals that like nothing better than taking up cases like yours, when they're satisfied there's something in them. I can manage all that for you, and in a few days look out for an article that will do Ashburn's business for him. You needn't be afraid of his fighting—he'll never have the nerve to bring a libel action! But you can't work this yourself; in your hands all that evidence is waste paper—it's the date and manner of its discovery which must be proved to make it of any value—and that's where I come in. I need scarcely tell you perhaps that I don't propose to mix myself up in all this, unless there is some better understanding between us in the future.'

'You had better be quite plain,' said Vincent. 'What is your proposal?'

'There has been a little unpleasantness about a letter which little Dolly Langton and I accidentally—'

'I know the facts, thank you,' interrupted Vincent.

'That makes it easier,' continued the other, unabashed, 'though you've probably been told the highly coloured version.'

'I've been told that you bullied that poor child into burning a letter of mine which you hadn't the courage to suppress for yourself,' said Vincent.

'Ah, that is the highly coloured version,' said Caffyn, 'but for the purposes of the present case we'll assume it to be correct, if you like. Well, we can't possibly work together if you won't make up your mind to let bygones be bygones: you understand.'

'I think I do,' said Vincent. 'Provided I forget that a letter of mine was intercepted and destroyed, unread, by a cowardly, cold-blooded trick, which if it was not actually a felony came very near it— provided I forget all that and treat you as an intimate friend of mine, I shall have your support?'

'Coarsely put,' said Caffyn, 'but you seem to have got hold of the main point.'

'And if I decline,' said Vincent, 'what then?'

'Why, then,' returned Caffyn, placidly, 'I'm afraid that my friend in whose custody the papers are, and who really is as casual a person as I ever met, may mislay those documents or go off somewhere without leaving his address—which would make things awkward.'

Vincent could stand no more; the anger he had suppressed for some time broke out at last.

'If you dare to make me an offer like that in any other place than a friend's house, if you even try to speak to me when we next meet, you will be unpleasantly surprised at your reception! Do you think any help you could give me would be worth the disgrace of having you for a friend? If I am asked my opinion of you, I shall give it, and it will not be one you would care to quote. As for the papers, tell your friend (you will not have to go very far to find him)—tell him he may do what he pleases with them, mislay them, suppress them, burn them, if he likes—perhaps he will be doing me a greater service than he imagines!'

He was afraid that he might have betrayed his real feelings in the matter; but Caffyn was too much a man of the world to believe him: he only thought that the other either had independent means of proving his claim when he chose, or felt convinced that it would be proved for him without the necessity of committing himself to any alliance or compromise. He could not help admiring such strategy even while it disappointed him.

'You're devilish deep, after all,' he said slowly: 'a little overdone that last bit, perhaps, but no matter—I can read between the lines. And now, as I am due for this first dance, and they seem to be striking up down there, I'll ask you to excuse me. One word—if you want me to play your little game, don't interfere with mine—you know what I mean!'

Vincent made no answer, and Caffyn went down to the music-room again, where about a dozen couples were already dancing. It was a small and quite informal affair, but one or two people had come in from other houses, and the room was filled, without the hopeless crush which it would have contained on an ordinary occasion.

He avoided Gilda, whose eyes, however, were following him watchfully, and made his way to where Mabel was sitting looking on at the dancing; for she had declined to take a more active part, and was intending to make her escape as soon as Mark should come to rescue her.

'I'll try one more chance,' he thought, 'and if that fails—'

Vincent had satisfied himself as he passed through the room after Caffyn had left him that Mark was not there. He went through a network of rooms, and out on the staircase, looking for him. Mark had had much to endure in the way of enthusiastic comments on his own work, and the delight he was supposed to feel at his wife's rendering of his heroine, while Mrs. Featherstone had driven him almost frantic by her persistent appeals, confidences, and suggestions with regard to the performance. He had chosen a moment when her attention was distracted to slip out unobserved. He knew he must return soon, but his nerves would bear no more just then, and, wandering aimlessly from room to room, he came to one in which some light refreshments had been placed for those engaged in the rehearsal, and he filled a small tumbler of champagne from a half-empty bottle he found there, and drank it, hoping it would give him courage to go back and play his part to the end. As he put down the glass Vincent came in.

'I was looking for you,' the latter began hurriedly, when he had satisfied himself that they were not likely to be overheard. 'I have seen Caffyn!'

'Well?' said Mark, listlessly.

'It is worse than I thought,' was the answer; 'he has got hold of some papers—Heaven knows how, but he can prove his case. He half threatened to destroy them, but if I know him he won't; he will use them to keep his hold over you—we must get the start of him!'

'Yes,' agreed Mark, 'I can disappoint him there, at all events. I'll go to Fladgate to-morrow, and tell him everything—it's all I can do now, and the sooner it is over the better!'

'You must do nothing without me!' said Vincent.

Despair made Mark obstinate. 'I wish to God I had spoken out last Easter! You stopped me then—you shall not stop me this time! I'll keep that book no longer, whatever the consequences may be.'

'Listen to me,' said Vincent. 'I will take back the book—I see no other course now; but I claim the right to tell the story myself, and in my own way. You will not be madman enough to contradict me?'

Mark laughed bitterly. 'If you can tell that story so as to make it look any better, or any worse, than it is, I won't contradict you,' he said: 'that is a safe promise!'

'Remember it, then,' said Vincent. 'I will tell you more when I have thought things out a little. In the meantime, the less we see of that scoundrel the better. Can't you take Mabel home now?'

'Yes,' said Mark, 'we will go home, and—and you will come to-morrow?'

'To-morrow,' said Vincent. 'Tell her nothing till you have seen me!'

They were returning to the music-room when Mrs. Featherstone passed.

'Have you seen Mr. Caffyn?' she asked Mark. 'I want to talk to him about the alterations in the fourth act.'

'He went to sit out one of the dances with Mabel, Gilda said, but I sent her to look for them, and she hasn't come back yet. I think they must have gone through the Gold Room, and out on the balcony—it's cooler there.'

When she had passed on out of hearing, Mark turned to Vincent. 'Did you hear that?' he said. 'Mabel is out there … with him—we are saved the trouble of telling her anything now … that devil means to tell her himself! I can't stay here!'

'Tell me where you are going—for God's sake don't do anything rash!' cried Vincent. 'You may be wrong!' He caught him by the arm as he spoke.

'Let me go!' said Mark, wrenching himself free.

Vincent would have accompanied him, but the excitement had turned him suddenly faint and dizzy, and he found himself obliged to remain where he was, until the attack passed and left him able to move and think once more.

CHAPTER XXXIX

CAFFYN SPRINGS HIS MINE

'I should like your opinion about those hangings in the Gold Room,' Caffyn had said to Mabel, for the benefit of any bystanders, as soon as he reached her chair: 'they seem to me the very thing for the boudoir scene in the third act. You promised to help me; would it bore you very much to come now?'

Tired as she was, Mabel made no demur. She knew, of course, that he wished to speak to her alone, and she had something to say to him herself, which could not be said too soon. He led her through the room in question—a luxurious little nest, at an angle of the house, entered by separate doors from the music-room and the head of the principal staircase; but he did not think it necessary to waste any time upon the hangings, and they passed out through one of the two windows upon the balcony, which had been covered in with striped canvas for the season.

He drew forward a seat for her and took one himself, but did not speak for some time. He was apparently waiting for her to begin. A tête-à-tête with a man to whom one has just forbidden one's house is necessarily a delicate matter, and, although Mabel did not falter at all in her purpose, she did feel a certain nervousness which made her unwilling to speak at first.

'As you leave me to begin,' he said, 'let me ask you if what your husband has told me just now is true—that you have closed your own door to me, and mean to induce Mrs. Langton to do the same?'

'It is true,' she replied in a low voice; 'you left me no other course.'

'You know what the result of that will be, I suppose?' he continued. 'Mrs. Featherstone will soon find out that two such intimate friends of hers will have nothing to do with me, and she will naturally want to know the reason. What shall you tell her?'

'That is what I meant to say to you!' she answered. 'I thought I ought in fairness to tell you—that you might, perhaps, take it as a warning. If I am asked, though I hope I shall not be, I shall feel bound to say what I know.'

'Do you think I can't see what you are aiming at in all this?' he asked; and under his smooth tones there were indications of coming rage. 'You have set yourself to drive me out of this house!'

'All I wish,' said Mabel, 'is to prevent you as far as I can from ever tormenting Dolly again—I am determined to do that!'

'You know as well as I do that you will do much more than that. Mrs. Featherstone does not love me as it is: your conduct will give her the excuse she wants to get rid of me!'

'I can't help it,' she said firmly. 'And if Gilda is brought to see, before it is too late, what things you are capable of, it would be the best thing that could happen for her.'

'It would be more straightforward, wouldn't it, if you told her at once?' he suggested with a slight sneer: 'it comes to very much the same thing in the end.'

Mabel had had some searchings of conscience on this very point. Ought she, she had asked herself, knowing what she knew of Caffyn's past, to stand by while a girl whom she liked as she did Gilda deceived herself so grossly? But of late a coldness had sprung up between Gilda and herself which made it unlikely that any interference would be taken in good part; and besides, there was something invidious in such a course, to which she could not bring herself without feeling more certain than she did that it was necessary and would be of any avail.

'If I was sure I should do the least good, I should certainly tell her,' Mabel replied; 'but I hope now that it will not be necessary.'

He bit his lips. 'You are exceedingly amiable, I must say,' he observed; 'but really now, why all this bitterness? What makes you so anxious to see an obscure individual like myself jilted—and ruined?'

'Am I bitter?' said Mabel. 'I don't think so. You ought to know that I do not wish for your ruin, but I can't help wishing that this marriage should be broken off.'

'Ah!' he said softly, 'and may I ask why?'

'Why!' cried Mabel. 'Can you ask? Because you are utterly unworthy of any nice and good girl—you will make your wife a very miserable woman, Harold—and you are marrying Gilda for money and position, not love—you don't know what love means, that is why!'

Even in the half-light which came from the shaded lamps in the room within she looked very lovely in her indignation, and he hated her the more for it—it was maddening to feel that he was absolutely despicable and repulsive in the eyes of this woman, to whose fairness even hatred itself could not blind him.

'You are unjust,' he said, bending towards her. 'You forget—I loved you! I expected that,' he added, for she had turned impatiently away; 'it always does rouse some women's contempt to be told of a love they don't feel in return. But I did love you, as I suppose I never shall love again. As for Gilda, I don't mind confessing that, on my side at all events, there is no very passionate emotion. She is handsome enough in her peculiar style, but then it doesn't happen to appeal to me. Still, she will bring me money and position, and she does me the honour (if I may say so without vanity) of caring very decidedly for me—it is fair enough on both sides. What right have you, what right has any one in the world, to interfere and make mischief between us?'

'None, perhaps—I don't know,' she said. 'But I have told you that I shall not interfere. All I am quite sure of is that I am right to protect Dolly, and, if I am asked, to speak the truth for Gilda's sake. And I mean to do it.'

'I have told you already what that will end in,' he said. 'Mabel, you can't really be so relentless! I ask you once more to have some consideration for me. We were old playmates together once, there was a time when we were almost lovers, you did not always hate me like this. You might remember that now. If—if I were to promise not to go near Dolly—'

'I trusted you once before,' she said, 'you know how you repaid it. I will make no more terms. Besides, even if I were silent, there are others who know—'

'None who would not be silent if you wished it,' urged Caffyn, eagerly. 'Give me one more chance, Mabel!'

'You have had my answer—I shall not change it,' she said: 'now take me back, please, we have been here long enough.'

Caffyn had been anxious from motives of pure economy to try fair means first, before resorting to extreme measures: he had tried irony, argument, flattery, and sentiment, and all in vain. It was time for his last coup. He motioned her to remain as she half rose.

'Not yet,' he said. 'I have something to say to you first, and you must hear it—you have driven me to it.... Remember that, when I have finished!'

She sank back again half quelled by the power she felt in the man. From the streets below came up the constant roll of wheels and 'clip-clop' of hoofs from passing broughams, intermingled now and then with shouts and shrill whistles telling of early departures from sundry awning-covered porticoes around.

From the music-room within came the sound of waltz music, only slightly muffled by doors and hangings: they were playing 'My Queen,' though she was not conscious of hearing it at the time. In after-time, however, when that waltz, with the refrain, part dreamy, part passionate, which even battered brass and iron hammers cannot render quite commonplace, became popular with street bands and piano-organs, it was always associated for her with a vague sensation of coming evil. Caffyn had risen, and stood looking down upon her with a malignant triumph which made her shudder even then.

'Do you remember,' he said, very clearly and slowly, 'once, when you had done your best to humiliate me, that I told you I hoped for your sake I should never have a chance of turning the tables?'

He paused, while she looked up at him with her eyebrows drawn and her lips slightly parted.

'I think my chance has come,' he continued, seeing that she did not mean to answer, 'really I do. When I have told you what I am going to tell you, all that pretty disdain and superiority of yours will vanish like smoke, and in a minute or two you will be begging my silence at any price, and you shall accept my terms!'

'I do not think so,' said Mabel, bravely: only her own curiosity and the suggestion of some hidden power in the other's manner kept her from refusing to remain there any longer.

'I do,' said Caffyn. 'Ah, Mabel, you are a happy woman, with a husband who is the ideal of genius and goodness and good looks. What will you say, I wonder, when I tell you that you owe all this happiness to me? It's true. I watched the growth of your affection with the deepest interest, and at the critical moment, when an unexpected obstacle to your union turned up, it was I who removed it at considerable personal sacrifice. Aren't you grateful? Well, between ourselves, I could scarcely expect gratitude.'

'I—I don't understand,' she said.

'I am going to explain,' he rejoined. 'You have been pitying poor Gilda for throwing herself away on a worthless wretch like me. Keep your pity, you will want it yourself perhaps! Do you understand now? I let you marry Mark, because I could think of no revenge so lasting and so perfect!'

She rose quickly. 'I have heard enough,' she said: 'you must be mad to dare to talk like this.... Let me go, you hurt me.' He had caught her arm above her long glove, and held it tight for a moment, while he bent his face down close to hers, and looked into her eyes with a cruel light in his own.

'You shall not go till you have heard me out,' he said between his teeth. 'You have married a common impostor, an impudent swindler—do you understand? I knew it long ago ... I could have exposed him fifty times if I had chosen! A few lines from me to the proper quarter, and the whole story would be public property to-morrow—as fine a scandal as literary London has had for ages; and, by Heaven, Mabel, if you don't treat me decently, I'll speak out! I see you can't take my word for all this. Perhaps you will take your husband's? Ask him if his past has no secrets (there should be none between you now, you know): ask him—'

He would have said more, but she freed herself suddenly from his grasp and turned on him from the window. 'You coward,' she cried scornfully, 'I am not Dolly—you cannot frighten me!'

He was not prepared for this, having counted upon an instant surrender which would enable him to dictate his own terms. 'I don't want to frighten you,' he said sulkily: 'I only want you to see that I don't mean to be trifled with!' He had followed her to the window, meaning to induce her to return, but all at once he stepped back hastily. 'There's some one coming,' he said in a rapid undertone: 'it's Mrs. Featherstone. Mabel—you won't be mad enough to tell her!'

'You shall see,' said Mabel, and the next moment she had taken refuge by the side of her hostess, her eyes bright and her cheeks flushed with anger. 'Mrs. Featherstone,' she said, almost clinging to her in her excitement, 'let me go back with you, anywhere where I shall be safe from that man!'

Caffyn was no longer visible, having retired to the balcony, so that the elder lady was somewhat bewildered by this appeal, especially as she did not quite catch it. 'Of course you shall go back with me if you want to,' she said; 'but are you all alone here? I thought I should find Mr. Caffyn. Where is he?'

'There, on the balcony,' said Mabel. 'It is no wonder that he is ashamed to show himself!'

At this Caffyn judged it advisable to appear.

'I don't exactly know why I should be afraid,' he said, with a rather awkward ease. 'Are you going to publish our little quarrel, Mrs. Ashburn? Is it worth while, do you think?'

'It was no quarrel,' retorted Mabel. 'Will you tell Mrs. Featherstone what you dared to say to me, or must I?'

Mrs. Featherstone looked from one to the other with growing uneasiness. It would be very awkward to have any unpleasantness in her little company when the play was so far advanced. On the other hand, she was not disposed to soften matters for a man she disliked so heartily as Harold Caffyn.

'Mabel, dearest, tell me what it is all about,' she said. 'If he has insulted you, he shall answer to me for it!'

'He insulted my husband,' said Mabel. 'I will speak, Harold, I am not afraid, though I know you have every reason to wish your words forgotten. He said—'

Here Caffyn interrupted her: he had made up his mind the only thing he could do with his secret now was to use it to spike the enemy's guns. Mabel was rash enough to insist on an explanation: she should have it.

'One moment,' he said. 'If you still insist on it, I will repeat what I said presently. I was trying to prepare Mrs. Ashburn for a very painful disclosure,' he explained to Mrs. Featherstone—'a disclosure which, considering my position in the family, I felt it would be my duty to make before long. I could not possibly foresee that she would take it like this. If you think a little, Mrs. Ashburn, I am sure you will see that this is not the time or place for a very delicate and unpleasant business.'

'He pretends that Mark is an impostor—that he knows some secret of his!' Mabel broke in vehemently. 'He did not speak of it as he tries to make you believe ... he threatened me!'

'Dear Mr. Ashburn, whom we all know so well, an impostor—with a secret! You said that to Mabel?' cried Mrs. Featherstone. 'Why, you must be mad to talk in that dreadful way—quite mad!'

'My dear Mrs. Featherstone, I assure you I'm perfectly sane,' he replied. 'The real truth is that the world has been grossly deceived all this time—no one more so than yourself; but I do beg you not to force me to speak here, where we might be interrupted at any moment, and besides, in ordinary consideration to Mrs. Ashburn—'

'You did not consider me very much just now,' she broke in. 'I have told you that I am not afraid to hear—you cannot get out of it in that way!'

Mabel was well enough aware that Mark was not flawless, but the idea that he could be capable of a dishonourable action was grotesque and monstrous to her, and the only way she could find to punish the man who could conceive such a charge was to force him to declare it openly.

Mrs. Featherstone's curiosity and alarm had been strongly roused. She had taken up this young novelist, her name was publicly connected with his—if there was anything wrong about him, ought she not to know it?

'My love,' she said to Mabel, taking her hands, 'you know I don't believe a word of all this—it is some strange mistake, I am sure of it, but it ought, perhaps, to be cleared up. If I were to speak to Mr. Caffyn alone now!'

'I shall be very willing,' said Caffyn.

'No!' said Mabel, eagerly, 'if he has anything to say, let him say it here—Mark must not be stabbed in the dark!'

'It's simply impossible to speak here,' said Caffyn. 'People may come in at any moment through those doors as soon as this waltz is over. Mrs. Featherstone will not thank either of us for making a scene.'

'The doors can be locked,' cried Mabel. 'There need be no scene. May they be locked, dear Mrs. Featherstone? He has said too much to be silent any longer: he must speak now!'

Caffyn stepped lightly to the doors which opened into the music-room; the key was on his side, and he turned it. The last notes of 'My Queen' were sounding as he did so, they could hear the sweep and rustle of dresses as the couples passed.

'We shall not be disturbed now,' he said, unable to quite conceal his own inclinations: 'they are not likely to come in from the staircase. If Mrs. Featherstone really insists on my speaking, I can't refuse.'

'Must I, Mabel?' asked the elderly lady, nervously; but Mabel had turned towards the door leading to the staircase, which had just opened.

'Here is Mark to answer for himself!' she cried, as she went to meet him. 'Now, Harold, whatever you have to say against Mark, say it to his face!'

Mark's entrance was not so opportune as it seemed; he had been standing unnoticed at the door for some time, waiting until he could wait no longer. He faced Caffyn now, unflinchingly enough to outward appearance; but the hand Mabel held in a soft close clasp was strangely cold and unresponsive.

Caffyn could not have wished for a better opportunity. 'I assure you this is very painful to me,' he said, 'but you see I cannot help myself. I must ask Mr. Ashburn first if it is not true that this book "Illusion," which has rendered him so famous, is not his book at all—that from beginning to end it was written by another. Is he bold enough to deny it?'

Mark made no answer. Mabel had almost laughed to hear so preposterous a question—it was not wonderful that he should scorn to reply. Suddenly she looked at his face, and her heart sickened. Many incidents that she had attached no importance to at the time came back to her now laden with vague but terrible significance ... she would not doubt him, only—why did he look as if it was true?

'Dear Mr. Ashburn,' said Mrs. Featherstone, 'we know what your answer will be, but I think—I'm afraid—you ought to say something.'

He turned his ghastly face and haggard eyes to her and at the same instant withdrew his hand from Mabel's. 'What would you have me say?' he asked hoarsely. 'I can't deny it ... it is not my book ... from beginning to end it was written by another.'

And, as he spoke the words, Vincent Holroyd entered the room.

His recent attack of faintness had left him so weak that for some time he was obliged to remain in a little alcove on the staircase and rest himself on one of the divans there.

His head was perfectly clear, however, and he had already perfected a plan by which Mabel would be spared the worst of that which threatened her. It was simple, and, as far as he could see, quite impossible to disprove—he would let it be understood that Mark and he had written the book in collaboration, and that he had desired his own share of the work to be kept secret.

Mark could not refuse, for Mabel's sake, to second him in this statement—it was actually true even, for—as Vincent thought with a grim kind of humour—there was a good deal of Mark's work in the book as it stood now. He grew feverishly impatient to see Mark and put his plan into action—there must be time yet, Caffyn could not have been such a villain as to open Mabel's eyes to the real case! He felt strong again now; he would go and assure himself this was so. He rose and, following the direction he had seen Mark take, entered the Gold Room—only to hear an admission after which no defence seemed possible.

He stood there just behind Mark, trying to take in what had happened. There was Mrs. Featherstone struggling to conceal her chagrin and dismay at the sudden downfall of her dramatic ambition; Mark standing apart with bent head and hands behind him like a man facing a firing party; Mabel struck speechless and motionless by the shock; and Caffyn with the air of one who has fulfilled an unpalatable duty. Vincent knew it all now—he had come too late!

Mrs. Featherstone made a movement towards him. 'Oh, Mr. Holroyd,' she said, with a very strained smile, 'you mustn't come in, please: we're—we're talking over our little play—state secrets, you know!'

Caffyn's smile meant mischief as he said: 'Mr. Holroyd has every right to be here, my dear Mrs. Featherstone, as you'll allow when I tell you who he is. He has too much diffidence to assert himself. Mr. Ashburn has admitted that he did not write "Illusion:" he might have added that he stole the book in a very treacherous and disgraceful way. I am sorry to use words of this sort, but when you know all, you will understand that I have some excuse. Mr. Holroyd can tell you the story better than I can: he is the man who has been wronged, the real author of "Illusion"!'

'I've done him a good turn there,' he thought; 'he can't very well turn against me after that!'

A terrible silence followed his words; Vincent's brain whirled, he could think of nothing. Mabel was the first to move or speak: she went to Mark's side as he stood silent and alone before his accuser, and touched his arm. 'Mark,' she said in an agonised whisper, 'do you hear? ... tell them ... it is not true—oh, I can't believe it—I won't—only speak!'

Vincent's heart swelled with a passionate devotion for her as she raised her fair face, blanched and stricken with an agony of doubt and hope, to her husband's averted eyes. How she loved him. What would he not have given for love like that? His own feelings were too true and loyal, however, to wish even for a moment to see the love and faith die out of her face, slain for ever by some shameful confession.

Was it too late to save her even now? His brain cleared suddenly—a way of escape had opened to him.

In the meantime two newcomers had entered. Mr. Featherstone, hearing voices, had brought up Mr. Langton, who had 'looked in' on his way from the House, and for some time remained under the impression that they had interrupted some kind of informal rehearsal. 'Still at the theatricals, eh?' he observed, as he came in. 'Go on, don't let us disturb you. Capital, capital!' 'Langton,' whispered the other, pulling him back, 'they're—they're not acting—I'm afraid something's the matter!' and the two waited to gather some idea of what was happening.

Before Mark could reply, if he meant to reply, to Mabel's appeal, Vincent had anticipated him. 'Mrs. Ashburn—Mabel,' he said, 'you are right to trust in his honour—it is not true. I can explain everything.'

The instant joy and relief in her face as she clung fondly to Mark's arm repaid him and gave him strength and courage to go on. Mark looked round with a stunned wonder. What could be said or done to save him now? he thought. Vincent was mad to try. But the latter put his hand, as if affectionately, on his shoulder with a warning pressure, and he said nothing.

'Do you mean,' said Caffyn to Holroyd, with an angry sneer, 'that I told a lie—that you did not write "Illusion"?'

'That was not the lie,' returned Vincent. 'I did write "Illusion." It is untrue that Mr. Ashburn's conduct in the matter does him anything but credit. May I tell my story here, Mrs. Featherstone?'

'Oh, by all means,' said that lady, not too graciously: 'we can't know the facts too soon.'

'I wrote the book,' said Vincent, 'before I went out to Ceylon. I was at the Bar then, and had thoughts of practising again at some future time. I had a fancy (which was foolish, I dare say) to keep the fact that I had written a novel a close secret. So I entrusted the manuscript to my good friend, Mr. Ashburn, leaving him to arrange, if he could, for its publication, and I charged him to keep my secret by every means in his power. In fact, I was so much in earnest about it that I made him give me his solemn promise that, if he could not shield me in any other way, he would do so with his own name. I did not really believe then that that would be necessary, or even that the book would be accepted, but I knew Mr. Ashburn wrote novels himself, and I hoped the arrangement would not do him any actual harm.'

Till then he had gone on fluently enough; it was merely a modification of his original idea, with a considerable blending of the actual facts, but he felt that there were difficulties to come which it would require all his skill to avoid.

'I was detained, as you know, for more than a year in Ceylon, and unable most of the time to write to England,' he continued. 'When I came home, I found—I was told that the book had obtained a success neither of us ever dreamed of: curiosity had been aroused, and Mr. Ashburn had found himself driven to keep his promise. He—he was anxious that I should release him and clear the matter up. I—I—it was not convenient for me to do so just then, and I induced him—he could hardly refuse, perhaps—to keep up the disguise a little longer. We had just arranged to make everything known shortly, when Mr. Caffyn anticipated us. And that is really all there is to tell about that.'

Throughout Vincent's explanation Caffyn had been inwardly raging at the thought that his victims might actually succeed in escaping after all. Forcing an indulgent laugh, he said, 'My dear fellow, it's very kind and generous of you to say all that, and it sounds very pretty and almost probable, but you can't expect us seriously to believe it, you know!'

For an instant this remark appeared to produce a reaction; but it vanished at Vincent's reply. His pale worn face flushed angrily as he faced him.

'No one seriously expects you to believe in such things as honour and friendship!' he said contemptuously. 'I am going to deal with your share in this now. Mrs. Featherstone,' he added, 'will you forgive me if I am obliged to pain you by anything I may have to say? That man has thought fit to bring a disgraceful charge against my friend here—it is only right that you should know how little he deserves credit!'

Secretly Mrs. Featherstone was only too glad to see Caffyn discomfited, but all she did was to say stiffly, 'Oh, pray don't consider my feelings, Mr. Holroyd!'

Vincent's indignation was enough in itself to make him merciless, and then, as a matter of policy, he was determined to disable the enemy to the utmost. Everything that had come to his knowledge of Caffyn's proceedings he now exposed with biting irony. He told the story of the letter, suppressed to all appearances out of gratuitous malice, and of the cruel terrorism exercised over little Dolly; he showed how Caffyn had tried to profit by his supposed discovery of the fraud, and how Mark had studiously refrained from undeceiving him, and gave a damaging description of the sordid threats and proposals he had himself received that evening. 'This is the high-minded gentleman who, acting under a keen sense of duty, has chosen to denounce Mr. Ashburn just now,' he concluded.

The victory was won. Caffyn's face was livid as he heard him—he had never foreseen such black ingratitude as this, and it upset all his calculations. He still had his doubts, after so many careful experiments, that the story of Vincent's was a fabrication, even though it was not absolutely inconsistent with what he had observed, and he could see no motive for shielding the culprit. But it was plain that every one there believed it—Vincent's word would be taken before his—he was thoroughly beaten.

No one had seen Gilda come in, but she had been standing for some time with red eyes and flushed face by one of the windows, and in the general stir which followed Vincent's explanation Mr. Featherstone came up to her.

'Well,' he said, 'we've been treated to a very pretty story this evening. This is the young gentleman you're going to give me for a son-in-law, is it, Gilda? But of course you don't believe a word against him!'

'I believe it all—and more!' she said with a passionate sob.

Caffyn turned to her. 'You too, Gilda!' he cried pathetically.

'You might have deceived me even after this,' she said, 'only—mamma sent me to go and fetch you—I heard you out there on the balcony, talking to Mabel, and—and I went out by the other window, this one, and along the balcony to the corner—'

'And, in point of fact, you listened!' he said.

'Yes, I did,' she retorted, 'and I shall be glad of it all my life. I heard enough to save me from you!'

She left him there and flew to Mabel, whom she embraced with a remorseful hug.

'You darling!' she whispered, 'what a wicked fool I was ever to be jealous of you—and about him. You will forgive me, won't you? And I am so glad about poor dear Mr. Ashburn.'

Mr. Featherstone tapped Caffyn lightly on the shoulder.

'Well, Master Harold,' he said, 'have you got anything to say? With all this suppressing, and plotting, and bullying, and threatening, and the rest of it—it strikes me you have made a d—d fool of yourself!'

The same idea had already occurred to Caffyn. He had been admirably cool and cautious; he had devoted all his energies to securing Mabel's marriage to Mark; he had watched and waited and sprung his mine with every precaution—and he was the only person it had blown up! His schemes had failed exactly like a common fool's—which was painful to reflect upon.

'If I haven't,' he said with a slight grimace, 'I've been made to look very like one.'

'You're more rogue than fool, after all,' observed the merchant, with distressing candour; 'and, by the way, I'm rather particular about getting all my correspondence, and I invariably prefer to burn my own letters. I don't think my offices are quite the place for such a gifted young fellow as you seem to be.'

'You mean I'm to go?' said Caffyn.

'I do,' was the reply. 'I never will have any one about me I can't trust. I did think once—but that's over— you heard what my girl said to you!—we'd better part now. I won't deny I'm sorry!'

'Not sorrier than I am, I'll swear!' said Caffyn, with a short laugh. 'Good-bye, Mrs. Featherstone,' he added to that lady, who stood by. 'You're not sorry, are you? Gilda will be a duchess after all—now!'

And he left the house, feeling as he passed out that the very footmen by the entrance knew of his discomfiture, and carrying away with him for a lasting recollection Mabel's look of radiant happiness as she heard Mark so completely vindicated.

'Revenge is sweet,' he thought bitterly, 'but I kept mine too long, and it's turned devilish sour!'

'Well, my dear,' said Mr. Featherstone to his wife, 'you've been leaving your other young people to their own devices all this time. Wouldn't it be as well to go and look after them?'

The dancing had been going on in the adjoining room while all this was taking place, now and then the doors had been tried by couples in search of a cool retreat between the waltzes, but no one suspected what important revelations were being made within.

Mrs. Featherstone was deeply mortified. It was true she had got rid of a hated presence, but her play—which she had meant to make the closing event of the season, and by which she had hoped to conquer one or two of the remaining rungs of the social ladder—her play was rendered impossible; this affair would get into the society papers, with every perversion which wit or malice could supply—she would be made thoroughly ridiculous!

'I'll go,' she said. 'I must get rid of everybody as soon as I decently can—this shocking business has completely upset me.'

Mark and Vincent were standing together at the door, and as she passed out she visited some of her pent-up displeasure upon them.

'Well, Mr. Ashburn and Mr. Holroyd,' she said, in tones that were intended to sound playful, 'I hope you are quite contented with your little mystification? Such a very original idea on both your parts, really. How it must have amused you both to see me making such an absurd exhibition of myself all this time. Seriously, though, I do consider I have been very, very shabbily treated—you might have warned me as a friend, Mr. Ashburn, without betraying any one's confidence! No, don't explain, either of you: I could not bear any more explanations just now!'

Mr. Langton, as he followed her, took Mark out with him, and as soon as they were alone gave full vent to his own indignation.

'I don't understand your conceptions of honour,' he said. 'Whatever your duty might be to Vincent, you clearly had duties towards my daughter and myself. Do you suppose I should have given her to you if I had known? It just comes to this, and no sophistry can get over it—you obtained my consent under false pretences?'

For he was naturally intensely humiliated by the difference these disclosures must make in his daughter's position, and did not spare his son-in-law. He said much more to the same effect, and Mark bore it all without attempting a defence: he still felt a little stunned by the danger he had passed through, and, after all, he thought, what he had heard now was nothing to what might have been said to him!

Obeying a glance from Mabel, as the others followed Mrs. Featherstone back to the music-room, Vincent had remained behind.

'When will you allow this to be generally known?' she asked, and her voice had a strange new coldness which struck him with terror. Had she seen through his device? Was it all useless?

'As soon as possible,' he answered gently. 'We shall see the publishers to-morrow, and then all the details will be arranged.'

'And your triumph will come,' she said bitterly. 'I hope you will be able to enjoy it!'

'Mabel,' he said earnestly, 'Harold Caffyn forced me to speak to-night—surely you saw that? I—I did not intend to claim the book yet.'

'Why didn't you claim it long ago?' she demanded. 'Why must you put this burden on Mark at all? Surely your secret could have been kept without that! But you came home and knew what a success Mark's (your book, I beg your pardon—it is strange at first, you know)—what a success your book had been, and how hard it was making his life for him—he begged you then, you said, to take back his promise, and you—you would not. Oh, it was selfish, Vincent, cruelly selfish of you!'

His sole concern in making that hasty explanation had been to give it an air of reasonable probability: he had never given a thought till that moment of the light in which he was presenting his own conduct. Now, in one terrible instant, it rushed upon him with an overwhelming force.

'I—I acted for the best,' he said; and even to himself the words sounded like a sullen apology.

'For your best!' she said. 'The book will be talked of more than ever now. But did you never think of the false position in which you were placing Mark? What will become of him after this? People might have read his books once—they will never read them now—they may even say that—that Harold Caffyn may have been right. And all that is your work, Vincent!'

He groaned within him at his helplessness; he stood before her with bowed head, not daring to raise his eyes, lest he should be tempted to undo all his work.

'I was proud of Mark,' she continued, 'because I thought he had written "Illusion." I am prouder now—it is better to be loyal and true, as Mark has been, than to write the noblest book and sacrifice a friend to it. There are better things than fame, Vincent!'

Even his devotion was not proof against this last injustice; he raised his head, and anger burnt in his eyes.

'You tell me that!' he cried passionately. 'As if I had ever cared for Fame in itself! Mabel, you have no right to say these things to me—do you hear?—no right! Have some charity, try and believe that there may be excuses even for me—that if you could know my motives you might feel you had been unjust!'

'Is there anything I don't know?' she asked, somewhat moved by this outburst, 'anything you have kept from me?'

'No. You have heard all I have to say—all there is to tell,' he admitted.

'Then I am not unjust!' she said; 'but if you feel justified in acting as you have done, so much the better for you, and we shall do no good by talking any more about it.'

'None whatever,' he agreed.

When he was alone that night he laughed fiercely to himself at the manner in which his act of devotion had been accepted. All his sacrifices had ended in making Mabel despise him for calculating selfishness; he had lost her esteem for ever.

If he had foreseen this, he might have hesitated, deep and unselfish as his love was; but it was done, and he had saved her. Better, he tried to think, that she should despise him, than lose her belief in her husband, and, with it, all that made life fair to her.

But altruism of this kind is a cold and barren consolation. Men do good by stealth now and then, men submit to misconstruction, but then it is always permitted to them to dream that, some day, an accident may bring the good or the truth to light. This was a hope which, by the nature of the case, Vincent could never entertain, and life was greyer to him even than before.

CHAPTER XL

THE EFFECTS OF AN EXPLOSION

Mrs. Featherstone made no attempt to detain Mark and Mabel as they took leave of her shortly after that scene in the Gold Room, though her attitude at parting was conceived in a spirit of frosty forgiveness.

In the carriage Mark sat silent for some time, staring straight before him, moodily waiting for Mabel's first words. He had not to wait long; she had laid her hand softly upon his, and as he turned, he saw that her eyes were wet and shining. 'Mark,' she said, 'it is you I love, not that book; and now, when I know all it has cost you—oh, my dear, my dear—did you think it would make me love you less?'

He could not answer her by words, but he drew her nearer to him till her head rested upon his shoulder, and so they sat, silent, with hands clasped, until they reached home.

Seldom again, and only under strong compulsion, did Mabel make any reference to 'Illusion,' nor was it till long after that he suspected the depth and reason of her resentment against Vincent—he was content to feel that her love for himself was unchanged.

But though she strove, and successfully, to hide it from her husband, this lowering of her ideal caused her a secret anguish; it had always been difficult to reconcile Mark as his nature seemed revealed in private life, with the Mark who had written 'Illusion.' One of her dreams had been that, as their intimacy grew, all reserve would vanish, and he would speak to her of his inmost thoughts and fancies, which it seemed almost as if he thought her unable to appreciate as yet.

Now all this was over, there were no hidden depths to fathom in his mind, no sublime heights to which she could rise; such as she knew him now, he was and must remain—not a strong and solitary genius with lofty thoughts of which he feared to speak freely, not a guide on whom she could lean unquestioning through life, only a man with a bright but shallow nature, impulsive and easily led. Even the Quixotic honour which had led him to entangle himself in complications at another's bidding showed a mind incapable of clear judgment—or he would have renounced the rash promise when it began to involve others. Sadly enough she realised the weakness implied in this, and yet it only infused a new element of pity and protection in the love she felt for him, and she adapted herself bravely to the changed conditions of her life.

After Holroyd had spoken, she had never questioned that his version was the true one, and Caffyn's charge an infamous fabrication—whatever she might have been driven to think in that one instant of sickening doubt.

To a more suspicious nature, perhaps, some of the facts connected with Vincent's visit to Laufingen might even then have presented difficulties, but if Mabel had remembered all that had occurred there more clearly than she did, she would have attached but little importance to it. The loyal faith she had in her husband's honour would have accepted as obvious a far less plausible explanation.

On the day following the rehearsal Messrs. Chilton and Fladgate were made aware of the facts relating to the authorship of 'Illusion,' whereupon they both expressed a not unnatural annoyance at having been, as they considered, made the victims of a deception. Mr. Fladgate, especially, who had always prided himself immensely upon the sagacity which had led him to detect Mark at once, and who had never wearied of telling the story, indulged in some strong observations.

Vincent vindicated as well as he could the scheme in which he was the most guiltless of accessories after the fact, and Mark kept in the background and said as little as possible; he felt distinctly uncomfortable, however, when Mr. Chilton drily inquired whether the same mystification attached to 'Sweet Bells Jangled,' and on being reassured as to this, observed that it was a little unfortunate that the matter had not been explained before the latter book had been brought out. 'If you think you are prejudiced in any way,' Mark said, flushing angrily, 'we can easily come to some other arrangement!' 'Oh,' said Mr. Chilton, 'I was not thinking of it from a pecuniary point of view exactly—we shall not lose much—as far as money is concerned, I dare say!'

'My partner,' explained Mr. Fladgate, 'was thinking of the results this will have upon our reputation in the trade;' on which Vincent tried to appease him by promising to make it abundantly clear that the firm were no parties to the concealment, and as soon as the partners understood that it was not proposed to disturb any existing arrangements respecting 'Illusion,' beyond disclosing the truth, and having some necessary revisions inserted in any future edition, they parted amicably enough, though Mark was made to understand his altered standing in the most unmistakable manner.

And in a few days, by means which it is not necessary to particularise here, the version of the affair given by Vincent at Grosvenor Gardens was made known to all those who might find it of interest.

The announcement, when it became generally known, caused a certain amount of surprise and remark, but not nearly so much as might have been expected. Hawthorne, in his preface to the 'Scarlet Letter,' has remarked the utter insignificance of literary achievements and aims beyond the narrow circle which recognises them as important and legitimate, and the lesson the discovery of this is to the man who dreams of literary fame. If Vincent needed to learn that lesson, he learnt it then; no fresh laurels were brought out for him—and the old ones had withered already; people were beginning to feel slightly ashamed of their former raptures over 'Illusion,' or had transferred them to a newer object, and they could not be revived in cold blood, even for the person legitimately entitled. Jacob had intercepted the birthright, and for this Esau there was not even the réchauffé of a blessing.

The people who had lionised Mark were enraged now, and chiefly with Holroyd; the more ill-natured hinted that there was something shady on both sides—or why should all that secrecy have been necessary?—but the less censorious were charitably disposed to think that Ashburn's weak good-nature had been unscrupulously abused by his more gifted friend.

Vincent's conduct, if it showed nothing more than a shrinking from notoriety, was sufficiently offensive, such distaste being necessarily either cynical or hypocritical. So upon the whole, the reaction which attends all sudden and violent popularity, and which had already set in here, was, if anything, furthered by the disclosure.

But this did not greatly distress him. Neglect and fame were alike to him, now that his lady had withdrawn her countenance from him. He had resigned himself to the loss of the fairest dream of his life, but it had been a consolation to him in his loneliness to feel that he might be her friend still, that he might see her sometimes, that though she could never love him, he would always possess her confidence and regard—not much of a consolation, perhaps, to most men, but he had found a sort of comfort in it. Now that was all over, and his solitude was left more desolate still; he knew there was no appeal for him, and that, so long as Mabel believed that he had sacrificed her husband to his deliberate selfishness, she would never relent towards him. There were times when he asked himself if he was bound to suffer all this misconception from the one woman he had ever loved—but he knew always that in clearing himself he would lay her happiness in ruins, and resolved to bear his burden to the end, sustained by the conviction, which every day became clearer, that he would not have to bear it much longer.

As for Mark, the announcement of the true authorship of 'Illusion' brought him nothing short of disaster, social and financial. It produced a temporary demand for 'Sweet Bells Jangled' at the libraries, but now that things had been explained to them, the most unlikely persons were able to distinguish the marked inferiority of the later book.

Those reviews which had waited at first from press of matter or timidity now condemned it unanimously, and several editors of periodicals who had requested works from Mark's pen wrote to say that, as the offer had been made under a misapprehension, he would understand that they felt compelled to retract the commissions.

Mark's career as a novelist was ended, he had less chance than ever of getting a publisher's reader to look at his manuscript, the affair had associated his name with ridicule instead of the scandal which is a marketable commodity, and might have launched him again; his name upon a book now would only predestine it to obscurity.

Mabel was made aware in countless little ways of her husband's descent in popular estimation; he was no longer forced into a central position in any gathering they happened to form part of, but stood forlornly in corners, like the rest of humanity. Perhaps he regretted even the sham celebrity he had enjoyed, for his was a disposition that rose to any opportunity of self-display—but in time the contrast ceased to mortify him, for most of the invitations dropped; he was only asked to places now as the husband of Mabel, and in the height of the season most of their evenings were passed at home, to the perfect contentment of both, however.

Mrs. Featherstone had given up her theatricals, in spite of Vincent's attempt to dissuade her; she had lost some of the principal members of her little company, and it was too late to recruit them; but her chief reason was a feeling that she would only escape ridicule very narrowly as it was, and that the safest course was to allow her own connection with the affair to be forgotten as speedily as possible.

But she could not forgive Mark, and would have dropped the acquaintance altogether, if Gilda had not, in the revival of her affection for Mabel, done all in her power to keep it alive.

Mr. Langton, deeply as he had resented the misrepresentation which had cost him his daughter, was not a man to do anything which might give any opening for gossip; he repressed his wife's tendency to become elegiac on her daughter's account, and treated Mark in public as before. But on occasions when he dined there en famille, and sat alone with his father-in-law over dessert, there was no attempt to conceal from him that he was only there on sufferance, and those were terrible after-dinner sittings to the unfortunate Mark, who was catechised and lectured on his prospects until he writhed with humiliation and helpless rage.

At Malakoff Terrace the feeling at the discovery of Mark's true position was not one of unmixed sorrow—the knowledge that he was, after all, an ordinary being, one of themselves, had its consolations, particularly as no lustre from his glorification had shone on them. Mr. Ashburn felt less like an owl who had accidentally hatched a cherub, than he had done lately, and his wife considered that a snare and a pitfall had been removed from her son's path. Cuthbert thought his elder brother a fool, but probably had never felt more amiable towards him, while Martha wondered aloud how her sister-in-law liked it—a speculation which employed her mind not unpleasantly. Only Trixie felt a sincere and unselfish disappointment; she had been so proud of her brother's genius, had sympathised so entirely with his early struggles, had heard of his triumphs with such delight, that it was hard for her to realise that the book which had done so much for him was not his work after all. But the blow was softened even to Trixie, for 'Jack' had been making quite an income lately, and in the autumn they were going to be married and live in Bedford Park. And of course Mark had done nothing wrong, she told herself, and he knew all the time what was coming, so she need not pity him so very much, and she was sure 'Sweet Bells' was nicer than 'Illusion,' whatever people chose to say, and ever so much easier to understand.

Several days had passed since the announcements with regard to 'Illusion' had appeared in the literary and other periodicals, and still Uncle Solomon made no sign—a silence from which Mark augured the worst. One afternoon Mr. Humpage came to see Mabel: he had heard of the whole affair from the Langtons, and reproached himself not a little, now that he knew how utterly without foundation had been his bitterness against Mark. Mr. Humpage did not approach the question from the Langton point of view, and was not concerned that Mabel should have married a man who had turned out to be a nonentity. He had done all he could to prevent the marriage in his resentment at finding the daughter of an old friend engaged to the author who had caricatured him, and his only feeling now was of complete reaction; the young man was perfectly innocent, and his nephew Harold had suspected it all this time and never said a word to enlighten him. So now the old gentleman came in a spirit of violent repentance which would not allow him to rest until he had re-established his old relations with his favourite Mabel. She was only too glad to find the coolness at an end, and he was just expressing his opinion of the part his nephew had taken, when, to Mabel's dismay, Mr. Lightowler was announced.

She wished with all her heart that Mark had not happened to be out, as she glanced apprehensively at her second visitor's face; and yet, as she saw almost at once, he came in peace—there was none of the displeasure on his big face which she had expected to see there; on the contrary, it was expanded with a sort of satisfaction.

Mr. Humpage rose as soon as the other had seated himself. 'Well, my dear,' he said, lowering his voice as he eyed his enemy with strong disfavour, 'it's time I went, I dare say. As to what I was saying about my scamp of a nephew—I only hope I did nothing to encourage him in the disgraceful way he chose to act; I never meant to, I assure you. But he won't trouble you any more for a little time, for I understand he's on his way with one of these theatrical companies to America, and I hope he'll stay there—he'll get nothing out of me, I'm ashamed of the fellow, and heartily glad his poor mother was taken when she was.'

He had spoken rather louder in his excitement, and Uncle Solomon overheard it, and struck in immediately. 'What, has that nephew of yours been turning out bad, hey?' he cried; he was quite a child of nature in his utter freedom from all conventional restraints, as may have been perceived before this. 'You don't say so, Humpage? Now I'm sorry to year it; I really am sorry to year that! Not but what, if you look into it, you'll find there's been a backwardness in doing one's duty somewhere about, yer know. P'raps, if you'd been more of an uncle to him, now, if you don't mind my saying so, he'd have turned out different. You should have kept a tighter hand on him, and as likely as not he wouldn't have felt the temptation to go wrong.'

'I was speaking to Mrs. Ashburn, Mr. Lightowler,' said the other, turning round with a rather ugly snarl.

'I 'eard you,' replied Uncle Solomon, calmly, 'that was why I spoke. Come, come, 'Umpage, don't be nasty—we've been neighbours long enough to drop nagging. It's no reason because I've got a nephew myself, who knows his duty and tries to be a pride to an uncle who's behaved handsomely towards him, it's no reason, I say, why I can't feel for them that mayn't be able to say as much for themselves.'

'I'm much obliged,' said Mr. Humpage, 'but I don't ask you or anybody else to feel for me. I am perfectly well able to do everything that's necessary in that way for myself.'

'Oh, certainly,' was the retort, 'no one can say I ever intruded on any one. I shan't take the liberty of feeling for you any more after that, not if you had twenty nephews and all of 'em in the "Police News," I promise you. And, talking of nephews, Mabel, I wonder if you came across a letter I wrote to the "Chigbourne and Lamford Gazette," a week or so back—I meant to send you a copy, but I forgot—I forgot.'

'No,' said Mabel, unable to make anything of this extraordinary mildness, 'I didn't see it.'

'Didn't you now?' he rejoined complacently, 'and yet it got copied into some of the London papers, too, I was told. Well, I brought a cutting with me, in case—would you like to hear it?'

Mabel made some assent—she always felt more or less paralysed in the presence of this terrible relative—and he drew out a folded slip, put on his spectacles, and proceeded to read:—

'"To the Editor.—Sir—I write you for the purpose of putting you right with respect to a point on which you seem to have got hold of an unaccurate version of a matter which I may say I have some slight connection with. In your issue of the—th inst., I note that your London letter prints the following paragraph:

'"Society here is eagerly anticipating the coming performance, at one of the most recherché mansions in Belgravia, of a dramatic version of Mrs. Ashburn (née Ernstone's) celebrated romance of 'Illusion.' I have been favoured with an opportunity of assisting at some of the rehearsals, and am in a position to state that the representation cannot fail to satisfy even the most ardent of the many admirers of the book. The guests will include all the leaders of every phase of the beau monde, and a repetition of the play will probably be found necessary. By the way, it is a somewhat romantic circumstance, that the talent displayed by the young authoress has already been the means of procuring her a brilliant parti, which will remove all necessity for any reliance upon her pen for a subsistence in the future.

'"Now, sir, allow me to correct two glaring errors in the above. To start with, the author of "Illusion" is not an authoress at all—his real name being Mark Ashburn, as I ought to know, considering I happen to occupy the position of being his uncle. Next, it is quite true that my nephew has contracted a matrimonial alliance, which some might call brilliant; but I was not aware till the present that the party brought him enough to allow him to live independent for the rest of his life, being under the impression that there would have been no match of any sort if it had not been for a near relative (who shall be nameless here) on the author's side coming forward and offering to make things comfortable for the young couple. But he will have to rely on his pen for all that, as he is quite aware that he is not expected to lay on his oars, without doing anything more to repay the sacrifices that have been wasted on him. Kindly correct, and oblige yours,

'"SOLOMON LIGHTOWLER (the author's uncle)."'

'You know,' he observed when he came to the end, 'it doesn't do to let these sort o' stories go flying about without contradicting them—but I put it very quietly and delicately, you see.'

Mabel bit her lip. Was it possible that this dreadful old man knew nothing—how was she ever to break it to him?

Mr. Humpage had listened to the letter with a grim appreciation. 'You don't write a bad letter, Lightowler, I must say,' he remarked, with an irrepressible chuckle, 'but you are a little behind the day with your facts, ain't you?'

'What d'ye mean by behind the day?' demanded Uncle Solomon.

'Oh, Uncle Antony,' cried Mabel, 'you tell him—I can't!'

It is much to be feared that Mr. Humpage was by no means sorry to be entrusted with such a charge. But if he was not naturally kinder hearted, he was more acquainted with the amenities of ordinary society than Mr. Lightowler, and some consideration for Mabel restrained him then from using his triumph as he might have done. He explained briefly the arrangement between Vincent and Mark as he understood it, and the manner in which it had lately been made known. When he had finished, Uncle Solomon stared stupidly from one to the other, and then, with a voice that had grown strangely thick, he said, 'I'll trouble you to say that all over again slowly, if you've no objection. My head began buzzing, and I couldn't follow it all.'

Mr. Humpage complied, and when he finished for the second time, his hearer's face was purple and distorted, and Mabel pitied him from her own experience.

'Dear Mr. Lightowler,' she said, 'you mustn't blame Mark; he had no choice, he had promised.'

'Promised!' Uncle Solomon almost howled; 'what business had he got to make a promise like that? See what a fool he's made o' me—with that letter of mine in all the London papers! I heard those Manor House girls gigglin' and laughin' when they drove by the other day, and thought it was just because they were idjits.... I wish to God I'd let him starve as a City clerk all his days before I let him bring me to this. I've lived all this time and never been ridiclous till now, and he's done it. Ah! and that's not the only thing he's done either—he's swindled me, done me out o' my money as I've earned. I could 'ave him up at the Old Bailey for it—and I've a good mind to say I will, too. I'll—'

'Stop,' said Mabel, 'you have gone quite far enough. I know this is a great disappointment to you, but I am his wife—you have no right to say such things to me.'

'No right!' he stormed, 'that's all you know about it. No right, haven't I? Let me tell you that ever since I was made to think that feller was a credit to me at last, I've bin allowing him at the rate of four hundred a year; d'ye think I'd 'a done that for kindly lending his name to another feller's book? D'ye think he didn't know that well enough when he took the money? Trust him for takin' all he could get hold of! But I'll 'ave it back; I'll post him as a swindler, I'll shame him! Look 'ere; d'ye see this?' and he took out some folded sheets of blue foolscap from his inner pocket. 'I was goin' to take this to Ferret on my way home—and it's the codicil to my will, this is. I was goin' to take it to get it altered, for I've not been feelin' very well lately, I've not been feelin' very well. This was made when I thought Mark was a nephew to be proud of—d—n him—and I can tell yer I left him a pretty tidy plum under it. Now see what I do with it. No fire, isn't there? Well, it doesn't make any odds. There ... and there ... and there;' and he tore the papers passionately across and across several times. 'There's an end of your husband's chances with me. And that don't make me intestit neither; there's the will left, and Mark and none of his will ever get a penny piece under it; he can make his mind easy over that, tell him.'

His coarse violence had something almost appalling in it, and at first Mabel had blanched under its force, but her own anger rose now.

'I am glad to think we shall owe nothing to you in future,' she said. 'If Mark has really taken your money, it was because—because he had this secret to keep; but he will give it all back. Now leave the house, please. Uncle Antony, will you get him to go away.'

Uncle Solomon, white and shaking, almost shrunken after his outburst of passion, was standing in the midst of a thick litter of torn paper, looking like a tree which has shed its last leaves in a sudden gust.

'Don't you touch me, 'Umpage, now,' he said hoarsely; 'I'm quite capable of going by myself. I—I dessay I let my temper get the better o' me just now,' he said to Mabel, rather feebly. 'I don't blame you for taking your husband's part, though he is a—ah, I shall go off my 'ead if I speak any more about it. I'll go—where's your door got to? Let me alone; I'll find my way. I shall get rid of this dizziness out in the air;' and he stumbled out of the room, a truly pitiable sight, with the fondest ambition of his later life mortally wounded.

'Dear Uncle Antony,' cried Mabel, who felt almost sorry for him, 'go after him, do. Oh, I know you're not friends, but never mind that now—he ought not to go home alone.'

'Hot-headed old ass!' growled Mr. Humpage; 'but there, there, my dear, I'll go. I'll keep him in sight at the stations, and see he comes to no harm.'

Mark had to hear of this when he came home that evening.

'And you really did take his money?' cried Mabel, after hearing his account. 'Oh, Mark, what made you do that?'

Mark hardly knew himself; he certainly would not have done it if he had ever imagined the truth would be known; perhaps his ideas of right and wrong had become rather mixed, or perhaps he persuaded himself that if he did not exactly deserve the money yet, he would not be long in doing so.

'Well, darling,' he replied, 'he would have been bitterly offended if I hadn't, you know, and I didn't know then that it was all done on account of "Illusion." But, after all, I've only had one year's allowance, and I'll give him back that to-morrow. He shan't say I swindled him.'

'I think you ought to do that, dear,' said Mabel. But in her heart she felt a heavy wonder that he should ever have consented to take the money at all.

Mark had received a fairly large sum for his second book, out of which he was well able to refund the allowance, and the next day he went down to Woodbine Villa, where, instead of the violent scene of recrimination he had prepared himself to go through, a very different, if not less painful, experience awaited him. Uncle Solomon had reached his house safely the day before, but, in relating what he had heard to his sister, had given way to a second burst of passion, which had ended in a seizure of some kind.

Mark was allowed to see him, on his own earnest entreaty, and was struck with remorse when he saw the lamentable state to which his own conduct had had no small share in reducing the old man. Were the consequences of that one act of folly and meanness never to cease? he wondered, wretchedly, as he stood there. His uncle allowed his hand to be shaken; he even took Mark's cheque with his stiff hand, and made a sign that his sister was to take charge of it. He could speak, but his brain had lost all command over his tongue, and what he said had a ghastly inappropriateness to the occasion. He saw this dully himself, and gave up the attempt at last, and began to cry piteously at his inability to convey his meaning; whether he wished for a reconciliation then or nursed his rage to the last, Mark never knew. He went down on several other occasions during his uncle's lingering illness, but always with the same result. Mr. Lightowler suffered all the tortures of perfect consciousness, combined with the powerlessness to express any but the most simple wish: if he desired to undo the past in any way, no one divined his intention or helped him to carry it out; and when the end came suddenly, it was found that he had not died intestate, and the will, after giving a certain annuity to the sister who had lived with him, left the bulk of his estate to go in founding Lightowler scholarships in the School for Commercial Travellers' Orphans. The Ashburn family were given trifling legacies; Mark, however, 'having seen fit to go his own way in life, and render useless all the expense to which I have been put for his advancement,' was expressly excepted from taking any benefit under the will.

But Mark had expected nothing else, and long before his anticipations were verified he had found it necessary to consider seriously how he was to support himself for the future. Literature, as has been said, was now out of the question; in fact, its fascination for him had faded. Mabel had a fair income settled upon her, but in ordinary self-respect he could not live upon that, and so he sought about for some opening. At first he had firmly resolved never to go back to his old school life, after having done so much to escape from it; but as he began to see that any profession that required capital was closed to him, and business being equally impossible, he was forced to think of again becoming a schoolmaster. And then he heard by accident that old Mr. Shelford was about to resign his post at St. Peter's, and it occurred to him that it might be worth his while to go and see him, and find out if the vacancy was unfilled, and if there was any chance for himself. It was not a pleasant thing to do, for he had not seen the old gentleman lately, and dreaded equally innocent congratulations and brusque irony, according to the state of his information. He went up to St. Peter's, timing his arrival after school, when the boys would all have left, except the classes which remained an hour longer for extra subjects. Mr. Shelford always lingered for some time, and he would be very certain to find him. Mark went along the dark corridors, rather shrinking as he did so from the idea of being recognised by a passing member of the staff, till he came to the door he knew.

Mr. Shelford was still in cap and gown, dictating the week's marks to his monitor, who was entering them, with a long-suffering expression on his face, into a sort of ledger. 'Now we come to Robinson,' the old gentleman was saying; 'you're sure you've got the right place, eh? Go on, then. Latin repetition, thirty-eight; Latin prose, thirty-six—if you don't take care, Master Maxwell, Robinson'll be carrying off the prize this term, he's creeping up to you, sir, creeping up; Roman History'—and here he saw Mark, and dismissed the monitor unceremoniously enough.

He evidently knew the whole story of 'Illusion,' for his first words after they were alone together were, 'And so you've been a sort of warming-pan all this time, eh?'

'That's all,' said Mark, gloomily.

'Well, well,' the old gentleman continued, not unkindly, 'you made a rash promise and kept it like a man, even when it must have been uncommonly disagreeable. I like you for that, Ashburn. And what are you thinking of turning to now?'

Mark explained his errand not very fluently, and Mr. Shelford heard him out with his mouth working impatiently, and his eyes wrinkled till Mark thought how much he had aged lately.

'Well,' he said, pushing back his cap and leaning back in his chair, 'have you thought this out, Ashburn? You were rid of this life a short time back, and I was glad of it, for you never were fit for it. And now you're coming back again! I make no doubt they'll be very willing to have you here, and if a word from me to the Council—but is there really nothing else but this? Why, I'm counting the days to my own deliverance now, and it's odd to find some one asking me to recommend him for my oar and chain! No, no, a dashing young fellow like you, sir, can do better for himself than a junior mastership for his final goal. Take warning by me, as I used to tell you—do you want to come to this sort of thing? sitting from morning to noon in this stifling den, filled with a rabble of impident boys—d'ye think they'll have any respect for your old age and infirmities? not they—they'll call you "Old Ashes"—for they're a yumorous race, boys are, they'll call you "Old Ashes," or "Cinders" to your nose, as soon as they think you're old enough to stand it. Why, they don't put any more kittens in my desk now—they've found out I like cats. So they put blackbeetles—do you like blackbeetles, eh? Well, you'll come to beetles in time. It's a mistake, Ashburn, it's a mistake for impulsive, hot-tempered men like you to turn schoolmaster—leave it to cold, impassive fellows who don't care enough about the boys to be sensitive or partial—they're the men to stand the life!'

Here a demon voice shrilled, "'Ullo, Shellfish, Old Shells, yah!' through the keyhole, and his footsteps were heard down the flags outside running for dear life. The old gentleman, crimson with rage, bounded to the door: 'Stop that scoundrel, that impident boy, bring him back!' But the boy had gone, and he came back panting and coughing: 'That's a commentary on what I've been saying,' he said; 'I'm an old fool to show I care—but I can't help it, and they know it, confound 'em! Well, to come back to you, Ashburn, you're married now, I hear; you won't find a mastership much support as time goes on, unless you started a boarding-house—the idea of never escaping from these young ruffians, ugh! No, no, didn't you tell me once you were called to the Bar?'

'Not called,' corrected Mark, 'I have passed the examination, though; there is only the ceremony to be gone through.'

'Why not go through it, and try your fortune as a barrister, then, you're just the man for a jury? We shall have you taking silk in ten years.'

Mark laughed bitterly. 'How am I to live till I get a practice?' he said; 'I've only a couple of hundred or so left in the world, and that would scarcely pay for my fees and chambers for more than a year.'

'Ah, is that so? I see,' said the old gentleman, 'yes, yes—but, see here, Ashburn, start all the same with what you've got, who knows how soon you may get work—can't your father-in-law do anything for you? and while you're waiting, why not take some pupils under the rose, eh? I was asked the other day to recommend a coach to two young rascals who want to be forked into the Civil Service. You could do that for them if you liked, and they'd bring you others. And—and I'm going to take a liberty very likely, but I've put by a little money in the course of my life, and I've no one to leave it to. I don't know how it is, but I feel an interest in you, Ashburn; perhaps I want somebody to be sorry for me when I'm gone, anyway, I—I wish you'd let me see you through any money difficulties till you're fairly started—it won't be long now, I'll wager, you can treat it as a loan if you prefer it. I want you to give yourself a chance at the Bar. Don't refuse me now, or I shall take it unkindly.'

Mark was deeply touched, he had not suspected Mr. Shelford of really caring about him, and the kindness and sympathy of this offer made him feel how little he deserved such friendship; and then the familiar class-rooms, dusty and stuffy at the close of a summer day, had brought back all his old weariness of school routine. He had outlived his yearning for literary fame, but he still wished to make a figure somewhere, somehow—why might not he do so at the Bar, in that line where solid learning is less necessary than the fluent tongue and unfailing resource, which he felt he could reckon upon.

He shook the other's hand gratefully. 'I don't know how to thank you,' he said, 'you've put some heart in me again. I will try my luck as you advise; perhaps with coaching and the money I have by me I need not take advantage of all your kindness, but there is no one I would come to for help like you when I can keep up no longer. I'll take my call at Michaelmas!'

And they walked out together, Mr. Shelford taking his arm affectionately through the streets. Mark, as has been said already, had a certain knack of attracting interest and liking without doing anything either to excite or deserve them in the slightest, and the old gentleman felt now almost as if he had gained a son.

He was anxious to prevent Mark from returning to the old life, because he had observed his unfitness for it; he himself, however, in spite of his diatribes against boys and scholastic life, was far fonder of both than he would have confessed, and would miss them as a few who knew him best would miss him when the time came for parting.

From that day he became a frequent visitor at Campden Hill, where he found with Mabel the appreciation and tender regard which he had never expected to meet again on this side of the grave.

Mark carried out his resolve, of which his father-in-law approved, allowing him to use his chambers during the Long Vacation. The pupils came there, and the coach's manner captivated them from the first, and made the work easy for both; they came out high on the list, and were succeeded by others, whose fees paid the rent of the chambers he took in the Temple shortly after. Call-night came, and as he stood with the others at the Benchers' table and listened to the Treasurer's address, he felt an exultant confidence in himself once more; he had been promised a brief from Mr. Ferret, who took this form of disapproving of Uncle Solomon's testamentary caprices, and this time Mark did not shrink from it—he had read hard lately, and with better results. He knew that he should be at no loss for words or self-possession; he had been a brilliant and effective speaker, as the Union debates had frequently proved, and he looked forward now to entering the legal arena as the field for retrieving his lost name. Mabel should be proud of him yet!

He was deceiving no one now, Vincent was not injured by the fraud—for he had his book back; it was true that Mabel did not suspect the real history of the transaction, but it would do her no good to know that he had once made a false step. Caffyn was over in America, and harmless wherever he might see fit to go—his sting was drawn for ever.

No wonder, then, that he seemed to look round upon a cloudless horizon—but that had been the case with him so many times since he had first complicated his life by that unhappy act of his, and each time the small cloud, the single spy of serried battalions, had been slowly creeping up all the while.

He forgot that—he generally did forget unpleasant reminiscences—it never occurred to him that the cloud might be rising yet again above the level haze on the sky line, and the hurricane burst upon him once more.

CHAPTER XLI

A FINAL VICTORY

It was an afternoon in January, soon after the courts had begun to sit again, and Mark was mounting the staircase to his new chambers with a light heart—he had made his début that day; the burden of the work had fallen on him in the absence of his leader, and he felt that he had acquitted himself with fair success. His father-in-law, too, had happened to be at Westminster, and in a Common Law court that day; and the altered tone of his greeting afterwards showed Mark that he had been favourably impressed by what he had heard while standing for a few minutes in the gangway. And now, Mark thought, he would go back to Mabel at once and tell her how Fortune had begun to smile once more upon him. But when he entered his chambers he found a visitor waiting for him with impatience—it was Colin. Mark was not exactly surprised to find the boy there, for Mr. Langton, judging it well to pad the family skeleton as much as possible, had lately sent him to his son-in-law to be coached for a school scholarship; and, as he was probably aware, he might have chosen a worse tutor.

'What a time you have been!' said Colin.

'It's not your day,' said Mark, 'I can't take you now, old fellow.'

'I know,' said the boy, fidgetting restlessly; 'I didn't come about that—it was something else.'

Mark laughed. 'You've been getting into another row, you young rascal,' he said, 'and you want me to get you out of it—isn't that it?'

'No, it isn't,' said Colin. 'I say,' he went on, blurting out the question after the undiplomatic manner of boyhood, 'why have you got Mabel to cut poor old Vincent? I call it a shame!'

Mark stopped half-way in taking off his coat. 'It would be no business of yours if I had, you know,' he replied, 'but who told you I had done anything of the sort?'

'Nobody, I can see for myself. Mabel told mother she would rather not come to dinners and things when Vincent was coming, and once she did meet him, and she only just spoke to him. And now, when he's so ill, she won't go near him—he told me himself that it was no use asking her, she would never come! She used to like him before, so it must be all your fault, and I call it a beastly shame, and I don't care what you say!'

All of this was quite new to Mark; Mabel had studiously avoided all allusion to Vincent, and it had never occurred to Mark to speculate on the light in which she chose to regard his explanation—that was all over, and he was little enough inclined to revive the subject. He began to be strangely troubled now. 'I don't know what you're talking about,' he said; 'is Holroyd ill? it—it is nothing serious, is it?' For he had seen very little of him lately, his obligation being too deep and too humiliating to make repeated visits at all desirable.

'He looks all right,' said Colin, 'but I heard mother say that he's very ill really, and she should have to put a stop to Dolly going to sit with him every day as she does, because—because he might die quite suddenly at any time—it's something wrong with his heart, she said, I believe. And yet he seems well enough. But oh, Mark, if—if it's that, you ought to let Mabel make it up with him, whatever he's done. You might let her go and see him—he would like it so, I know he would, though he wouldn't own it when I asked him. Only suppose he died! I know Mabel would be sorry then!'

Every word the boy said cut Mark to the heart—he had never suggested to Mabel that she should avoid Vincent, and he could not be satisfied now until he had found out why she had done so; his insight not being nearly keen enough to discover the reason for himself.

'Give me his address,' he said, for he did not even know where Holroyd was living, and as soon as the boy had gone Mark drove to the place he had mentioned, a house in Cambridge Terrace, instead of returning home at once as he had previously intended.

He did not believe that the illness was as serious as Colin had implied; of course that was exaggerated— but he could not be quite easy until he had reassured himself by a visit, and some lingering feeling of self-reproach drove him to make this atonement for his long neglect.

The Langtons' carriage was at the door when he arrived; and, as he came into the sitting-room on the second floor, he heard Dolly's clear little voice and paused, hidden by the screen at the door. She was reading to Vincent, who was lying back in an arm-chair; it was Hans Andersen's 'Story of the Shadow,' a choice to which she had been guided by pure accident.

Mark heard her read the half-sad, half-cynical conclusion as he stood there unseen:

'"The Princess and the Shadow stepped out on the balcony to show themselves, and to receive one cheer more. But the learned man heard nothing of all these festivities—for he had already been executed."

'How horrid of that wicked Shadow!' was Dolly's indignant comment as she finished; 'oh, Vincent, aren't you very, very sorry for the poor learned man?'

'Much sorrier for the Shadow, Dolly,' he replied, a reply of which Dolly would have insisted upon an explanation had not Mark then come forward.

He murmured some confused sentence accounting for his visit.

'I have been wondering whether I should see you again,' said Vincent. 'Dolly, you had better go now, dear, it is getting late—you will come and read me another story to-morrow?'

'If mother will let me,' said Dolly; 'and I tell you what, next time I come I'll bring Frisk; you want amusing, I know, and he's a nice, cheerful dog to have in a room with you.'

When Mark returned from putting her into the carriage, Vincent said, 'Is there anything you want to say to me, Ashburn?'

'Yes,' said Mark; 'I know I have no right to trouble you. I know you can never really forgive me.'

'I thought so once,' said Vincent, 'but I have done with all that. I forgave you long ago. Tell me if I can help you?'

'I have just heard for the first time,' said Mark, 'that—that my wife has not—has not treated you very kindly lately. And I came here to ask you if I am the cause.'

Vincent flushed suddenly, and his breath was laboured and painful for a moment. 'What is the use of bringing that up now?' he asked; 'is it a pleasant subject for either of us? Let it rest.'

'I had no intention of paining you,' said Mark, 'I ought not to have asked you. I—I will ask Mabel herself.'

'You must not do that!' said Vincent, with energy; 'you might have spared me this—you might have guessed. Still I will tell you—it may do good. Yes, you are the cause, Ashburn; the lie I told on that evening of the rehearsal has borne its penalty, as lies will, and the penalty has fallen upon me heavily. Ask yourself what your wife must think of the man I made myself appear!'

'Good God!' groaned Mark, who saw this now for the first time.

'You see,' Vincent pursued, 'I am dying now, with the knowledge that I shall never see her face again; that when I am gone she will not spare me a single regret, that she will make haste to lose my very memory. I don't complain, it is for her good, and I am content. Don't imagine I tell you this as a reproach. Only if you are ever tempted again to do anything which may put her happiness in danger, or weaken the confidence she has in you, remember what it has cost another man to secure them, and I think you will resist then.'

'Vincent!' cried Mark brokenly, 'it can't be; you are not—not dying!'

'My doctor tells me so,' said Vincent. 'I have been prepared for it a long time, and it must be coming near now—but there, we have talked enough about that. Don't fancy from anything I have said that I have lost all faith in you—you will find, very soon, perhaps, how little that is so.... Are you going already?' he added, as Mark rose hastily; 'good-bye, then; come and see me when you can, and—if we are not to meet again—you will not forget, I know.'

'No, I shall not forget,' was all Mark could say just then, and left the house. He could not trust himself to bear any longer the unhoped-for expression of confidence and regard which he saw once more upon his friend's face.

As he walked home his mind was haunted by what he had just heard. Vincent dying, his last hours embittered by Mabel's coldness. Mark could not suffer that—she must see him once more, she must repair the horrible injustice she had shown—he would urge her to relent!

And yet, how could she repair it, unless her eyes were opened? Gradually he became aware that a final crisis had come in his life, just as he thought all was well with him. He had said to himself, 'Peace, peace!' and it had only been an armistice. Would the results of that shameful act always rise up against him in this way? What was he to do?

He had felt as deep a shame and remorse for his past conduct as he was capable of, but hitherto he had supposed that the wrong had been comfortably righted, that he himself was after all the chief, if not the sole sufferer.

That consolation was gone now; he knew what Mabel had been to Vincent, and what it must be to him now to feel that he must bear this misconception to the end. Could Mark accept this last sacrifice? More and more he felt that he stood where two paths met: that he might hold his peace now, and let his friend go down misunderstood to the grave, but that all his past baseness would be nothing to that final meanness; that if he paltered this time, if he chose the easy path, he might indeed be safe for ever from discovery, but his soul would be stained with a dishonour that nothing would ever cleanse; that he would have done with self-respect and peace of mind for ever. And yet if he took the other path, the right one, where would it lead him?

And so he reached his house in miserable indecision, driven this way and that by contending impulses, loathing the prospect of this crowning infamy, yet shrinking from the sole alternative. He found Mabel sitting alone in the firelight.

'How did you get on?' she asked eagerly; 'you won your case?'

'My case?' he repeated blankly, so far away did all that seem now. 'Oh, yes, my case—the Lord Chief sums up to-morrow. I think we shall get a verdict.'

'Sit down and tell me all about it,' she said. 'I will ring for the lamp. I can't see your face.'

'No,' said Mark, 'don't ring; it is better as it is.'

She was struck by something in his voice.

'You are tired, dear,' she said.

'Very tired,' he confessed, with a heavy sigh; and then, with one of his sudden promptings, he said, 'Mabel, I have just seen Vincent—he is very ill.'

'I know,' she said. 'Is he—worse?'

'Dying,' he answered gloomily. 'I want to ask you a question—is it true that you have been thinking very harshly of him lately?'

'I cannot think well of him,' she replied.

'Will you tell me why?' he demanded. Even then he tried to cherish the faint hope that her resentment might have another cause.

'Cannot you guess?' she asked. 'Ah, no, you are too generous to feel it yourself. How can I feel kindly towards the man who could let you sacrifice your name and your prospects for a caprice of his own, who persuaded you to entangle yourself in a manner that might, for all he knew or cared, ruin you for life?'

'Even if that were so,' said Mark, 'he is dying, remember. Think what it would be to him to see you once more—Mabel, will you refuse to go to him?'

'He should not have asked this of me,' cried Mabel. 'Oh, Mark, you will think me hard, unchristian, I know, but I can't do this—not even now, when he is dying ... he ought not to have asked it.'

'Mabel,' he cried, 'he did not ask it—you do not know him if you think that. Do you still refuse?'

'I must, I must,' repeated Mabel. 'Oh, if it had been I who was the injured one, I do not think I should feel like this; it is for you I cannot forgive. If I went now, what good would it do? Mark; it is wicked of me, but I could not say what he would expect—not yet, not yet—you must not ask me.'

Mark knew now that the decisive moment had come: there was only one way left of moving her; there was no time to lose if he meant to take it.

Must he speak the words which would banish him from his wife's heart for ever, just when hope had returned to his life, just when he had begun to feel himself worthier of her love? It was so easy to say no more, to leave her in her error, and the shadow would pass away, and his happiness be secure. But could he be sure of that? The spectre had risen so many times to mock him, would it ever be finally laid?

And if Mabel learnt the truth when it was too late?—no, he could not bear to think of what would happen then?

And yet how was he to begin—in what words could he break it to her? His heart died within him at the duty before him, and he sat in the firelit room, tortured with indecision, and his good and bad angel fought for him. And then, all at once, almost in spite of himself, the words came:

'Mabel,' he cried, 'Holroyd has done nothing—do you hear?—nothing to call for forgiveness ... oh, if you could understand without my saying more!'

She started, and her voice had an accent, first of a new hope, then of a great fear.

'Is Vincent better than he seemed? But how can that be if—tell me, Mark, tell me everything.'

Mark shrank back; he dared not tell her.

'Not now,' he groaned. 'My God! what am I doing? Mabel, I can't tell you; have pity on yourself—on me!'

She rose and came to him. 'If you have anything to tell me, tell me now,' she said. 'I am quite strong; it will not hurt me. You must not leave me in this uncertainty—that will kill me! Mark, if you love me, I entreat you to save me from being unjust to Vincent. Remember, he is dying—you have told me so!'

He rose and went to the sideboard; there was water there, and he poured some out and drank it before he could speak. Then he came back to the fireplace, and leaned against the mantelboard.

'You will hate me before I have finished,' he said at last, 'but I will tell you.'

And then he began, and painfully, with frequent breaks and nervous hurrying at certain passages, he told her everything—the whole story of his own shame and of Holroyd's devotion. He did not spare himself; he did not even care to give such excuses as might have been made for him in the earlier stages of his fraud. If his atonement was late, it was at least a full one.

She listened without a word, without even a sob, and when he had come to the end she sat there silent still, as if turned to stone. The stillness grew so terrible that Mark could bear no more.

'Speak to me, Mabel,' he cried in his agony, 'for God's sake, speak to me!'

She rose, supporting herself with one trembling hand; even in the firelight her face was deathly pale. 'Take me to him first,' she said, and the voice was that of a different woman, 'after that I will speak to you.'

'To Vincent?' he asked, half stupefied by what he was suffering. 'Not to-night, Mabel, you must not!'

'I must,' she replied; 'if you will not take me I shall go alone—quick, let us lose no time!'

He went out into the main road and hailed a cab, as he had done often enough before for one of their journeys to dinner or the theatre; when he returned Mabel was already standing cloaked and hooded at the open door.

'Tell him to drive fast—fast,' she said feverishly, as he helped her into the hansom, and she did not open her lips again till it stopped.

He glanced at her face now and then, when the shop-lights revealed her profile as she lay back in her corner; it was pale and set, her eyes were strained, but she had shed no tears; he sat there and recalled the merry journeys they had had together, side by side, on evenings like this, when he had been sorry the drive should ever end—how long this one was!

The cab reached Cambridge Terrace at last. Mark instinctively looked at the upper windows of the house—they were all dark. 'Stay here, till I have asked,' he said to Mabel before he got out, 'we may—we may be too late.'

Vincent had been moved to his sleeping-room, where he was sitting in his arm-chair; the trained nurse who had been engaged to wait upon him had left him for a while, the light was lowered, and he was lying still in the dreamy exhaustion which was becoming more and more his normal state.

He had received his death-warrant some months before; the harassing struggles against blight and climate in Ceylon, the succession of illnesses which had followed them, and the excitement and anxiety that he underwent on his return, had ended in an affection of the heart, which, by the time he thought it sufficiently serious to need advice, was past all cure.

He had heard the verdict calmly, for he had little to make him in love with life, but while the book in which he had already begun to find distraction was unfinished, there was still work for him to do, and he was anxious to leave it completed. If the efforts he made to effect this shortened his life, they at least prevented him from dwelling upon its approaching end, and his wish was gratified. He fixed his mind steadily on his task, and though each day saw less accomplished and with more painful labour, the time came when he reached the last page and threw down his pen for ever.

Now he was on the brink of the stream, and the plash of the ferryman's oar could be heard plainly; the world behind him had already grown distant and dim; even of the book which had been in his mind so long, he thought but little—he had done with it all; whether it brought him praise or blame from man, he would never learn now, and was content to be in ignorance.

The same lethargy had mercifully deadened to some extent the pain of Mabel's injustice, until Mark's visit had revived it that afternoon. He had come to think of it all now without bitterness; it might be that in some future state she would 'wake, and remember, and understand,' and the wrong be righted—but it had always seemed to him that in another existence all earthly misunderstandings must seem too infinitely pitiful and remote to be worth unravelling, or even recalling, and so he could not find much comfort there.

But at least he had not been worsted in the conflict with his lower nature. Mabel's happiness was now secure from the worst danger, the struggle was over, and he was glad, for there had been times when he had almost sunk under it.

So he was thinking dreamily as he sat there while now and then a cloud would drift across his thoughts as he lost himself in a kind of half slumber.

He was roused by sounds on the stairs outside, and presently he heard a light step in the farther room. 'I am not asleep,' he said, believing the nurse had returned.

'Vincent,' said a low tremulous voice, 'it is I—Mabel.' Then he looked up, and even in that half light he saw that the figure standing there in the open doorway was the one which had been chief in his thoughts.

Unprepared as he was for such a visitor, he felt no surprise—only a deep and solemn happiness as he saw her standing before him.

'You have come then,' he said; 'I am very glad. You must think less hardly of me—or you would not be here.'

She had only obtained leave to see him on her earnest entreaties and promises of self-restraint, but his first words sorely tried her fortitude; she came to his chair and sank down beside it, taking his hands in both hers. 'Vincent,' she cried, with a sob that would not be repressed, 'I cannot bear it if you talk so.... I know all, all that you have suffered and given up ... he has told me—at last!'

Vincent looked down with an infinite pity upon the sweet contrite face raised to his. 'You poor child,' he said, 'you know then? How could he tell you! Mabel, I tried so hard to spare you this—and now it has come! What can I say to you?'

'Say that you forgive me—if you ever can!' she said, 'when I remember all the hard things I said and thought of you, when all the time—oh, I was blind, or I must have seen the truth! And I can never, never make it up to you now!'

'Do you think,' he asked, 'that to see you here, and know that you understand me at last, would not make up for much harder treatment than I ever had from you, Mabel? If that were all—but he has told you, you said, told you the whole sad story. Mabel—what are you going to do?'

She put the question aside with a gesture of heart-sick pride: 'What does it matter about me? I can only think of you just now—let me forget all the rest while I may!'

'Dying men have their privileges,' he said, 'and I have not much more time. Mabel, I must ask you: What have you said to Mark?'

'Nothing,' she said, with a low moan, 'what was there to say? He must know that he has no wife now.'

'Mabel, you have not left him!' he cried.

'Not yet,' she said, turning away wearily; 'he brought me to this house—he is here now, I believe.... You are torturing me with these questions, Vincent.'

'Answer me this once,' he persisted, 'do you mean to leave him?'

She rose to her feet. 'What else can I do,' she demanded, 'now that I know? The Mark I loved has gone for ever—he never even existed! I have no husband beyond the name. I have been in a dream all this time, and I wake to find myself alone! Only an hour ago and Mark was all the world to me—think what he must be to me from this time! No, I cannot live with him. I could not breathe the same air with him. I am ashamed that I could ever have loved him. He is all unworthy, and mean, and false, and I thought him noble and generous!'

'You are too hard,' said Vincent, 'he is not all bad, he was weak—not wicked; if I had not felt that, I should never have tried to keep his secret, and forced him, against his will, to keep it himself. And now he has confessed it all to you, when there was no fear of discovery to urge him, only because he could not endure the thought of my bearing your displeasure to the end. He did not know that that was so till this afternoon, and I told him without thinking it would have that effect on him—I did him an injustice there. He must have gone back and accused himself at once. Think, Mabel, was there nothing unselfish and brave in that? He knew what you would think of him, he knew that he was safe if he kept silence— and yet he spoke, because he preferred the worst for himself to allowing me to bear the penalty for his sins. Is a man who could act thus utterly lost?'

'Lost to me!' she said passionately, 'the confession came too late; and how could any confession atone for such a sin! No, he is too unworthy, I can never trust him, never forgive him!'

'I do not ask you to forgive him now,' he urged; 'he has done you a great wrong, your love and faith have received a cruel shock; and you cannot act and feel as if this had never been. I understand all that. Only do not close the door on forgiveness for ever, do not cut him off from all chance of winning back something of the confidence he has lost. The hope of that will give him strength and courage; without that hope to keep him up, without your influence he will surely lose heart and be lost for ever. His fate rests with you, have you thought of that?'

She was silent, but her face was still unconvinced.

'You think your love is dead,' he went on, 'and yet, Mabel, something tells me that love will not die easily with you. What if you find this is so at some future time, when the step you are bent upon has been taken, and you cannot retreat from it? What if, when you call him back, it is too late; and he will not, or cannot, return to you?'

'I shall never call him back,' she said.

'You will have no pity on him for his sake or your own,' Vincent pleaded, 'will you not for mine? Mabel, let me say something to you about myself. I have loved you for years—you are not angry with me for telling you so now, are you? I loved you well enough to put your happiness before all other things; it was for that I made any sacrifices I have made; it was for that I was willing even that you should think hardly of me.'

'For me!' she cried, 'was it for me you have done all this? How I have repaid you!'

'I was repaid by the belief that it secured your happiness,' he answered. 'I thought, rightly or wrongly, that I was justified in deceiving you for your own good. But now you are taking away all this from me, Mabel! I must die with the sense of having failed miserably, when I thought I was most successful, with the knowledge that by what I have done I have only increased the evil! Must I leave you with your happy home blighted past recovery, with nothing before you but a lonely, barren existence? Must I think of you living out your life, proud and unforgiving, and wretched to the end? I entreat you to give me some better comfort, some brighter prospect than that—you will punish me for my share in it all by refusing what I ask, but will you refuse?'

She came back to him. 'No,' she said brokenly, 'I have given you pain enough, I will refuse you nothing now, only it is so hard—tell me what I am to do!'

'Do not desert him, do not shame him before the world!' he said; 'bear with him still, give him the chance of winning back what he has lost. Peace may be long in coming to you—but it will come some day, and even if it never comes at all, Mabel, you will have done your duty, there will be a comfort in that. Will you promise this, for my sake?'

She raised her face, which she had hidden in her hands. 'I promise—for your sake,' she said, and at her words he sank back with a sigh of relief—his work was over, and the energy he had summoned up to accomplish it left him suddenly.

'Thank you!' he said faintly; 'you have made me happier, Mabel. I should like to see Mark, but I am tired. I shall sleep now.'

'I will come to-morrow,' she said, and bending over him, she kissed his forehead. She had not kissed him since the time when she was a child and he an undergraduate, devoted to her even then; and now that kiss and the touch of her hand lingered with him till he slept, and perhaps followed him some little way into the land of dreams.

Mark had been waiting in a little dark sitting-room on a lower floor; he had not dared to follow Mabel. At last, after long hours, as it seemed, of slow torment, he heard her descending slowly, and came to meet her; she was very pale and had been weeping, but her manner was composed now.

'Let us go home,' was all she said to him, and they drove back in silence as they had come. But when they had reached their home Mark could bear his uncertainty no longer.

'Mabel,' he said, and his voice shook, 'have you nothing to say to me, still?'

She met his appealing gaze with eyes that bore no reproach, only a fixed and hopeless sadness in their clear depths.

'Yes,' she said, 'let us never speak again of—of what you have told me to-night—you must make me forget it, if you can.'

The sudden relief almost took away his breath. 'You do not mean to leave me then!' he cried impulsively, as he came towards her and seemed about to take her hand. 'I thought I had lost you—but you will not do that, Mabel, you will stay with me?'

She shrank from him ever so slightly, with a little instinctive gesture of repugnance, which the wretched man noted with agony.

'I will not leave you,' she said, 'I did mean—but that is over, you owe it to him. I will stay with you, Mark—it may not be for much longer.'

Her last words chilled him with a deadly fear; his terrible confession had escaped him before he had had time to remember much that might well have excused him, even to himself, for keeping silence then.

'My God!' he cried in his agony when she had left him, 'is that to be my punishment? Oh, not that—any shame, any disgrace but that!'

And he lay awake long, struggling hard against a terror that was to grow nearer and more real with each succeeding day.

Vincent's sleep was sweet and sound that night, until, with the dawn, the moment came when it changed gently and painlessly into a sleep that was sounder still, and the plain common-place bedroom grew hushed and solemn, for Death had entered it.

CHAPTER XLII

FROM THE GRAVE

The days went by; Mark had followed Vincent to the grave, with a sorrow in which there was no feigning, and now the Angel of Death stood at his own door, and Love strove in vain to keep him back. For the fear which had haunted Mark of late had been brought near its fulfilment—Mabel lay dangerously ill, and it seemed that the son she had borne was never to know a mother's care.

Throughout one terrible week Mark never left the house on Campden Hill, while Mabel wavered between life and death; he was not allowed to see her; she had not expressed any wish as yet to see him, he learnt from Mrs. Langton, who had cast off all her languor before her daughter's peril, and was in almost constant attendance upon her. Mabel appeared in fact to have lost all interest in life, and the natural desire for recovery which might have come to her aid was altogether wanting, as her mother saw with a pained surprise, and commented upon to the conscience-stricken Mark.

Day after day he sat in the little morning-room, which looked as if she had but left it for an instant, even while he knew that she might never enter it again; sat there listening and waiting for the words which would tell him that all hope was at an end.

The doctors came and went, and there were anxious inquiries and whispered answers at the cautiously-opened front-door, while from time to time he heard on the stairs, or in the room above, hurried footsteps, each of which trod heavy upon his aching heart.

People came sometimes to sit with him. Trixie, for instance, who had married her artist, and was now comfortably established in a decorative little cottage at Bedford Park, came daily, and as she had the tact to abstain from any obviously unfounded assumption of hopefulness, her presence did him good, and perhaps saved him from breaking down under the prolonged strain.

Martha, too, even though she had never been able to feel warmly towards her sister-in-law, cast aside some of her prejudice and held aloof no longer.

Martha was inclined to take a serious view of things, having caught something of her mother's gloomy Puritanism, which her own unhappy disposition and contracted life had done nothing to sweeten, and not a little to embitter. She was not, perhaps, incapable of improving the occasion for her brother's benefit even then, by warnings against devotion to perishable idols, and hints of chastenings which were intended as salutary.

But somehow, when she saw his lined and colourless face, and the look of ghastly expectation that came and went upon it at the slightest unexpected sound without, she lost hold of the conviction that his bereavement would work for his spiritual benefit; her words in season died unspoken on her lips, and she gave way at parting to tears of pity and sympathy, in which the saint was completely forgotten in the sister and the woman.

And now it was evening, and he was alone once more, pretending to read, and thinking drearily of what was coming; for the doctor had just left, and his report had been less encouraging than ever—a change must come before long, he had said, and from his manner it was too clear what he thought that change would be.

Mark let his thoughts wander back to his brief married life, doomed to be cut short by the very fraud which had purchased it. They had been so happy, and it was all over—henceforth he would be alone.

She was leaving him after all, and he could not even feel that her love would abide with him when she had gone; oh, the unspeakable agony of knowing that she welcomed death as a release from him!

Never now could he hope to regain the heart he had lost, she despised him—and she was dying.

No, she must not die, he cried wildly in his extremity, how could he live without her? Oh, that she might be given back to him, even though he could never make the dead love live in her heart again! Had he not suffered enough—was not this a punishment beyond his sin?

And yet, as he looked back, he knew that he himself had brought about this punishment, that it was but the stern and logical sequence of his fraud.

There was a low tap at the door, and he started to his feet—the summons had come; no need to question the messenger who brought it, he heard the first words and passed her hastily.

He entered the room where Mabel was lying, and fell on his knees by her bedside, bowing his head upon the quilt in agonised despair, after one glance at her pale sweet face.

'My darling—my darling!' he cried, 'don't leave me ... you promised—oh, remember ... this is not—not good-bye!'

She laid a weak and slender hand on his dark hair in a caress that was more in pity than in love. 'They have not told you?' she said; 'I asked nurse to prepare you. I knew you would be so anxious. No, dear, it is not good-bye. I feel much better, I am quite sure now that I am going to get well. I wanted to tell you so myself. I must live for baby's sake—I can't die and leave him alone!'

And even in the ecstasy of relief which Mark felt at her words there was a spasm of sobering jealousy; she only cared to live for the child's sake—not for his.

Those who know Mark now are inclined to envy his good fortune. His literary mistakes are already beginning to be forgotten; the last breath of scandal was extinguished when it became known that Vincent Holroyd had dedicated his posthumous work to his college friend, to whom he also confided the duties of editor—duties which Mark accepted humbly, and discharged faithfully.

His name is becoming known in legal circles—not as a profound lawyer, which he will never be to the end of his career, but as a brilliant advocate, with a plausibility that is effective with the average juryman, and an acquaintance with legal principles which is not too close to prevent a British unconsciousness that a cause can ever be lost.

Society has, in a great measure, forgiven the affront he put upon it, and receives him to its bosom once more, while his home life can hardly fail to be happy; with his young and charming wife, and the only child, to whom she devotes herself.

If the story of his life were better known than it will ever be now he would certainly be thought to have escaped far more easily than he deserved.

And yet his punishment still endures, and it is not a light one. It is true that the world is prospering outwardly with him, true that the danger is over, that Harold Caffyn has not been heard of for some time, and that, whether alive or dead, he can never come between Mabel and her husband again, since she knows already the worst that there is to tell.

But there are penalties exacted in secret which are scarcely preferable to open humiliation. The love which Mark feels for his young wife, by its very intensity dooms him to a perpetual penance. For the barrier between them is not yet completely broken down; sometimes he fears that it never will be, though nothing in her manner to him gives him any real reason to despair. But he is always tormenting himself with the fancy that her gentleness is only forbearance, her tenderness pity, and her devotion comes from her sense of duty—morbid ideas, which even hard work and constant excitement can only banish for a time.

Whether he can ever fill the place he once held in his wife's heart is a question which only time can decide: 'Le dénigrement de ceux que nous aimons,' says the author of 'Madame Bovary,' 'toujours nous en détache quelque peu. Il ne faut pas toucher aux idoles; la dorure en reste aux mains,' and in Mabel's case the idol had been more than tarnished, and had lost rather its divinity than its gilding.

But in spite of all she loves him still, though the character of her love may be changed; and loves him more than he dares to hope at present; while the blank that might have been in her life is filled by her infant son, her little Vincent, whom she will strive to arm against the temptations that proved too strong for his father.

Vincent Holroyd's second book was received with cordial admiration, though it did not arouse any extraordinary excitement.

It cannot be said to possess the vigour and freshness of 'Illusion,' and betrays in places the depression and flagging energy of the writer's condition, but it has certainly not lessened the reputation which he had won by the earlier work, to which it is even preferred by some who are considered to be judges.

And there is one at least who will never read it without a passion of remorseful pity, as its pages tell her more of a nature whose love was unselfish and chivalrous, and went unrewarded to the end.

F. Anstey – A Concise Bibliography

Vice Versa (1882)
The Black Poodle And Other Tales (1884)
The Giant's Robe (1884)
The Tinted Venus (1885)
A Fallen Idol (1886)
Burglar Bill And Other Pieces (1888)
The Pariah (1889)
Voces Populi (1890)
Tourmalin's Time Cheques (1891)
Mr. Punch's Model Music-Hall Songs And Dramas (1892)
The Talking Horse And Other Tales (1892)
The Travelling Companions (1892)
The Man From Blankley's And Other Sketches (1893)
Mr. Punch's Pocket Ibsen (1893)
Under the Rose (1894)
Lyre and Lancet (1895)
The Statement of Stella Maberly, Written By Herself (1896)
Baboo Jabberjee, B. A. (1897)
Puppets At Large (1897)
Love Among The Lions (1898)
Paleface And Redskin (1898)
The Brass Bottle (1900)
A Bayard From Bengal (1902)
Only Toys! (1903)
Salted Almonds (1906)
Winnie, An Everyday Story (1909)
In Brief Authority (1915)
Percy and Others (1915)
The Last Load (1925)
The Would-Be Gentleman (Adapted From Molière's Le Bourgeois gentilhomme) (1927)
The Imaginary Invalid (Adapted From Molière's Le Malade imaginaire) (1929)
Humour and Fantasy (1931)
A Long Retrospect (1936)

www.ingramcontent.com/pod-product-compliance
Lightning Source LLC
Chambersburg PA
CBHW060533260626
47161CB00003B/880